Two Feet Press

D1227937

UNHINGED

An UNLIKELY SERIES Novel

Book 1

JB SCHROEDER

Lily —
Reading is
one of life's best pleasures!

♡ JB

Two Feet Press
PO Box 351
Chatham, NJ 07928-9991

Unhinged © 2016 by JB Schroeder, LLC

www.jbschroederauthor.com

Cover photographs ©Digital Vision/Thinkstock

Print Edition 1.0

ISBN-10: 1-943561-03-6
ISBN-13: 978-1-943561-03-2

To my mom, who is the absolute best.
Daughters everywhere should have one just like you.

PROLOGUE

All is not as it seems. Not here, where so many of the players are not who they pretend to be. Even, to a certain degree, not exactly who they believe themselves to be.

But oh, they'd learn. Surprises were in store.

The loser would find that second chances were a delusion—that's simply a sad fact of life.

The loner would find unexpected, yet permanent attachments—as it should have been all along.

The wronged would finally be satisfied—and likely silenced.

And the untethered—after so many years of uncertainty—would find warm, solid ground.

Yet years worth of planning and devotion meant the fear of failure was very real. On rare occasions, gut-curdling, debilitating doubt reared up deep inside, each time with unexpected ferocity. The only way to combat that was thorough preparation. The better the groundwork, the greater the chance for a satisfactory outcome. Hard won, but worth it. Ultimately, the end result was the only thing that mattered.

And it was almost time. The waiting, the interminable waiting, was *this* close to coming to an end once and for all.

Yes, the landscape of life as they all knew it was about to change very, very soon.

For some, the new terrain would feel unsteady—shifting and precarious. Scary mainly because it was unexpected, like a sudden slide of sharp rocks underfoot: scrambling feet, flailing arms, pounding pulse, hitching breath. Panic rearing up and taking over.

At least until they accepted this fact: no one escaped their past, because the past existed. Lived and breathed and clawed at the future.

CHAPTER 1

SHORT ON CASH for far too long, Tori Radnor knew exactly what was in her wallet—down to the dollar, the denominations, and yes, the cents, too. Honest mistake on the cashier's part or not, she wasn't budging without her change. Uh-uh—that money was earmarked for her son.

"I only had two twenties," Tori said, attempting to keep a waver from entering her voice. She thrust the thin leather piece at the young employee, the dark slot where money sometimes nestled now gaping empty. "The total was twenty-six sixty-five, yet this"—she opened a fist with the change the young woman had given her—"is only three dollars and thirty-five cents." She refused to look at the people behind her in the express line of this giant, buzzing Miller's Market, all trying to get home with a prepared dinner or groceries after a long day of work.

The cashier—Haley, according to her nametag—flipped her glossy, dark brown hair over her shoulder, revealing a tiny pearl earring and a simple pendant that was only just noticeable within the V of her navy company polo shirt. She pursed glossy lips and narrowed her brown eyes under deep blunt-cut bangs.

"That proves you need reading glasses," Haley retorted.

Tori's mouth dropped open. The girl looked like every mom's dream babysitter: college age, preppy, and sweet—until she opened her mouth. And, Tori bristled, she was clearly nowhere near needing reading glasses.

She did, however, hate to draw attention to herself. She'd had enough drama the last two years—yet apparently there'd be no help for becoming a bit of a spectacle today. At least three people fidgeted in line behind her.

Tori set her jaw. The change due to her now was meant to last Luke for the rest of the school week, and this was only Monday.

The kid was growing at warp speed and shoveled down food just as fast.

"It proves that you owe me a ten," Tori replied.

"You gave me thirty dollars. A twenty and a ten." The young woman stuck out a hip, and planted her hand on the slim curve.

Tori wanted to scream, but managed to keep her voice level. "I gave you forty. Two twenties. I know, because that's what the ATM gave me."

She dug the white slip of paper out of another flap, unfolded it, and waved it at the girl. "See? Bank receipt. The time stamp is no more than a half an hour ago."

The girl's eyes flashed with malice, before a blank mask dropped over her features as fast as a slammed door. Tori blinked. Surely she'd imagined that look.

When the cashier just stood there staring past the proof, Tori said, "Call your manager."

She heard huffs of annoyance and hasty rustling as the shopper behind her began to gather up his things from the belt, and the ones further back abandoned the express line. "Sorry. Really," she said, turning only halfway. Then she pinned Haley with her eyes and strung her voice with steel. "I'm not leaving without the ten."

"Fine," the girl spat as she reached for the phone, staring Tori down all the while.

Tori glared right back, while she silently thanked her lucky stars that her own teen was polite and respectful. She couldn't picture Luke pulling this attitude in a million years. Whether the girl was skimming bills or had made an honest error didn't matter in the least. The customer was always right and should always be treated courteously. Tori taught all her clients those golden rules, and would be shocked if the expectations of the staff at this chain weren't the same.

"Mr. Miller. I need you at register one, please," Haley said in a calm and clear voice that reverberated over their heads on the speaker system, proving that she was capable of professionalism.

Tori raised an eyebrow.

Haley smirked. "The *owner* should be here momentarily."

"Excellent," Tori replied. She crossed her arms and settled in to wait, as Haley flipped off the green light above her. The girl straightened her nametag, then patted the rectangular plastic, and aimed a pointed look at Tori.

Tori's eyes widened as she read the block letters. Haley Miller. Oh, crap. The owner's daughter? Niece? Cousin?

Haley winked—actually winked—at her. But surely the man didn't play favorites when it came to customer satisfaction.

Leaning against the register, the insolent young woman ignored Tori and made a big show of painting her pout.

Tori rolled her eyes at the cashier's on-the-clock makeover routine, and dug out her phone. No texts, no voice messages. Not that she'd expected any. Hopefully Luke had finished his homework and found something to tide him over until she made it out of this ridiculousness with dinner. She stuck the cell back in the outer pocket of her purse and raised her gaze.

A man—without doubt the legendary Aiden Miller—strode purposefully toward her. She noted Haley straightening, but Tori kept her eyes on the owner of the ever-growing chain of top-notch groceries boasting high-end food courts. According to the papers, he was like the Midas of Markets, turning each store he acquired—even here in a largely seasonal area like the Poconos—into pure gold.

Much of that profit came directly from the customers, in the form of higher price points on everything from toilet paper to imported specialty items from abroad. Consequently, Tori herself rarely shopped here. She imagined, however, that the upscale crowd who could afford organic everything and ready-to-go gourmet meals found the experience well worth every extra cent.

Or maybe all the women just hoped to get a glance of Miller himself, because newsprint didn't do the man justice. Tall, with broad shoulders that tapered to a narrow waist, he appeared perfectly pressed in a tailored shirt, tan slacks, and shined shoes that matched his leather belt. Thick, dark brown hair rose from his forehead, only to dip and curve back to show off a classically handsome face, but it was the way he moved that really captured a woman's attention. Full of purpose, yet unhurried. Athletic, powerful, and coming straight at her.

"How can I be of assistance, Haley?" Aiden Miller began before he'd even fully arrived. Tori amended the thought that he was handsome. Striking blue eyes, lips that quirked up only to the one side, and a crooked nose made him not plain good-looking, but undeniably sexy. Wow.

The girl beamed at him, then managed a sweet frown. "I gave this customer the correct change. I'm sure I didn't make a mistake, but she insisted I call you."

"Ma'am," Miller said, "we're sorry for the misunderstanding. How much change do you believe you are short?" The corners of his mouth lifted, but his eyes were flat.

"Ten dollars. I gave her two twenties, but she claims it was less."

"It says right here, thirty dollars even." Haley pointed to the display.

"You must have entered it wrong," Tori said.

"Haley," Miller said, "please open the drawer and give Mrs. ...?"

"Radnor."

"Mrs. Radnor. Give her a ten-dollar bill, please."

Haley didn't move, except for one slow blink. Then a flush stole into her cheeks, and she said, "Yes, sir." She stabbed a button to slide open the drawer, and passed over the ten.

"Thank you," Tori said on an exhale to Aiden Miller, rather than to Haley. Just having that money in her hand made the tension lowering her brows disappear like magic. She even felt the corners of her mouth lift.

"Again, I'm sorry for the inconvenience."

The side of his mouth that curled notched up a bit higher,

and this time, the smile did seem to reach his eyes. Likely he was pleased to be shooing her away.

Miller turned his head. "Haley," Miller continued, "close out your drawer, please."

The girl waved to the lines on either side of them. "During the dinner rush? While we're short-staffed here?"

"We're also short in the deli."

"Oh," Haley said.

Tori watched the exchange but her mind spun in a different direction as well. Should she? Could she? Opportunity was definitely knocking. She'd be nuts to ignore it. Now, or tomorrow?

Miller told Haley, "It's policy. I need to check your drawer, *and* we need help at the deli. Besides, managers do need to be familiar with every position in the store."

"Of course," Haley said. "I'm on it."

Miller caught Tori's gaze, and the twinkle in his eye shared an adult-to-adult commiseration on the ego of the young, before he said, "I apologize for the discrepancy today. Haley is actually one of my very best. A real asset to Miller's."

The girl's smile broadened and her chin notched up, though Tori thought Haley's eyes narrowed ever so slightly at her, as if to say, *See, you witch?*

Tori said, "Like father, like daughter, then."

Miller laughed, and the girl's attention shot to him.

"No relation," he said.

Out of the corner of her eye, Tori saw Haley flinch. Quick as lightning, a look of disgust passed over her features, before a pleasant expression appeared for her boss.

Tori looked at Miller, but he must not have even glanced at his employee. Instead, he faced Tori, and the heated look in his eyes could mean only one thing—he'd been checking her out.

Her skin warmed, but before she could wonder about that response, he said, "Allow me to escort you out."

No time like the present. "Actually, Mr. Miller"—Tori sucked in a deep breath and prayed she could work some magic without coming off like an ambulance chaser—"I believe I can help you with at least one of your problems. Could I bother you for five more minutes of your time?"

He raised an eyebrow. "Of course."

Tori could feel the cashier's eyes on her. "In private, perhaps?"

"Sure." His eyes flashed, and that raised brow twitched. She was out of practice with men's signals. Did he think she was coming on to him?

She reached for the reusable bag that held her groceries, but Miller leaned in close and snagged the handles.

"Let me," he said.

As she thanked him, it crossed Tori's mind that she found him way too sexy.

As they left the checkout lane, Tori tucked her wallet in her purse. She refrained from acting on the urge to stick out her tongue at the two-faced cashier and stifled a bubble of inappropriate laughter. Aiden Miller, at least, knew how to behave around a customer, and, apparently, around women, too. She wondered how old he was, and put him within a couple of years of her age. Late thirties. Oh, who was she kidding? She'd be forty in a matter of months. Aiden Miller looked like he was in far better shape than many men his age, however. No paunch— no extra pounds at all, as far as she could see. Even his hair had decided to stick around. Her eyes slid from a trim waist to tight buns. She felt a blush bloom on her face and thanked her lucky stars nobody seemed to be watching.

Tori attempted to concentrate as they weaved around customers, past the far end of the checkout counters. For her clients' sakes, and her own, she needed to focus on this pitch. That she'd even noticed Aiden Miller's sexy rear end unnerved her big time.

She tamped down the appreciative smile that threatened, just as he opened a smooth oak-colored door and motioned her inside.

"Please sit," he said, and walked around a desk crammed

with papers and ledgers and photographs. "And ignore the store manager's mess."

"I hope we aren't inconveniencing him."

"We're not. He's out unexpectedly for a couple of days, which is why you're dealing with me." He looked at her pointedly. "What was it that you wanted to discuss, Mrs. Radnor?"

"Tori, please."

"Tori."

She cleared her throat and sat up as tall as her five feet, six inches allowed. "I fear you'll find this in bad taste, and yet, for the sake of my clients, I simply can't pass up this opportunity to speak to you on their behalf."

He raised his eyebrows—likely he'd expected that come-on, or even a rehashing of her altercation with the cashier. Tempting, but she had far more important things in mind. Tori consciously relaxed her fingers on her thighs. "I run a placement service for homeless adults and teens."

"I'm sorry. We don't sponsor charities, except for—"

"Oh no, you misunderstand. I'm not asking you for even a penny. In fact, when UpStart finds a client a position, we pay their salary for the first month. After that point, if you'd like to keep them on, you take it over. That way there's no risk to you, only incentive. Essentially you'll have an extra employee, for free, for one month." She reminded him, "You did say you're short-staffed."

Miller frowned. "Your company can sustain that? Why wouldn't the applicant just come directly to apply for a job?"

"Two weeks of the cost will eventually be reimbursed by the state's pilot program, but we also rely on private donations." Tori moved on to address the more important issue. "One of my clients' biggest hurdles is that all employers require an actual address and telephone number on the application, usually an email address as well. It's a vicious cycle," she explained. "They can't get a job because they have no addresses, yet they can't secure anyplace to live because they are jobless. We give them both the skills and the missing pieces they need to enter the workforce in a professional way. I promise you, they have the desire to succeed. It's a simple matter of providing them the right opportunities."

"Do you"—Miller rubbed his temples—"house these people, too?"

The words themselves were innocent enough, but Tori sensed an undercurrent within his tone. She hoped he wasn't one of *those people* with prejudices. Why he would find the conversation stressful otherwise, though, she couldn't figure. "No, that's up to the state of Pennsylvania. We provide a business office—a professional home base of sorts."

"As I understand it," Miller said with a slight frown, "so often, the homeless have other issues that prevent them from maintaining employment."

Tori had heard it all, though many took less care in their phrasing. She didn't miss a beat. "UpStart doesn't represent the chronically homeless or mentally unstable. Unfortunately, they need more than we can provide. The folks we do champion are those who are temporarily down on their luck and wish to improve their circumstances."

Miller frowned again. He snatched a round glass paperweight off his manager's desk and seemed to focus on tossing it up and down with his right hand.

"Please, just give one of my clients a chance," Tori said. "They really want to work. They need to work. I promise, you won't be disappointed."

Miller shook his head, and Tori's fists clenched. He looked like a reasonable adult. A smart, classy, educated, sexy hunk of a man—what a disappointment! Those good looks hid a narrow, dispassionate—

"Fine," he said, surprising the hell out of her.

Tori blinked, then stilled, fearing that she'd misunderstood.

"Only because," Aiden continued, reluctance edging his voice, "I've already tried and failed to find Butch's applicant file in this mess." He swept a hand over the desk, before he clunked the paperweight down and leaned back in the chair. "For all I know, there isn't one. But it's clear we need more bodies on the floor, and soon."

Tori found she'd been holding her breath. She wanted to squeal in delight, but she simply let her grin erupt instead.

A smile eased its way onto Miller's face as he held her gaze. He had incredible eyes, but she was thinking about his mouth— such a sexy smile framed in that strong jaw. When her cheeks started to heat, she looked hastily away. Glancing back, she noted that his brow had creased and his lips had flattened.

"You won't be disappointed," she said.

"So you said."

"Would you prefer someone for the day shift, afternoons, or evenings?"

"Afternoons, evenings, weekends. They'll have to fill out our standard application and interview with me. If I don't think they are a good fit, I will still pass."

"Of course. I'll have someone here tomorrow, and I'll bring along UpStart's contract as well."

"Make it Wednesday. Butch, my manager, should really meet your client as well. Another day won't sink us," Miller said. He came around the desk and opened the door behind her. Tori stood. As soon as they exited, the ex-cashier crossed their path. She held a durable-looking white jacket in one hand.

"Don't forget the cap, Haley," Miller said.

"I've got it." She produced a navy cap with the Miller's logo on it from under the jacket. She smoothed her bangs carefully to the side, before placing it on her head.

"Be glad it's not a hair net," he said, and winked, obviously teasing.

Haley's eyes widened, and her lips curved. Out of Miller's range, she turned slightly and glared at Tori.

Tori gave her own smile some wattage. Nothing was going

to bring her down this evening, especially not Aiden Miller's spoiled employee.

Miller put a hand behind Tori's back, presumably to guide her. Though the pressure of his large palm lasted only a few seconds, a warm tingle remained. She drew a deep breath, surprised, for it had been a long time since she'd been so aware of a man.

When they reached the automatic doors, she turned. A flash of white caught her eye, vanishing down an aisle, distracting her for just a moment. She looked up at the serious face of Aiden Miller, hoping this moment would mark the beginning of a long, fruitful partnership.

"Thank you, Mr. Miller." *On behalf of my clients, myself, and even my son,* she thought with a squeeze of emotion near her heart.

"You're welcome." He started to walk away, then stopped and gave her a hard look. "Please don't make me sorry."

CHAPTER 2

TORI MANAGED TO walk calmly to her car. She kept from skipping, leaping, or fist-pumping—until she sank into the driver's seat of her beat-up Toyota and slammed the door, at which point she drummed her feet on the floor, shimmied her fists, and squealed with glee. Adrenaline still surged from the altercation with that little beast of a cashier, yet euphoria from the successful pitch to Aiden Miller bubbled up and took over.

Confident she and her new Miller's employee would conquer all his doubts, Tori dismissed his negative reaction. Hope erupted like a geyser, as ideas swirled. If she could get a foothold in a store like Miller's, UpStart would really be up and running. A single placement here and there at the local dry cleaner's, coffee shop, and diner was great, but so limited. Miller's must have hundreds of employees and loads of turnover. All along, she'd had big plans—Miller's could well be the turning point.

Tori put a hand to her chest and shut her eyes for a moment to savor this feeling. Then she started the car, blasted the radio with pop music, rolled down the windows to let the wind whip at her hair, and sang all the way to UpStart's offices in a small warehouse enclave called Pocono Hill. A ridiculous name given that the area was one of the flattest sections in Monroe County.

Her father had handed her the building free and clear for two reasons only: one, the blue-collar property didn't fit with the rest of his portfolio or his vision of himself, and two, her parents had wanted her and Luke out from underfoot. If he'd had any idea they'd choose to live in the warehouse, he'd have never agreed. Tori slid her car between the buildings, parked in the back, and looked up at the second-floor windows as she hopped out.

In fact, it'd been Luke's idea to squeeze their living quarters out of the back storage area of UpStart. She'd planned to rent an apartment until they could afford a two-bedroom house in a nice neighborhood. Luke, quite the budding businessman, had insisted, pointing out that the elimination of rent would allow far more of her percentage-based salary to be reinvested more quickly. Furthermore, the property fell within the boundaries of the best public school in the area—known for both quality academics (her priority) and a good lacrosse team (Luke's). The silver lining? Luke was getting quite the education in business, too. A win-win all around.

She rushed up the narrow flight of stairs from the back alley and entered their floor. The galley kitchen had a two-burner cooktop and enough room on the counter for a dishtowel as a drying rack, and a cutting board for prep space. On a rolling cart, they had a George Foreman Grill and a convection toaster oven. A tiny wooden table and two folding chairs were smashed up against the wall.

Once upon a time, she'd had top-of-the-line appliances and a showroom-style kitchen big enough to park a car in, but she was all right with this. Much like her clients, she and Luke had experienced hardship and learned to live with less. A lot less. And this, though meager, was actually a step up from the hell they'd been faced with not long ago. Tori counted the odd living arrangement as a blessing, and Luke didn't seem to mind the tight quarters at all.

Of course, she wanted more for her son. She ached for what she couldn't yet provide, cried for what he'd had to deal with, and yet, although he was only sixteen, he'd handled it all with a practical maturity. Unlike most kids, he'd already learned that the important things in life had nothing to do with one's trappings.

"Luke!" she called as she shut the door and hustled through the spacious common area where they'd arranged UpStart's workstations.

"Hi, Mom." Luke emerged from the back rooms, and as

always, she had a moment's marvel that she had to look so far up at her only child. In their old house, she'd made pencil marks on the wall of his walk-in closet to mark his growth. When they'd left, she'd been too preoccupied—frantic and terrified, actually—to think to transfer those marks to paper. The briefest pang of grief squeezed her before she let it go. Dropping her purse, she reached for his hands.

"Guess what?"

"What?"

"You'll never guess! I got us a placement at Miller's Markets!"

"Mom, that's huge!" He leaned down, wrapped her in his arms, and lifted her off her feet to spin her around.

She laughed. "Put me down before you drop me."

She heard his stomach growl before he released her.

"You're starving, aren't you?" She reached for her bag, then stopped and conked one hand on her head. "I was so excited I left the groceries in the car. Be right back."

As they ate some thin chicken cutlets that Tori had quickly rubbed with spices and grilled up on George, she told Luke about her talk with Aiden Miller, including the fact that he seemed to harbor some reservations.

"He sounds like a dick."

"Luke!"

He shrugged. Since his green eyes, the exact same color as hers, revealed a decided twinkle, she knew he'd aimed to get a reaction. Sixteen-year-olds did that. Tori couldn't help the small smile that escaped.

"He seemed like an okay guy overall." The unnerving physical reaction she'd felt aside, why defend him? She'd been unable to decipher the mixed signals she'd caught behind Miller's gorgeous blue eyes. He *could* be a total jerk, for all she knew. Tori shook her head. "He agreed, so that's all I care about."

"Who are you gonna put in there?" Luke said around a mouthful of food.

"Manners," she reminded him. "I'm torn between Alan, Clarice, or one of the teenagers."

Luke's eyes lit up. He spent a fair amount of time at the shelter and had become close with both Alan Hammerton and Clarice Stokes. They each adored him, and acted like pseudo-grandparents.

Tori sighed. "They all need a job so badly."

"Do either of them have experience in a grocery?"

"Clarice has almost no experience of any kind. Housewife syndrome." Tori tapped her fingers on the table. "I'll have to look back over Alan's résumé. As I recall, he listed mainly physical labor."

"Can't Miller take them both?" He stabbed another piece of chicken and transferred it to his empty plate. Had he inhaled the first round?

"That's my plan," Tori said. "Once we get our foot in the door. Don't mention anything just yet, please."

"No problem." Luke's eyes slid away, a frown formed, and he busied himself slicing and shoveling a too-big bite of chicken in his mouth. She knew that particular look.

"What?" she asked, as only a mother of a teen can.

"Nothing."

Tori raised her eyebrows as she lowered her chin. Was he in trouble at this school now too? Did he fail a test? Lose the phone she'd finally managed to purchase for him?

He continued to eat, then said, "It's nothing I can't handle." *Uh-oh*, she thought.

"But I know you want to know, so..." Luke bit his lip.

Tori's fist crushed her paper napkin under the table. "Out with it. You're killing me."

He sighed. "I spotted Dad again outside school."

Tori tossed her the crumpled ball on the table. "Shit."

"Mom!" Luke feigned shock.

"Sorry." She blew out a breath and tried to read his face. "Same as last time? Just watching?"

"Yeah. I pretended I didn't see him—again."

"What is he thinking? I should just go over there and confront him."

"No scenes, pleeeaaase, Mom."

Tori pressed her fingers to her forehead hard in a feeble attempt to dispel the tension there. "He's making you uncomfortable."

He shrugged, his shoulders just nipping his surfer-style golden hair. "He's not really hurting anything, though."

"I should call the police."

"Then what?" Luke's voice nearly cracked, something it hadn't done in months. "They haul him in as a suspected *pedophile* or something? That's just what I want to add to my list of Radnor Humiliations." He crossed his arms over his chest and slumped back in his chair, avoiding her gaze.

Tori felt that one like a stab to her heart. How had she let things get so out of hand? Would they ever get past it all? And sheesh, the word pedophile hadn't even made him cringe. Her little boy was awfully world-weary.

"No." She swallowed hard to force words out of her tight throat, for Holden wasn't a sicko; he was just a supreme ass. "I'd just mention the deadbeat dad thing. Maybe we'd actually see some money."

Though she doubted it, since they hadn't been officially granted a divorce yet—though she'd begun the process. Then again, she could prove abandonment.

Luke was shaking his head. "No way. He's a piece of shit, so just let it be. We don't need his money. If he talks to me, I'll tell him to F off. End of story. Until then, I'm good if I don't have to ever hear a word out of his mouth."

Tori narrowed her eyes. Goddamn Holden. He'd really done a number on their son, and she'd allowed it to happen. Holden had always said, "I'll handle the financials. You don't need to worry about a thing." Hah. Her worry factor had exploded exponentially thanks to him. Truth be told, she didn't want her almost-ex's money either, yet every penny helped right now.

She said, "I'll leave things alone on two conditions."

Luke remained in the defensive position, but raised his eyes to meet hers.

"One: can the swearing."

He rolled his eyes. "Look who's talking."

"Two. Keep me posted about your dad."

Luke sat up fast and opened his mouth to speak, so she held up a hand. "I won't make a single move without talking to you. But I'll worry terribly if I feel like you're keeping me in the dark."

The combative posture Luke had donned like instant armor deflated, and he put his elbows on the table. "I have a condition of my own."

"Okay, lay it on me."

His eyes twinkled again, and Tori knew he—they—were okay, or would be shortly.

"Dessert. I gotta have it." Luke placed a fist against his chest as if a sweet was his life's greatest desire.

Indeed, her son had become quite skilled at defusing heavy moments. "Too easy," Tori said.

"That depends. What'cha got?"

The kitchen was so tight, Tori had only to lean from her chair and grasp the knob of the lower cupboard. She slid out a white bakery bag of double-chocolate cookies—Luke's favorite and a rare treat. In fact, it'd been the reason she'd chosen Miller's Market this evening.

"Is that what I think it is?"

"Yep."

"Then we have a deal." Luke rubbed his hands together.

Tori beamed, as he dug in. Her son was thriving. Her new business hopefully would be soon.

She pushed away the sense that she ought to look over her

shoulder. Just a knee-jerk reaction. A holdover from the slippery slope of the last few years—that was all. For this moment, all was right with her world. And damned if she didn't deserve to enjoy the foreign feeling.

Tomorrow was soon enough to worry about keeping it all afloat.

————

Aiden flipped on all the lights, tossed his car keys on the island, and slid the takeout bag from Miller's onto the counter next to the fridge. Only Monday. Nine thirty p.m. Not remotely hungry for dinner. Aiden ran both hands through his hair, ending up with them on his hips, elbows akimbo. He looked at his behemoth fridge, didn't bother opening it. He knew exactly what it held: half a case of beer, a wedge of cheese and a hunk of salami, milk, orange juice, eggs. That left some serious Sub-Zero-sized empty space.

Too quiet. This damn house was too friggin' quiet. Finally, Aiden yanked open the stainless steel door, wrestled a beer out of the torn cardboard packaging, and enjoyed the entire two seconds of noise he made as the bottles clanked together.

Furthermore, he decided as he blew out a breath to release some tension, the place was way too big. It was meant for a family, or at least a raucous gathering of singles on occasion, which was probably more in line with what he'd been thinking back when he'd built the Adirondack-style home. Right now, he could just use another body. Somebody else breathing in this cavernous, quiet-as-a-tomb house. Maybe even somebody making a delicious commotion right up against him, under him.

Aiden's thoughts jumped to the woman he'd met earlier this evening, Tori Radnor. Sexiest woman he'd seen in a long time. Because she was real. Fresh and full of life. Not some female souped up on body enhancements like pro ball players were jacked on chemicals. Her personality was straightforward too.

She hadn't batted her eyelashes once. Not even for the benefit of her little business. Nope, she was the real deal, classy through and through.

Aiden shook his head. Didn't matter that his libido actually woke up around gorgeous, green-eyed, apparently available Tori (no wedding ring; he'd looked). No way did he need the stress a relationship entailed. Even the easy home runs—straight to sex—somehow ended up messy. He was willing to bet that playing with Tori would be incredibly complicated. Hot—hell yes—but loaded with curve balls.

What really got him, though, was her heavy involvement with the charity circuit. In his experience, those who appeared to be the most passionate about their causes were usually the most self-aggrandizing. And often focused to a fault—at the expense of the people around them. Hell, she may as well have a brand right across her lovely forehead: "Do-Gooder. Beware."

Aiden's shoulders shifted with discomfort. Given his history, there couldn't be a worse moniker.

When she brought her client for an interview later this week, he'd simply avoid looking at her sexy mouth and touchable hair—man, those straight strands looked like honey poured through sunshine. Even now, his fingers itched to slide in and grab on to all that natural beauty. And that smile—so pure he'd ached to taste it.

No—no looking, no touching, and definitely no tasting. Instead, he'd picture a scoreboard hanging over her head. In blinking neon, it'd say, "Bad Odds. Sure Loss."

Damn, but he needed a physical release. He wished he'd gotten out of the store in time to spar with Eddie at the martial arts school they owned. Exercise was an approved part of the plan. Stress was not. Doctor's orders. Anti-anxiety meds? Those he was determined to avoid. Doc hadn't mentioned sex. Nah—the cure-all properties of that pleasurable pastime would be short-lived.

Aiden crossed the great room and yanked open the sliders

to the deck that looked out over the lake. A lot of cloud cover. No moonlight highlighting the lake. No breeze to make the tops of the pines sway and the leaves of the oaks rustle. He took another swig of his beer.

He rolled his shoulders, rotated his head to pop his neck. He dragged in a deep breath, but the air still felt heavy and muggy in his lungs. Aiden dropped into a deck chair, leaned his head back, and shut his eyes. Tried hard to concentrate on breathing, only breathing.

But there was that unsettling creeping along the back of his neck again. His eyes popped open, and he stood abruptly. He scanned the lakefront, the undergrowth, the dark edges of the shed. Nothing. Not even a raccoon.

Jesus, he was losing it.

That sense that something was off, that inability to relax, was just the usual. Inner turmoil manifesting itself. The same sense of unease that plagued him everywhere. Same reason he'd left Philly, taken a time-out here in the Poconos, where work was supposed to be less stressful and relaxation was supposed to be more attainable.

But he was coiled too tight, his head all fucked up, his body always paying the price.

Aiden stomped back into the house in search of his phone.

One text and thirty minutes later, Aiden and his oldest friend Eddie had their asses planted on barstools at The Granary, a local pub. The pails of peanuts were the safest best, but they ordered some appetizers anyway. The trick was to stick with items that went straight from the freezer to the fryer. The back of the place, once a feed store with a loading dock, opened up wide to a cement slab patio. Sure, it looked over a bunch of other parking lots, but here in the Poconos trees were everywhere, too. Neon signs provided most of the lighting and hid the fact that cleanliness wasn't exactly a priority. Sometimes noisy and not much to look at, the place usually failed to attract tourists and high-end grocery shoppers.

In other words, the dive was perfect.

They discussed some Sunrise Martial Arts business and kept one eye on the suspended televisions. One played news, the others sports. Little by little, Aiden felt his edgy disquiet ease.

By the time the food arrived, their few comments centered on nothing more important than the ball game, the announcers, and the commercials.

Eddie's eyes shifted now and then over Aiden's shoulder. They'd already greeted the guys outside, a couple of whom had kids that attended their martial arts classes. Aiden wondered if a fight was brewing or somebody was bordering on too drunk to drive. Finally, he craned his head around to check.

"Wish you hadn't done that," Eddie muttered.

"Why?"

"'Cause now she's gone."

"Who?" Aiden frowned. There hadn't been any women back there.

"Some woman was taking pictures."

"Of?"

"Don't know. Maybe you."

"Why not you? Why not them?" He gestured to the men out back. "Or the bar in general?"

Eddie shrugged. "She was half behind the tree, not taking open shots like a tourist or reporter. Wasn't till you turned around that she fled."

Aiden grimaced. His money and success had occasionally attracted the Philadelphia media, not to mention women on the prowl for a wealthy lover—or worse, loaded husband. "Great," he muttered, and signaled for more drinks. Usually, around here, at least the reporters left him alone.

"What'd she look like?"

Eddie raised his eyebrows. "You hoping she's hot or worried your loony-bird stalker is back?"

"Jesus, I'd forgotten about her." Aiden shuddered. Even as a male, strong and skilled in karate, it'd been unsettling.

"How's that possible?" Eddie pulled a face. "Even I have nightmares about Audra Smelty."

Aiden laughed. "Because, thank God, I haven't had to deal with her in years."

"Fucking nuts, that one." His friend shook his head. "Whatever happened to her? The restraining order didn't really work, did it?"

Aiden scoffed. "Hardly. She just got more creative." He'd never have considered filing—too fucking embarrassing—except she'd broken into their house. *While* Pops had been awaiting the transplant—too weak to yell or pick up the phone, let alone defend himself if he'd had to.

"Maybe she died, or moved," Eddie said.

"More likely she found someone else to stalk, or got her crazy ass thrown in jail." Aiden frowned. How many years had it been since he'd seen the last of her? Eight? Ten? More? "Shit, what if she's out?"

Eddie laughed. "Didn't mean to freak you out, man."

Aiden rolled his shoulders. Ridiculous. But just in case... "So what did this woman look like?"

"Not sure. She was well past the cars, halfway hidden behind the trunk of a tree. Boxy windbreaker, a ball cap pulled down low, and a camera with a big lens in front of her face."

"That's helpful," Aiden said. "Age? Weight? Height?"

"Hard to tell," Eddie said.

"Hair color?"

"Couldn't see her hair. Might have been tucked into the hat."

Aiden smirked. "So it might have been a man, for all you know."

"Nope. Didn't move like a man."

"You'd know, all those years in the sandpit." A marine, Eddie had served numerous tours in the Middle East. "You sure you even remember how women move?" Aiden meant the comment as friendly ribbing only, but practically choked when he thought the shithead comment through. Eddie was a widower.

Thankfully, Eddie cracked a smile. "Asshole."

"Back at ya. Audra Smelty. Shit." Aiden laughed.

———

"Mom?" Luke asked, startling Tori as she set the phone back in the cradle. He jerked out his earphones and tossed them behind him, presumably to his bed, then padded on bare feet to the common area of the apartment.

"Sorry. Did the phone wake you?" she asked. Unease was edged out by concern. Mothers were no less protective of their teens' sleep than they were of their babies' naps, and it was past eleven.

"Nah. I was still doing homework."

"Luke," she said, unable to help the admonishing tone, "you'd be finished earlier if you'd kill the music."

"It helps me concentrate." He rolled his eyes. "Who keeps calling?"

She shrugged. "I don't know. Nobody. I think maybe somebody's accidentally dialing from their cell. There's music in the background, and they can't hear me."

The phone trilled, and she answered. "Hello? Hello? Hell-ooooo?" She said it louder each time, though still the caller didn't respond.

"See?" Tori shrugged and hung up.

The blasted thing rang almost immediately. Tori groaned.

Luke snatched for the receiver. "Maybe it's for me, and they won't talk to you. Hello?"

He held Tori's eyes as he waited.

"Hellooo? Dude, pay attention to your phone! Hey!"

Luke lifted one shoulder. "Still only music. It's Pink. She's big with the girls at school. This one's called 'Blow Me.'"

Tori raised her eyebrows. "Nice," she muttered.

Finally, Luke hung up. The unit was still in Luke's hand when it rang again. He hit speaker, allowing Tori to hear the music loud and clear.

"Yeah?" he said, the receiver held out in front of his mouth now. "Hello?" He set the phone on the nearest desk and started strumming an air guitar. "Come on, Mom, rock it."

She laughed and banged her head to the music, although her tastes ran more to stuff like seventies and eighties pop. Ancient crap, according to her son.

Luke laughed, too, as they got silly and danced in the wide-open space between desks. He sang along about having *a shit day.* In the spirit of fun, Tori ignored the swearing and even joined in as she caught on.

Pink crooned to the close, then a moment of silence. Tori put a hand on her chest and waited, as Luke shoved his hair out of his face. The next tune began with a fast electronic swish, then switched into a quick beat. Tori threw her arms out and danced.

"Stop," Luke snapped, making a slicing motion with his arm as his eyes narrowed and pinned on the phone. "It's on repeat. Same song."

Tori frowned. He was right. And the music, she realized, wasn't distant or background. The volume blared. On purpose, right into the phone.

Luke grabbed up the receiver, hit end, slammed the phone into its base, and ripped out the jack.

Tori's gut clenched. This was no butt dialer. Rather, it was a direct message.

Blow me.

―――――

The voice came from behind. "I'm getting sick of that song."

Shrug. Earphones wouldn't help, so whatever.

And it'd been a crap day. The musical salute was just blowing off steam—directionally. Mere minutes worth of effort, and it felt good.

"Who's on the other end?"

Same shrug, but cheeks heating. Fists clenched under the

desk. Didn't want to explain today's embarrassment. And, hopefully, the cause was a non-issue.

Disapproval filled the air. But the printer, jets zipping back and forth, made plenty of noise to mask the silence. On screen, the photos were even better.

"Those are good. That one especially, nice addition."

A nod. "I thought so too." They usually could agree on pictures.

A nod at the phone, the speaker. "Don't get distracted."

And there it was. The criticism. Never good enough.

Someday, though. Someday soon it would be.

The trouble was *when*. Such a fine line.

The final piece of the plan had finally been set in motion, the cops tipped off. That meant a conversation had to happen. *Before* they wrapped up their little investigation, got off their asses, and made an arrest. But not too far before. Couldn't risk him taking pity on that loser, or giving him too much time to think or mess with the plan.

Unlike most things, this part couldn't be monitored or controlled. That was uncomfortable. Even unsettling.

Think. Plan for every possible contingency. Reach up. Twist and pull. Focus.

Finger throbbing, pulsing. Yes, focus.

CHAPTER 3

TUESDAY MORNING Tori and Luke cut through the alley alongside their building. He was headed for the bus stop; she to the shelter to speak with Clarice Stokes about the Miller's placement.

The other warehouse buildings around them were dilapidated, none too attractive, and built one after another in city block style—except they were wider than a standard row house, and metal rolling fronts were more common than doors. Company logos painted directly on brick had mottled long ago from weather exposure. Some buildings had closed up shop decades before. Now, though, a few startups were taking advantage of the cheap rent and providing a much-needed facelift.

Yes, the area could feel like a bit of a ghost town in the evenings, but after the last couple of years, privacy was a relief. And it *was* safe. You didn't need white picket fences and backyard barbecues. What few neighbors there were looked out for one another. Besides, she thought, at times like this, living near the shelter was incredibly convenient.

Early June made for a mild morning, and a few folks sat out on the sidewalk on folding chairs they'd carried outside. Two children sat cross-legged, scraping rocks on the sidewalk. She made a mental note to donate some bright chalk. Although these two, she knew, would be moving on—Grandpa was due today from Ohio to collect his daughter and her children.

Alan Hammerton greeted them with an incline of his head. "Mrs. Radnor. Luke."

An older African-American, he was raised in the South with a heavy dose of manners and religion. She smiled, picturing him as a child sitting in a pew with a shirt and tie for lessons, an imposing mama with a jaunty Sunday hat standing over his shoulder.

"Good morning, Mr. Hammerton." He insisted on calling her Mrs., so she addressed him in kind. "How are you?"

"Just fine, thank you. And you, ma'am?"

Conversations with Alan always began this way. He saw no reason to skip the niceties just because he happened to find himself in an impoverished condition. In fact, he was always one of the most well-dressed men here—pressed, tucked, and buttoned at the wrists.

He handed Luke a bulging, napkin-wrapped package. "Clarice asked me to give you this."

Clarice had been taking care of men and boys all her life and knew the way to their hearts. Every chance she got, perishable extras were smuggled out to Luke.

"Let me guess," Tori said. "She's helping the staff clean up the kitchen?"

Alan inclined his head. That was the other thing: Clarice simply didn't know how to be idle.

Luke asked Alan to pass on his thanks, and the bus rattled up.

"I remembered to give you the lunch money, right?" Tori asked Luke.

He patted the back pocket of his shorts.

The hard-won ten bucks. Tori still couldn't believe that awful cashier. She'd only barely managed to keep her cool. But even now, she could hear her mother's voice in her head. "Above all, Victoria, remember to act the lady."

Ugh. Grossly unfair that she had to contend with the woman, even when she didn't.

Luke was still half asleep, but he stood back and gestured with a lanky arm for the younger kids to go ahead of him up the bus steps.

Manners as nice as Aiden Miller's, Tori thought, even if he was only sixteen.

Aiden Miller. Tori squeezed her crossed arms. There was a topic that could derail both thoughts of her mother and worry about Luke's constantly growling stomach. Tomorrow, when she introduced Clarice, she'd face Aiden again—a prospect that both unnerved and excited her. A warm flush stole over her cheeks—half desire, half bewilderment. Why she should feel all tingly because the man was so good-looking was beyond her. Especially when she wasn't at all sure he was a decent guy down deep. He'd definitely had misgivings about her clients working in his stores, and Tori had zero tolerance for wealthy people who lacked empathy for those less fortunate.

Not that it mattered. She wasn't remotely in the market for a relationship, and even if she was, he'd be the last kind of man she'd go for. Too used to being in charge, to giving orders. And his wealth didn't help. Probably no one ever even questioned the man. She grimaced. Uh-huh. She'd been down that road once, and it had caved like a sinkhole. No way would she or her son ever take a backseat again.

And wasn't that getting a little ahead of herself for a woman who couldn't afford distraction right now anyway? She huffed a little breath of disgust at her own foolishness.

She had a teen to raise, a business to run, a bank account to build. Even so, it was good to know she could feel the heat of attraction, the rush of anticipation, the—

The bus shifted into gear, and she waved hastily.

Then she slipped through the shelter door. At the end of the corridor, she stopped at the office.

"Got one more," she announced to her friend Stefan Cruz, who ran the shelter.

He pumped his fist. "You go, girl!"

She laughed. Stefan had been behind her homeless-to-work idea from the beginning, recognizing that jobs would get folks off the streets better than any free meal ever would. Besides that, he was her closest friend. Despite a nearly ten-year age gap, different genders, and opposite upbringings, she and Stefan had bonded like nobody's business.

She told him about the upcoming interview at Miller's. He whistled.

"I know, right?" She still had the urge to jump up and down. "I'm so hopeful. I was torn between Clarice and Alan. He's such a gentleman. She's such a sweetheart."

"It won't matter," Stefan said. "Either one will work their ass off, which means you'll have the other one placed there in no time."

"God, I hope you're right. Tonight?" she asked, as he often stopped over after his shift.

"You know it."

Tori smiled. At present, Stefan pretty much constituted her entire social life. Which was just fine, as he'd proven a more reliable friend than any of her old ones. And Luke enjoyed his company as much as she did.

She entered the main room—really just a gigantic, wide-open space set up with rows of framed cots and thick foam floor pallets. Dividers separated the one end of the room where there was a table with jugs of water and juice, carafes with hot water and coffee. Breakfast had already been cleared. Usually, it was packets of oatmeal or boxes of cereal, single-serve cups of syrupy fruit, or some hand fruit, depending on the season. Today, given the hand-off to Luke, they must have had a coffee cake or muffins as well. Lunches would be brown-bag donations from a nearby church, then the shelter would open the kitchen for a more substantial dinner. Round tables dotted the space where people ate meals or simply sat to wait—for what, they didn't always know.

As Tori scanned the room for Clarice, she spotted the mom of those kids she'd seen outside. Head bent into her knees and arms wrapped around her shins, a spray of tissue stuck out from both ends of her fist. One duffel bag, two backpacks, and a garbage bag filled to the brim sat beside the young woman.

Tori's heart squeezed in sympathy. Going home, for lots of people, was a last resort. Perhaps home was the last place they ever wanted to be, or pride kept them from calling. Maybe they had no support system to access. Tori herself somehow fell into all those categories.

After Holden had disappeared on them—unearthing a shocking financial situation, damn him—she'd done all she could. No matter how many jobs she took, how little she spent, there was no getting out from under. Still—even with Luke to consider—she hadn't been able to go to her parents, until the situation became downright terrifying. Both too proud and too humiliated. Plus, she'd known instinctively they wouldn't help her.

She'd been right. They'd stowed her and Luke in the guest room suite only to save face—their own reputations, the family name. Besides qualifying as rich cheapskates, they despised charity cases. She hadn't been surprised, but that didn't mean it hurt any less.

Tori sighed. The polar opposite of her parents, *she* had never wanted anything but to help people.

Tori found Clarice as she exited the showers, and they sat on her cot to talk. This one, Tori thought, knew hard work, yet barely knew how to help herself. She'd never held a job, instead cooking and cleaning and serving three generations of men in her household. Tori suspected they'd lived only a margin above the poverty line. Therefore, despite knowing how to stretch a dollar, when her husband had died unexpectedly and his income disappeared, Clarice quickly found herself in dire straights.

Tori had been contacting cleaning agencies for her; however, she hadn't yet found a reputable enough one that paid a decent wage. Luckily, Miller's Markets was a better option by far.

Clarice wrung work-worn hands in front of her barrel-shaped middle.

"Don't worry, you are going to do just great."

"But I don't know how to do anything but cook and clean."

"It's a grocery store with some kiosks that prepare meals," Tori said. "I don't know specifically what position they'll put you in. But there's lots of things you'd be good at."

The woman did not look convinced. Wet hair that normally made a thin cloud framing her face was combed flat, making her brown eyes look huge in her pale face. She clamped her bottom lip between crooked teeth.

"Clarice. When you come home from the grocery, you put anything new in the cupboards and pantry and organize them, right? Well, a store is just the same. They stock their shelves, just on a bigger scale. They also need people to mop or sweep, and I know you know how to do that. You might even be asked to chop vegetables for the salad bar or cook alongside one of the chefs."

She nodded now, and Tori reached out to squeeze her hand.

"We'll practice for the interview. Miller's is a perfect place for a hard worker like you. And it's a classy place, with a good reputation."

Clarice's head dropped to her chest, and Tori barely caught her whispered words. "I'm white trash. I won't fit in."

Tori's heart twisted. "That's not true. I promise you'll feel comfortable at Miller's in no time. Everyone there will be so welcoming."

Tori returned to her office determined to drum up some UpStart donations. The notebook on her desk contained a constantly morphing list. She added names line by line every time she walked out the door and saw another company, business, or person she thought might be worth calling. She also crossed names out. Too often, unfortunately.

The bulk of the grant she'd secured had gone toward cleaning up this space, buying equipment, materials, informational brochures, et cetera—simply getting up and running. The business plan was a solid one, although Tori knew it would take time before the financials worked like well-oiled gears. Although UpStart was a for-profit company, it provided social benefit, and therefore enjoyed some non-profit advantages. This early in the game, however, profit was awfully slim. She brimmed with ideas for long-term sustainability—both UpStart's and her own. In the meanwhile, donations were a necessity. Money had to flow in to pay first-month salaries, especially with the lag time of the state's reimbursements—doubly so, if this new affiliation with Miller's Markets continued.

Tori sat, figured out where she'd left off in the notebook, and reached for the phone. Dead.

Oh. The hang-ups, or rather hang-ons, from last night. She rounded the desk and squatted to retrieve the cord. As soon as she had the jack connected, the phone rang, making her jump.

"UpStart. Tori Radnor speaking," she said, tense and primed, even though she knew logically that any of Luke's ex-pals—for surely they were behind the crank calls—would be headed to school right now, just like her son.

"Hey, Tori, it's Mitch Saunders."

Tori sank into her chair. "Mitch, good to hear your voice. How are you holding up?" Mitch was a cop she'd worked with over the years through various social services. He was a good man, and nowadays, she owed him everything. But he and his loved ones had been contending with some heartbreaking events recently.

"Getting by." He cleared his throat and said, "Listen, I'm calling about something else."

"Are you checking up on me?" she asked, because Mitch had saved her butt big time.

"Why, is there something I should know? You need sprung?"

"No, thank God," Tori said, marveling that they could even joke about all this. She stood to walk around as they chatted. "Everything's going real well. Luke is so much happier in his new school. UpStart has made some strides."

"See that? I knew you could do it."

"Well, there's a long way to go, still, but thanks...for every-thing."

"No need, as I've told you before."

Didn't matter. Tori would never stop thanking him. "It was good to talk to you, Mitch," she said, hugging her arm to her side. She counted him a true friend, though she didn't see him all that often.

"Hey, not so fast," he said. "Your box showed up."

Tori gasped. "Oh my God, really?" Her albums chronicling Luke's childhood—at the time the only thing she had left to give him that meant anything. Stupid cardboard box full of mem-ories she'd broken the law to save, risking way too much. That damn box marked rock bottom—but also the turning point. "After all this time?"

"Yep. Had word a while ago, but I was hesitant to say any-thing until I had it in hand."

"How?"

"We lucked out, big time. The top split open during the trash-out, but the guy had kids, so he couldn't make himself ditch it. Except he also had no idea how to find you. Eventually my inquiries reached him. The thing's been riding around in his trunk all this time. Honestly, I only expected confirmation that it was long gone, but I figured you could put it to rest if you knew that for sure."

Tori had been temporarily renting a crappy little house, the third that year. She'd barely unpacked, as the property was in foreclosure, the owner squeezing out a smidge more income before he couldn't. She hadn't known or cared about the details. Cheap and safe was all that had mattered. But everything had fallen apart when her movers didn't show. She and Luke had been escorted out, with no time, no choices, no resources—only utter despair and a panicked rush to grab what they could.

Tears welled in her eyes. "Oh, Mitch, thank you, I can't tell you…" This was turning out to be a stellar week. A placement for Clarice, an in at Miller's Markets, and now this—what felt like Luke's whole childhood in one container—returned to her.

"Any days better than others for me to bring it down?"

She laughed. "I work, eat, and sleep here. Trust me, I'm about the easiest person on the planet to corner."

———

As Aiden headed past the freezers toward the rear exit on Tuesday evening, he cursed Butch with every stressed-out cell he possessed. If it hadn't been for Haley tag-teaming the worst of it with him… He scowled. He'd have to have a serious sit-down with Butch, which he hated to do while the man was worried about his wife, but it couldn't wait.

He pushed open the rear exit alongside the loading docks. The rank stench from the Dumpsters was heavy in the moist air, and the fog swirled like a living thing. The second his feet hit pavement, the shadows moved too, lurching in the dark, dank corner underneath the mounted motion-sensor spotlights.

Decades of martial arts under his belt, Aiden fell into a defensive stance, his whole body strung tight, ready to flash into motion at the slightest provocation. Adrenaline spiked, but in the back of his mind, he noted with relief that his blood pressure and respiratory rates increased normally, instead of off the charts. No gasping for air, no shooting daggers in his chest, no pouring sweat.

A start, a stop, a scuffle, then pounding footsteps fleeing through shallow puddles and loose cinders.

His first thought was Eddie's maybe-woman with a camera. Just what he didn't need after a shitty day. Reporters, at least, didn't play hide-and-seek.

But no—not one set of footsteps, but two. And heavy treads, he thought. Men? Probably, but not necessarily.

The fuzzy cone of light from overhead was for shit. It covered about a ten-foot radius. Beyond that, between the hour and the dense fog, it was near to pitch black. And the building jutted in and out, providing plenty of visual cover anyway. He had only his hearing to go by.

Two car doors slammed. An engine started up. He heard the tires spin for purchase, and the vehicle—something large, a truck probably—roared out of the lot.

Who the hell was slinking around Miller's back lot? And why?

Even though he relaxed his stance, Aiden's breath became shallow.

He'd known that something was off at this branch. Today, it'd become ultra clear, as if it'd all converged suddenly. Declining profits, an increased rate of staff turnover, for-shit vendor contracts, an uptick in customer complaints, and something else—an odd undercurrent he hadn't been able to put his finger on. Something was up.

What, he couldn't imagine. But he didn't like it one bit.

On the other hand, tonight's visitors could have nada to do with the store.

Aiden ran through the possible scenarios. Vandals, thiefs, reporters. None good, and none made sense. Neither did stalkers. That sort usually worked alone. And although women looking for an intro to a wealthy single man sometimes did attempt to corner him in unusual places, he doubted they'd choose to cozy up to a smelly Dumpster while they waited.

His chest started to hurt. Forcibly, he flexed his fingers, rolled his shoulders back, attempted a slow inhale of dense, smelly air.

Aiden struggled to breathe. *Shit.* He couldn't even trust his body to cooperate. How would he know if what he'd heard tonight was accurate?

Okay, chill. He'd check the video feeds later. Maybe they'd crossed under the light at some point. He'd also check with Butch. Maybe there were occasionally kids looking for somewhere to hang out or punks looking to spray-paint a nice big surface... He'd even humor Eddie and call the private investigator he had on retainer for Miller's to check Audra Smelty's whereabouts…

Shit. Usually a plan of action helped, but Aiden still fought to calm the rising panic.

Nothing was working. He started to freak.

Aiden yanked open the door, rushed to get inside. No way was he suffering an attack among the garbage and rats.

Goddammit. This supposedly quiet, underachieving store was going to be the death of him.

CHAPTER 4

AIDEN GAVE BUTCH about thirty seconds back on the clock before he stalked into his office Wednesday afternoon and slammed the door behind him. They'd already checked in by phone, so he knew Butch's wife was in the clear. This morning had topped yesterday for crap days, however, and he was this close to blowing.

Butch took one look at Aiden's expression and stood. The manager frowned, which wrinkled his forehead right up through the bald. "What's going on?"

"You tell me," Aiden said, knowing full well Butch likely didn't have much to say for himself, but giving him the opportunity anyway.

Butch shrugged and sent both thick black brows skyward. "You're gonna have to fill me in."

"Where should I start? The expired ground beef in the case? The truckload of seeping vegetables you accepted?"

Butch shook his head.

"The for-shit contract you agreed to with Runion's?" Aiden had a helluva list. "Or how about the specialty bread guy who refuses to show because he doesn't have a signed contract?"

Butch's mouth opened and closed like a dying fish— appropriate enough, because Aiden was this close to canning his ass like a friggin' sardine.

"I signed that!" he finally spat out. "I know I did."

"Or how about the fact that the staffing is in the shitter? Christ, man," Aiden said, "I cleaned the john myself yesterday!"

"Oh man, boss, I'm sorry. I—"

Aiden waved him off. He didn't care about cleaning the damn toilets. "Seriously. What's going on?"

"I thought Anna was miscarrying. I rushed out—"

Aiden shook his head in a sharp motion. "I'm not saying you shouldn't have taken off; you should have. And dammit, I am glad Anna and the baby are safe." Aiden blew out a hard breath. "One or two issues because of a hasty leave would make sense, but this mess didn't happen overnight. You're not doing the work, you're costing us money, and you're cheapening our reputation."

Butch waggled his head, hanging it low.

"I knew there were some problems, but man…" Aiden shook his head in disgust. Yeah, he was ticked at himself, too. "I can't even figure how I didn't see it before, except that it all seemed to converge and implode at once." That and he'd been rather preoccupied with his damn health.

"I'll do better, Aiden, really."

"You'll have to." He didn't need to say or else.

Butch knew. He knew Aiden had high standards, that he valued diligence and honesty. Normally Butch met those marks and made it all look easy. That was what didn't make sense. Aiden had taken a chance on the guy, and the ex-con had made good. He gave it his all, and he cared.

Now? Shit. This wasn't your average employee getting a little lax after the trial period. This was something more.

"I'm on it now," Butch said. "You don't have to worry about anything."

"No?" Aiden snorted. "You know anything about some low-lifes hanging around the rear door?"

Butch's dark eyes widened. His meaty hands wiped the thighs of his chinos. "Out back?" he asked.

"Yeah."

Butch shrugged. "Sometimes kids like the dark corners. Smoking and drinking, but that's nothing new."

Aiden narrowed his eyes. "Did you look into installing some more light back there?"

Butch blanched.

Christ, he'd get about as much out of Butch today as the empty bread bins.

Disgusted, Aiden turned his back on his manager and wrenched open the door—only to nearly plow into a body. A feminine, fresh-smelling, golden-haired—whoa—Tori Radnor. Working to erase his scowl, he said, "Sorry, I didn't hear you out here."

"We hadn't knocked yet," Tori said.

Wow, but the woman had a killer smile. She radiated...what? Health? Sunshine? Goodness? He noticed even when he was feeling like a son of a—

Butch grunted behind him, yanking Aiden back to reality. Tori was standing in Butch's doorway, and she wasn't alone.

Her companion was middle-aged and sweet looking, but her expression read one hundred percent terrified. The woman clasped a manila envelope like a life raft to her chest and bit her lip so hard Aiden worried she'd break skin. This had to be Tori's client.

Damn. Between the late night visitors, his attack, the morning's chaos, and Butch's idiocy, he'd completely forgotten the time. He hadn't forgotten Tori, though. In fact, she'd been slipping into his thoughts the same way the smell from the bakery hit your olfactory nerves. Just a hint, and then bam—you were drooling.

Tori gave the woman a reassuring nod, before turning to him. "Mr. Miller, I'd like you to meet Clarice Stokes."

She remained poker faced, but reached out slowly to offer a handshake. He was pleased to discover that her icy fingers didn't wilt in his much larger hand.

Forcing an easy smile, he said, "We're glad you're here, Clarice."

"Thank you, sir." She spoke barely above a whisper.

He noted Tori's arched eyebrow. Mimicking the gesture, Aiden gave her a slight nod. He could admit that he hadn't been on his best behavior when they'd discussed this arrangement. Her work made him draw parallels to his mother, and, invariably, his mother brought out the worst in him.

A look of amusement crossed Tori's face, and Aiden somehow felt satisfied that he'd pleased her—a fact that had nothing to do with his mother.

"Come on in." Aiden stepped back. He introduced them to Butch, then explained, "Mrs. Radnor helps people find work. Since we seem to be somewhat short-staffed"—he shot Butch a glare—"she's brought Clarice to interview with us."

"Is that right?" Butch said. He shot the females a goofy look. "Gotta love it when the big boss makes my job easier."

Aiden frowned. Butch's down-to-earth, friendly demeanor was one of the reasons he was normally damn good at his job. The staff responded well to him. Customers loved him. But Butch's engaging personality had been largely MIA lately.

"We're quite pleased ourselves," Tori said. "Thank you again, Mr. Miller."

Aiden nodded. "I'll take this interview off your hands, Butch, so Mrs. Radnor can explain how her placement company works." That irked. He had this crazy urge to hoard Tori's time. Keep her all to himself. But he'd promised to interview her client himself.

"Sounds good," Butch said.

Aiden turned to Clarice. "How about if you and I find a café table to sit at for an informal interview? Then you can fill out the application."

Butch shuffled through some messy stacks before handing Aiden an application and a pen, then waved Tori to a chair.

"Come find us as soon as you're through," Aiden said to Tori, ushering her client out of the office and across the store to the food court.

Aiden offered Clarice a soda from the pizza kiosk in the food court, but she said, "No thank you, I'm not thirsty."

Of course she wouldn't accept anything she couldn't pay

for—not that he would have let her. Damn. In trying to put her at ease, he'd made her uncomfortable. He kicked himself for not focusing on the task at hand and the person with him, filled two courtesy cups at the water fountain, and chose a corner that was slightly out of the fray. The dinner rush was an hour off, but there was enough action to make the open space noisy.

Aiden linked his fingers and casually rested his hands on the table. "So, tell me. What kind of jobs have you done in the past?"

"I clean and cook and organize. I'm strong and I rarely tire. I'm a hard worker." She slumped, as if it'd been an effort to spit out those words.

Aiden nodded. "That's—"

"Mrs. Radnor says I'm to focus on my strengths and to be truthful." She sat taller and looked him in the eye. "And the truth is I've never worked anywhere but my home. For my father and then for my husbands and sons."

Aiden said, "I'm told there's no job harder than that of a wife and mother."

Her lips curled up a bit. "Being the breadwinner isn't easy either."

Aiden wasn't sure if she was giving kudos to her husband or commenting on her recent struggles. Either way, he'd add diplomacy to his mental list of her strengths.

He'd already made up his mind, and therefore he determined to make the interview as easy as possible on the nervous woman. Well, damn. If he didn't watch out, his sudden urge to help the less fortunate would soon rival his mother's extreme proclivity toward philanthropy.

Aiden said, "Running a household involves planning and organization, along with the skills you already mentioned. Is there anything you like more than something else? Say working with food over cleaning? Or organizing things?"

"No, sir. I'm grateful for any work." She twisted her hands on the table.

"Well, Miller's is a big place. I've got ideas about where you could help us the most. But I also want you to gain all the experience you can. You should try out a number of different positions. If you are happy with the variety, you can remain a pinch hitter."

She nodded, and he figured she'd watched some baseball with her family of men.

Aiden smiled. "But if there comes a point when you decide you'd prefer one department or position over another, I want you to let me know. Okay?"

"Yes, sir. Thank you, Mr. Miller, so much," she said with a waver in her voice.

Aiden realized her eyes were starting to well up, so he uncapped the pen and slid the application across the table. "This is just a formality."

She lifted the manila envelope from her lap. "I have a résumé, too."

"Good. Attach it to the application, and I'll look them both over later."

Aiden spotted Tori weaving through the tables. Somehow, he zeroed in on her smooth, honey-colored head, the graceful carriage, and her perfect figure amidst all the other people that milled about the kiosks. Her eyes connected with his, as if she'd sensed his heated gaze.

Tori approached them with a hesitant smile. "Hi, how'd it go?" she asked.

"Great," he said. "She's hired."

"Oh, that's wonderful!" Tori said, and—proving herself as wholesome as he suspected—actually clapped her hands together before leaning down to give her charge a hug. "I knew you'd have no trouble."

"I need to get back to things," Aiden said, "so just leave the papers on Butch's desk on your way out. I'll tell him to put you on the schedule right away."

Aiden saw admiration in Tori's eyes and felt a pang of guilt. He'd almost told her no that day she'd pitched him. All because he had rules about charities. But he was glad he'd bent a little. He hoped the job would allow Clarice to get her feet under her again financially and to gain some paid work experience. Now to get this store in order, so that the experience would be a positive one. But even if it all went to pot, at the very least, she'd be able to put the Miller's name on any future résumé.

"Wait, Mr. Miller," Tori said, catching up to him as he turned. She wore loose linen pants and a cotton top, jeweled sandals, and tiered earrings that swung from her hustle. She managed what few women did—a perfect balance between classy and casual.

"Call me Aiden. The formal address is for the staff, not my counterparts."

"Aiden it is." She nodded. "I just wanted to thank you, again, for taking a chance on Clarice and UpStart, and"—her gaze hit the tile between their feet—"well...even me."

Aiden felt a little tug in his chest, protectiveness and desire both, as he looked at the crown of her head, the tips of her dark blonde hair spraying out from a loose twist in the back. His fingers itched to lift her chin, shift those big green eyes in his direction.

"I had some doubts," he said. "But Clarice is great."

"Oh, she is." Tori watched Clarice scribbling away. The more she avoided his gaze, he discovered, the stronger the urge to make her to look at him.

"You, however," Aiden said, "look like trouble."

Score. Her face swung to his, with her brows arched in surprise. The green of her eyes danced with light—actually sparkled.

Out of nowhere, Haley appeared at his side, breaking the spell that had caused him to notice eye color of all things. What the hell was up with him?

"Mr. Miller, we could use your input in the deli."

"Okay. I'll be right there."

Haley remained rooted.

"Haley?"

She blinked up at him. Then she nodded once to Tori, spun an abrupt one-eighty, and marched back toward the deli.

Tori bit her lip, then cleared her throat. "So…I look like trouble, huh?"

He grinned. "Capital T."

"Here I was thinking I looked like a savior," she teased, "making your applicant process so easy."

"That's how you see it, huh? I thought I was doing you the favor."

"Just you wait," she retorted with a wink, which gave him the craziest urge to haul her to him and kiss her. "Clarice," she said, "is going to blow the socks off your other employees."

She inclined her head as if to say your turn at bat, but he stood at the plate, frozen with the thought that he'd like Tori to peel his socks off—and not stop there.

"Sorry," she said, lowering her eyes. "I…"

He said, "I'm sure you're right."

Tori practically glowed with pleasure. "Well…" she said, and gestured toward Clarice, who was still bent over the application. "I'm going to see if she has any questions."

A whiff of…vanilla, with a hint of something warm and earthy, like toasted pine nuts, drifted in her wake. Aiden caught himself. Yeah, he'd become something of a foodie because of the markets, but damn—surely he couldn't smell her in the midst of all the scents emanating from the various stations?

Aiden watched her go, toned arms swinging from the sleeveless top, a set of thick silver bangles flashing on her wrist—until the sway of her hips drew his gaze. He thought he could just see a faint outline of lacy thong underwear. The hint of sexy under all that class was a total turn-on.

He swallowed hard and tore his eyes away.

Jesus, he was eyeing up a customer. Or partner. Or whatever the hell she was. Right here in the store. Get a grip, Miller. Before you do something you'll regret.

CHAPTER 5

THURSDAY MORNING, Tori was blessedly occupied with work. At UpStart, she helped a client build a résumé and walked another through a personality profile assessment. However, the minute her clients were focused on a short series of videos related to successful interviewing, Tori's mind jumped back to the issue she'd worried over all night: Aiden Miller. Specifically, flirting with him. On the job. Ugh—as unexpected as it was unprofessional.

Until that moment, she'd forgotten flirting existed. Neurons she didn't know she possessed started zinging around when she saw him—hell, even when she was simply thinking about him. Like now, Tori thought, and pressed her palms to her warm cheeks. She wouldn't act on those feelings, of course. No way, no how. Yet, she'd conceded, she wasn't as immune to the man as she'd prefer.

Once her clients left, Tori yanked the notebook she always kept on hand out of her purse. Flipping past the cover—doodled on everywhere because the mindless act helped her think—she found her running cold-call list and tried to focus on it.

When the phone trilled, she jumped, cringing all over again, as if she'd been caught smooching Aiden's photo.

Then she remembered to brace herself. Last year, whenever the phone rang, Luke's school was on the line reporting another infraction. Plus, there were those prank calls the other night.

Tori grasped the phone and took a deep breath, steeling herself. "UpStart. Tori Radnor here."

"It's Butch Kovacs from Miller's Markets. I was trying to reach Clarice Stokes."

Tori froze. She hadn't expected to hear from them so soon. Were they questioning Clarice's paperwork? Reneging?

"Hello, Mr. Kovacs. Our employees list UpStart's number on their application. Most of them don't own cell phones." She left unsaid the fact that they often didn't have access to landlines either.

"Got it. And call me Butch."

"Likewise, please call me Tori."

"Sure thing."

She frowned down at her list, where she'd begun to draw patterns in the margins, and prompted him, "Can I have Clarice call you, or shall I pass on a message?"

"Tell her she can come pick up her uniform anytime."

Tori pressed a hand to her chest in relief.

"It's just the company polo," Butch continued. "She'll need to wear khakis on the bottom. Shorts or pants or skirt, doesn't matter."

"No problem. Do you know how long until she starts?"

"If she can come on Friday, I've got enough staff that afternoon to pull somebody to train her. Same with Saturday."

Friday was tomorrow! "I'm sure that'd be fine."

"Shift is five o'clock to ten thirty. I'll put her on Sunday morning, too. That shift is slow, so it's a good time for her to try the registers."

"Sounds just great, Butch. Thanks."

"Fantastic. And um, Tori...another thing."

Uh-oh, she thought, pausing in the linked diamonds she'd been doodling. Here we go with a warning about her clients toeing the line—just like Aiden.

"There's more turnover here than I'd prefer," he began. "We're always looking for new hires. It occurs to me that your clients might value their jobs more than some of these kids who're only working because their parents insist they earn something toward all those lattes and music downloads."

Tori caught her breath and gripped her pen tight. Was he saying...

Butch continued, "So let me know whenever you think you've got some good candidates."

Tori's heart leaped, though she managed to control her voice. "Someone comes immediately to mind. Are there specific positions you need to fill?"

"Truthfully, I'm pretty sure I could find a use for nearly anybody—especially if they are willing to do the dirtier jobs."

"It'll likely be me dropping Clarice off on Friday. Shall I bring him to meet you then?"

"Well, that should be Clarice's day, don't ya think?"

Sensitive for a guy with tattoos all over his forearms, she thought, impressed. "You're right. How about Saturday?"

Butch asked, "Would it be easier if I came to your office?"

"Either way."

"All right. I'll come to you. Saturday before I head to work," he said. "I'll give Clarice a ride over when we're through. Save you a trip."

"You really don't have to do that."

"No trouble. Ridiculous for you to drive to the same place I'm going."

Tori hardly knew what to say. He'd met her less than twenty-four hours ago, and yet he was going above and beyond. "Thank you, Butch. You sure are making my day."

"I aim to please." He chuckled.

When they'd hung up, Tori slid down in her chair and clasped her hands tightly in her lap. My God. If she could continue to feed to Miller's, UpStart was really going to make it. Maybe turn a healthy profit sooner than she'd dreamed. More immediately, these folks she'd come to care so much about were going to have jobs—soon! Clarice would gain so much confidence. Alan—

Oh, Alan! Tori shot to her feet. She snatched up her purse, bolted the door, flipped her new sign to "Back Soon," and trotted down the stairs.

She paused to catch her breath when she reached the common area inside the shelter. She caught sight of Alan, who stood and waved.

"Mrs. Radnor." He inclined his head and pulled out a chair for her.

"Thank you, Mr. Hammerton. I'm glad I found you in this morning."

"Well, I'd prefer to be out knocking on doors, but the ankle sure is smarting today." Old injury on a construction job, Tori knew. Unfortunately, without quality healthcare and the luxury of time off for therapy, it hadn't healed correctly. Usually he managed well enough.

"About that. I've got something for you," Tori said, excitement bubbling up.

"Is that right?"

She nodded. "The same place Clarice is starting: Miller's Markets. The manager, Butch Kovacs, is looking for some additional staff."

"Is that so?" A slow smile spread across Alan's face.

"Yes. We'll go through their application process, of course, but it sounds *really* promising."

"Well, ma'am, that surely is some fine news." He placed a large hand on the table and pressed down hard, as his eyes closed.

Tori wasn't sure if he was sending up a prayer or simply trying to refrain from getting ahead of himself. Life was bleak without hope, and yet an open window of hope meant you risked gale-sized gusts of disappointment, too.

"Mr. Kovacs is coming to us. The interview will be Saturday morning at UpStart. How about if you and I meet tomorrow to prepare?"

"Will do."

"Great." Tori stood, and so did Alan.

He looked her in the eye, and said softly, "Thank you, Mrs. Radnor."

She nodded, feeling the prick of tears in her eyes, for that simple expression of gratitude was so earnest.

———

Tori couldn't remember the last time Luke had come to the mall without grumbling, but he adored Clarice and needed a few items, so she'd lucked out. Tori couldn't help feeling a little giddy. Things were working out so well.

Tori had insisted that Clarice try on khakis for her new job at Miller's Markets. There was nothing like a perfect fit to boost your confidence level.

"Luke, you need t-shirts, right?"

"Yeah, and black pants for the end-of-the-year concert. The old pair is too short."

Luke played the saxophone. He'd wanted to quit time and again, except he was actually talented. Everything Tori read maintained that colleges looked favorably on well-rounded applicants. In other words, lacrosse alone wouldn't cut it, especially if they harbored hopes of a full scholarship.

"Did you check the hem?" Clarice asked Tori.

She nodded. "There's no more room to let them down."

Tori handed Clarice a selection of khakis in various sizes. She could see the men's rack from here. To Luke, she said, "Why don't you—"

"Victoria Radnor! Why it's been such a long time!"

Tori spun, automatically pasting a smile on her face. When she saw who had spoken, tension pulled her shoulders toward her ears in defense. A fair-weather friend from the old days of overpriced everything: designer clothes, prestigious schools, and well-to-do neighborhoods.

"Cynthia, how nice to see you," Tori fibbed. The woman's makeup was flawless, and her clothing could have walked right out of this month's *Cosmo*. Tori tried to imagine what she was doing in Sears at the Stroud Mall. Probably buying an extra fridge or foosball table for her son's game room—the one in her summer place near Skytop.

"And Luke," said Cynthia Sutton, "you've gotten so tall."

"Hello, Mrs. Sutton," Luke said.

Tori decided maybe this wouldn't be so bad after all. "We were just discussing the fact that he's grown out of pants again. And this is Clarice," Tori said.

Clarice nodded and clutched the hanging pants to her middle.

Cynthia's eyes narrowed with a distinctly speculative gleam.

Luke stepped closer to Clarice even as Tori shot off a quick question for distraction. "How's school been this year for Tripp?"

"Oh, you know. All honors, but the sports schedule really keeps us jumping."

Her mahogany hair was smoothed into a sleek bob, not one perfect strand out of place, or, God forbid, a single hint of gray. But then, Tori knew Cynthia spent enough money at the top Philadelphia salon to have set up direct deposit.

Cynthia said, "He'll be sorry to have missed you, Luke."

Luke responded in kind, though Tori knew he wasn't exactly a fan of Tripp Sutton. Both boys had gone to Demorrow Prep, a private Catholic school—however, Tripp wasn't exactly a kid who was grateful for the education.

"Are you already here for the summer season, then?" Tori tried.

"I should ask the same question of you, but I expect that's no longer an option, is it?" Cynthia cooed.

Tori's face began to burn. As a girl, she'd loved summering in the Poconos, and later, during her marriage, the social work she'd managed in this area during Luke's school breaks had renewed her purpose. Her fondness for the region had been both a comfort and an escape after the pressure cooker of high-society Philly. Screw Cynthia for attempting to taint any of that.

"I summer all year long, Cynthia. We live here now."

"Of course you do. The Main Line was out of the question after—well, I was just so sorry to hear about your financial woes." Cynthia placed a hand to her chest—better to display the glittering diamonds on her fingers.

"We're fine—" Tori began.

"When I heard that you'd actually tried to break in—to your own house!" Her voice dropped to a whisper, like the word wasn't fit for speaking aloud. "Foreclosed—how awful. My word, Victoria, what you must have gone through. And Holden"—she leaned in, feigning concern—"has he returned?"

Tori fisted her hands. Cynthia's details weren't quite right—technically the owner of the tiny house had been foreclosed on, Tori had paid her rent—but it didn't matter. The woman was unbelievable. Such a snobby, nosy bitch.

She snuck a glance at Luke. He wore disgust plain as day on his face, so she stepped between Cynthia and Luke. "Men's is that direction," she said, turning his shoulders.

Bless his heart—he looked back at Clarice, concern for the sweet woman outweighing his own discomfort. Tori directed Clarice to a dressing room and added, "Holler if you need a different size."

She scurried off at once. But Luke shot Cynthia one more wary look over his shoulder before he left.

Calling forth every ounce of restraint, Tori said, "I've moved on, Cynthia. So should you." She pushed past the toxic woman.

But Cynthia scooted ahead of her with tiny taps of her impractical shoes. "Lovely visit, Tori. I've enjoyed it immensely." Her eyes and mouth turned up with ill-gotten glee. Then she spun on her snakeskin-patterned Jimmy Choo heels and slithered away.

Tori seethed. She'd tolerated the woman in years past. Now, she could admit that she truly despised the bitch.

She stalked back down the center aisle and between the

racks, too agitated to stand still. Yes, breaking back into the rental she and Luke had just been evicted from was quite certainly the stupidest thing she'd ever done.

She'd been prepared, had known from day one the rental was cheap precisely because they'd be forced to vacate when the eviction date was set. But it had all gone south at the end. From bad—unable to secure an apartment in time, she'd been forced to rent both a storage unit and a hotel room—to worse—her cheap-assed movers pocketed her deposit and never showed.

Tori'd been forced to root frantically through boxes to find the most important items to take for the kitchen and bath. Luke grew so fast he had only the bare minimum for clothing; however, she tossed yet more of her own, keeping only the quality items in classic styles, because they'd last. Meaningful keepsakes had already been pared down as much as possible and were still packaged from the last move. Determinedly, she blocked the worry about how in the world she'd manage to replace their furniture from her mind.

As memories flooded Tori, anger at Cynthia Sutton gave way to a quake deep inside. She sought out the cushioned chair by the dressing room, hugged herself tightly, and squeezed her eyes shut.

They'd dragged boxes and bags to the bus stop, with some help from the not-unsympathetic officers. Still in view of the rental, she'd watched with tears of humiliation streaming down her face, as men nailed another big sign to the door and tromped inside with their clipboards.

And worse again: the bus driver had taken one look and shaken his head. "Sorry. Too full for all that," and he'd gestured to what little was left of their life and snapped the doors shut.

Without transportation, there could be no hotel. Time was well and truly up. She and Luke were homeless.

Finally, she'd borrowed a passerby's cell phone—she'd been unable to pay for hers for months—and called her father. The ultimate last resort.

Doubling the mortification, both her parents had come—why, she'd never know. Her father Bernard, outwardly polite on the street, obviously seethed inside. Her mother sat facing forward, sunglasses on, fury vibrating in her stiff posture. She refused to even look at her daughter and grandson. The humiliation must have been as great for Grace Winterspoon as it was for Tori herself.

Later, after the garage door had been closed behind them so that the neighbors wouldn't see—a move Tori was simultaneously disgusted and relieved by—they'd unloaded the trunk.

Intense distress had swamped her—somehow they'd missed the most important box. The albums marking Luke's birth, his first tooth, the first day of kindergarten, right on through T-ball and later, his first lacrosse championships. Although she had begged, her father wouldn't hear of returning to "that hovel."

At midnight, she'd snuck out in her dad's car to retrieve the one set of memories she could give to her son that wasn't a lie. Her heart sank when she saw the padlock. Desperate, Tori tried the windows. Every single one. The rattling—or maybe her sobs—alerted a neighbor, who called the police.

No matter that she'd only wanted one box—her own box—she'd been booked for attempted breaking and entering. Tori shuddered even now. The back of a police vehicle was a terrible, horrible place. Close and suffocating, with nothing to grab on to, no hope of escape.

"Tori? What happened?" her old friend, Detective Mitch Saunders from the Blakes' Ridge P.D., had asked when he showed up unexpectedly that night at the station, pulling her into a hug. He'd seen her name come through the wire and called in a favor, hence her long wait.

The familiar face and kind tone had Tori collapsing into his shoulder. Despite being out of his jurisdiction, he managed to escort her out sans charges, and promised to do what he could about getting her box of albums. They retrieved her father's car, then he followed her to her parents' house.

In the dark driveway, she approached the driver's side of his truck.

"I know how easily things can spiral into a bad situation, but you've got to get it together," Mitch said with sympathy threading his voice. "Press charges against Holden, file bankruptcy, sign up for social services, do whatever you have to, to get back up onto stable ground. For Luke's sake. For your own."

She nodded, and Mitch eyed her family's palatial home. "If help is available to you," he said, "you have to swallow your pride."

"It's not like you think," she'd said, feeling her features pinch. The shame she felt when she thought about the kind of people her parents were twisted together into a tight rope bound with the humiliation she felt about her own horrendous situation.

He shrugged. "Maybe it's not like you think, either."

It hadn't been. It'd been worse.

Tori jumped up and entered the fitting room area. She couldn't sit here in public rehashing the worst period of her life yet again.

"Clarice," she called, "do you need me to grab another size?"

"No," Clarice said, and swung open the half door. She bit her lip and searched Tori's face. She'd tucked in her t-shirt, and the slacks fit perfectly.

She looked…like she was on her way. Tori smiled, tears stinging her eyes.

They selected a knee-length skirt in the same size and two pairs of khakis for Alan—for she felt sure that tomorrow's interview with Butch Kovacs would result in another hire. She wanted both of them to have an extra, since they couldn't wash clothes as easily as most people.

Luke rejoined them, a pair of pants crunched in a fist and a package of black t-shirts tucked under his arm.

Tori felt the anger boiling beneath his clenched jaw and clipped responses. She felt a pang of regret, as always, for what she'd put him through. And an incredible urge to kick the shins of that Sutton witch for stirring up the muck with her nasty broomstick.

Clarice attempted to cheer Luke up by teasing him, threatening to stop her sweet smuggling efforts if he didn't stop growing out of pants. He forced a corner of his mouth up, but the gesture was halfhearted at best.

The memories had surfaced, for both of them. As she stood in line to pay, her mind continued to replay last year in nauseating Technicolor.

"Ma'am," the cashier said, her annoyance evident as she waved a paper under Tori's nose. "Your receipt."

Luke gathered up the bags, and Tori said, "Let's go home."

"Finally. I hate shopping," Luke muttered.

Tori tried to shake it all off. Cynthia's rotten pleasure in taunting her. The bad memories. And worst of all, the ever-present fear that reared up, reminding her that they weren't exactly on solid footing yet.

But it was no good. The threesome left the mall, their moods far weightier than their purchases.

CHAPTER 6

AIDEN HAD GIVEN Clarice the tour of the store himself when she arrived for her shift on Friday. Then he'd suggested that Butch rotate her through a few different tasks. He'd continued to keep tabs, however, wanting to make sure she felt comfortable right off the bat. She didn't talk much, but had a sweet disposition. And she took pride in doing even the smallest job both well and fast. He could see why Tori had suggested her.

At shift's end, Aiden went in search of Clarice, only to find that Butch had had some time to give her instruction on the registers. The two were deep in conversation, Butch gesturing and Clarice nodding.

As he approached, he passed Haley, who was also focused on the exchange.

"Hey, Haley. All set?" he asked as he gestured to her drawer. She preferred to be up front. Tomorrow, however, she'd have no choice, as Saturdays were deli-heavy, and they couldn't put anyone under eighteen on the slicer.

She blinked. "Yes, Mr. Miller."

"Great," Aiden said.

She'd been a go-to employee since she started working a few hours a week at age fourteen. Although Aiden had offered both his recommendation and his blessing when Haley had graduated college, she'd chosen to stay on and learn management his way. Her hospitality degree didn't mean squat without real-world, down-and-dirty experience—meaning every position from sushi chef to toilet cleaner, from bookkeeper to—yes—deli staff, too.

"How'd it go?" Aiden asked Butch.

"Excellent," Butch said. "Clarice handled things like a

champ, and"—he slammed the now empty drawer shut with a flourish—"she's even, right down to the penny."

She shook her head. "Not really. I haven't tried it on my own yet."

"You've proven a fast learner on everything else. You'll be fine here, too," Aiden said. "Let me be the first to say we're glad you're on board."

Clarice's smile grew; however, it faltered as she noticed something behind him.

Aiden turned to look, but got distracted by a movement outside the front windows. A tall teen with shaggy hair waved, obviously trying to get someone's attention. "Anybody know him?" Aiden hooked a thumb toward the plate glass.

Clarice and Butch both turned toward the windows, and her face brightened once more. She waved back, and the kid pointed to the lone car in the front lot. She nodded at the boy, who turned and loped away.

"That's Mrs. Radnor's son," she said. "They're here to pick me up."

"Well, let's not keep them waiting. Go clock out, and I'll walk you to the car."

The lot was fairly dark, but Aiden could see Tori leaning against her car as her son jogged back to her. No wonder she seemed so wholesome. Tori had "mom" written all over her—while Aiden had been looking at her solely as a woman. A desirable, sexy, complex woman he'd best avoid getting to know better.

Right now, though, she looked decidedly unprofessional. Baggy t-shirt, drawstring-type pants, and flip-flops?

"Mr. Miller." Haley stepped into his line of sight, hands on hips.

"Yes?"

"I *said* I'm taking off," she said.

"Sorry, I didn't hear you."

"That's okay." Haley's expression was a bit pinched. She was a good kid, but so serious sometimes that it was difficult to bond with her.

"See you tomorrow, then. Be careful."

"Oh, I always am," she murmured, and slid around him toward the back, where the employee lockers were located.

Clarice returned and he unlocked the front door, ushering her ahead of him. The air was warm and fresh, unlike the cool chill of the store, and he felt his spirits lighten the minute he set foot off the curb.

He told himself it was the polite thing to do—escort Clarice out.

When she spotted them, Tori straightened up off the dark blue car and used both hands to tuck her hair behind her ears. She wore it loose today, the length reaching her collarbone. He liked her in comfy clothes. She'd look right at home on his couch. Odd, though, the juxtaposition of the dinged-up, ancient Toyota and casual attire, when her daytime outfits suggested an abundance of wealth—or at least credit.

Tori said something to Luke he didn't catch, and the boy looked him over warily.

"Evening," he said as he neared. Aiden couldn't help himself; he checked—again—for a wedding ring. Single or divorced definitely, and, he sensed, unattached.

"Hi," Tori replied. "Luke, this is Mr. Miller. Aiden, my son, Luke."

"Sir," Luke said as he extended his hand.

Aiden shook it and replied, "Nice to meet you, Luke."

Tori crossed her arms over her middle. Trying to hide her outfit?

"He looks like you," Aiden said.

"Except for the height," she said, the corners of her mouth lifting a bit. "So, how'd it go tonight?"

"You'll be glad to learn that Clarice here is a natural fit."

Clarice blushed, and Tori grinned—a true smile now.

"You're not sorry?" she said.

Aiden shook his head, then ran a hand through his hair. "I, uh, apologize...for that."

Tori nodded, her eyes holding his. Amusement seemed to play at their corners.

"Thanks for walking her out," she said. Her lips lifted in a sweet curve.

"No problem." Aiden waved his hand. "I figured you'd like an official report."

"You were right."

Clarice thanked him as well, and Aiden lifted a hand in farewell. As he turned back toward the store, he noticed an older-model SUV idling at the side of the building.

Oh—just Haley. A bluish light illuminated her face. She held her cell phone up to check it, the cool glow diminishing as she switched the cell to her ear. Ah, a pause for a call before she hit the road. Good—she played it safe. Most young people seemed to have little common sense when it came to cell phone use and driving. Or, for that matter, gaming and walking, texting and working... But Haley had been on her own at a young age. He'd never seen her act like a typical carefree, impulsive kid.

He took a last look back at Tori and her crew as he reached the doors. They'd piled into that crappy little sedan—an old Toyota Corolla, he thought—Luke in the backseat, Clarice in front. The car started up with a rattle and groan.

Tori needed a tune-up—and damned if Aiden's pulse didn't kick-start the second that double entendre hit home.

He watched them pull away, and Haley's brake lights winked off. He wondered when Clarice's next shift was scheduled, or rather Tori's next chauffeur duty. He made a mental note to check, then immediately erased it, shaking his head.

Remember, dip wad, all the reasons Tori Radnor is off limits. Recommend your mechanic for her vehicle. Keep your own damn pump locked in the garage.

CHAPTER 7

AIDEN HAD COME straight home after work. He'd forgotten to leave a light on, and the house looked big and cold, despite the fact that the sensor light was already on in the driveway. Not that unusual. It popped on in the middle of the night pretty often. The bigger animals like bears or deer often tripped it. Just in case, though, Aiden pulled in, then went to the switch. He flipped it on and off. Yeah, it was set correctly.

He walked out to the middle of the drive and looked up. Nice clear sky tonight. Lots of stars. Aiden breathed deeply.

A clicking caught his ear and he dropped his head, cocking it.

Crickets. Had to be. Such a racket from the tree line a person couldn't hear much else. Aiden shook his head, rubbed his neck, and turned to go in.

He hit the buttons for the garage door and made his way to the kitchen, unloading his keys and phone on the counter. Aiden grabbed the mail from the front door, dumping it, too, on the counter. He washed his hands and splashed some water on his face before grabbing a beer from the fridge.

Here he was again. Same old.

Twisting off the top, Aiden raised the bottle, tipping his head back to drink.

The doorbell rang—loud and startling enough to make him jerk. The mouthful of cool brew he'd been about to enjoy splattered onto his chin and dripped onto his shirt. Shit, he thought as he tried to eyeball his own chest, when was the last time he'd even heard that bell? The only visitor he'd had since he'd relocated was Eddie, but his oldest friend entered through the garage, same as Aiden usually did himself.

He traded the beverage for a dishtowel, rubbed the cloth

over his well-past-five-o'clock stubble, and headed for the front door.

What could be up this late on a Monday night? And who?

Aiden flipped on the front deck lights and pulled open the door to find two men he'd never seen before.

"Mr. Miller," said the stocky one wearing a boxy suit and a gray buzz cut, "I'm Detective Lundgren. This is Detective Smaltz." Each one flashed a badge, the metal catching the light.

Smaltz nodded. He was a big guy, bulky and tall, with blond hair, droopy eyes, and a placid expression.

"Detectives," Aiden said, "what can I help you with?"

"We need to speak with you—privately," Lundgren said.

Aiden raised an eyebrow—his house wasn't exactly on top of his neighbors'. "Of course. Come in."

He led them to the great room, which boasted cushy furniture, a state-of-the-art entertainment center, and massive fireplace built with local stone. Vaulted ceilings and wide-planked natural hardwood floors connected the space to a dining area and the kitchen. Open living, everyone called it. Aiden had decided the bigger the space, the more a person felt the emptiness.

"I'd offer you a beer, but since you're on duty, how about a soda? Water? Coffee?"

Lundgren waved away the offer. "Thanks, we're fine."

"Please, sit, then." They chose the far ends of the couch. He sat in the leather armchair at their right, braced his elbows on his knees, and spread his hands wide. "So what can I do for you?" He imagined a property dispute or a background check on an employee.

"Mr. Miller," Lundgren began, "we have reason to believe drugs are being sold out of your store."

What? Aiden blinked, his synapses as stunned as if he'd been hit with a fastball in the head. "I'm sorry—drugs? In my store? This store?" He straightened and grasped his knees, every individual muscle in his hands straining.

"Yes, the Poconos branch."

Aiden shook his head. "No way."

"Oh, it's true," Lundgren insisted. "There's more than one arrow pointing directly to your store. We need a set of inside eyes, however. Someone we can trust, who's got a lot at stake. Figure you wouldn't want news to get out Miller's was running a drug ring."

"Jesus, no," Aiden said. My God, his father would keel over if the markets were associated with something like this. Then there was the bad press, tanking customer confidence—all attached to a branch already at risk due to poor profits.

Lundgren inclined his head before moving on. "You didn't suspect something? That's not why you've suddenly gotten more involved in this store?"

"No." Aiden shook his head. "I had no idea. This location hasn't been doing well, so I've moved here, indefinitely, to get it on track." They didn't need to know about the doctor-required rest and relaxation. Translation: avoidance of the more high-maintenance stores in Philly, his workaholic nature, and plaguing anxiety.

Smaltz finally spoke. "What? The Midas touch doesn't extend out here to the Poconos?" His voice was easygoing, and his lips curled up.

Aiden cringed. "Not lately." Midas of Markets, they called him. Aiden would love to get his hands on the idiot reporter that first came up with that. Admittedly, it was usually true. Even here, where he'd opened a store almost on whim and had the ebb and flow of seasonal population to contend with, he'd easily made the branch a success. He'd gotten bored, though, and returned to Philly. Little by little, the store's bottom line tilted, until the downhill incline became too steep to ignore.

Not for the first time, Aiden wished he'd sold the troubled branch to Barry King when he had the chance. But King's increasingly aggressive offers to buy the store had ceased. He didn't know why, but it damn sure wasn't because King's

FreshRite chain had suddenly recovered the market share Miller's had stolen. FreshRite sucked, and so did its profits, but at least King wasn't housing a drug ring.

Aiden leaned forward again, clasping his hands together. "Why aren't you questioning me? Instead of enlisting my help?"

"Oh, we checked you out when we first got the anonymous tip." The older detective, Lundgren, shrugged. "It's not you—that's clear. If we just wanted to bust an individual or two, run a few kids through on possession, we'd have done it already. But this operation is nasty. We want every individual involved."

Smaltz leaned forward, and if the gleam in his eye hadn't clued Aiden in that his easygoing demeanor was a ruse, his words would have. "Gotta yank the whole thing up like a ball of roots. Eradicate every single fucker bringing drugs into our community."

"Okay." Aiden breathed deeply, then braced himself. "What kind of drugs are we talking about?"

"Prescription drugs, large volume. You know, painkillers like OxyContin, depressants, which are your anti-anxiety meds and sleep aids like Xanax, stimulants like Ritalin, and maybe even tranquilizers."

"Tranquilizers?" Aiden asked, only able to envision marauding bears shot with dart guns, a common occurrence out here.

"You know, like roofies."

At his blank look, Smaltz added, "Date-rape drugs."

Aiden closed his eyes as a sick feeling washed over him. He forced himself to speak, needing the facts. "It's not just some kids raiding their parents' medicine cabinets, reselling pills out of my store? We're talking"—he swallowed hard—"an actual dealer?"

Lundgren's expression was grim. "The dealer, we believe, is Butch Kovacs."

"Butch?" Pain sliced through Aiden's chest with enough

intensity that he pressed a fist to his sternum. "Fucking A."
Aiden shook his head. "I gave him a chance... I trusted him."
No way. He looked hard at the detectives. "Wait—how sure are
you?"

"Ninety-nine percent," Lundgren said. "But he's a peon. He's
the black market distributor. In other words, he's the guy they
send stuff to in dribs and drabs when it's become too hot to
unload to the secondary wholesaler."

"A wholesale business for stolen prescription drugs right
under my nose..." Aiden murmured, trying to wrap his mind
around this news.

"Oh, yeah," Smaltz confirmed. "But that's just a small
piece of the pie. These guys'll take anything—cigarettes, cancer drugs, alcohol, even hair-care products. Cargo theft is a
multibillion-dollar business. Highly skilled teams of criminals
raid warehouses or hijack tractor-trailers. They print fake labels,
then offer huge discounts under the guise that the units are
nearly expired, and presto, the pedigrees pharmaceuticals are
supposed to have to show that they originate from an autho-
rized dealer..." He shrugged.

"Jesus," Aiden muttered as he rubbed his forehead. "I
wouldn't have though Butch had it in him." He still couldn't
fathom it. He hoped, prayed, that somehow these men were
wrong.

Lundgren shook his head. "Like I said, we think he's only an
end guy, the local distributor. One of many. The guys supplying
him? That's who we're really after."

Huh. The guys supplying him. That was who Aiden must
have heard in the rear lot the other night. Butch's cohorts,
but...

Aiden felt the pressure stabbing his chest worsen and his
breathing turn shallow as the gravity of this situation hit home.
This was a big fucking operation. People could be hurt. Beads of
sweat erupted on his forehead, and he managed, "So my store—
and Butch—is a means to an end. For them, and you."

———

The panic that flared in the woods had receded, but anxiety and anger only increased during the trip home, eventually roaring louder than the whir of multiple blenders at the juice bar.

Those two men—God. At first, it seemed they'd meant harm…that glint of metal could have been guns. So scared— just for one second—but whoa, that second had just sucked.

Because what if they had been some jackasses—robbers or blackmailers or something—and they'd killed him?

No, no. He couldn't die. It would ruin literally everything.

But a person could die. Just walking out the door any given morning. An aneurysm explodes gray matter without warning. Too much rain and a falling tree smashes a skull. Focus is else- where and bam, a car crushes a body as easily as a soda can… That last could be called up from memory like it'd been yester- day. A hard shake—block it out.

Accidents. Some things simply couldn't be controlled or foreseen. A split second, and the world changed irrevocably. Made a person feel every ounce of vulnerability.

But the event had certainly illuminated the situation. Too close, and yet not close enough all at once. Time to step it up. That'd been reality check part A.

Reality check part B? The men were cops. Badges, not guns. Idiot.

"Too much TV."

Humiliation flared, with a surge of anger in its wake. Quick check over each shoulder, lip curling. TV? No, more like taught to believe the worst.

Unbelievable, just un-fucking-believable. All good buddies now, the police shaking Miller's hand on the way out. Never dreamed the cops would involve him, when it was all set up. But should have realized it was a possibility. Dumb, so fucking dumb. Frustration churned, building.

Not the cops' secret to tell, goddammit, but mine. Mine, mine, mine.

That was supposed to be the ace in the hole. A blockade removed, coupled with the cementing of trust and gratitude, proof of loyalty. A serious bonding session. Superglue. Welding. Insurance...before The Big Reveal.

Fuck and double fuck. Those damn cops had totally screwed up the insurance policy. Now it was back to mustering courage, sweaty palms, doubt...always the doubt.

Rage erupting—palms pounding the desk. Over and over. Stinging and pain. Finally, palms numb, head hanging in acceptance. Hard truth was, it was not only the cops' fault. It had been years of staging, needing surety. So close to the perfect setup, finally, finally in place—but the length of time had also been a negative, allowing problems to creep in.

"I should have done it already. Long ago."

"You blame me for talking you out of it."

"I blame you for all of it." Yanking photos off the floor. Frowning at a close-up of the prize. "I am such a chickenshit."

"Only when it comes to this, and it's for the best anyway."

"I have to be sure."

"You can't trust him."

"So you've told me. A million friggin' times."

"Especially him."

"I know, I know." Turning back to the screen. "Shut up now. I have to concentrate."

Shake it off. Regroup...get a handle on all of it before forming a new plan.

Oh, yeah. Reality check C. To see the way he'd looked at that dumpy woman during the interview. It was disgusting. Puke-worthy. So concerned and caring and pleased. On day one. Ridiculous. Hurtful. Another vulnerable moment. Made the blood boil. Even now.

And part D? The woman who'd orchestrated the new hire.

Trouble—big time. Used to be women, lots of them, and sometimes a steady one here or there. But not lately, and not here in the Poconos. This one, though… He'd never laughed so easily before or looked so fascinated…so hungry. Simply not fair, not after all this time. Friggin' weakling, Miller was, responding like that. Traitor.

Entirely unacceptable. Doubly so now, when things were so close to being set to rights. All that hard work, careful planning, and patient waiting nearing an end.

God, the fucking waiting. Biding. Time. Fucking. Sucked. Tenfold worse when it looked like it was all going to hell.

How to handle these developments? These sudden side streets appearing out of nowhere, when it was supposed to be a one-way, no-exit highway…

They had to be cut off. Roadblocked.

Reaching up, pulling hard. Think, think.

"You shouldn't have involved the police. That plan was too complicated."

Gritting teeth. "You're the one who always said I could control anything with a smile and a well-placed suggestion. That cunning was best served sweet. That planning and patience are key. That the trail should always be invisible, and dirty hands are a last resort."

"You can still use the Kovacs drug thing. Telling will still paint you in a good light."

"Maybe, but it's lost its impact. As for the other—"

"I told you he wasn't to be trusted."

Again? Already? Heaving a sigh. "I wanted you to be wrong, okay?"

"You don't know him like I do."

"Yeah, well, I'm learning the hard way. It doesn't matter now anyway. I have to regain control, before I even have any options. Clear the path for me. Make the distractions disappear."

Disappear. Vanish. A string of ideas. Scare off. Eradicate. Eliminate. Exterminate.

"That little project you started after the Radnor woman showed back up?"

Instinct had called for a just-in-case gift. Yes, gifts were fun. One begun...perhaps another from the other end, delivered via third party. A two-pronged warning should make the message clear. A real smile, a rarity. "For starters."

CHAPTER 8

DEEP IN THE SHADOWS and flush against the brick wall. Backpack at the ready on the asphalt. Despite the late hour, the pavement was still toasty underfoot. The plan was crafted and set it in motion right after Radnor and her little pull-toy, Clarice, had visited Miller. And now it was ready. Ripe for delivery. Thankfully, because obviously action was necessary. The bitch deserved far more than she was going to get. The heat wave in the next couple of days would certainly help in that regard, delivering the warning with that much more impact.

Peeking around the corner of the building one more time. No one on the street. Windows dark upstairs and in the neighboring businesses as well. Almost too quiet. Extracting the small lock pick, slipping away from the wall and setting to work.

With plenty of previous experience, it didn't take long. Piece of junk trunk creaked loudly as it opened, however.

Straining to hear once more…nothing. Then donning rubber gloves over the black ones. Hefting the gift out of the bag and laying the bundle in the trunk, the heavy plastic crinkling. Unwrapping it with as little noise as possible. The timeline unclear—annoying that the internet had little concrete information on this one. Still, utter confidence in the end result.

All done. Folding the wrapping neatly into itself and tucking it into a heavy plastic bag, along with the rubber gloves. Not all that nasty yet. Still, best not to take the stench, or the evidence, home. Better to ditch the garbage a few blocks away.

This little present would get better with age, however, and that meant it was necessary to jam the trunk lock but good. Resources were scarce on this part, too, but rather like accidentally snagging fabric in a zipper, there were anecdotes about catching jackets or blankets in car trunks. It should work. To that end, a piece of tough nylon fabric (thin enough to catch, durable enough not to tear), a large tube of superglue (extra insurance maybe), some careful placement, and a bit of luck...

Two failed tries. Dammit, the glue would be dry in seconds...

Third time—yes! It felt right, and the trunk stayed closed.

Too focused to notice if it'd been loud. Retreating to the shadows to wait.

Nothing.

Stupid people slept like the dead.

Give it five more anyway. Another brilliant idea had surfaced. Might even be the better of the two. So, just wait it out.

Always the waiting. Waiting for things to change, waiting for people to take the hint, or suffer the consequences. Waiting and watching, too. Sometimes to see which way the cards needed to fall. Sometimes to gather information. Waiting to be sure. Had to embrace the waiting. A necessity that always, eventually, paid off.

Focus. Still all quiet. And more work to be done.

Peeling away from the wall, surveying the car. A blank canvas.

Not for long.

Excitement surged. Two for one.

———

Saturday morning's interview went well for Alan, and Tori couldn't have been more pleased that she'd pushed Aiden Miller in the first place. Butch had been impressed by Alan's manners and undeterred when she'd mentioned on the sly that he sometimes had trouble with his ankle.

Although Butch looked every inch a tough guy under his official store polo—sporting tattoos on both forearms, a silver stud on the left ear, a shaved head, and heavy-duty work boots jutting out from under his khakis—he was as jovial and friendly as could be.

Luke had been in and out of the room during the interview, listening in, while not appearing to. Tori knew that he felt as protective of Alan as she did.

As soon as Butch officially welcomed Alan on board, Luke approached. "Mr. Kovacs? You got room for one more at Miller's?"

"Who do you have in mind?" Butch asked.

"Me," Luke said.

"Luke!" Tori's jaw nearly hit the floor.

"I would never take a job from any of the UpStart people"—he glanced between them—"but I really want to earn some money, so if you really are hurting for workers?"

Butch looked to her.

She rubbed her forehead. "We've talked about this. You're helping out at that lacrosse clinic this summer. It looks good for college."

"So does a job," Luke said. "And lacrosse is, like, three hours a day. It's nothing. Do you really want me underfoot all summer?"

Tori noticed that both Alan and Butch's lips were twitching. She sighed.

"I can do both easy," Luke said. "Besides, there aren't even any jobs I can walk to around here. But if I'm at Miller's, they could put me on the same shifts as Clarice and Alan, so it's one trip for you." Then: "It'd take the pressure off you, Mom, if I could earn—"

Tori groaned. "Stop right there." The last thing she needed was Butch knowing how much she worried, what little income she made, or anything else.

Butch said, "Well, I don't want to get in the middle of family stuff here, but would it help if I told you I could just about guarantee some more UpStart hires going forward?"

Tori glanced at Alan, hoping for a gauge on what some of her other clients might feel about this. But the man sported a grin so big his eyes squished up.

"Okay, fine," Tori said.

Alan let out a hearty laugh, Luke pulled his fist in with a yes, and Butch chuckled.

"You didn't stand a chance," Butch said to her.

"I guess I didn't," she said. "Interview him as you would anyone else."

Alan thanked both Butch and Tori. On his way out, he said, "Clarice is going to love this. Yes-sir-ee."

After Luke's application and impromptu interview, they awaited Clarice, who was to catch a ride to the store.

"That your car down in back?" Butch asked.

"Yes."

She assumed he was just making conversation, but Butch shook his head and pursed his lips. "Such a shame."

"What do you mean?"

"The graffiti." He frowned when he saw her confusion. "You haven't seen it?"

"Graffiti on my car?" Tori rushed for the door. Couldn't possibly be finger painting in grime, given Butch's reaction. Spray paint, maybe?

Tori burst out the ground-level door into the sunshine. Her little dark blue Corolla sat in its usual spot and looked the same as always. Butch's vehicle, a black four-door pickup truck, sat on its far side, also parked head in to the wobbly six-foot wooden fence dividing her chunk of asphalt from the one the left.

When Tori rounded the tail end, she gasped, her hands snapping up to cover her mouth. There were jagged scratches—like a child's drawing of a rudimentary mountain range, the peaks and valleys zigzagging up and down from under the trunk lock all the way to the right side.

"Oh, man," she heard Luke say from behind her.

Butch, who'd followed her, lifted his hands, palms up. "It's been keyed—bad."

Luke squeezed her shoulder with one of his big paws.

"Who would do such a thing?" she murmured. "Everybody knows us here."

Butch cleared his throat, looking extremely uncomfortable as his nearly black irises shifted away from her. "Uh, unfortunately, there's more." He gestured between their two cars to her car's passenger side.

Tori moved slowly, her feet feeling leaden. How much worse could it be?

She froze and stared, hardly able to believe her eyes. Not only was her poor car further defaced, but the vandal's scratches spelled out an awful—simply horrid—message.

DISAPPEAR OR DIE, BITCH.

Tears sprang to her eyes, making the sunlight sparkle, and she squeezed her arms around herself. The temperature had already climbed to seventy this morning, probably more in the direct sun as they were, but she shivered—cold through and through.

Butch squeezed her shoulder gently. "I'm really sorry. That's... Well, it blows all the way around."

Tori nodded.

"Those scratches are deep," he said. "Not going to just buff out. You'll need to take her in."

Tori knew her crappy insurance policy wouldn't cover this. She'd gone for covering people, not the car, which wasn't worth squat. And she couldn't afford a big outlay of cash. Tori shut her eyes. My God, she'd be forced to drive Luke and her clients around like this.

"I know a guy," Butch said. "He owes me. I'll get him to give you a hefty discount."

Tori told herself that a car was just a car, yet she rubbed her hands up and down her arms anyway. "Thanks, Butch. I'd appreciate that."

"What you're doing here, with UpStart, it's a good thing,"

Butch said. "So don't give up. Take precautions, but don't give in to that threat." His voice had hardened with anger, and his expression became fierce.

Tori shook her head. "I can't imagine that is really meant for me. Probably a case of mistaken car identity," she said with a wry smile. "Or some hoodlum's poor idea of a joke."

"Maybe, but if it happened overnight, back here in your parking lot, doesn't it figure someone local did it? Someone who knows you, who chose your car specifically?"

Tori was shaking her head before he even finished. "Around here, they do know me—and support our mission. This had to have happened while we were somewhere else. I wouldn't have spotted it in the dark last night, nor would anyone coming in or out of the building on foot this morning. Only you, because you parked on the far side."

Butch angled his head as if considering; however, she could see by his narrowed gaze that he didn't agree.

Her neighborhood, sketchy as it seemed to outsiders, was safe. They all watched out for each other. There was simply no way anyone from the shelter would have done this, nor her few business neighbors who largely vacated the area at night anyway. A passerby, maybe. But doubtful.

The threat—well, that definitely upset her, but who knew? It could mean nothing to her.

Finally, she reminded herself, things could always be worse. In fact, they had been, not all that long ago.

Tori put her hands on her hips. As soon as she had some ready cash, she'd take Butch up on that offer. She sucked in a fortifying breath, then quickly covered her nose with her arm. "Ugh, do you smell that? Something reeks."

"I do," Luke said, making a face.

Glad for the distraction, she headed for the Dumpster at the rear of the narrow lot. She lifted the lid and scrunched up her nose. "Hasn't been picked up yet."

Butch asked, "Are they due to come today?"

Tori grimaced. "Not until Monday. Unfortunately."

"Listen, are you all right?" he asked.

"Yeah, thanks." Tori took a fortifying breath. "This is one bitch who's way too busy to disappear or die."

CHAPTER 9

AIDEN AND HIS DAD exited the store at five p.m., just as Tori rolled by in her little sedan, windows down, her dark gold hair half blown out of its clip. She smiled brightly and gave a slight wave before turning down an aisle to look for a spot.

"Who's the lovely lass? A customer?" Patrick Miller asked, with a hint of the Irish that still nuanced his words. Pops was in a fine mood, as he liked nothing better than visiting the store, especially with Aiden at his side. He'd been incredibly proud when Aiden's novel ideas—organic everything, specialty imports, and ready-made, hearty meals for dine-in or takeout— had made the chain such a huge success.

"More like a business associate. Her name is Tori Radnor. She does..." He frowned, momentarily distracted. What the hell had happened to the back of her car? "...some charity work placing homeless people in jobs." Aiden waved a hand. "I took on one of her clients."

"You did, eh?" his dad said, a note of surprise clear in his voice.

"I know, I know," Aiden said, "I've made a point to avoid stuff like that. Hate the constant hounding. I give a set amount, yearly, to the same charities every year, period. But we were short-staffed, Butch was out, and Tori..."

He'd tried hard at first to be annoyed by all that goodness oozing from her like maple syrup. Given his upbringing, warning bells should have been sounding off like an evacuation siren. Instead he'd agreed to hire her client, getting sticky despite himself. All because he couldn't bear to tell her no when her incredible green eyes shone with such hope.

Granted, he wished he could renege now. Someone in Clarice's position didn't need to be anywhere near a drug operation.

But he couldn't. Detective Lundgren didn't want a single pink slip—nobody leaves, he'd insisted—until after the police made their big sting. Similarly, nobody was to know…which all sucked, because his hands were tied.

Aiden shrugged.

"Tori what?"

Pops was like a hunting dog when he caught a scent. Aiden shook his head. "Decide for yourself."

They watched Tori traverse the crosswalk in loose linen pants and a pleated white blouse, sleeves rolled up to show slim wrists, laced with beaded bracelets. Aiden felt like a puppy, nearly panting and drooling with pleasure. Christ, it was crazy how this woman made him feel.

After Aiden had made the introductions, Tori said, "Mr. Miller, how nice to meet you," even as Patrick took her hand in his gnarled ones.

"You as well, lass."

Then both men spoke at once: Aiden inquiring after her car, Patrick saying, "Aiden here tells me you do good work helping the less fortunate."

Tori slanted Aiden a look, ignored his question, and responded to his dad. "I do."

"Tell me a little about it."

Aiden listened to her spiel again—this time less of a sales pitch, more conversational. God, she really was beautiful, he thought, and found himself in awe of the light in her eyes and excitement in her voice. He didn't experience an ounce of that passion in his own work.

Sure, there'd been a time, long ago, when he'd been making big changes and had felt jazzed. Except that feeling had been about starting something new, being a maverick, giving the community something they didn't even know they needed. Not simply running a grocery day after tedious day.

In no time at all, Aiden could see that Tori and his father were both enamored.

"Where are you and your son off to?"

"The ballpark, of course!" Patrick said.

"The minor league one in Scranton with the funny name?" Tori put a finger to her lips. "The IronPigs?" she asked.

"Close," Aiden said. "That's the Lehigh Valley team. Scranton has the RailRiders."

"Tonight it's the Wilmington Warriors at home against the Arlington Armed Angels," Patrick said, then explained further at her blank look. "Still Triple-A ball, but in the East Division of the International League, along with the Morgantown Miners and the Frostburg Jacks."

"Ah," Tori said, "I've heard of them."

"I hope so." Patrick beamed. "My boy here played for the Jacks."

Aiden only rolled his eyes.

"That's a long way for an evening ball game."

Aiden agreed. They'd chosen that game on purpose, though, because rumor had it that after this season, the franchise may be no more.

Patrick shrugged. "We always go to a ball game to celebrate our birthdays, ever since Aiden's mother decided that any gifts should go directly to the needy."

"Pop," Aiden said.

"What? It's true. The time together is a real silver lining, especially now. When he was young, though, boy was he angry."

Tori shot Aiden a quizzical look.

"Hey," he said, feeling ten all over again. "It would have been one thing if it had been my idea. But it wasn't. I desperately wanted those DC Comics action figures."

"Not to mention that signed ball."

"We're not going there, Dad." Aiden crossed his arms.

"She didn't even let him keep them an hour," Patrick said.

True. His mother, Marjorie, had taken the whole lot, unwrapped but not yet opened, allowing him to keep only her own gift—hand-carved chopsticks she'd bought from some orphan selling wares on the street of whatever Asian country she had recently aided.

No way did Tori need to hear any more about his crazy mother. "Pop—"

Patrick yapped on. "Once Marjorie gets an idea in her head, well…" He looked at Aiden. "Tell her what you did, lad."

"Absolutely not." Tori would think he was deranged.

"It was quite inventive, really, and healing, too, I suspect."

Tori raised her eyebrows, and Aiden glared hard at his father.

"Anyway," Patrick whispered to Tori, "after that, we gave up on presents. Aiden and I both love baseball. Marjorie doesn't get it, so every year off we'd go without her—"

"Tori's heard enough about my sorry upbringing."

"Your childhood wasn't bad!"

Aiden held up a hand. "I was very blessed. I'm just saying—enough."

Patrick hooked a thumb at Aiden, simultaneously winking at Tori. Great, Aiden thought, clenching his jaw. Make it official. They'd ganged up.

"So whose birthday is it?" Tori asked.

"His," Patrick said, "and he still tried to get out of it."

"No!" Tori exclaimed with mock horror.

"I'm busy. The store—"

"Bosh," Patrick said. "You're overdue for some time off. Butch can handle everything for an evening."

Exactly the issue. Butch *handling* things. Though he really did love a good ball game, especially with Pops. Didn't matter if it was big league, farm team, or even a decent high school match-up. He could always sink into the game and lose track of his worries.

"Happy birthday," Tori said, meeting his eyes.

"Thanks." Holding her gaze, he mentally flashed on a more intimate birthday celebration. Her wish, followed by a hot kiss, a deep moan. He'd slide that clip out of her hair and—

The breeze picked up, sending Tori's hair right into her face.

"Oh," she said, breaking eye contact, "I didn't realize I was such a mess."

She whipped out that clip and fastened it to the V-neck of her blouse. Aiden swallowed hard.

"Ach, lass, ye look fetching any which way," Patrick said, making Tori scrunch up her nose.

"And you," she said, "have a way with words." She stuck her keychain between her teeth and reached up with both arms to smooth then twist her hair up in back.

Aiden gulped. He should *not* be noticing the way her breasts strained against the now taut cotton...and he for damn sure shouldn't be fighting the urge to grab the material and...

She mumbled, "I had to ride with all the windows down." Task complete, she snatched the keys from her teeth. "There was a stink in our area that really seemed to linger in my car."

Aiden grasped that like a lifeline. "What happened to the back of your car, anyway?"

Tori's face fell. "Somebody keyed it."

Aiden got a twinge in his chest, except it wasn't the usual sharp pang signaling an impending attack.

"Really? How terrible," Patrick said. Aiden was glad his dad's old eyes hadn't spotted the damage, or he'd be just as concerned as Aiden found himself.

Tori bit her lip and glanced away, and Aiden frowned. That was some serious vandalism, but why did she seem embarrassed?

"Well," Tori said, "I enjoyed talking with you, Mr. Miller, but I'd better collect Clarice."

"The woman you hired, Aiden?"

"Yes."

"I'd like to meet her. And, I daresay, I wouldn't mind spending a little more time in your presence, my dear." He chuckled as he patted Tori's hand. "Let's all go in, but you must call me Patrick, or better yet, Paddy."

Aiden remembered why the corner store had held on so long

amidst the influx of the big-box chains. Good old-fashioned customer service, personal connections, and a heavy dose of Irish
charm. He chuckled to himself as he followed the pair inside.
They'd definitely miss the first inning.

He didn't mind, though. His dad wasn't the only one who
craved more time with Tori.

————

Huh, Tori thought to herself as she followed Aiden through the
market, the senior Miller bringing up the rear. Outside, other
than desperately trying to derail his dad, Aiden had been as
relaxed as she'd seen him. His eyes had lit with pleasure, his
smile had been genuine, and even his embarrassment had been
charming. Now, however, she watched his wide shoulders creep
closer to his ears with every step he took.

Just past the refrigerated section, Haley—Tori's favorite—
joined them. Aiden asked, "Have you seen Clarice?"

"Shift's over," Haley said. She held Tori's eyes with a small
smile playing about her lips. "She's probably getting ready to
go…home."

Tori narrowed her eyes, but Haley had moved on. Her smile
adjusted to disgustingly sweet, as she gazed at Aiden. "I'm
headed to the locker room, if you want me to check."

"No, thanks. We're almost there anyway."

"Haley, lass. How have you been?" Patrick said, patting the
girl on the back.

"Hi, Mr. Miller," she said, and they continued to chat as the
gang tromped past the rear of the dining area.

Out of nowhere, a high-pitched scream erupted. A loud
metal bang, then another series of short screams.

Aiden rushed forward, his dad on his heels. Tori had some
first-aid training. She didn't think, just followed.

The men pushed through a set of swinging doors, paused,
then headed right. Tori kept up, only to skid to a halt in a room
full of tables and chairs, modern sofas, and lockers ringing the

space. Clarice sat on the floor, her back against the rear of a couch, knees tucked up, hands fanning her face, eyes squeezed shut.

"Clarice!" Tori said. "What happened, what's wrong?" she asked.

Far more pale than normal, Clarice only made a high-pitched noise behind her closed mouth.

Aiden reached her first, taking her hands, pulling her up to stand. "Are you hurt?"

She bit her lip and pointed.

"Your locker?

She nodded, eyes wide.

Tori wrapped her arm around the poor woman, tucking her into her own side as she watched Aiden. He took a few steps toward the lockers and touched a handle. "This one?"

Clarice shook her head. He shifted one over to the right, and she nodded.

Tori held her breath. What in the world could have upset her so much?

She heard the clang of the latch lifting, saw that he'd opened the door. His broad back filled the space and Tori craned to see. A pause, then he slammed it shut. When Aiden turned around, his scowl was fierce.

"Son?" Patrick Miller asked, concern etched on his face.

Aiden whipped his phone off his belt, pushed a button, and held it sideways like a walkie-talkie. "Butch," he barked. "I need you in the staff room now. And for God's sake, call the exterminator."

"What the hell?" Tori muttered, and charged forward.

"Take Clarice out of here." Aiden crossed his arms over his chest, the phone crackling with static in his palm.

She scowled.

"I need my purse," Clarice said from behind her, sounding shaky.

"Aiden." Tori's voice vibrated with warning.

"I'll bring it out. Please. Wait for me on the other side of the doors."

"Absolutely not. Clarice is under my care. And if this store is infested—"

Patrick told Aiden, "Whatever it is, she's got a right to know." The he turned to Clarice. "Come," he said, gently taking her arm.

Tori raised her chin and narrowed her eyes at Aiden. His jaw ticked and he held her stare until she heard the swinging door swish open and settle closed.

"You're not going to like it," he said, stepping to the side.

Tori reached for the metal handle. Took a breath. She jumped at a noise behind her, and turned to look over her shoulder.

Butch barreled through the doors. "What's up?" he asked. Tori realized Haley lingered in the room as well and stood only a few feet to her left.

Aiden's voice was clipped as he gestured toward Tori. "See for yourself."

Tori lifted and pulled. Gasped and jumped back.

Directly at eye level, was an obese but definitely dead rat, hanging from a coat hook. Tori looked closer. His tail was looped around the metal curve. No...not looped, but...double-knotted.

CHAPTER 10

AFTER YESTERDAY'S BIZARRE rat incident, Tori felt somewhat uncomfortable sending Alan and Luke for their first shift at Miller's on Sunday, along with Clarice, who'd already been scheduled. She simply couldn't understand it, couldn't remotely fathom a rhyme or reason for something so cruel and sick. Butch had sworn that nothing like this had ever happened before. He and Aiden both promised they'd get to the bottom of it, and it wouldn't happen again.

Clarice had been shaken, of course, and on the way home, Tori noticed that every so often she shimmied her shoulders as if trying to dislodge the heebie-jeebies. Later, Luke had seemed fascinated with the details, like every teenage boy who thought the grosser, the cooler. And Alan had only frowned and shaken his head as if disappointed in the human race in general.

But to a one, even Clarice, they felt it had been some sort of twisted prank, probably not even meant for Clarice. They'd speculated: perhaps a joke gone awry, the wrong locker number, or some kind of sick dare from one idiot to another...

More importantly, no one would hear of delaying their shifts until Aiden and Butch had ferreted out the culprit.

"Not like it'd happen twice," Luke had said.

And she supposed he was right.

Tori didn't feel at ease, however, until she saw her little clan troop out of the store together at shift end. They chatted amongst themselves, and Luke responded animatedly to something Alan said. Clarice patted him on the shoulder.

On the other hand, her relief was tempered by an unreasonable kick of disappointment. Aiden hadn't escorted them out. She told herself it was only that she'd wanted to know if they'd gotten to the bottom of the prank, and chose to forget that she'd taken extra care with her outfit and her lipstick.

"So, how'd it go?" she asked.

"Great," Luke said. "Mr. Kovacs put me up front on registers."

"He got the hang of it in no time, even memorized some of the codes already," Clarice explained. "I decided I'm happier *not* on registers."

Luke said, "You just got a little flustered."

"I got a lot flustered." Clarice shook her head, but was smiling.

"And you, Alan?"

"It went just fine. I sure am happy to have something to occupy my day."

Tori wanted to cheer. "Awesome. Let's celebrate."

Both Clarice and Alan tried to tell her it wasn't necessary.

"It most certainly is," she said.

A short time later, they settled at a picnic table, the cool June breeze making Tori wrap one hand in her hair to keep it out of her black raspberry ice cream. Cars zipped by, headlights on, but only an older couple and one family shared the space with them. Most kids were home, being forced to bed, by parents who knew Monday morning would be a struggle.

Luke was quiet and seemed distracted.

"What's up?" Tori asked her son.

"Huh? Nothing," he said.

Tori narrowed her eyes but didn't press him.

"Mmmn," Alan said. "Just about as good as my momma used to make."

"She made it herself?" Luke asked incredulously, and Tori laughed.

Details ensued, and Tori forced herself to wait until they were tossing their napkins in the trash before she asked, "Did Mr. Miller update any of you on Clarice's scare?"

Alan said, "I don't believe Mr. Miller was in today. I was looking forward to thanking him for hiring us all."

"Mr. Kovacs made sure to check in with me a few times," Clarice said. "But he said he didn't know anything more than last night."

Tori sighed. They returned to the car, but Luke stopped her from getting in with a tug on her wrist.

He waited until Clarice and Alan had both slid in and then said quietly, "Dad was across the street."

"What!" She spun and scanned the parking lots of the businesses on the other side but couldn't spot him.

"I think he's gone now," Luke said.

"Why didn't you tell me?"

"I *am* telling you."

"Before!" Tori said. "When I could have *done* something about it."

"Because you *would* have done something about it." He flicked a glance at the car, indicating their passengers.

Tori blew out a hard breath. Sometimes it sucked when her teenager actually used his head.

———

Out of sight but too far away to hear the conversation. Disgusted by the happy smiles. So sappy.

And Radnor, all fancy. Sunday best for Miller, surely. A far cry from Friday's pickup outfit.

Practically overnight their numbers had gone from one to three. Damn that Kovacs. He really had to go. He was fucking things up with his Mr. Nice Guy routine. Three new employees through that stupid UpStart program meant that bitch Radnor was going to be there virtually every damn day, slithering up to Miller like a snake twists around a branch.

Grip tightening so hard the shutter nearly made one continuous sound: *clickclickclickclickclick*. Not okay. Because unlike all those women from before, this particular one, for some reason, he wasn't ignoring.

Not remotely okay. His life needed to be empty. Dead and cold. Ripe for someone new—only one someone had the right to be there.

They were all laughing now. One big smiley family. UpStart. *Click*. More like upchuck. Commuting to work together and ice cream trips. Sickeningly sweet. So TV family. Not real life.

Definitely not something they'd have done as a family, or non-family as it were. Ice cream had come from the grocery store. Or once in a while a fast-food milkshake off the highway during their camping trips. Car camping, they'd called it. No roasted marshmallows, because there'd been no fires. No tents, no pillows, no pajamas, and no plan. Impromptu excursions, nearly always an unexpected destination. Full of possibility. And sometimes disappointment. Twice, they'd ended up at the beach with no swimsuits.

All the hours in the car meant plenty of time for stories, though. A favorite pastime. "It's time," one of them always began. Then, "Which one do you want to hear first?" The memory fond. The voice in it so pleased.

Until it wasn't. A shift always occurred. Tripping a downward spiral: frustration, bitterness, depression. And for one of them, invariably: hunger. Rarely any food on those trips. Learned early to take what was needed. If caught, the other rules, smiles, and well-placed suggestions came in handy. Learned preparation and planning, too. Back then that meant handfuls of pretzels in pockets. Pop-Tarts hidden under the seat.

Now it meant weighing every possibility, calculating reactions and risk, long-term assessments...predicting all nine innings.

Hah. That was the other thing they'd done together. Family time inevitably meant a lot of ball games. Even as the years went on. Here, there, anywhere within driving distance.

Radnor's kid finished his cone long before the others. But his attention kept shifting...

There... Another watcher?

Zoom lens on the camera worth every single penny: old guy, preppy, hangdog expression, but intense eyes.

Watching who? *Click, click, click.*

Interesting. He'd glanced at the others and lingered on Radnor, but his overall focus remained bull's-eyed on her boy. Surprised the kid didn't go up in smoke. Who was he? Weirdo with a grudge? Some perv? Some loser Radnor had screwed and discarded, who maybe held a grudge? That'd fit.

Bore checking into. Could be useful.

Information was power, after all.

———

Even though his desk at home faced a stretch of wall-to-wall windows, Aiden stood up and moved to stand in front of the glass. Rolled his shoulders, tipped his neck side to side, cracking it, and tried to draw a deep breath.

A riot of untamed trees, brush, and vines covered the property past his clearing, and a short path through it led to the lake just below, where his dock tethered a speedboat and two jet skis. On the bank, well away from the lapping water, lay two kayaks—his preferred water sport, as it quieted the mind. The sun highlighted the treetops as it rose, although the air wouldn't feel like June until close to noon. The water would be ball-shrinking cold until mid-July, so he kept wet suits in the shed to lengthen the season.

The view brought him little peace today. He'd slept like shit and had already downed two cups of coffee. What with the worry over a sick prank on his newest employee, a drug-dealing manager, and a store that was now surely doomed, not to mention all the good people he'd have to let go...

He shook his head. Yeah, this was some extreme shit, but truth be told, he hadn't been sleeping well before all this. Hell, it was why he was in the Poconos in the first place. Stress. Aiden blew out a breath, but his chest still felt tight. So much for doc's orders to take it easy.

About thirty-six hours, and Aiden still had no info pointing him toward a culprit. Whoever had planted that rodent in Clarice's locker was lying low. He'd considered every bizarre possibility—but the only one that made a lick of sense was a sort of warning to someone involved in the drug scheme. An *If you rat us out, you're dead* kind of message. Conveniently, the two security cameras in the staff room had lost their feed that evening. Wouldn't that point to a higher level of criminal? Still, he was surely reaching. Anybody distributing drugs would be aiming to stay under the radar, not draw attention to themselves.

Chances were better that the dead rodent was just somebody's sick idea of a joke.

Or an insult. Rats were associated with the streets. Clarice was homeless.

A bias extreme enough to plant a dead animal? Crazy. But then, he wouldn't have believed Butch was capable of selling drugs here either—not at the place he'd been given a second chance.

Theories swirled, but didn't really fit. Like two puzzles that had gotten mixed up in the same box, the pieces wouldn't connect. He shook his head hard. He had to stop speculating. Pointless, until they knew something definitive.

He'd hoped that by now someone would have come clean or maybe—hah—*rat* someone else out. He'd gotten a text from Butch last night: Clarice had worked a trouble-free shift on Sunday. One occurrence and done? He should be relieved. But he wasn't. He felt somehow that he'd be disappointing Tori, not doing right by Clarice, if he didn't have answers. Regardless, today he owed Tori a call.

Truth be told, he hadn't been avoiding only Tori yesterday by taking a day off. He was finding it extremely difficult to act normal with Butch.

He'd taken a chance on the guy—record and all—because his gut had told him he could trust the ex-con. Aiden had never been so dead wrong.

He clenched his fists. Once upon a time, Butch had done a good job. Now? No wonder the store was in the shitter. Running drugs. The man couldn't possibly have any energy left to give the actual job.

Christ, if only he could fire the fucker. But he couldn't. Lundgren had been ultra clear on that point.

He crossed to the custom display shelves lining one wall. Ignored the various framed photographs, business awards, and signed baseballs, and picked up instead the worn-out, well-loved glove he'd used in high school. Aiden removed the old practice ball nestled in the fold, put the mitt to his nose, and took one long sniff. He shut his eyes for just a moment, then chucked the glove back on the shelf. He spun to face the lake and tossed the familiar ball in his right hand, over and over, with a cadence he knew well.

Gradually, he calmed. Aiden stopped tossing the ball and spun it in increments instead. He focused by feel on the strings, the leather, the weight.

Too early to call Tori, anyway. Maybe a workout first to shake the last of the grogginess. Not the lake, though. Aiden needed distraction, not more time to think. He turned and grabbed his cell off the desk. Texting Eddie, he wrote, *30 min?*

The reply came back: *1 hr. Stressed already?*

Aiden blew out a breath. He'd been there just last night, after the detectives had caught him in the early evening to update him with *nothing* helpful.

Damn straight, he typed.

Talking to Eddie acted like a reminder: he still hadn't called his private investigator to check on Audra Smelty.

Nick Shepard picked up on the first ring, and promised that Aiden hadn't woken him. "I'm deep into a case. Haven't even been to sleep yet," Nick explained in a gravelly voice.

"This can wait."

"Good. I'd hate to ditch this just because you pay so damn well." Nick laughed. "Give me the particulars. I'll get on it the minute I'm free. Probably a week or so."

Aiden explained briefly about Eddie's feeling that the photographer outside The Granary had been focused on him, and the mental leap to checking up on his ex-stalker. "Unlikely she's made a reappearance. She hasn't bugged me in years."

"Time period?"

"Jesus—senior year of college to maybe my early to mid-thirties?" He snorted—human nature to not notice right away when something awful had ended. Only looking back did you realize it hadn't happened in a while. "Early on, it was awful—I literally couldn't go anywhere without her showing up. Even places she had no right to be. Once she scared the shit out of one of my teammates. She'd hid in a locker—thought it was mine."

"Jesus."

"Push came to shove the day she broke into my dad's house. She sat at his bedside for an hour." Aiden's temper flared thinking back. "He was ill, and was too weak to throw her out. When she finally left the room, he managed to get to the phone, and called the cops. They found her rooting through my childhood room, trying to shove a trophy down her shirt. I did the restraining order thing, but it didn't matter. I could still sense her, or she'd stay just out of range. Occasionally she'd show up somewhere crowded, like a bar or a game, pretending she didn't know I was there. She'd leave, but always tried to touch me first." Aiden's lip curled in distaste. "Got to where I'd scope out a cop or security guard anywhere I went."

"Phone calls and deliveries too?"

"Yeah. Some weird shit in the mail. A lock of hair or a picture of her in something skimpy—the head cut off, the envelopes unmarked." He snorted. Like that made it untraceable.

"Last time I saw her was in my Philly store. She'd disguised herself as an old woman, tried to get me to help her."

"That's a new one I haven't heard," Nick said. "Inventive."

Aiden laughed. "Yeah, but seriously, it's been probably eight to ten years since I've seen her, so finish your job and catch some sleep. I'm only looking into this because I promised my buddy I would. I'm sure it's nothing."

And he was. It'd be a waste of Shepard's time, not to mention his own. Aiden shook his head and swore. Now that Nick was on it, he wouldn't give crazy Audra another thought.

CHAPTER 11

FEELING A LITTLE LOOSER after the sparring session, Aiden entered the store through the back door, glancing up at the security camera as he did so.

He'd already scrolled through Saturday's tapes for locker tampering, but he'd seen nothing unusual in terms of how his staff or customers treated the woman. Trouble was, his system seemed to be on the fritz. Some of the feeds worked, others seemed to go on and off. Loose wires? Or tampering?

The detectives had requested a month's worth of video, and Aiden had managed to scan through most of those before passing them on. The only suspicious incident was only a couple of weeks ago. Butch had been accosted by two big men when he'd left the rear door one night. Hooded sweatshirts and shaved heads. Buddies from the joint? Old cohorts that had landed him there? They'd shoved him and gotten in his face. Although his body language read defensive and angry, Butch hadn't appeared to say much until he'd held up his hands and seemed to placate the pair. The tapes were fuzzy and angled from above, not to mention dark. Aiden doubted they'd provide conclusive IDs, but who knew? In the meantime, he just hoped Butch would avoid pissing the thugs off. Avoid any major altercations. Keep any violence—and messages in the form of dead animals—far away from his employees.

Yeah, discovering that hadn't helped Aiden's stress level a bit. He'd be lucky if he didn't develop ulcers to go along with the panic attacks.

Unfortunately, the only peace he'd had lately had been the workouts with Eddie and the ball game with his dad—even though they'd missed the first three innings because of the damn rat thing. As he dug out the key to his office—new habit, locking it—he fantasized for a second about selling the entire Miller's chain after this drug debacle went down. Except what would he do with himself? Floundering around bored and aimless would drive him batshit in a week flat. Besides, these stores were his dad's pride and joy—even now, after being benched for so many years.

He'd love to call Pops, tell him to come and stay with him for a few months, act as another set of eyes in this place. But he'd take the gory details very hard, and Aiden couldn't risk compromising his dad's health with the stress.

He sought out Haley at the customer service desk, then waited, outwardly patient at least, while she finished helping one of the regulars, giving him just the kind of attention he liked.

"Thank you, dear," the older man said. He stopped to peer up at Aiden and winked. "This one's a keeper, Mr. Miller. You owe her a raise."

"Don't I know it, Mr. Cranford," Aiden said.

"Why isn't she working at some important job instead of this old place?"

"You got me," Aiden said. "I told her she should take that degree and run. Even offered my highest recommendation."

Haley piped up. "There's nowhere I'd rather learn the ropes than here, under Mr. Miller."

"King Midas." Cranford chuckled. He slapped Aiden on the back as he turned to go. "She probably thinks you'll rub off."

"Wish that name would rub off."

"I'll just bet you do," he said without turning around.

Aiden chuckled—he could always count on receiving a dose of humility along with Cranford's compliments.

As soon as they were alone, he leaned his elbows on the high counter. "Have there been any new developments concerning Clarice's locker thing?" God forbid a customer heard him utter the word *rat*.

"No, none," Haley said.

"Any theories?" he asked.

Haley frowned and cocked her head. "Well, I can't be sure, but it seems she's been targeted for some reason."

"You don't think it could have been accidental? Maybe a bizarre joke meant for someone else?"

She crossed her arms and began to tap a pen against the counter—*tick, tick, tick*—apparently thinking.

"Haley?"

"I suppose," she said, "but who could it have been meant for?"

"Jesus, I don't know." Aiden scrubbed his hair in frustration. "You haven't noticed anybody giving her a hard time, have you? Anything unusual or suspicious?" He held his breath.

"Other than a dead rat showing up in her locker?" she asked, as Aiden cringed. She shook her head and answered her own question: "No. Not a thing."

He raised a hand to his neck. "Do me a favor, watch out for Clarice, okay? Be my eyes and ears."

Haley raised an eyebrow.

"The last thing she needs is to feel unwelcome. Her confidence is shaky at best," Aiden explained. "And while she's here, her well-being is my responsibility."

Haley nodded. *Tick tick tick* with the pen. "You're right, Mr. Miller—under our roof, it's up to us."

"Exactly. So, let me know if you hear or see anything, anything at all, okay? Maybe you can even take her under your wing."

She set the pen down, only to reach up and twirl a piece of hair around and around her finger. He thought for a second she'd spaced out, until she looked him right in the eye. "Sure," she said. "You can count on me."

"Great," he said. "I appreciate that more than you can know."

"No problem."

Aiden smiled. Haley might be young, but she'd been a model employee since her teens, when she'd started at the branch outside Philly. Smart, serious, courteous, hardworking, and willing to go the extra mile. Like Cranford said, she was a keeper.

Butch was next on Aiden's list, in order to make sure he was giving Tori the most current information. He clenched his jaw—it irked him to go to Butch for anything. Still, it was an excuse to keep tabs on the jerk.

The hell of it was, Aiden still cared. Because he knew Butch's wife and kid? Because he harbored a ridiculous hope that Butch was a halfway decent individual underneath all his fucked-up choices? Because he was usually a good judge of character and hated to be wrong?

As he strode through the store—taking care to see and be seen—he was swamped with feelings of nostalgia mixed right in with dismay and melancholy. The thought of his dad's legacy being tainted by Butch's mess—it was sickening. Aiden dug his fingertips into his neck and shoulder muscles as he walked. Damn, the pretense of not knowing about the drug ring was making him crazy with the need to *do* something.

He was stopped three times in short order, by employees saying hello or making suggestions that added to his to-do list, although he didn't mind.

As much as this work had been smothering him, it was also a part of who he was. He'd grown up in his dad's corner store, greeting customers and helping out. He'd built the business into the hit it had become by figuring out what people needed and taking big chances. One store at a time and a helluva lot of hours, but he'd succeeded—nearly solo. And the people—some of the original employees still worked at the Haddon Township location his dad had owned. Yet he cared about all the newer folks, too. Even Clarice, the newest, who'd only been here a few days.

Even the ones he'd never met, Aiden thought, spotting an older African-American man down the aisle in Miller's attire wheeling a dolly full of boxes.

"Mr. Miller, sir," the man said as they met midway. "I'm Alan Hammerton." He released the utility cart for a handshake.

"Welcome to Miller's, Alan."

"Thank you, sir. Thank you for taking us on. It really means a lot."

"Us?" Aiden asked. They always hired on an individual basis, interviewing each candidate on their own merit.

"Yes, sir. Myself and the others from UpStart."

His stomach pitched. Brain spinning, he managed, "You're welcome. How many of you are there?"

"Just three. We'll all work hard, sir, not just for you, because we're grateful, but because we wouldn't want to disappoint Mrs. Radnor."

"She is quite the champion, isn't she?" Aiden forced a smile. Even he had already stepped up to please her—and look where it got him. Holy shit. Not one, but *three* new employees who desperately needed jobs. Jobs they were probably about to lose. Even worse: their employment history would be tainted because of a crime ring they had the bad fortune to share a roof with...or maybe they'd even end up plagued by nightmares because some shitbag was into stringing up dead animals.

Just then, a teen with longish blond hair rounded the end of the aisle. Aiden recognized him: Tori's son, Luke—except, oh Christ, he was wearing a Miller's apron, too. Aiden's gut clenched like he'd taken a sudden hit.

"Hi, Mr. Miller."

"Ah," Alan said, puffing up like a proud dad or grandpa, "here's our third."

Aiden's pleasant expression felt as stiff and heavy as dried cement. "Nice to see you again, Luke. Thanks for introducing yourself, Alan."

Aiden kept calm until he was out of their sight, then he aimed for Butch's office with anger pumping his limbs. The tension in his neck and shoulders suddenly dug at his muscles like talons.

He planted himself squarely in front of Butch's desk, where

the man was hunched over his paperwork, his cue-ball skull shiny in the fluorescent light.

Butch raised his head, took one look at Aiden's expression, placed his palms on the desk, and stood to his full height. Still, Aiden, about five inches taller, looked down at him.

"What the hell is with you trying to circumvent me at every turn?" Aiden growled in a low voice.

"I don't know what you're talking about."

"Oh, no?" Aiden took a breath, ready to thrash the man for pushing opiates—then caught himself. Livid or not, he had to be careful, goddammit. Aiden paced back and forth, ran his hands through his hair in frustration.

He leveled a stare at Butch. "I just met Alan Hammerton."

"He's great isn't he?" Butch said, but Aiden could hear the strain of forced levity through the words. "Love the guy's old-time manners."

Aiden scowled. "And Luke Radnor? He can't be considered an UpStart employee."

"No. Great kid. Smart." Butch chuckled, but he seemed to watch Aiden carefully. "Convinced me and his mom to let me hire him on his own merits."

Tori's clients *and* her son. Great. What a goat fuck. "No more, Butch."

"No more what?"

"No more UpStart employees."

Butch blinked. "You started this. Don't tell me now you're prejudiced."

Aiden looked pointedly at the tattoo on his manager's right forearm—the one that covered a cruder, smaller tat Aiden knew Butch had gotten in the state pen—before raising an eyebrow. "You know I'm not."

Butch frowned. "I don't get you. They're perfect candidates. The kind that could end up lifers. And we get a month free—"

"I said no more." Aiden tried not to yell, afraid his voice would carry through the whole friggin' store.

Butch mimicked Aiden's belligerent posture and full-on scowl. "Care to explain?"

"It's time I micromanaged. No hiring anybody—period—without my okay."

He'd just keep saying no until Butch was in handcuffs. Chances were, after that, nobody would be applying anyway.

"What the hell, Aiden? You know I've got to hire somebody nearly every week the way they turn over. You've never wanted veto power over hires before—you trusted me."

"Now I don't."

"That's bullshit," Butch said as he slashed a hand through the air. "I might have screwed up a few things lately, but you know I'm a damn good manager."

"Not these days." Aiden couldn't say more, or he'd go off. Let Butch assume what he would.

"But—"

"Enough." Aiden held up a hand. Aiden couldn't manage even one more person to worry about. Jesus, his chest hurt just thinking about it. "I'm not going to explain myself to you."

"Then explain yourself to me," said a furious-sounding female voice from behind him.

Aiden spun. Tori—of course—seethed in the doorway. Her eyes were narrowed, her nose flared, and every line of her body looked tension-rod tight. Damn, she'd *definitely* overheard way too much.

"Tori, I…" Shit. What could he possibly say? Aiden looked back at Butch. Not here, for sure.

"Come with me to my office, and I'll explain." He approached her warily. She wore a deep blue silk top that made her green eyes pop and her cheeks glow pink—or maybe anger caused the heightened color.

She glared at him with narrow eyes, one hand on a hip, the other gripping the doorframe.

"Please." He held out his arm, palm up. "So we can talk in private."

"Fine," she said, and marched out Butch's door.

He walked beside her, leading only at the turns, and watching her cautiously out of the corner of his eye. Like most of the women in this store, her shoes looked brand name, and her bag, too. The jewelry, he guessed, was handcrafted and probably high-end in its own way. Yeah, except for the crappy car she drove, she looked very expensive—one of the many kinds of women he normally avoided.

She wore her hair in a braid today. When he realized how his blood heated at the thought of licking the exposed curve of her neck, he tore his gaze away.

Try to remember, dumb ass, Tori Radnor's got two strikes. High-end *and* a good-cause junkie. He didn't plan on putting her up to bat to unearth a third.

Aiden nodded to customers and employees alike as he went. He tried to focus on how to pacify Tori, while giving her as little information as possible.

Unfortunately, the cheesemonger practically reached out and grabbed him. The man was at his wits' end with a high-maintenance customer, who was in no hurry despite the queue forming behind her. Ah, Madeline Baumgarten. An attractive woman in her early thirties. Always perfectly coiffed, nails shiny, jewelry over-showy. She liked to complain—mainly, he thought, just to flirt with him.

"Just a minute," Aiden murmured to Tori, and slipped behind the counter to butter the woman up with compliments and sample tastes.

Finally, he stickered the last of the paper-wrapped chunks of cheese and handed it across. "Do you care for anything else, mon cherie?"

"This should do, thank you, Aiden." She practically purred his name, and even blew him a kiss. "Next time, Albert," she said to the cheesemonger before sauntering away on her heels.

"She knows your name, too?" Aiden asked his employee as he watched her go.

"*Oui*," he said with a heavy French accent, "she entertains often, and we, *bien sur*, have the best *fromage* around."

Aiden smiled at his employee. "So we do."

He turned to Tori, who was regarding him suspiciously.

"One of your old girlfriends?" she asked, then winced as if she wished she could take the words back.

"Not my type," he said. He came close to shuddering at the thought.

Except all of a sudden as he regarded at Tori—all class, natural beauty, a bright and focused mind, a caring heart, and yet a woman who was not afraid to stand up to him—he realized *she* could be.

His type.

Instead of a tight chest or shooting pain, he felt...oddly calm.

Aiden cleared his throat. "Need any cheese while we're here?"

"No." Her pretty green eyes flashed. "I need answers."

CHAPTER 12

TORI FUMED as her flats slapped along the store's aisle. Butch had reported that he'd been extremely pleased by Clarice and Alan's performance thus far, so why in the hell didn't Aiden want more UpStart clients?

Aiden kept pace at her left, taking her elbow at the turns, and Tori wished he wouldn't touch her. She was all too aware of his size, strength, and even his scent. Anger pumped through her blood, yet still her libido ignored her brain.

She clenched her fists. It seemed that no matter the situation, she felt this pull toward him. An intense tug of desire that made her insides warm, her breath come more quickly, and all her senses pay attention. An attraction that flared despite all her better, smarter instincts. She was an intelligent woman. She'd never succumbed to lust without an awful lot of thought. She didn't want to want Aiden, she sure as hell didn't need him, and she was determined to avoid any entanglements.

Instinctively she knew that sex with Aiden would, once and for all, prove that the ladylike behavior her parents had bred into her hadn't taken root.

Of course, if she didn't get a lid on her temper before she and Aiden discussed his stupid, sudden, baffling directive, she'd be proving that in the next five minutes.

God, but she was pissed off at her own trusting nature as well. She knew better than to count too heavily on goodwill—never reliable—and yet she'd already started thinking big with the lure of Miller's Markets.

Aiden ushered her into his office. The cube, seemingly repurposed, had no windows, cream walls, and a crummy wooden desk smack in the middle. With surprise, Tori registered that Aiden's sparse office was smaller by far than Butch's, and hidden away in the rear of the store. Not what she'd expect from King Midas.

Tori took a deep breath. Where to start? She'd come here to demand answers on Clarice's behalf, yet had stumbled into another issue that warranted stripping off the gloves.

"Please," Aiden said, gesturing to a sturdy wooden chair that faced his desk.

The last thing she wanted was to get comfy, but manners may as well have been one of the chromosomes in her gene pool, so she sat. He rounded the desk and slid into his own cushioned chair. Forearms on the desk and strong, lean fingers laced together, he bowed his head just enough that she couldn't see his expression.

Good, she thought—let him squirm.

"So?"

"So," he said.

"You've had Clarice on the time card for less than a week. Alan and Luke for—"

"They were hired without my knowledge, by the way."

"What's that got to do with anything?" Tori tried to remain calm, but her voice rose as her temper flared. "Have they offended you? Done a terrible job? Did you get complaints?"

"No, no. I only just discovered that Alan and Luke are employees here."

"And Clarice?"

"She's great. Hardworking, a quick study, pleasant, and sweet."

Tori fought to stay seated. She wanted to burst out of her chair. "Then what exactly is the problem?"

"Tori, I…"

Tori stared hard at him, leaned forward. Just let him try to wriggle out of this.

He looked her in the eye then. "It's purely a business decision."

"Meaning what? You're worried about your long-term bottom line because"—Tori cleared her throat pointedly—"their free wage costs you too much?"

He was shaking his head, but she was on a roll now. "Maybe you've decided your customers will be turned off if they realize there are homeless people working in the store?"

Aiden answered, "No," with an emphatic shake of his head.

"Well then, what?" In her head, she decided he must just simply be a bad person. Perhaps small-minded, self-centered, shortsighted—

"The store's..." Aiden began.

During his pause, she wondered if her thoughts showed on her face. Did it matter? This relationship was pretty much severed anyway.

"...in jeopardy."

Tori stared at him for a moment. Then flopped back in her chair with an audible woof, rather like the odd groan of the pipes in their building when she turned the water off abruptly.

"So..." she said, unsure of what that admission meant. "You think you won't be able to pay them when the time comes?"

"They'll get paid. But"—he grimaced—"it seems unfair to be hiring—making implied promises that I may not be able to keep."

"Butch?"

"He doesn't know yet. He hired Alan and Luke in good faith."

Tori thought he gulped, but she couldn't be sure. She narrowed her eyes. "What about Clarice? You knew then?"

"I was confident I could salvage things, but the...severity... of the situation became clear rather suddenly." Aiden rubbed the back of his neck. "And then I justified that the income would help her, even short term, and that the experience would be invaluable. You know, give her something official on her résumé and essentially give her me as an ongoing reference."

Tori caught herself, mouth open. She wasn't quite ready to give up the angry head of steam she'd built or to suddenly conclude he was a nice guy. However, she couldn't argue with that reasoning.

She frowned. "So when I first pitched you, things were already rocky…"

"It's not like me," he said, "but I couldn't say no to you." Aiden met her eyes. "Or to her," he said with that silly quirk of his lips.

She rolled her eyes, rather than stare at his sexy mouth. "Most people have no trouble saying no to me and my clients. Even though I know I get overly passionate."

Tori felt her cheeks warm. Shoot, that word had way too much sexual connotation. Although she wouldn't even twist it that way herself if she were sitting here with any other man. Would he miss it entirely if he had no interest?

She chanced a glance at his cornflower-blue eyes—they twinkled at her. Her heart sped up. Still, she reminded herself, the twinkle didn't necessarily mean anything. Most men walked around with sex on the brain.

"You're not so over the top," Aiden said. "I have experience with worse."

"Is that right?" Tori knew he was teasing because of that lopsided lift to his full lips, so she played along, more comfortable with him than she probably should be, considering that theirs was, after all, an awfully precarious working relationship.

"Uh-huh. Would make you embarrassed to call yourself a champion of the underdog."

She laughed, but shook her head. "My parents would beg to differ." He looked younger, she decided, when he forgot about the stress. "And that's an interesting description for a job title."

"What would you call yourself?" Aiden looked suddenly serious, like this answer was important to him.

So she gave a straightforward answer: "I'm a business-woman—who cares."

He considered this thoughtfully, his eyes roaming over her

face, making her blood heat. Tori looked away and squirmed in her seat.

"So," Tori said, "this experience with worse. Your mom?"

Aiden grimaced, then nodded.

"I'm dying to know what your dad was talking about. After she gave away your toys?"

He laughed, shook his head. "You'll be worrying about my mental health."

"Oh, come on. I have a seriously difficult relationship with my own parents. I doubt it'll shock me as much as you think. Besides, children get a lot of leeway."

Aiden raised his eyes to the ceiling, then let out a breath. "She'd given me carved chopsticks, and the birthday before, a little hand-stitched doll."

Tori raised an eyebrow.

"Yeah, and trust me, I was all boy." Aiden shook his head. "I reincarnated it—into a voodoo doll. Of her. Splintered the chopsticks and went to town until that thing looked like a por-cupine."

Tori covered her mouth, trying not to laugh outright. "I guess she didn't die."

"She didn't even clutch her stomach." Aiden's smile grew, until he laughed.

Tori said, "I'd say your dad was right. Heck, they probably teach that technique in therapy."

They held each other's gaze, and she felt warm through and through.

Then Aiden's eyes sobered. He got up and moved around the desk until he was standing over her. His proximity made her nerve endings stand at attention. She had no choice but to look up at him. Past the silver belt buckle, his French-blue shirt—custom-made certainly, as it didn't have that bagginess around his trim abdomen and was monogrammed at the cuffs. No cuff links, she realized, and was glad—they would have smacked even more of the world she grew up in. The one where net worth and class were the be all and end all. Past the march of buttons over his chest and up to that strong jaw, bent nose, and steady blue gaze, only a few shades lighter than his shirt color.

When she met his eyes, Aiden spoke. "I'm sorry about the hiring freeze. I would have liked to warn you, but it's important that anything that might send the staff into a tailspin remains quiet."

"I get it. Your secret is safe with me."

This was far too intimate a position to be in, so Tori stood. The wooden chair barely budged behind her knees, though, stuck somehow on the painted concrete floor.

And Aiden didn't step back. They faced each other nearly nose to nose—well, nose to collarbone, as he was well over six feet compared to her five feet, six inches. So close that if she lifted a hand, she'd touch his. She tilted her head up to speak, but words vanished when she realized he was staring at her lips. All he had to do was dip his head and they'd be...kissing.

Tori cleared her throat in an attempt to regain her equilibrium and her brainpower. "We're not finished here," she stated.

"Not even close," Aiden said, his voice rather rough. And all of a sudden she knew without a doubt that he felt the attraction between them as strongly as she did. Desire traveled in a swift surge from her dry mouth to her toes. Like a lighting bolt grounding into the earth under this building.

His eyes telegraphed so much: everything she couldn't think about yet—or maybe never. She had a kid to take care of, a business to build, people to help—she didn't have room for...

She broke eye contact, her gaze skittering past his tempting mouth with its lopsided smile. "We have more business to discuss."

"Do we?" he asked with that glint still in his eyes.

She nodded, more forcefully than was warranted. "The rat incident."

Aiden blinked. "Of course." He took a full step backward,

putting two feet between them. The life in his face vanished, a mask of professionalism taking over.

He ran a hand through this hair as he rounded the desk again. Back to neutral corners, Tori thought, watching him slide out a drawer and pull out a scuffed-up baseball. He stared at it, spinning the ball in his fingers and passing it from hand to hand before he spoke.

"I wish I had something concrete."

Tori scowled. "You mean to tell me—"

"I mean"—Aiden's cheek above his jawline ticked—"that I have nothing. Nada. Zilch. Nobody's talking." He blew out a breath and leaned back, crossing his arms over his chest. "I hope that means it's an isolated incident. It's possible, probable even, that it was a prank or a dare or some kind of mischief that wasn't even meant for Clarice."

He gripped the ball tightly, and Tori wondered if there was something he wasn't telling her. Then again, she'd thought the same herself. Still, she'd hoped for a resolution, a culprit, a firing, a something.

"I know it's only been a few days, but it means the world to Clarice to be working," Tori said. "I'm not sure she'd say anything if something else happened."

He held up a hand. "Say no more. I'll keep an eye out." Aiden dumped the baseball in the drawer and shut it before he stood.

"Will you let me know? Keep me filled in?" Tori asked, her gaze searching his.

"I will," Aiden said, and he felt an odd little flip in the region of his heart that signaled his pleasure to have an excuse to contact her. He grimaced mentally. Tori Radnor was not someone he should pursue; she was all wrong for him. Right?

She pulled him like a magnetic force—hell, earlier he'd come *this* close to taking her head in his hands and covering her lips with his. Again, he resisted and strode right past her to open the door.

"Are you shopping before you leave?" Aiden asked.

Tori shifted her gaze away from him. "Not today."

"Then I'll walk you out."

As she brushed past, he caught her scent. No heavy perfume. Just light and fresh. A hint of sweet vanilla again, and that elusive something else he couldn't put his finger on, but it suited her.

Aiden set his hand to the small of her back, found the silk both warm and thin. Thoughts of his palm actually caressing her skin flashed through his mind, and he forced himself to stop touching her.

Rather than walking through the congested food court, Aiden aimed left. Out of nowhere Tori stopped abruptly, put one hand on a hip, and stared toward the deli.

Aiden followed her gaze. Haley raised a plastic-gloved hand in his direction and smiled, before returning her focus to the slicer. Tori stalked away from the deli toward the front of the store.

"Tori?"

She moved fast, her hand clenching her purse strap to keep it from falling. Aiden lengthened his strides to match her pace.

She turned after she passed by the registers. "I'll be popping in—unexpectedly. I'd better not see anything questionable—"

"I said I'd keep an eye, and I will."

Tori stopped, crossed her arms over her chest, and pinned him with a sharp look. "You need to keep an open mind, too."

"All right," Aiden promised. "Don't worry. I won't hesitate to act swiftly if I see anything unacceptable."

She blew out her breath, shut her eyes for just a second, then spoke, her voice still rich with emotion. "Thank you."

He'd put her through the wringer today, and sought to reassure her by giving her shoulder a squeeze—even had a crazy urge to pull her against his chest. And he *still* wanted that kiss. Too damn much. "I'll keep you posted."

She nodded once, then turned and left.

Conflicting emotions rioted inside him, much like the silver ball inside the pinball machine his dad had once rented to draw kids into the store to buy Ring Pops and baseball cards. Tori was both sweet and tart, same as the green-apple-flavored hard candy he'd worn on his finger, and as addictive as those trading cards had once been for a boy who'd breathed baseball.

Aiden followed. She exited the store and crossed the parking lot, digging out her sunglasses and keys on the way. Inexplicably, he kept watching. The way she pulled her hair out from under her purse strap, the way the strands caught the sunlight, the graceful way she sank into the car...

Crap, that car. Again he'd forgotten to ask her about the marks on her trunk. The fact that she'd avoided the topic on Saturday made him wonder. She drove right past the front door, and—what the hell? The rear panel on the passenger side had scratches all over it too. Either she'd been hanging out in a rotten neighborhood, or somebody really had it out for her.

CHAPTER 13

DISHRAG TIED AROUND her mouth like a bandana, Tori growled in frustration as her eyes watered—the smell was that bad, though tears threatened, too. With rodents fresh in her mind, she assumed maybe a mouse or squirrel, or, God help her, a kitten had gotten stuck under the hood or in a wheel well. Because this smell had to be something decomposing.

She'd thought a rat in Clarice's locker and the subsequent bombshell of a hiring freeze at Miller's was as bad as the week could get. She was dead wrong. That stink she'd assumed was garbage Saturday morning? It had gotten worse each day. She'd finally realized Tuesday—when it was time to drive Alan and Clarice to their afternoon shift—that the smell radiated directly out from her car. She had called them a taxi service and intended to take care of her car with time to spare before pickup.

Except she'd also discovered that her car key was useless: whoever had keyed her car had also ruined the trunk's locking mechanism. Even the trunk release latch under her driver's seat didn't work. The trunk was stuck shut but good. Which doubly sucked, because she didn't have AAA and really couldn't afford to pay a garage to pop this sucker just to unearth a dead animal.

Luke had yelled the minute he'd gotten home from school, "Mom! How could you wait so long? It's awful!"

Now, facing the smell up close and personal, she conceded that she should have gone sleuthing earlier. With temperatures hitting eighty degrees, the stench was now officially unbearable.

Luke called down from the second-floor window, "Mom, your friend Mitch is on the phone."

She gave her son a thumbs-up and darted inside. Phew, she thought, yanking down her makeshift mask and sucking in air.

Still, she crinkled up her nose. That awful stench lingered in her nostrils.

Luke handed her the phone as soon as she entered the apartment. Tori took a calming breath. "Hey, Mitch."

"Hi. I'm in the area. Thought I'd drop off your box."

"This really isn't a good time."

"Headed off somewhere?"

"No, dealing with a crisis."

"Anything I can help with?"

Tori bit her lip. He'd done so much for her already. Besides, the graffiti on her car was humiliating, the smell horrifying. She looked at Luke, who frowned. Mortifying as this was, she had to do something—fast. And here was a gift horse...

"Any chance you have a crowbar in your truck?"

A short while later, Tori met Mitch at the curb and indicated he should park on the street.

"Whoa," Mitch said, rounding the cab of his truck. "That decomp's your crisis?"

Of course, Mitch, being a detective, would know that smell in a split second. And she must be carrying it on her clothes and hair for him to catch a whiff out here in front.

"Yeah." She scrunched up her face. "A dead animal must have gotten stuck in my trunk, which I can't open. I'm sorry you had to walk into *this*." She waved her hand.

He shrugged. "Actually, I'd say it's good timing." Mitch opened the built-in tool caddy on the back of his truck and was rooting around. He waved a crowbar then moved to lean into the cab.

Mitch passed her a little blue jar. "Here, wipe some under your nose."

Noxzema, she realized.

They tromped the narrow side drive to the back, at which point Luke exited the building. "Hey, Luke," Mitch said, tucking the crowbar under his arm and shaking her son's hand.

"Luke, please go inside," Tori said. Her stomach was turning even with the camphor and menthol scent masking the worst of the stench.

Her kid grinned at Mitch. "You gonna tell me 'Nothing to see here, move along'?"

Mitch laughed, even as he took the keys from Tori and tried the lock. "Have you seen a rotting carcass before? 'Cause it's not going to be pretty." He didn't seem the least bit fazed.

Luke shrugged. "In the woods, where we used to live."

Tori sighed and handed him the Noxzema. "Like this." She pantomimed how to apply the scented cream.

"All right." Mitch didn't waste any more time as he fitted the crowbar in the gap. "Get ready for the flies."

Oh God, Tori thought, clenching her teeth. She'd been trying her damnedest not to think about what that noise meant.

Mitch leaned down, arms braced, straining for only a second, and pop—the trunk swung up. Flies swarmed, rose like an angry cloud, only to loop maniacally and dive down again. Mitch had stepped back, then leaned forward. Tori crept closer, too. Not wanting to see, but needing to know.

The stench was even worse now that the trunk was open, and she cupped her palms around her nose and mouth.

All she could see was flies and squirming white—eewww—maggots!

Mitch reached in with the crowbar, poked around, shoulders tense.

"What is it?" Luke asked. "I can't tell."

Boys, Tori thought. She was just glad it didn't look furry—not a cat.

Mitch reached up to shut the trunk, but it kept popping open. He slammed it, but the thing wouldn't catch. Finally, he set the crowbar on top to weigh it down.

She frowned. The lock was probably permanently busted now.

"That's no dead animal," he said with a grim expression. "That's a hunk of meat."

"What do you mean?" she mumbled, brain stumbling, trying to latch on to something that made sense.

"I mean, whoever keyed your car left you a present."

Tori just stared.

Gently, he squeezed her hand. "It's a giant slab of beef, like an eye round or something."

Tori gagged, vomit rising up, even as she spun and ran. Reaching the sewer grate only a few feet behind Mitch's truck, she bent and lost her lunch, tears streaming down her face, even once she'd caught her breath.

"Mom?"

She waved Luke off, needing some time.

After a few minutes, she became aware of Mitch rummaging in the truck. Tori remained bent in half, hands braced on her knees until some napkins and a bottle of water entered her field of vision. She straightened, wiped her tears, and took a mouthful of water. Swooshed and spat. Wet another napkin and cleaned her face.

Looking at Mitch, she felt her eyes well up again. "I thought it was going to be something accidental. A dead squirrel, or something that rolled out of one of my grocery bags. First that horrid message, now this…" She shook her head as a tear slid onto her cheek. "What does it even mean?"

He didn't hesitate, just leaned in and gathered her up in a hug.

"Who would do such a thing?" she whispered, her voice shaking.

He squeezed harder, rubbed her back. Tori couldn't remember the last time she'd had a hug from anybody other than her son. She let go, had a thorough cry.

When she pulled back and looked up, he said. "I called it in."

Tori gasped. "It's twisted, but surely it was just a prank."

"Maybe, maybe not. But between the graffiti and this?" He shrugged. "You've gotta file a report."

She was mortified. Besides, she really didn't ever want anything to do with the inside of a police station again, ever. "But—"

"It's already done. And Tori"—he held her eyes, his tone dead serious—"you need to document these kind of things, in case they escalate."

She took a shaky breath and nodded.

————

The patrol officers, a white male and an African-American female, and then another younger set of male officers who only stayed long enough to be sure they weren't needed, were as kind as could be. They shared pats on the back, sympathetic looks, and even some really gross jokes.

"This is how we lighten the mood," Mitch had said. But in the end, he'd pulled her aside, given her strict instructions to be careful, to call him, and not to be a martyr or, God forbid, a hero if anything else should happen.

Tori had been surprised that the responding Pocono Area PD officers dusted the car for prints, as well as taking elimination prints for her and Luke, plus contact information for Clarice and Alan, since their prints also had cause to be on the vehicle. The officers' report would travel the required channels, and a property crimes detective would be the one to contact her if a match showed up in a national database called AFIS. Mitch warned her that that could take weeks.

One of the officers had jotted down the name and number of a crime scene cleanup service.

"This isn't a crime scene," Tori had insisted.

The woman had hooked her hands on her loaded utility belt and arched one eyebrow. "I wouldn't touch those maggots with a hazmat suit if it was me."

Tori had actually called, too, but they charged extra for rush service, and the estimate she'd wrangled out of the person on the phone had nearly given her palpitations. Her business plan didn't have much wiggle room financially—a couple of hefty unexpected outlays like this could sink them. It wasn't as if another grant was going to come down the pike, and a loan was out of the question. No, she'd have to buck up and do the dirty work herself.

Tori had donned thick rubber gloves, bagged the squirming meat in multiple, heavy-duty black garbage bags, and shut the lid of the Dumpster on it. Far more concerned about lingering odor than discoloring decade-old carpet, she poured bleach over the maggots, hoping the chemical would also deter the flies. In the interior of the car, she used a deodorizing cleaner on all of the fabric, emptied a full can of air freshener, and even lit candles in the cup holders.

Her mind swirled as she worked, running over possibilities, struggling to figure out who she'd made enough of an enemy of to warrant all this. Holden? She couldn't see it. That bitchy cashier, Haley? Tori shook her head. A minor altercation over monetary change and some rude behavior didn't mean she'd pull something like this. It just didn't follow; too extreme… Someone she'd worked with? Anyone she or Luke had offended before they'd moved to the Poconos? Since they'd arrived? No, no, and no.

In the end, Tori had to believe, these things were just a string of unrelated incidents, bad luck, and a rotten week. Literally.

She'd missed a call from Aiden in the late afternoon, and seethed at the message he left. "I promised to keep you updated, so I'm calling… Unfortunately, I have nothing new to report on Clarice's incident yet. I did speak with both my legal counsel and my employee relations team. Please…let's keep this particular issue between us."

How dare he, she thought, scrubbing with all her might the floor of the trunk as bleach fumes stung her eyes. As a mother and an employer who was more invested in her clients' well-being than most, she wished she could yank everybody from Miller's and never look back. On the other hand, as a business owner herself, she—to some degree—understood Aiden's request. Unfortunately, business-wise, UpStart and its clients needed Miller's.

Regardless, she'd have a serious talk with them all about

harassment and hazing, even bullying. If there was another occurrence they'd face it head-on, and she'd make sure Aiden Miller held his people accountable.

Tori had gone back to wearing the dishrag bandana-style, along with liberal swipes of Noxzema, which Mitch had left, under her nose. Again, she hosed everything down, sprayed, and scrubbed once more. Hours ago, she'd sent Luke down the block to visit, then called to have him borrow some bleach and another pair of rubber gloves from the shelter.

But it was no use. Everything smelled. She smelled. She left the windows down, turned off the interior lights so she wouldn't find herself with a dead battery too, and even left the car doors open. She trudged upstairs feeling weary and defeated. Just when things had really started to look up.

She bagged her clothes, scrubbed her body raw, washed her hair twice, spread aloe on the back of her neck where she'd gotten sunburned, and finally emerged from the bathroom feeling slightly better.

Luke said, "I made you a sandwich."

Again her eyes filled with tears, though she managed a smile. "Thanks, hon." She didn't have any appetite, but knew she needed to eat.

"Wanna watch TV with me?" he asked.

"Sure. Anything but *CSI*," she said, pulling a half-grin out of him.

He settled on his bed, she on the chair in the corner. The room was dim, as it had only a small bedside lamp and no windows. Luke flipped through the channels and picked an older action flick with Bruce Willis. One of the *Die Hard* movies, she thought.

Tori picked at the chips he'd put on her plate and tried a bite of the sandwich—had to force it past the lump in her throat.

Luke looked at her, the glow of the tube playing on his left side. He tossed the remote in his right hand with just a flick of the wrist, reminding her of the twist of the lacrosse stick.

"Did we miss a game today?"

He shook his head. "Mom." He set the remote down. "Crank calls. Your car. The meat. The rat."

"The rat *has* to be unrelated to the rest." Tori shut her eyes for a moment. Regardless of her urge to shield and protect him, he was more mature than many adults she knew. "Even the prank calls could even have been one of your old schoolmates or some other bored kid who picked our number randomly." Was she trying to convince him, or herself?

He pulled a face. "You really think that? After today?"

Tori rubbed her forehead with both hands, her plate balanced on her lap. "I don't know what to think."

"Could it be Dad?"

Tori flicked a hand out with a dismissive motion.

Luke ignored it, and said, "I know you put the notice in the newspaper to serve him…could he be retaliating? Freaking out?"

Indeed, in Pennsylvania, the law required that to serve a petition of divorce to an absentee spouse—after doing due diligence in order to find him—she had to post a public notice in the newspapers where he last lived for a certain period of time. It was called divorce by publication, and until Tori needed it, she hadn't even known such a thing existed.

She set her plate on the floor beside her and leaned forward, elbows on her knees. "I don't know that he's even seen the post; certainly he hasn't notified the court." Tori watched Luke closely. "He hasn't shown up since we got ice cream, right?"

He snorted. "Not that I know of."

"He hasn't tried to contact me at all," she said, and considered Holden. Blue blood in his veins, a personal tailor, a controlled voice, and long ago, a nice man…the father of her son. "I just can't see it. Unless he's gone completely off the deep end. I mean, you know—"

"I know." Luke rolled his eyes. "*Further* off the deep end."

Holden couldn't have done this. She shook her head hard. "No. There's no way your father would do something like this."

But someone had. And despite what she'd said to Mitch, she sensed that someone meant her harm.

Tori reached for his hand, squeezed, and held his eyes. "I need you to be extra careful."

"Same goes for you," her son said, gripping her tightly.

CHAPTER 14

DESPITE HER PHYSICAL and emotional exhaustion, Tori spent most of the night sorting and re-sorting too little information, grasping hard to find some sense in the disturbing events of the week. She groaned when she heard Luke's alarm go off, but she got up anyway, determined. The minute it was reasonable to make phone calls, she dialed Miller's. Then she called every half an hour until she reached Aiden himself and asked him to meet her for lunch.

She arrived at Marie's Place early. She was strung tight with apprehension, for she couldn't guess how he was going to take her theory. Tori waved to Marie, who was behind the counter packing up a sandwich for an older male customer in golf attire. When Marie had thanked the customer for coming in, she beckoned Tori forward and reached over the counter to hug her.

Marie was tiny, but strong. She never stopped moving, her energy and work ethic making this little shop thrive. At first, Tori had frequented this eatery because she felt like she'd discovered gold in the personal setting and healthy, homemade fare, and later because she hoped to see Marie—a kindred spirit—and her little place stay in business. Now, she owed her loyalty and thanks.

"How are you, stranger?" Marie asked.

Tori laughed. It had only been a couple of weeks since she'd come in. Well, maybe closer to a month if she really counted. "Busy, which is good."

"UpStart's making progress, then?"

"We're coming along."

Marie smiled. "I'm so happy to hear it. Just keep on trusting your instincts, and it'll be fine."

Trusting her instincts was exactly why Tori had called

Aiden. Because the one idea she'd kept coming back to over and over again was that Haley might well have planted that meat. As turnabout for deli duty. Nothing else made sense— not that there could be much rationality in something like that.

"Let me get our guy so you can say hey." Marie moved quickly to the kitchen's swinging door and hollered, "Emilito! Surprise visitor!"

The dark-skinned Mexican, who looked like a young man because of his slight stature, was really forty-five, and a much older soul underneath all that. "Mrs. Tori!" He smiled with a set of large, overly white choppers.

Vaguely, Tori registered the jangling of the bell on the door behind her, but she stared wide-eyed at her friend. "Emilito, your teeth!"

He bowed. "Thanks to you, Mrs., I have finally bought my smile." His eyes crinkled in deep grooves, and he posed as if he was in an advertisement for teeth whitening.

Tears pricked her eyes, even as she grinned back. "I'm so glad. You look incredibly handsome."

He flashed the new teeth again, and Tori marveled. When she'd placed him here about five months ago, he'd mumbled rather than opened his mouth. His upper front two teeth had been knocked out long ago in a street fight, and others she suspected had been pulled for infection. These, then, must be a full set of dentures.

Emilito bobbed his head and then slipped off to the kitchen, and Marie said, "Yes, sir," as she looked past Tori.

She stepped to the side, then started at Aiden's familiar voice.

"I'm actually meeting Tori," he said.

She turned, and her traitorous tummy fluttered as she looked up into his blue eyes. Didn't her body get it? This wasn't a date. This was a meeting to start a damn tough conversation. If she were braver—and less tactful—she'd just blurt it out now and be done already. *Hey, handsome, you float my boat, but I can't help thinking your trusted assistant manager might be borderline certifiable, or at the very least an immature, impulsive bitch with a really gory sense of humor.*

"Morning," he said, mouth turning up on one side.

There was an awkward moment in which Tori briefly considered a handshake. Technically they *were* business associates. Except somehow, with Aiden, the pressing of palms would feel both too formal and too intimate. Angling herself to face both parties, she said, "Marie, this is Aiden Miller, the owner of Miller's Markets. Aiden, Marie Sandoval."

"Obviously the owner of Marie's Place." He stretched his hand over the counter. "Nice to meet you."

Tori noted again how charming he became when his voice melted into smooth and his eyes twinkled.

"You too," Marie said. "Why don't you take one of those tables near the window?"

"So, how's it going?" he asked, waiting for Tori to be seated before pulling out a chair for himself.

"I'm glad it's a new day. You?"

That was as far as they got before Marie arrived with menus, water, and a push for the scones, baked just this morning. She rattled off flavors, and Tori laughed. "Enough. You know I'd try all of them if I could, so just give me your latest creation."

———

Aiden found he had to tear his gaze away from Tori's shining face. He hadn't heard her laugh outright before. Plus, her hair was up in that sloppy twist again. Strands around her face had escaped, and he had the crazy urge to brush them back just so he could touch her.

"Give me a minute to look at the menu," he said to Marie. "I may do an early lunch." He felt good for a change, sitting here with Tori. The friggin' store could wait.

"You got it," Marie said, retreating.

"The specials are the way to go," Tori said, and pointed to the blackboard behind the counter.

Aiden stood up to look, let Marie know he'd settled on the pulled pork sandwich, then slid back into his chair.

Tori quickly bent her head to the backside of a writing tablet where she'd begun an intricate doodle in one corner of the cardboard.

Interesting, Aiden thought, as Tori had been the one to request this urgent meeting—apparently calling numerous times before she'd been put through to him. Plus, she'd insisted they talk away from Miller's. Now she'd rather draw than speak?

"So," Aiden said, putting his elbows on the table, hands clasped. "Small talk? Or do you want to tell me what's on your mind?"

Tori huffed a quick breath, lifting the pen as she straightened. "I don't think I can manage small talk today." She tucked a chunk of that smooth hair behind her ear. She seemed to zone in on something in the parking lot, then her mouth turned down as she faced him. "I know no one's come forward, but... do you have any ideas who might have planted the rat?"

Aiden gave a half shrug. "Not a clue." He couldn't tell her about his theory about drug dealers leaving a warning.

Just then, Marie showed up with their plates. Aiden thanked the owner, and Tori gave a distracted smile as she set her notebook and pen to the side.

"Let's eat," Aiden said, gesturing to her plate.

Tori's brows drew down, causing a little crease between them, as she broke off a bit of scone. He could picture his thumb smoothing that frown, and he admonished himself. Why he ached to ease and comfort this particular woman every time he saw her, he couldn't figure.

"You haven't noticed anything from a particular employee that made you raise your eyebrows?"

Did the tiny diamond piercing Haley had shown up with

today in her nose count? He shook his head and picked up his sandwich, the gooey chunks threatening to spill right off the bun.

"Oh, wow," Aiden said after the first bite. He'd had a hearty breakfast, but had burned through the calories working out with Eddie again this morning.

Tori spared him a quick glance, but didn't speak. She seemed as if she needed a little time, and this, he could tell, would be a heavy conversation. Possibly one he wouldn't like. Until then, Aiden intended to enjoy the food, the downtime, and the scenery—not the stellar view of the strip mall's parking lot, but the beautiful class act sharing his table.

Yet guilt crept into his subconscious and tension marched slowly up his back to his neck.

His level of frustration wasn't Tori's fault, Aiden knew. He was ticked at himself, because he had nothing to offer. Without a culprit and with his hands effectively tied, he had no way to make amends to her or Clarice.

Once he'd tossed his napkin on his plate, Tori asked, "So, nothing suspicious at all?"

Aiden glanced out the window. In the glass's reflection, he watched Tori bulldoze a little pile of crumbs with her finger. She pinched them together and popped some in her mouth. He enjoyed the smooth expanse of skin he saw when she tilted her head up to catch the bits. And he liked that she'd chosen a treat—not zero-calorie lettuce—and eaten every bite. He saw enough bobblehead stick figures in the stores. Where the hell, he always wondered, did all that food they bought actually go?

"No, there's been nothing unusual."

She shook her head as if arguing with herself, then wrapped both arms around her middle. "In the light of day, it seems crazy...but I just can't shake the idea."

Aiden watched her. She wasn't making much sense, but she was obviously both truly concerned and very serious.

She shut her eyes for a beat of one, two, three, while Aiden studied her. Then she opened her eyes, sat up straight, and placed both palms flat on the table.

"There's no easy way to say this." She took a breath, her chest rising under the ruby-colored silk blouse, and tucked her chin before she spoke in a rush. "I suspect your employee Haley is behind everything."

"Everything?" Weren't they talking about the rat incident? Aiden relaxed back in his chair and laughed outright. "Haley? That's absurd."

"Actually, it's not. She isn't the golden child you think she is."

Aiden shook his head. She was grasping at straws. "Haley is responsible, professional, friendly, always on time. She works hard, supports herself." He started to get angry, the more he thought about the *wrongness* of her claim. "I've never had a single problem with her. Nor has there been even one black mark on her employee record. Period."

Tori started to speak, but Aiden plowed on. "I've known her for years. She's a serious kid. Good grades in school and a good college. Constant compliments from the customers. I'm telling you, Haley's had it all together since I met her in her teens—probably since she was, like, six."

Tori rubbed her forehead, looked pained. "I can't speak to her past. I can only speak to now."

"Hell, you can't speak to her at all," he snapped. "You don't even know her."

"I know enough," she said, brows drawing down.

"Tori," Aiden said, lowering his voice, but letting his exasperation show. "There is no way that Haley killed a rat and tied it to a hook in one of my lockers. The girl eats and breathes Miller's."

Questions slammed around inside his head like fastballs. How could she even think that Haley would do such a thing? What the hell was Tori trying to pull?

She leaned in over the table. "Seriously, Haley's had it out for me from that first day I challenged her at the register. I got prank calls that very night. My car was keyed the same week. And the rat? Haley could absolutely have been targeting my client, just because she has an issue with me."

"That's..." Aiden snorted. "Laughable. Insane."

"I can understand that you want to think the best of your employees, especially someone you've known that long, but—"

"She's a nice kid."

"You're wrong there. You don't have any idea at all who that girl really is. I'm telling you, she presents a sweet smile to you, then sprouts fangs the very second your back is turned. She's playing you."

Aiden shoved his plate aside in frustration. He didn't like this conversation. He was usually a decent judge of character, yet somebody was duping him—and for all he knew, it could be Tori with her expensive clothes, earnest eyes, and do-gooder mask.

Haley? Come on. He'd known Haley for years, and Tori only—what? A week? Two?

"I see you doubt me," Tori said. "Unfortunately, I can't *prove* anything, but hear me out. That day I met you over the discrepancy in change? She was so *rude* before you arrived that I was shocked. I couldn't believe that Miller's would put up with that kind of behavior—to a customer, no less. Until I saw her morph into a perfect angel when you showed up. Then she sneered at me again later."

Aiden crossed his arms over his chest. This was bullshit.

Tori wasn't done. "Then when we left your office, yesterday? She glared at me with such animosity."

Aiden shook his head. Surely Tori had misinterpreted.

"Mark my words, one of these days, she'll shock you."

"Let's think about this another way." He leaned forward, getting in her space as much as he was able with a table between them. "You have any enemies yourself? Anybody who'd want to sabotage your business? A direct competitor or some old stalker boyfriend?"

"Believe me," Tori said, "I've been over all of that. Far as I know, I'm the only one providing this particular service around here. And yeah, there are people who might not mind seeing me fail." She blanched, then raised her chin a notch. "But the only person who holds actual animosity toward me would be Haley."

"Except you barely know her."

"What can I say? Instant hate." Tori shrugged.

Aiden stood and took his wallet out of his back pocket.

Tori stood, too, hands braced on hips. "I haven't told you all of it."

He shook his head, disgusted.

"Just hear me out," she said. "Then you can tell me to go to hell."

Aiden ran his hand through his hair and smacked his wallet down onto the table. "Fine," he said, as he yanked his chair out. He sat further from the table this go round, crossed his arms over his chest again, and angled himself at forty-five degrees. "You've got two minutes."

Tori took a deep breath and shut her eyes once more. He shook his head and looked away. He'd had it with the drama.

"Those scratches on my car? The vandalism? I don't know how much you saw, but there's a message on the passenger side."

Aiden tensed. This should be good, he thought. What? Was there a signature for Haley Miller? *HM* etched right into the paint?

"Disappear or die, bitch." Tori's voice shook.

Aiden gripped his upper arms hard, but didn't speak. She damn well should be upset. Personally, he'd be happy to take whoever had done it by the neck and throttle them. Maybe Tori herself *was* the target. Except she had to face facts: that message in no way pointed to Haley. She was so friggin' far off base.

"And maybe just as bad…" She hesitated. He waited, ceased to breathe. As bad as that?

"The vandal left a chunk of beef, like an eye round. Rotting meat, Aiden. With the God-awful smell and maggots and everything locked in my trunk."

Aiden's words refused to form in coherent order, as his mind scrabbled for a foothold. That was sick. Twisted.

Tori looked at him with sad eyes. "Who else would leave a gift like that, but the girl who got demoted to deli duty because I challenged her at the register?"

Aiden's lunch roiled in his stomach and his chest started to pain him. He fisted one hand and pressed the thumb knuckle into to his sternum.

"I don't understand it, it's so…*extreme*," Tori continued. "Yet I can't get past that connection. I can't help but feel that the rotting meat was some kind of sick signature, a message in itself."

Aiden sat forward, elbows on knees, head lowered into his hands. He couldn't believe this. It was all royally fucked up. He sincerely hoped things got no worse for Tori. Prayed too that these incidents didn't originate somehow from her association with his store. Regardless, the conclusions she'd drawn were pure supposition. Too weak for him to put the reputation of a good kid through the meat grinder simply because some woman he barely knew asked him to.

"I filed a police report," she said quietly. "And I'm looking for new jobs for my clients—and Luke, of course."

Dammit, Aiden thought, the detectives weren't going to like this. Neither did he, actually, as they were all hard workers, and he felt he owed them more than that. Still, probably best for Tori Radnor to exit his life as quickly as possible.

Tori said, "I'd feel better terminating the contract right now, but they'll fight me on that." She looked out the window as she spoke. "I can understand that this might be hard to accept."

Aiden dropped his hands and sat up. "Accept?" He shook his head. "I can at least see why you've connected those particular dots, but you're grasping at straws. I'm telling you, I just can't see Haley...ever..."

Aiden saw that her green eyes pleaded with him.

"Christ." Aiden shook his head. There was nothing else to say, really.

"You know," she said, "I hope you're right. Really, I do." She clasped her hands together, tucked them in her lap. "I'm only asking you to consider the possibility. That Haley is less—or more—than she appears."

CHAPTER 15

AIDEN HAD INSISTED on paying the bill, which he could see that Tori didn't like.

"I can expense it," she'd said, brows drawn together. Well, so could he.

Tori had paused outside the shop to check her phone. Aiden watched her as he waited at Marie's counter. He'd asked the woman to package up dinner and a late night snack: a cold caprese and chicken pasta salad with some rosemary focaccia and a scone like the one Tori had enjoyed so thoroughly. As good as Miller's food was, he got tired of it. Besides, even though they were competitors to some degree, he liked to see the little independents—which invariably made him think of his dad's original store—succeed.

Another reason, he supposed, that he was drawn to Tori despite all the red flags warning him away. Tori was an underdog, fighting against the general malaise of the American people and the shortcomings of the government.

Great. He was thinking just like his mother now. If that was what Tori Radnor did to him, then he hoped she'd find new placements for her people and move on quickly. Hell, he'd give them recommendations to speed the process along. Aiden scowled out the front window and saw that she had reached her vehicle. With an empty parking space on her driver's side, he had a fairly clear view. Suddenly, as she put her key to the driver's-side door, she froze. Tori turned toward the rear end of her car, her posture stiff and wary.

Unease shot through Aiden, followed immediately by a hot rush of adrenaline. A man approached Tori from the next row. Average height, close-cropped brown hair, and dressed much like Aiden himself in casual business attire.

Aiden glanced at Marie, who was just bagging his food. At less than a hundred yards away, he could be at Tori's side in no time. He tensed, waiting and watching as Tori shook her head and stuck out a palm, as if to stop the guy's approach. He didn't look crazed or violent, though he kept leaning toward Tori. She kept inching backward.

She must know him, Aiden decided, as she planted both fists on her hips. She appeared to be yelling, getting aggressive.

Aiden had to smile. He knew from experience the venom Tori's tongue could deliver.

"Here you go—" Marie began, but the man reached out, grabbing Tori by the upper arms.

Aiden bolted, shoving through the shop's door, the bell jingling cheerily in direct opposition to the black anger that had seized him at seeing Tori manhandled.

Thoughts raced through his mind as fast as his feet covered the distance. Could it be the same person who'd defaced her car? A stalker, perhaps? Shit—Aiden knew what that felt like. Had to be ten times worse for a threatened woman.

Or was Tori married to this jerk, or possibly dating him? Her fingers sported only a chunky silver ring on the right hand. He'd go back for his food. He'd pay Marie another time if he forgot. Maybe the guy was some stranger, a total wack job. Maybe Aiden was overreacting—

No, the bastard shook her now.

Aiden came at him from a slight angle, ensuring that his approach would go undetected. Tori had been so focused on this asshole that her eyes widened when Aiden entered her line of vision. He slammed his own arm down from above, hitting the guy's elbows to break his hold on Tori. Rationally, he knew he should have done that from behind the guy, then pinned him, except the urge to bust between them and block Tori with his own body couldn't be denied.

Aiden shoved the guy in the chest to back him off a few feet. Off balance, the man bounced off Tori's rear door. Aiden ached to deck him for touching a woman that way—especially Tori—but he knew that given his training, his fists could do an unprepared man serious damage.

And there was no way this guy was trained in anything—except straightening paper, or maybe, given the quality of his clothes, stacking up stock certificates. He didn't have his feet, his reaction time was for shit, and he looked around wildly for Tori, as if Aiden had made her vanish into thin air.

If Aiden weren't so pissed, he'd be laughing.

———

Tori waited a few beats, then peeked around Aiden's broad back. Shock and confusion showed plainly on Holden's face. Served him right, she thought.

She drew a fortifying breath and stepped to the side. Aiden lifted his arm, palm toward her, to block her from coming forward. She realized that while he looked at ease—standing straight and tall, not crouched like a boxer or ninja or any of the other fight-style video games Luke used to play—his senses were on full alert.

She cleared her throat, hating that she had to do this. Wishing away the mortification she already felt. "Aiden, this is"—she saw a flicker in the tense muscle of his cheek and forced herself to go on—"my ex-husband."

"We're still married!" Holden said, too loud and raw.

"Only because you left us in the lurch and disappeared like the coward you are! If you'd been anywhere to be found, I would have had you divorced and held accountable faster than you could blink." Tori was angry, so angry, which made her voice waver as if she was on the verge of tears. "Besides, I've served you by public notice, so it's only a matter of days."

Holden looked miserable, like he could cry himself. Physically, he sagged.

Aiden dropped his arm, allowing Tori to pass. She stepped forward only far enough so that she couldn't see his face—that he was watching made her feel safe and yet all the more embarrassed.

"How could you, Holden?"

He bent his head, then raised his eyes to hers. They glimmered with tears. "I'm sorry."

"After years of deceit, your 'sorry' doesn't hold much water with me."

"I know. I don't expect... I just want to see Luke. Regular visitation or something," he said, although Tori was already shaking her head.

"Absolutely not."

"He's my son. You can't keep him from me."

"Oh, yes I can. Legally, all decisions are mine. *Abandonment*, Holden."

"I'll take you to court. I'll—"

"Take me to court? Are you insane? Have you suddenly hit the lottery? Or did you steal someone else's kid's college fund?"

"Please," Holden said.

"It's not just me," she admitted, crossing her arms. "Luke doesn't want to see you."

Holden looked stricken, and just like that, Tori felt drained. All the fight went out of her at the thought of her son. How much the boy had lost, what could have been. All Luke had from Holden was anger, disgust, disappointment, and hurt—and a complete loser for a father.

"He's been pretending he doesn't see you," Tori told him. She noted the dejection that slid over his features, a face she'd once considered handsome, but now could see only as weak. She couldn't feel sorry for him. Not after the hardships she and Luke had suffered. There were things Holden deserved. Things he had to hear. "You're making him uncomfortable. Stop following him—or I will call the authorities, and you'll find yourself in a far deeper mess than you've created already."

Holden opened his mouth to speak.

Low and menacing, Aiden said, "Time to go, man."

Aiden reminded Tori of a cobra she and Luke had seen on some National Geographic show—towering over them, vibrating with tension, poised and ready to strike at the slightest provocation.

Tori watched Holden's eyes shift up to Aiden's face and then slide back to her. He turned without another word, shoulders slumped, and moved woodenly across the parking lot away from them.

Tori could only stand and watch, frozen. She'd dreamed of that confrontation for ages. Dreaded it, too. Knew instinctively it was far from over. So much left unresolved, yet she could, if she chose, just be done with him for good. When Holden was two whole car aisles away, she drew in a shaky breath that probably telegraphed all the opposing emotions playing for space in her chest.

Aiden turned her to face him, maneuvering her view away from her almost-ex, his big hands gentle on her upper arms. His thumbs rubbed her skin, warming her, at least there. He searched her face, dark eyebrows angled down in concern.

"Are you okay?" he asked, his voice belying a remaining intensity his soft touch had hidden.

"I am, I think," she said, realizing she felt a measure of relief. "But I really wish you hadn't had to witness that."

He smiled, that half-smile she liked so much, and said, "I, on the other hand, am very glad I was here." He dropped his hands from her arms only to reach up and cup her face in one palm. Tori's breath caught as he traced her cheekbone with the pad of his thumb. She in turn traced his face with her eyes. Clean-shaven jaw—relaxed now. Full lips. That crooked nose, and the blue eyes, so striking with his dark brown hair. The look she saw there was both tender and heated—he was going to kiss her now, she thought with only a little surprise and no resistance.

Except he didn't.

That look vanished, his eyes suddenly shuttered. He raised his head, retreating, and his hand disappeared from her skin to run through his own hair and settle on his neck. He'd done that before, she'd noticed. Did she make him nervous? Of course she did. Between her employees, the Haley thing, and the crazy ex, she was like a walking, talking minefield of stressors.

Disappointment flooded her, making her face surge with color. More humiliation to add to this awful situation. Yet it was just as well he'd come to his senses. Things between them were complicated enough. Her own life, even more so. Plus, she had big goals. A man—even a temporary one—would only get in her way.

"Tori," Aiden said, his voice serious and demanding her attention. "I want you to let me know if he bothers you—or your son—again."

She sighed. "I appreciate that, but he's not your problem."

Aiden shrugged. "Still. Sometimes a well-placed threat from an outside party—another man—can go a long way."

Tori wasn't sure how to respond. That he'd be willing to go to bat for her was...overly macho, but sweet. Definitely intriguing. Yet he wasn't her boyfriend or lover. She wasn't even sure they were friends. Most accurately, perhaps, they were business associates at cross-purposes. People who didn't see eye to eye.

"You'll be okay getting home?"

Tori nodded, then realized she didn't know what had happened to her car key. It wasn't in her hand. Aiden bent and reached just under the door of her car. He stood, put the key in the lock, and opened her own car door for her. When she reached out for the key, his thumb pressed it into her palm, his large hand cupping hers from underneath, a gesture so intimate in its simplicity that Tori's breath hitched.

"Take care," he said, and released her.

He didn't turn to go, though, and Tori hesitated. Normally, she would have aired out the stink mobile big time before daring entry.

She clenched her teeth and slipped into her seat. He shut the door for her—quickly, thankfully, because she could already smell the stench.

Tori forced a smile and wiggled her fingers at him through the window. He bent slightly, in order to see her, still hovering.

She put the key in, turning it only enough to roll the window down a couple of inches.

"Bye," she said.

He didn't budge. Dammit, he left her no choice. She resigned herself to misery and sucked in a big breath, knowing the rancid smell would have built up again in the ducts, cooking in the heat, simply waiting for the signal to attack.

She started the car. The rattling of her heart felt as unsettled as the uneven rumbling of the engine before it caught. Both had been in a holding pattern, needing attention, even though she'd been withholding service—her heart tucked away for protection, her disaster of a vehicle ignored for lack of funds.

Damn Holden Radnor, and God save her from Aiden Miller, too.

Aiden stepped forward as if to say something.

Panicked, Tori dialed up the force of the air—hot air, since her air conditioning hadn't worked in ages.

Ugh! The wrong move.

She chanced a glance at Aiden.

His nose was buried in the elbow of his dress shirt. Only his eyes, narrowed under frowning brows, were visible.

Voice muffled, he asked, "Is that…?"

Tori's face flooded with heat, and she knew color leaped to her cheeks. She tore her eyes away, unable to face him. He knew already, yet the unreasonable mortification of that scent and everything behind it—being a target of something cruel and still driving this garbage can because she couldn't afford to just junk the thing—swamped her.

Hastily, she powered the windows all the way down.

"It's better when I get moving," she said, knowing just how lame that sounded when the vents spewed foul air.

"Goddammit, Tori," Aiden nearly growled.

Aiden's long fingers clamped onto her door.

She scowled up at him. "Let go."

"You can't drive this car."

"I can, I have, and I will. Let go."

"For Christ's sake." His arm shot across her, to turn off the key and remove it, then he yanked open the door. With a firm hold on her left elbow, he tugged. She pulled away.

She heard a massive sigh of frustration before he braced his hands on the frame of the car's door. "This is me asking—*please*—come out so we can talk."

Tori clenched her fists. The last thing she wanted to do was talk some more about *this* with *him*.

Knowing he wasn't going to take no for an answer, she climbed out, forcing him to straighten and back up a step. She crossed her arms and set her jaw as she glared. "There's nothing to talk about."

They were still too close. With no one parked in the spot beside her, he could back up. He didn't. He ran both hands through his hair. Good. She'd stress him out, just like he was stressing her out.

"Why," he said through clenched teeth, "are you driving this car?"

"It's my dream car," she said, sarcasm screaming from every syllable. "Give me my key."

Aiden scowled. "Could you just, for one second, drop your armor, and—"

"No," Tori said. "Because King Midas couldn't possibly understand."

His face got harder, if that was possible, and Tori regretted that comment instantly. "Sorry," she said, her gaze dropping. "But it's not your problem."

Aiden spun, stalked around the tail of her car, eyeing the scratches and the frayed rope she'd been forced to tie the trunk shut with after they'd pried it open. Stood staring at the horrid etched words. His jaw clenched, ticking furiously, as Tori felt another wave of humiliation grip her middle.

He raised his eyes to hers, looking like hell come to roost. "You driving Miller's employees around in this shit bucket?"

She flinched, even as her face flared like fire.

"Then it *is* my problem," he said. "Grab your things. You're coming with me."

CHAPTER 16

TORI SAT IN the passenger seat of his Mercedes, a belligerent statue, face turned away, avoiding him the entire ride from town. That awful smell clung to her, just enough to make him lower the windows a couple of inches.

Questions plagued Aiden about the altercation Tori had had with her soon-to-be ex-husband. What kind of lurch? Accountable for what? Aiden already thought the guy was an asshole, but as he speculated, he became even less impressed. Tori Radnor, even with her bleeding heart for the underprivileged—okay, okay, Aiden knew most people would find that admirable, but they hadn't grown up with an extremist do-gooder like Marjorie Miller—seemed a class act. How she'd become tangled up with that loser of a husband, he'd never know.

When they'd traversed his drive—nearly a half-mile long—her eyes swung toward his. "Where are we?"

"My house."

Her chin jutted forward. "Why?"

"I've got an extra car you can borrow."

"Yeah? And for how long?"

He shrugged. "As long as it takes."

"I can't—"

"Save the arguments, okay? Just come inside and talk this through like a reasonable person."

Tori's eyes flashed, but she held her tongue. Aiden turned off the ignition and climbed out.

She slammed the car door and hoisted her purse to her shoulder, her doodle book sticking out of it. She took one look at the front of his home then, with a shake of her head, marched toward the front steps. He unlocked the door and motioned her inside. Her eyes swept the entryway, then the great room as the space opened up. Her fingers balled into fists.

He looked at her quizzically, tossing his keys up and down in his palm. All of a sudden, it came to him. "You hate my house," he said, amazed. The last woman who'd seen the inside of his Poconos home, Diane, had drooled when she'd seen the place for the first time, running her hands along everything as if she could literally feel dollar signs beneath wood, stone, and granite.

"I don't hate your house," Tori mumbled, waving a hand.

"Then why so uncomfortable? You're safe with me. You know that, right?"

"I know." She nodded, although something he couldn't pinpoint passed like a shadow across her features. "It's just…" She shrugged, then sighed as she put one hand palm up, as if she didn't have the energy for sugarcoating. "You're rich."

He raised an eyebrow. "Yeah. And?"

"I don't like rich."

Aiden burst out laughing. "Everyone likes rich."

He tossed his keys on the hall table with a clatter and ushered her forward into the living area. Secretly, he was pleased. He didn't want a groupie who got off on the team uniform. He wanted *her* to like *him*, period. Except there was that umpire on his shoulder, yelling and red-faced, making the call. Throwing him out of the game, before he'd even gotten up to bat. Insisting he follow the playbook he himself had written regarding Tori—despite the urge to act otherwise.

Tori was frowning, and Aiden couldn't resist reaching out a finger to tip up her chin. "Tori. You have a fledgling business that relies heavily on people with money to burn. You need to love rich."

She scrunched up her nose.

"I'm betting this has something to do with that ex of yours."

"You weren't kidding when you said you wanted to talk, huh?" Tori said. "Fine, let's get a few things said, so you know where I'm coming from." Tori dropped her bag on the floor and made to sit on his couch.

"Whoa." Aiden jumped into action, grasping both of her elbows to pull her upright. "How about a shower first?"

Tori's eyes widened.

"No, I mean—" *Real smooth, ace,* Aiden thought. "No offense, but that smell is kinda lingering. On you."

Her face turned pink again and her nostrils flared. "If you'd let me go on my merry way, you wouldn't have to smell me."

He took a step back and clasped his hands together out in front of him. "Just…take a shower. I'll give you some clothes so you can leave in a clean ride feeling fresh. It'll allow me time to make some calls about your car. See how fast we can get it back to you."

"I've been trying to tell you," Tori said, "right this minute, I cannot afford to pay to have the stupid car repaired."

He held up his hands. "We'll sort it out. Payment plan or a loan or something. Not fixing your car? Not an option. Period." Tori's brows lowered, but she remained silent. "Shower, take a deep breath, and then we'll deal—calmly. Okay?"

He could see she didn't like taking orders, yet she allowed him to lead her by the hand to the door of his bedroom. Aiden fought to ignore the pleasure of touching her. She halted there, digging in her heels like a mule.

"I don't even have shampoo in the hall bath," he said. "If you'll be more comfortable, I'll move what you need, though it's probably faster if you just use mine. Your call."

Tori hesitated, entered the master bedroom, and studiously avoided looking at his California king bed. Hiding his amusement, he turned to dig out a pair of gray sweats with elastic at the ankles and a soft navy t-shirt.

"They're gonna be huge," he said. "How 'bout I run your clothes through the wash real quick?"

"You do your own wash?" This time, her green eyes teased.

"Only on Wednesdays." He winked. "Leave them outside the door."

"No, uh, I don't want to keep you that long from work. These have a drawstring. They'll be fine. I'll just take a plastic bag for my clothes and return yours later."

Aiden was going to insist—found that, inexplicably, he didn't want her to rush off—however, she slipped past him and shut the bathroom door with a quiet whoosh, right in his face. The lock clicked into place.

"Towels under the sink," he called.

No answer, only the sound of the water surging forth. He liked this woman. A lot. Good-hearted, feisty, and mysterious— she certainly kept him guessing.

His instincts had been right. Association with her had definitely proved complex, and sex wasn't even on the table—yet. Damn. Even now, his head level and Tori behind a locked door, he couldn't deny that he wanted her. Big time.

He'd been so close to kissing her in the parking lot. Demure as it had been, that red silk blouse she'd been wearing had made him think sex all through lunch. Then, after the adrenaline surge, believing she was in danger? God, but he'd have devoured her there, if he hadn't come to his senses in the nick of time. Mixing pleasure with their already-complicated business arrangement was pure stupidity. And yet he'd invited her home, insisted she get naked.

No matter the good intentions behind his strong-arming, the fact was that sexy Tori Radnor was now in his bathroom, stripping out of that incredible blouse. A red bra? Or maybe black. *Don't even think about the panty options…or the bubbles of soap catching on her nipples, the water cascading over her smooth skin…*

Aiden groaned and forced himself to leave the room. What was he supposed to be getting? Oh yeah, a kitchen garbage bag for her clothes. He didn't have anything smaller that would contain the smell. His chain didn't do cheap plastic. He tossed it to the floor outside the master bathroom, then exited, closing the bedroom door to give her an additional measure of privacy—and him an extra barrier between them.

Remember, horn ball, he scolded himself, *she's absolutely the wrong woman for you.* Bad for his stress level, awfully stubborn, too focused on her charity work.

That was puzzling, actually. She dressed like she had money, but drove an old, horribly defaced car that smelled like hell rotting, when she should have been ditching the thing. Contended that she couldn't pay for repairs or cleaning. Perhaps her ex really had cleaned her out. If so, what the hell was she doing with the charity work? Why not get a higher-paying job?

He frowned as he unclipped his phone. Was she playing him? Poor me and all that, so he'd pick up the bill?

No, he didn't think so. She would have driven off in that shit-mobile in a flash, if he'd let her. He shook his head and headed for the living room, where the cell reception was better.

He'd table the Haley argument for today. Surely they could agree to disagree until something gave on that front. Either Tori would eventually come around and see that she'd built suspicion out of dust, or the real culprit would be exposed. For the moment, Aiden vowed to also set aside the worries about the upsetting pranks, the drugs, the store's reputation, the safety of his employees...

One thing at time. He blew out a long breath. First, Tori's car. Aiden dialed Eddie, who'd lived in this area longer. He'd know who did the best detailing, who was reasonable for body work. Action was always better than inaction, and already Aiden felt lighter.

One action he wouldn't be taking? Making a pass at Tori. Nope, he'd table the lust, too. For now.

Unless, of course, she walked out in a towel, dripping wet and flushed...

Fantasies, Aiden decided, were exempt from the *smart* thing.

———

When Tori padded into the living room, Aiden had sunk deep into the couch cushions, feet propped on the rustic coffee table, hands loosely clasped over his middle, his eyes shut.

Was he actually asleep, she wondered? He looked more at peace, not so wired, with his eyes shut and his jaw less tense. She regretted having to tell him her theory about Haley. Really did hope she was wrong. She gave him a lot of points for coming to her rescue today. He'd been misguided, of course. She'd have handled Holden. And she still wasn't happy about the car thing. But Aiden meant well and hadn't let their disagreement stop him from doing what he felt was right.

Tori set down her purse and the plastic bag her clothes were tied up in.

Her eyes traveled down Aiden's length—broad shoulders, trim waist, big hands, long legs—all the way to his crossed ankles and now bare feet. He was one fine specimen of a male, she thought with a tsk. Too damn bad she wasn't looking.

Tori eyed the other love seat. Should she wait or wake him? She glanced back at his face.

Blue eyes twinkled under lazy lids, and a slow smile grew on his lips.

She blushed, feeling exposed. Not only had he caught her ogling him, but she stood here without makeup or bra, like a drowned rat in his oversized clothes.

Tucking the still-wet hair behind her ears, she said, "All set." She nearly groaned. Embarrassment had made her sound far too perky.

"Feel better?" He swung his feet to the floor and stood, closing the distance between them.

"Actually, yes. Thank you."

He leaned in, nose nearly nestling in her neck, causing her to catch her breath in anticipation. Just as fast, he straightened. "You definitely smell better."

He grinned, and she rolled her eyes.

"Warm enough?" he asked. "I can shut the doors."

He'd opened the sliders to the deck wide. What a view. Green forest, blue lake, summer sunshine. She shouldn't have been so snarky earlier. His home was gorgeous. Huge and amazing, yes, but somehow cozy and comfortable, too.

"I'm fine." She walked over to take a look. Some cleared lawn and weathered Adirondack-style chairs. Rustic shed, a short dock, orange kayaks. Luke would love this. Oh, who the hell was she kidding? She, too, would feel like she'd gone on vacation, just sitting for an hour in one of those chairs, soaking up the sun and the view.

"It's really beautiful," she said, turning back around. "You kayak often?"

"Few times a week now. July and August, I expect I'll go out nearly every morning."

"Must be cold in the morning, though."

"I don't get wet." He shrugged one shoulder. "Plus, those kayaks have drink holders. Nothing like a hot cup of joe on the water at sunrise. Speaking of, you want some coffee? I did pour us some water." He gestured to the low table.

She shook her head. "Water's good."

"Sit for a minute."

She perched on the edge of the couch, took a sip of water.

"So, why couldn't I smell it at Marie's?" he asked quietly.

Tori tucked her hands into her armpits. "We weren't sitting that close together."

He raised an eyebrow.

"Okay, fine," she huffed. "At home I can let the car run for a while, windows and doors open, vents blasting, to air it out before I get in. It's far worse when it's closed up and the heat builds."

"Ah," he said. "Well, the good news is I've got your car all set. Towing, detailing, and they've even got an industrial ionizer that should knock out the stench. Same shop can take care of the trunk and side panel. I'm meeting the guy there in an hour with your key."

Tori frowned. "But—"

"A friend of a friend is doing the work. He'll give us a good price, and I'll pay for it."

"No, I don't want—"

"You can pay me back. I promise." He held her eyes. "But wait until we get an estimate before you decide what makes sense in terms of reimbursement."

Tori hated this, but oh what temptation not to breathe that stink ever again. What relief not to drive around with a sick threat emblazoned on the side.

"I'm not going to charge you interest, even if it takes a year, so really—don't stress, okay?"

Tori looked out at the lake. A year and a half ago, Mitch had told her to swallow her pride when it came to accepting help. Stable ground was just around the corner, so near she could almost grab it. And now she had not only herself and Luke to consider, but her UpStart clients, too. A payment plan would work, especially with no interest. In fact, in a matter of weeks, when her clients' first month was up, Miller's would take over payroll, freeing up some of her funds. And eventually, UpStart would be due the government's reimbursements as well. Yes, surely, she could make a sizable dent in the money owed on her car before long.

Tori turned to Aiden and nodded. "Thank you." Silently, however, she vowed to ramp up her efforts to find other big employers. The last thing she wanted was to become dependent on Aiden and Miller's.

"I am wondering, though...why?" she asked, searching his eyes for hidden motives.

Like her, he looked out at the lake, took his time responding. In the end, he shrugged. "Because I can. Because it's the right thing."

Tori nodded again, relieved. Midas had a heart.

"Can I ask you a question now?" he asked, holding her gaze, those blue eyes serious and caring.

Tori felt that connection again, prompting her to agree to take this—this whatever it was—to a more intimate level.

"Yes," she said.

"Is it because of your ex? This thing you have against the rich?"

Tori grimaced. "Partly. But it started long before him." She scooted back onto the couch, tucked her bare feet beneath her, and pulled a couch pillow in front of her for comfort. "My parents."

"Your parents what?"

"They're rich—the worst kind of rich."

Aiden's brows lowered. "What does that mean?"

"You want an illustration? All right, here goes." Tori sighed. "I was about thirteen. Our housekeeper had a stroke. Alma was her name, though I called her Myalma, for "my Alma," ever since I was little. She was everything to me—nanny, playmate, nurse, teacher, idol. I was heartbroken. One day Myalma was there, and the next she simply wasn't. I was told she was okay but unable to work, and nothing more. Then, one night, her husband came to the door completely distraught and desperate, begging and sobbing. They could no longer afford their apartment, let alone an aide, yet he couldn't care for Alma and still work…"

Tori picked at the fringe of the pillow, then met Aiden's gaze. "I would have given her the whole house, anything, and couldn't understand why they wouldn't help. Later, I pieced it together. My parents hadn't provided healthcare, a severance, a bonus, or anything. She'd worked for us for sixteen years."

God, she could still remember it like it was yesterday. The despair and disbelief from Alma's husband. The disgust and anger from both her parents. The salt of her own tears. Her heart-wrenching, whispered cries from under her covers at night—*Myalma, Myalma.*

Even now she teared up, but covered it with a wry smile.

"Sadly, that's what I consider the defining moment of my childhood." Still to this day, it mortified her, this stained movie reel that highlighted who her parents really were: tight-fisted, hard, selfish, awful people.

Aiden ran a hand through his hair and his jaw clenched. "That's why you do what you do? Why you've dedicated yourself to helping others?"

She nodded. "Pretty much." God, she couldn't believe she'd actually shared such a painful, personal story with Aiden. He certainly didn't need to know the rest. "What was your upbringing like?"

"Fairly normal, I guess. You know how Miller's started?"

"Your dad owned stores and then you took over?"

"Dad had one store. An old-fashioned corner market." His expression was nostalgic. "I worked there as a kid. Just the two of us, mainly, and sometimes a part-timer so that Dad could attend my ball games and tournaments. The store was barely hanging on by the time I was in high school, but the neighbors tried to support us, because of my dad."

"I can see why." Tori smiled. "He's very personable. Awfully charming."

Aiden smirked. "He liked you, too."

Tori laughed. "Baseball, huh? Travel leagues and everything?"

"No travel ball, not with my dad being tethered to the store. I meant local karate competitions."

Ah, that was why he moved with such power and grace. She skimmed her gaze over his athletic build before she caught herself. "Where did you grow up?"

"Outside Philly, but in Jersey. Haddon Township. A real neighborhoody kind of place."

"I know of it. We were on the Main Line."

"I'm getting the picture now. A house with manicured grounds and balustrades? Private school? A sweet sixteen gala to rival a wedding, maybe at the Union League?"

Tori grimaced with embarrassment. "Unfortunately, yes."
To all of the above.

"If you've got blue-blood money behind you"—Aiden
frowned—"why such an issue to pay for your car?"

Tori felt a moment of panic, shook her head, and pressed
her lips together. It was either that or crawl onto his lap, bury
her face in his chest, and fall apart. She was too raw and fragile
from the events of the last few days.

"Sorry. Too personal." Aiden held up his hands, his lips
forming the quirky smile that threatened to melt her. "My dad
could have gotten away with that kind of question. I forget
sometimes that I don't have half his charm."

She appreciated the attempt to lighten the awkward moment,
but he was wrong. Aiden was far too charming, too enticing. The
more she got to know him, the more her heartstrings stretched.
But unlike a chunk of Silly Putty that could be pulled beyond its
limits and then massaged back together, Tori doubted she would
recover well.

"It's fine," she said, waving her hand. "I just really need to
get going."

"Of course." Aiden's brows lowered slightly, but he nodded
and stood.

Tori felt an irrational surge of disappointment. What had
she expected? That he'd try to get her to stay? That they'd waste
another couple of hours together talking and laughing and getting to know each other? What purpose would getting cozy
serve?

None. That was what. Despite the fact that she'd be working with him and even—*cringe*—driving his car, it was best she
didn't delude herself. The only relationship between them was,
and would remain, all business.

CHAPTER 17

TORI HAD JUST LEFT an interview at FreshRite, Miller's Markets' main competitor in the Poconos, and was *this close* to securing new placements for Clarice and Alan.

After a series of phone conversations, a high-level manager had finally passed her on to the CEO, Barry King. Today, he'd had been engaged, interested, and, she could tell impressed. She realized, of course, that much of King's interest stemmed from her mention of Miller's Markets as a client. FreshRite stores were large and well stocked and did big business, offering constant sales—however, they looked like discount dumps compared to the high-end, specialty niche Miller's claimed. Besides, if the Midas of Markets was doing something, well then, it had to be cutting edge and glinting like gold. Tori only needed a foot in the door—didn't matter how said door was opened.

She tipped up her chin and grinned into the sun.

She'd been testing out her business plan with smaller venues to start, making sure the salary breakdown was viable against the government's commitment, confirming that she was providing her people the right kinds of preparation, matching client personality carefully to position and company. She didn't intend to slack on any of that; however, she'd also known all along that places with loads of staff on the payroll were going to be of the most benefit to UpStart—the trick had always been in getting them to commit.

Now that she could claim a foothold at reputable Miller's—even if she yanked her employees tomorrow—she envisioned rapid growth. Case in point: Barry King's interest.

Tori hugged her purse to her side, hoping for the best. Clarice and Alan swore there'd been no more awful surprises on the job. Luke, however, worried her. He'd been employed just shy of a week, but his initial enthusiasm had taken a nosedive. He didn't moan and groan. Instead, he was...stoic. Increasingly withdrawn and reticent. And yet, when she thought things over, she realized he'd asked a fair amount of questions in the days after the rat incident. Timing that would coincide with his own first few shifts.

"Mom, when's your interview with FreshRite again?"

"What's the Miller's contract say? Any hanging rat clauses?"

"How bad would it look for UpStart if you pulled Clarice from Miller's?"

"Would we lose a lot of ground?"

Tori leaned against the car and used her cell to call Stefan. He'd be spending some time with Luke this afternoon. Maybe, just maybe, he'd have better luck with her kid.

"Listen," she said, "Luke's still insisting that he work exactly the same shifts as Clarice and Alan."

Stefan said, "Very altruistic of him."

True, it saved her some shuttling. And Tori knew he enjoyed their company, as well. But... She chewed her lip. "What if it's not that?"

Stefan told somebody to hang on, then asked, "You think he's protecting Clarice? Acting as a buffer because of the rat thing?"

"Maybe." Tori frowned, thinking back. Last night, she'd had enough and pressed Luke. He'd slammed his bedroom door in her face and refused to come out, even for dinner. When she'd demanded he apologize, he dismissed her with a rude *Whatever, Mom.* "But that wouldn't explain the surliness. Or avoiding me and my questions."

"Yeah," Stefan said, "he's not usually like that. He seems sort of closed off suddenly."

"Right. And it's a common response when somebody's being bullied." Or abused or harassed. Given Tori's years in social work, she knew well that shutting down was a form of self-protection.

"You think someone at Miller's is bullying him?" Stefan's tone was skeptical.

"If my theory about all the various incidents is correct—that *I'm* the target? That the perpetrator is in the store—maybe even Haley? What better way to get to me than through my son?"

"That's…" She pictured Stefan shaking his head, brow furrowed under expertly gelled hair.

Diabolical? Awful? Unlikely, but possible? All of the above?

"I know," she said, as if he'd spoken. "But consider this. Luke's a remarkable kid, really well adjusted. But all of a sudden, he's a completely miserable teen? Pulling away from me out of nowhere, when normally we're super close?" She pushed off the car and paced. Her tight relationship with Luke was one of the only good things to come out of their difficult past. "The only thing that's changed lately is that damn position at Miller's Markets."

"I'll see if I can get anything out of him," Stefan said. "Don't worry."

"Worry is my middle name," Tori said. But her shoulders dropped, as a measure of tension eased.

Stefan asked about the FreshRite interview and Tori sent up another prayer to the universe. If that worked out, the difficult situation at Miller's was a non-issue. Null and void. Her son would go back to his normal self, and she'd stop peering into shadows in her own parking lot.

Tori pulled out the new key fob and bleeped one of the buttons. The lights on Aiden's SUV blinked and she heard the locking mechanism switch. She sighed. She'd gotten used to that perk fast.

Hmm, transportation, she thought. Most of the bigger-box stores, including the home repair chain she was talking to and some of FreshRite's branches, were a longer drive. Another year, and Luke would have his license, and could help with the shuttling, at least until he went to college. When UpStart really began to thrive, she'd need to purchase a used minivan and could hire one of her own clients to drive the others.

Tori climbed into the car and tossed her presentation folder and purse on the passenger seat, where a bag with Aiden's clothes sat waiting to be returned. She shut her eyes, attempting to put concern over her son aside, reminding herself that nothing else had happened lately. Nothing that she knew of, anyway.

She focused on the feeling of the sun on her lap and visualized Luke laughing, Clarice and Alan in FreshRite uniforms, and not one but two minivans sporting the UpStart logo.

She nodded once, and then enjoyed a deep inhale of this glorious vehicle. Not a whiff of stench, just sun-warmed leather. Only temporarily hers, but so pleasurable. Aiden had claimed he used it primarily in the winter and sometimes to haul gear—nothing special.

His old was her new. She started the car and lowered all the windows at once. The air conditioning worked, too—at goose-bump level. The built-up heat dissipated like magic. And hallelujah, no rattling, grating, or groaning from the engine, eliminating the need to send up a prayer each time she drove.

She'd be spoiled beyond belief by the time her own car was finished. Aiden had estimated four weeks, if they could find the panels for her older-model Toyota nearby. He'd also quoted a number that sounded suspiciously low.

"I told you," he'd said. "Friend of a friend."

Tori wasn't so sure, but it didn't matter now. The car would be fixed, and she'd simply insist on an invoice from the shop. A month, minimum—meaning she'd enjoy this icebox well into July. Maybe longer.

She pulled out of the lot and focused on the next item on her agenda. A trip to the courthouse in Philly to confirm that Holden had not filed a response to her public notice and to submit forms requesting a default divorce judgment. Would the judge require a court hearing, or simply grant the divorce? She hoped for the latter.

She was probably required under oath or something to admit that he'd been following Luke and had approached her. But she feared the court would insist she start the due diligence process of contacting him in person all over again. A pointless exercise, given that she still didn't know where he was living or how to reach him. And the more time this took, the more she worried.

Surely he couldn't touch the grant money or UpStart, given that they'd come about well after his disappearance. As for other holdings, he'd cleaned them out so thoroughly there was nothing left. In terms of their son—he had no ground to stand on. Desertion meant she held all decisions in the palm of her hand. Holden had no say, no rights. Even if he did, she'd have fought for Luke's wishes not to see him.

Yet she wanted that piece of her life done, the lid sealed tight. Stashed away in the deep recesses of a garage, like a used can of paint. Existing, but ignored, even sometimes forgotten. An annoyance you'd gratefully dispose of, if only it was that easy.

Did it matter day to day, in the way she and Luke lived their lives? No, not in the least. But inside she yearned to be free of her non-marriage.

If she were being truthful, she'd felt that desire more keenly lately—because of Aiden.

He'd almost kissed her.

Awaiting the press of his lips, a secret part of her had begun to unfurl. She knew instinctively that, like a blade of grass, if that something was fed, it would grow fast and sure, at an astounding rate. Because, God, how she'd wanted him. Not simply a physical yearning. With Aiden, something connected. Tugged. As natural and strong as the pull of the sun to new growth.

"No, I can't," she said inside Aiden's car.

For she sensed he'd be way too easy to lean on, and awfully hard to say no to.

Tori grimaced. This luxurious ride was a prime example.

And she'd never give up control—financial or emotional—of her life, or Luke's, ever again.

Gripping the steering wheel tight, Tori merged onto the highway. Mentally, she set aside any prospect of a romantic future with Aiden, even as she drove toward slamming the door on her past.

———

"Counter?" Aiden asked Haley on Friday afternoon, once he had his Starbucks coffee, and she her hot chocolate. Like Tori midweek, Haley had insisted that she needed to speak with him privately—away from the store.

"Sure," Haley said. She seemed tense, her movements stiff as she climbed up onto the high chair.

Even though he'd felt like a traitor, he'd been watching her closely ever since Tori shared her crazy theory. Other than continued—and rather dramatic—changes to her appearance, he couldn't see anything but the same hardworking, well-mannered, conscientious employee.

Today, she wore her newly dyed jet-black hair loose. The ends were jagged, the hair stiff. Faint smears of purple near her temple—the dye, he guessed—looked like a skin condition.

Aiden took the adjacent stool. "Interesting new look you've got going."

"Do you like it?" she asked, searching his eyes.

"It's a little extreme, but cool."

Seemingly satisfied with that, Haley popped the lid off her hot cocoa and stirred the whipped cream with a little plastic stick. "It's not so out there," she said. "Lots of people my age dye their hair funky colors and get piercings."

She'd swapped out the tiny diamond in her nose for a spiky silver stud. He wished she'd stuck with the diamond. "Just wouldn't have expected it from *you*," he said.

She leaned back and sucked the cream off the stirrer. "I'm feeling like I need to branch out a little, you know? I got good grades, I worked hard in school and at the store, I took care of my mother…I finally graduated. This is the first time I have a little bit of freedom, a chance to carve my own path."

"I get it. I really do. Just don't branch out so far that you scare off my customers, okay?" Aiden caught her eye and winked. "I'm not sure Mr. Cranford will even recognize you."

She looked at him, her mouth twisted in half of a small smile—then returned her gaze to her cup.

That was the other thing—her lipstick was a chalky white that showed through some pink. A ghastly look, like a specter or evil clown. He'd definitely need some time to get used to this harsh new style. And he hoped that she'd get tired of it soon.

"So, what did you want to talk to me about?"

The girl took a big breath, filling her chest. "It's going to upset you, but you have to know."

She'd found the culprit behind the rat, Aiden thought.

"It's…"

He nodded and leaned toward her, silently urging her on.

"Butch."

Aiden froze.

Haley said, "You won't believe it. I really couldn't myself." She shook her head. "But…"

"Spit it out, Haley." Aiden knew what was coming. This wasn't about the rat at all.

Another dramatic inhale, and her voice dropped to a whisper. "I think—no, I'm sure of it—he's selling drugs." She paused. "From Miller's."

Aiden scrubbed a hand over his mouth.

"I know it must be a shock. Hard to believe and all, but—"

"Listen, Haley, I need you to keep quiet about this."

"What?" She looked at him, eyes and mouth wide with disbelief.

"I'm already working on it," he said.

"What do you mean, 'working on it'? Shouldn't we just call the police?" she asked, big blue eyes narrowing.

"We can't, not yet, and I've got to leave it at that."

"But—"

"Thank you for telling me. Really, I'm glad I have you in my corner, but this has to stay between us for now."

Haley pursed her lips and her brows lowered, her expression somewhere between confused and angry. Aiden couldn't blame her. That was shit for an answer, and they both knew it. But once again, his hands were tied—he didn't have the leeway to be forthcoming. Besides, the details would only upset her anyway.

They sat for a minute, watching the passersby. Most young girls were chatty, nervous. Not Haley. A plus, right? And look, she'd just leveled with him, trying to help him and protect his store, and his people. More proof that Tori's theory was bogus.

He swigged the dregs of his pick-me-up. "It goes without saying that Butch isn't going to be here much longer," he said.

She looked up at him expectantly, like a puppy.

"I don't know what's going to happen with the store."

"What do you mean?" she asked.

"Well, if the Butch thing gets out, it'll be bad. There's a real possibility I'd need to close this store," he said. "You've always got a job with us, though. Back in Haddon Township, where you started, or any of our locations."

She inclined her head, chin cocked toward him, crown angled away. Her eyes locked on his paper cup, his hands. "Thank you."

"Of course. I still think you'd be smart to gain other experience, though."

"I'm hoping the store will come through okay," she said, "and that I could be promoted into Butch's position. I've worked hard for it."

"I'm not discounting that. You're a dependable, dedicated employee, and smart as can be. However"—he had to be frank with her—"you still have a long way to go to manager. You're very young."

She stared at him, her jaw jutting forward in disbelief—the most emotion he'd ever seen from Haley.

"Age shouldn't be a basis for qualification," she said, setting down her cup hard enough that hot chocolate sloshed over the side. "I've worked for you for eight years."

"And Miller's has been lucky to have you."

"I'm ready," she insisted.

"Haley," Aiden said gently. "Managing people takes a special skill set, and managing them well requires a *lot* of experience."

Her mouth dropped open, and then she faced forward, eyes trained out the front window.

He almost put a hand on her shoulder, then thought better of it. "You're about the most mature twenty-two-year-old—"

"Twenty-three," she corrected through gritted teeth.

"—twenty-three-year-old I've ever met," he said. "I know you had to grow up fast with your mom sick and all, but there are some things that only come in time. Besides, in a position like that, it matters how others perceive you."

Haley crossed her arms over her chest, and her foot went tick tick tick—fast—as she bounced her leg up and down, her heel just nicking the metal support under the counter each time.

Aiden was shocked to realize she'd thought the position was right within her reach. She'd wanted management training. He was providing that—but apparently over a much longer term than she had envisioned.

"The other thing," Aiden said, thinking of Tori's claims, that Haley acted differently when he wasn't around, "is to always remember the golden rule."

"The one you taught me way back when I first started?" she asked.

"Yes. Same one I teach all my employees. The customer is always right. Always catered to, pampered, treated like gold."

Haley nodded, and the swinging of her foot slowed to a less insistent pace. She uncrossed her arms, seemed to relax as she reached up and twirled a piece of hair. The other hand tucked between her crossed thighs.

"Well, it still holds," he said.

Haley looked him right in the eye, her foot suddenly still. "Is someone implying that I—"

He held up a hand. "It's something I remind anyone on the management track, and anyone who's lasted long-term. It's too easy to get a big head. You know, the big fish in the small pond kind of thing."

Haley didn't react, and Aiden continued, "In fact, as assistant manager or someday manager, the golden rule is even more true—"

"*Someday*?" Haley repeated. "You say that like it's questionable."

"Well—"

"I can't help my age," Haley said. "But I have a real way with people…better than you can imagine." She narrowed her eyes. "You *do* believe I'm manager material, don't you?"

"Of course I do." Aiden set a foot on the floor and stood, pushing back his stool with a *scrumpf.* "Let's get back to the store."

As they walked out to their respective cars, Haley said, "I've been meaning to ask you, is that your car Mrs. Radnor is driving?"

"Yeah. She needed a loaner while hers is being repaired." He shrugged. "The Land Rover was just sitting there."

"That's thoughtful of you, Mr. Miller."

Back at the store, Aiden and Haley crossed through the dining area to let Butch know they were back. He said, "Stay away from Butch, okay? I don't think anyone's in danger, but I'd rather know you're safe."

"Thanks," she said, "but you don't have to worry about me."

They greeted Clarice, who was sweeping up in the café. Then, as they continued toward the front of the store, Haley said, "Mr. Miller, there is one more thing I wanted to mention. I've heard… murmurs from some of the staff." She shook her head.

"About?"

Haley cleared her throat. "Let me just preface by saying that I know you want to do right by Clarice and those other two Mrs. Radnor brought, and really, I admire you."

She angled closer to him, put a hand on his forearm. "But people are worried"—her voice dropped to a whisper—"about what the customers might think of the homeless working in the store."

Her expression was apologetic. Aiden narrowed his eyes.

"You know," she continued, "we sell food. The new hires look normal, of course, but you never can tell. I mean, what if they have *fleas* or something?"

"For God's sake, Haley."

"Don't shoot the messenger, Mr. Miller. I'm on your side." She held up her hand. "Except it seems I'm the only person willing to level with you."

Aiden tried to breathe deeply, but his chest clamped tight. Instead of being reassured by her candor, he felt...uneasy? Why hadn't she mentioned it before? Why hadn't Butch? He'd wondered if Clarice could have been targeted because of her situation, but discarded it as unlikely. Goddamn—were people so prehistoric that—

Speaking of UpStart—there was Tori, just coming through the automatic doors to the right of the registers. She looked amazing. Fresh and pretty in business clothes that somehow managed to be both understated and feminine. The pain in his chest eased some.

Aiden veered off to meet her, practically sweeping Haley, who was still on his right, into his abrupt turn.

"What's *she* doing here?" Haley asked under her breath, but he caught it.

"Don't know," he said, shooting her a sharp look. Attitude? Now?

He intercepted Tori, startling her, as she'd been focused dead ahead.

"Aiden." She blinked. "Haley."

"Hi," Aiden said. "What brings you in?"

"Oh, uh, here." She shoved a shopping bag at him. "Your things."

"Drawstring did the job, I hope?"

Tori blushed, and Aiden felt a warm rush.

"Yes," she said. "They're clean. Thanks again."

"Anytime," he said, but Tori was already darting between the registers to the exit.

Haley just looked at him. "Boy, you work fast."

"It's not what it looks like. Certainly, it's none of your business." His temper flared. "You want to be manager?" Aiden's words were clipped. "Keep your suppositions to yourself."

She scowled, eyes hard under that jagged black fringe. As he watched, her pupils shrank and her focus seemed to draw inward, while the corners of her mouth turned up.

Aiden's brows lowered. That was *weird*.

"Sorry." She reached up to twist a piece of hair around her finger, so hard the tip of her digit turned dark purple and bulbous. "I was just so taken aback."

Her voice sounded sweet and genuine again, like the Haley he knew...*thought* he knew.

CHAPTER 18

EVERYTHING WAS TURNING to shit. He'd given Radnor his car. Handed it over. The bitch was driving around town in his car.

Which was not the point of gifting the woman with rancid beef. Instead of *disappearing or dying*, as the message demanded and the smell of death and decomposition should have underscored, Radnor had slipped one hand in Miller's pocket already—lifting his car keys.

And apparently, she'd been fingering his dick too.

They'd disappeared after that cozy little lunch. The tracer had shown that they'd gone to his house, which, unfortunately, was the one place there weren't any microphones. Add in the returned clothing? Some down and dirty was a pretty safe bet.

What'd he do, blow his load before he managed to get her clothes off? Was he that far gone?

Miller had denied fucking Radnor—but his red-faced reaction was telling.

Maddening that Miller had such a thing for *her*. Why? Why her? Why now?

Couldn't figure that out. So fucking unfair.

Whatever. Didn't matter which base they'd reached; he had it bad. And if Miller was getting attached to a woman—then the original plan was for shit, too.

Just as awful, the kid. Miller was too taken with Luke Radnor. The fatherly routine was sickening. Always putting his hand on his shoulder. Praising him. Pumping him up. Talking ball and sports. Why? Because he was a boy?

But pair them together in Miller's life? Mother and son? Just add water and there was an instant happy family, all warm and cozy and filling like oatmeal?

No way, no fucking way. No, no, no.

Far fucking past time to step it up.

Working on that right now, in fact. The weapon was in place. An item that wouldn't draw suspicion. Not when it was combined with a toppled pallet from the high stock shelves.

A little adjustment had been made to the schedule. Lukey would be clocking out alone, soon. The setup was all planned out. Circle around and be back out on the floor, no one the wiser. Best of all, it would all look like an accident afterward.

Getting excited as imagination took flight… Oh, poor little Luke. There was a bolt loose on the shelving—causing just enough slant to make the wooden pallets slide off, toppling the heavy goods. How totally unlucky.

No one would be the wiser. That was important.

Because the situation *was* salvageable—but only if there was no suspicion cast in this direction.

Miller may not feel any love—yet. But there was attachment, fondness, reliance… Solid ground still, mostly. Not right-hand material yet, though—that was a brutal blow.

"That should be a lesson to you. You let yourself think he could be trusted."

"Did not."

"Did too. You fell under his spell. Gave him the benefit of the doubt."

"I thought we were getting somewhere."

Scoff. "How many times have I told you? Never wear your heart on your sleeve. Aiden Miller will rip your whole arm right off."

She was right, of course. But it'd been so close—finally ready to tell. Then out of nowhere, it'd all gone south. Hoping hoping hoping that all wasn't lost—because giving up wasn't an option. But she was right about something else, too—the situation had to be brought back into control. Immediately. No more pissing around. Because now everything had changed, a point *she* kept hammering.

"He's sleeping with her—"

"You don't have to remind me! The knowledge is burning me like it's acid." Blood surging hotter with remembrance.

"He'll never pay you any mind now."

Hotter still with humiliation, failure looming. Because it was fucking true. He'd never be receptive if he was in a relationship. All his brain blood would pool in his dick.

Had never understood that. Drugs could mess with your mind, make you need, fool you. Make you forget for a while even, a nice respite.

But sex? A tool only. Useful sometimes for getting what you wanted, but it wasn't a mind fuck like the drugs.

Except not to Miller, apparently. He'd looked like he'd found his own personal heaven, Kingdom Cum.

Worse still, it appeared that his heart was involved. The fact that he'd gone all alpha and rushed out of the restaurant to confront that bitch's husband—for that was who it had to be, given the public notice posted by one Victoria Radnor.

So fucking sappy. And stupid. Only stupid people let their emotions have any say. And all this time, they'd been counting on him being only a *little* stupid. Just emotional enough to be swayed by guilt, duty, loyalty, and hopefully pride, too.

"You've got to do something about it."

"I am. Can't you see that?"

"This is dicey. You might be seen. Something off site is safer."

"No shit, but the kid is never alone. And I took care of the camera. Besides, it's ideal if Miller's is at fault."

Unsafe work environment. Because they had to go. *Radnor* had to pull her employees, sever all ties with Miller's. Unless they were gone, there was no hope.

No response.

"You got something better?"

Silence.

"No? I didn't think so. So chatty when it's time to put me down. You get real quiet when it's time to plan, huh? 'Cause you were so shitty at it. You couldn't have gotten half this far—could you? It's no wonder the hard work was left to me."

Climbing down. Tucking into the corner. Taking position to wait.

Doubt creeping forth…it *was* risky. But there was little choice. These UpStart workers were stubborn as all get out. Keeping silent, so grateful to have stupid jobs. Ignoring all the warnings, refusing to take the hint.

Had to do something drastic, something physical. Radnor must come to understand.

This. Was. Not. A. Game.

Period.

Reaching up. Twisting round and round. Tugging tight. The sensation, the throb, sometimes narrowed the focus. Brought clarity with it.

No time left for doubt—Lukey boy was approaching fast.

A smile stretched unbidden from ear to ear. God, how she'd wanted to do this and more, for such a long time. Bash in some faces, let loose her frustration.

It was so hard to be a good girl all the time.

Gripping the wooden handle tight, Haley raised it over her shoulder. Three, two, one…

———

"Hey," Aiden said Sunday evening, as he entered Butch's doorway and saw him facing out the small windows behind his desk, which, as usual, looked like a box of papers had upended to land where they may.

Butch didn't turn, though. He stood stiff, the line of his beefy shoulders hunched up around his ears. His arms hung at his side, but one hand gripped the cordless phone tight at his thigh.

"Butch," Aiden tried again. This time, the manager turned. An intense look, so serious and clearly upset, hovered on his features for an instant, before he forced a neutral expression.

"Everything okay?" Aiden asked.

"Yeah," Butch said. He seemed to remember the phone, and placed it back on the cradle with a plastic clatter. "Family stuff."

Aiden frowned, thinking of the miscarriage scare Butch and his wife had had. "Anna okay?"

"Yeah. Yeah, she's feeling good. Extended family, I meant." Now Butch waved his hand. "What's up?"

"The issue with the fruit vendor."

Butch motioned Aiden to the chair—free of clutter, surprisingly—and took his own.

"I spoke with—"

There was a flurry behind him, and Aiden turned.

"Mr. Kovacs, Mr. Miller." Clarice wrung her hands. "You have to come. Luke's hurt."

Both men jumped up and practically rushed her.

"What happened?" Butch demanded.

"Where is he?" Aiden asked.

He watched Clarice's mouth open, but the words didn't come fast enough to suit him. Aiden propelled her out the door. "Show us," he said more softly.

As Clarice jolted forward, her voice jump-started as well. "In the back. By the lounge. Alan's with him, and Haley. He got hit on the head and fell, I think."

The trio made fast progress, cutting through the store, pushing open the industrial swinging doors to the back, where they hung a quick right to the "lounge," as the staff called the break room.

Luke sat at a chair that had been yanked a few feet away from a table. Alan Hammerton sat to his right pressing a wad of paper towels to the boy's face.

Shit, Aiden thought. An eye injury. He grabbed the first-aid kit by the door. Had they had an emergency drill or offered first-aid classes since the UpStart staff had all begun? He guessed not. Past time, then.

Both Aiden and Butch knelt before Luke. Clarice hung back.

"What happened?" Butch asked.

Luke shook his head, mouth pressed tight with strain.

"Let me see," Aiden said, nodding at Alan to remove the paper towels. Blood welled immediately, but Aiden managed to get a look at the gash first, and felt a measure of tension leave him. Not the eye. The forehead, slashing into the eyebrow. Only about half an inch in length in terms of split skin, but a much larger area swelled. He pressed clean gauze there. Shouldn't need to clean it with the blood flowing like that, but he'd bet Luke needed stitches. Head wounds often needed help staying closed because the skin stretched so taut.

"Ah, not so bad," Butch said. "Still, looks like you have a good story to tell us."

Alan spoke up: "Haley said she found a spill of water near the doors, and had just grabbed the mop when Luke walked into it."

Aiden heard the skepticism in the older man's voice, and raised an eyebrow.

Luke tried to nod under the pressure Aiden was placing on the square of gauze.

Luke said, "She was just yanking it out of the bucket. I didn't see her."

"Where is Haley now?" Aiden asked.

"I sent her to get ice from the café." The timbre of Alan's voice didn't change, but his eyes held Aiden's and said it all. "Expected her back by now."

A few minutes later, Haley showed up, ice in a sandwich-type baggie that they used for many of the items in the café. He felt Luke stiffen under his hand.

"How is your head?" Haley asked, but didn't stop for the answer. "Oh, Luke, I'm so sorry," she gushed, and put a hand on the boy's knee. Luke seemed to harden from the knee upward, like an ice cream dipping flavor—liquid until you changed the temperature. Even his one visible eye had frozen.

"Hold this," Aiden said to Alan, and motioned to Butch.

"Haley. Come talk to us." Aiden moved across the room to give Luke some space. "What happened?"

Haley clasped her hands in front of her. "Mr. Miller, Mr. Kovacs, I feel so bad." A little crease appeared between her brows. "I noticed some water on the floor right by the doors. I was going to clean it up, but the mop was stuck in that part that does the wringing. I yanked hard, and it came loose all of a sudden." Haley reached out and squeezed Aiden's arm, just above the wrist.

Aiden twisted his forearm to dislodge her, not remotely in the mood for drama.

"Really," she whined as tears welled in her eyes. "It was an accident."

"It's all right," Butch said. "Accidents happen."

Aiden looked hard at Haley. Lip just barely quivering, hands clasped to her chest, concerned glances in Luke's direction...

Tori's warnings rang in his ears, and Luke's physical reaction to Haley's touch flashed through his mind.

Accidents did happen, but Aiden wondered: would he get the same story from Luke?

CHAPTER 19

TORI RUSHED INTO the emergency wing's waiting area and spotted them immediately. Two tall forms: Aiden, fully grown and fit, with layers of lean muscle, and Luke, still stretching, lanky between each knobby protrusion, head wound in white gauze. Although they both stared at the TV mounted in the corner, Tori could tell each was lost in his own troubled thoughts.

Aiden's eyes shifted to meet hers before she'd even passed the admittance desk. He nudged Luke, who looked up. Now Tori could see a patch of brown over his eye, dried blood, but thankfully not much.

She weaved her way between seats and people. Aiden stood and squeezed Tori's arm gently, a show of support, she supposed. Tori smiled, ignoring the flutter of her pulse from the contact, though words were more difficult. On one hand, she should thank him for taking care of Luke, bringing him directly to the ER. On the other, she wanted to fire questions at him. What the hell happened? Who was involved? What had Luke said? Was this truly an accident?

Tori leaned down to hug Luke. "Are you all right? Does it hurt?"

"It throbs a little, but it's okay."

"I haven't seen any signs of concussion," Aiden said.

"Good," Tori said.

"They aren't too backed up, the nurse said," Aiden told her. "Still, I thought I'd go pick up some dinner for you guys before I go."

"You don't have to do that."

Aiden insisted, and they decided on sandwiches from

Marie's Place before Tori followed Aiden outside. Although they stood under the drive-up's portico, the day's build-up of heat traveled from the concrete through the thin soles of her flats.

Aiden inclined his head toward the building. "You've got a great kid."

"He's the best," she said, pride pricking her eyes. Sheesh, her emotions were close to the surface this evening.

Aiden nodded and looked out over the busy lot, people and vehicles coming and going. When he faced her, his expression had settled into a tense mask. "You'll want to know what I think about this accident."

"Yes."

"I…" He blew out a hard breath as he bowed his head. "I don't know what to think."

"Aiden," Tori said with disgust. "That's a total cop-out."

His hand shot up like a stop sign. "Before you skewer me further, let me say one thing. If this had happened to anybody but someone connected with you, I wouldn't even consider the possibility that it was anything but a random accident."

She scowled and he blew out a breath.

Aiden said, "I tried to talk with Luke, but he won't say a word."

"He's been that way when it comes to work. Won't tell me a thing. Insists everything is fine, even though I can tell it's not." She crossed her arms over her chest. "I wondered if Haley's been harassing him."

"Why wouldn't he say something?" Aiden's brows were drawn down in concern, the lines of his mouth tight.

"Because keeping silent, isolating oneself, is pretty typical in kids who are bullied or anybody who's been abused. There's embarrassment, humiliation, and, of course, fear of making it worse."

A car zoomed up to the curb. Aiden took Tori's elbow to

shift her along the curved driveway, farther away from the doors to the emergency room. Out from under the overhang now, the early evening sun shot through Aiden's hair, and Tori noticed for the first time a few slivers of gray.

He'd turned to face her, his face clouded. He slid his hand from her elbow to her upper arm. His other hand did the same. Tori's breath caught as his thumbs gently caressed her bare skin, and his eyes searched hers.

"You seem to know a lot about it..." Aiden drew a breath. "Was your husband abusive?"

Tori blinked, stunned, then remembered the way Holden had manhandled her in the parking lot—was that only two days ago? "No," she said. "What you saw was...out of character."

Aiden closed his eyes, bent his forehead to touch hers—just a moment only—then straightened and looked into her eyes.

"Good," he said, and squeezed her arms gently before releasing her. Tori felt full and bereft all at once, and wondered at the way the slightest gesture from this man could affect her. She wondered, too, if she was making too much of everything he did and said.

Tori cleared her throat, searching for words to deflect her blossoming feelings. "I'm a social worker. Besides my training, I've spent tons of time with abused women and children over the years. A lot of time in shelters."

Aiden frowned and nodded.

Tori glanced over her shoulder in the direction of the glass of the sliding doors, though she couldn't see inside for the angle. "As for Luke, it's also possible he's keeping mum because of the income, for my sake." She grimaced and forced herself to look at Aiden. "And because he knows I'll pull Clarice and Alan. He wouldn't want to risk their newfound employment. He's protective, of all of us."

Aiden rubbed his neck. "Maybe after this, Luke will tell you something he wouldn't have told me," Aiden said. "So far, both parties tell the same story: unfortunate accident."

Tori eyeballed Aiden. Lowered brows and clenched jaw. Eyes that avoided hers.

A chill raced up Tori's arms. "Who's the other party?"

He ran both hands through his hair—his tell, she'd already discovered.

"Haley? Goddamn it, Aiden." She threw out both hands. "You've got to believe me now."

He shook his head.

"Oh, come on—"

"Damn it, Tori. I can't throw away eight years of a perfect record on your suspicion," Aiden said. He sucked in a deep breath, his chest expanding under his dress shirt. "Luke or Clarice or somebody has to start pointing fingers, or my hands are pretty much tied. No one else has seen or reported a damn thing. There's still a reasonable possibility that it's all happenstance. Bad luck or clumsiness."

"You don't believe that." Tori narrowed her eyes. "There's too much coincidence."

Both of Aiden's hands slid to his shoulders to squeeze the tense muscles of his neck, and his eyes shifted away again, too. The movements telegraphed stress. Doubt must be creeping into his consciousness.

She pushed. "You have to do something."

"I'll take care of it."

Tori planted her hands on her hips. "How? Like you have been?"

Aiden scowled at her. She knew it was a low blow. She looked at her feet and tried to get hold of her temper. Antagonizing Aiden was stupid. Better to work together, if possible. Except she wasn't sure there was much point.

She said, "Luke won't be returning to work. And as far as I'm concerned, if there's danger, there's no choice for Clarice and Alan either."

"I wish you'd wait. Let me sort it out," Aiden said.

Tori scuffed the toe of her ballet flat on the sidewalk.

"As soon as I drop off dinner to you," he said, "I'll head back to Miller's to talk to the other staff, see if anybody witnessed the accident."

Tori crossed her arms over her chest. Not good enough.

"If nothing new comes to light," Aiden said, "I'll have a sit-down with Haley before shift end."

"She'll never admit to a thing."

"Maybe not." He raked his hands through his hair. "But if Haley is behind everything—I'm still saying if—then all your people, even Luke, should stay." His blue eyes held hers. "Because she'll never set foot in Miller's again."

———

Aiden stood on his balcony looking over the moonlit lake, barely seeing the landscape, let alone the beauty in it. He gripped his cell tight, counting the rings.

"Lundgren."

Thank God, Aiden thought before he spoke. "Detective, it's Aiden Miller."

"Hang on," the gruff voice said. Aiden heard some scuffling and a door slam before Lundgren said, "What's up?"

Aiden said, "That's what I'd like to know."

The sounds of the crickets and frogs beat in a near-constant symphony, but from Lundgren? Silence.

"Detective, are we any closer to doing this bust? Did you manage to get IDs from the tapes?"

"We're working on it. You got more for us?"

"No, I have nothing." Nothing except problems stacking up like a precarious end-cap display, primed for a cart to bring it all crashing down. He paced the deck in his bare feet.

"Look," Aiden said, "you've got to do something sooner

rather than later. I've got all kinds of weird shit going on that I can't address because you've got my hands tied."

"Calm down, Miller."

"People are threatening to quit." Aiden spoke as evenly as possible given his level of frustration. "Like you asked, I'm not firing anybody, but I can't force them to stay either."

He pivoted, traversing the length of the house again.

Lundgren asked, "Are these people you think could have anything at all to do with the movement of drugs?"

"No. No way." Aiden shook his head in emphasis, not that Lundgren could see him. "They are all essentially new hires."

"Then let them go, but make sure I have their names and contact info."

Aiden felt his shoulders drop just a bit. Okay, then. "You can't move up this mystery time table?"

"We're working on it."

Work faster, he thought, and gnashed his teeth. "When?"

Lundgren heaved a sigh. "There's a couple of trucks on the move in Florida. I don't know yet what the deal is, though. If the load feels too hot, they'll sit tight and wait, possibly for months, even a year. If they're anxious to unload, they'll hit one of their distributors. Hopefully Kovacs."

Aiden heard the scooping of ice and clinks against glass from the detective's end. He'd already had a stiff one himself. Hadn't helped.

"Miller, listen. We're watching the trucks, anybody who even waves at them, and your sorry-assed manager. So try not to worry."

"Can you promise me nobody's going to get hurt?" Aiden shut his eyes as he waited for Lundgren's answer.

A cupboard door shut across the line, and Lundgren grunted. "Somebody's gonna get hurt. That's almost a given."

"My employees," Aiden said. Christ, he'd be lucky if his molars didn't end up as smooth as his granite countertops by the time this was over.

"Like we told you, Butch is small potatoes. It's doubtful anything would go down at your store."

"I hope you're right about that."

"So do I, Miller. So do I."

Aiden heard a slurp of liquid and ice shifting in the glass. Lundgren seemed to take a healthy swig.

Not reassuring. Not at all.

CHAPTER 20

AIDEN HAD SPENT more of the wee hours standing at his bedroom windows watching the moon's progress across the sky than actually lying in his bed. At four thirty, he'd had enough and brewed a pot of Miller's own high-end, fresh-ground beans large enough to keep a bear awake through a Pennsylvania mountain winter. Geared up in a light windproof jacket and pants, water boots, and a knit hat he pulled low, he poured the steaming liquid into a spill-proof insulated cup. Then he headed down to the lake and hauled the kayak off the dock and into the water.

Normally, just the act of shoving off began to calm him. Today, Aiden went round and round about Luke, Haley, Tori, Butch, drugs, detectives... Talk about a whopping list of concerns.

Arms just beginning to burn with the continued rhythmic effort of propelling the kayak, he'd finally begun to think about the issues that had been coming to a boil *before* current circumstances had put the lid on the pressure cooker. About why he was here in the Poconos, fighting anxiety and panic attacks, spinning his wheels in frustration. Because those problems hadn't disappeared with his retreat to a place he loved. They'd traveled with him, like baggage always did.

When he'd first met Tori, he belittled her career choice in his mind. He'd come to realize, however, that she wasn't the self-aggrandizing zealot his mother was. And he gave Tori a lot of credit. Despite the shitty financial situation her ex had apparently landed her in, she was at least true to herself. Unlike him, she seemed fulfilled professionally and emotionally.

What about sexually?

He shook his head, sending one end of the oar in just a little deeper than usual, far enough to throw off the perfect cadence of his dips, pulls, and resulting lapping water.

Aiden set the oar across the center of the kayak and sucked in a deep breath of the cool lake air as he watched the horizon. No rays of sun yet, only a vague lightening of the sky. He wiggled his coffee cup out of its holder and took a hefty swig.

He still felt the press of tension on his neck and shoulders, but at least his brain seemed to be firing in a straight line now. Aiden shifted his lower back more comfortably into the sling support and rested his forearms loosely on top of the oar, the coffee cup still held in one hand.

He let himself float on the water as he watched the sky. His Dad. Baseball. Tori Radnor. Sparring with Eddie. Kayaking. Comfortable, enjoyable, good times. No panic attacks, no trouble breathing.

Out here alone, he had to face facts. The culprit behind the anxiety? The markets. In Philly, in the center of the hive, or all the way out here at his lone Poconos branch...

The chain wasn't his dream. It had never been his. It'd been his father's.

Not even his, Aiden scoffed, thinking of the crummy little corner store his father had owned and run before Aiden took over. The markets had outgrown either of them. Multiplying like chicken pox and a fever, infecting him from head to toe and burning up his well-being.

He shoved his to-go mug back in place to rub that hand over his face, scratching the beard that had grown overnight, then slid his hand to his neck muscles, pressing hard.

Aiden had to get out. The question was how? Without crushing his dad, abandoning his employees, laying it all to waste? How to just walk away and leave it all intact? He could leave it to his executive team to run things, elevating the COO or CFO to president. But instinct told him Miller's needed a non-corporate-bred leader. At its heart, his chain still felt like a family business.

And there was no one suitable, family-wise or other, to step up. Even people he might have trusted once, or trusted eventually, to run a store or a region—though hardly the whole chain—seemed laughable now.

Butch or Haley here in the Poconos? Yeah, right. An ex-con manager who was pushing drugs instead of groceries, or a possibly unstable, maybe even violent, assistant manager who'd left the store manager-free last night. Supposedly, she'd been too upset to stay at work after Luke's accident.

No, he definitely needed to sell the entire chain, find a way to make it palatable, or to somehow not give a shit, and just walk away.

"Damn," Aiden muttered.

The first rays of streaming light hit the water as he was coming into the home stretch. No peace to be found in the sunrise today. Stress had settled on his shoulders like a pile of bricks—a miracle he hadn't sunk to the bottom of the lake.

A text message awaited him. Haley—finally—in response to his repeated calls last night, letting him know that a family member was ill and so she was unexpectedly taking a few days off.

Despite the early hour, Aiden dialed her immediately. No answer. He left yet another message: "Haley, we need to talk. The sooner the better. Call me."

Aiden realized he had his cell in a death grip, and made himself loosen it.

Despite Tori's surety, Aiden needed facts before hanging Haley out to dry. Both parties told the same story. And a bit of odd behavior lately from the girl didn't automatically indicate dangerously crazy. Yet...

By the time he'd showered, the pressure cooker inside him was whistling. Frustration and tension rattled, building like they could blow him apart.

At six fifteen, he texted Eddie. *You there?*

The response: *Here waiting to kick your ass.* No surprise; the guy still kept a military schedule.

Aiden grabbed the Harley's keys from the counter, instead of the car's. Maybe the noise would drown out his brain. Errant thoughts circled around themselves again, making him feel out of control. He was damn tired of it.

Eddie was just dropping into a split by the time Aiden arrived at Sunrise Martial Arts, which meant he'd been up long before Aiden had texted, running through his own personal workout. Aiden grunted at him as he passed by the open doorway. Bastard. He'd always been more flexible than Aiden, which occasionally gave him an edge with the kicks. Luckily Aiden was taller, which evened them back out.

Since Eddie's service did his laundry—one of the perks of being part owner of the school—Aiden's locker held multiple sets of clean sparring clothes. Aiden donned the loose pants and a t-shirt sporting the school logo, before knotting his belt.

Eddie'd often kept him sane over the years. He loved his dad dearly, but Pops was inexorably linked to his mother—whom he could barely tolerate. He should probably be in counseling for the animosity he still held toward her. Except baring his soul to some stranger in an office was not his idea of soul cleansing. He preferred to work off his frustrations physically. A punishing run, kayaking as the sun came up...

Well, shit. Lately almost nothing worked.

Aiden grimaced and slammed his locker with a bang. Hopefully kicking Eddie's ass would do the trick, clear his head. Otherwise, figuring out a plan of escape from the markets would be near impossible.

He and Eddie padded up, the goal being cardio and practice, not a bare-knuckle pummeling. Once Aiden had pulled on his gloves, the two men fell into a familiar pattern. They started slow with thrusts and jabs as they circled, then ramped up the aggression when they got warm.

They almost never spoke until they were mopping their faces and chugging water. Most times, they traded insults and tidbits of information, and occasionally they'd manage to open up and really spill.

By the time Aiden's face poured sweat, he was still thinking about Luke's stitches, the worry flattening the light in Tori's eyes, the niggling suspicions concerning Haley, and, last but not least, Lundgren's for-shit assurances on taking down Butch's ring.

He took a front kick—one he absolutely should've seen coming—in the gut and grunted hard. Neither Eddie nor Aiden aimed to inflict damage, but both could take a hit, and for damn sure they both kept score—which meant the two competitive men didn't pansy-ass it either. Eddie crowed, enjoying his point. Soon enough, he'd landed another.

"Fuck," Aiden spat around his bulky plastic mouth guard. He stepped back and ripped off his gloves.

"Your focus is for shit this morning," Eddie mumbled through his own chunk of protective plastic.

Aiden grunted. "No kidding."

Eddie simply inclined his head toward the rear wall. They'd snag bottles of water from the cooler behind the counter and sprawl out on the bleachers. Not the set inside, but the ones outside, facing some cleared grass and the mountains. Sometimes they'd hold class out here. More often Eddie and Aiden used it as a hangout.

Even grown men needed to feel they were sneaking out back for a smoke or a beer, or, in their case, pure hydration. Like going to a pub, except healthier. When you watched the sun rise or set, a deer leading her fawn, or an eagle swoop, you didn't need to talk. If you did mutter something worth saying, well, somehow the words worked their way out of you easier in the open.

Aiden grabbed hand towels and tossed one to Eddie as they climbed up far enough to lean their backs against the building.

"You're lucky I didn't add to your ugly," Eddie said.

Aiden snorted. "Just wait until I've had some sleep."

Eddie shook his head. "It's not the lack of sleep, man. It's whatever's eating you."

Aiden slugged some water, scrubbed his face. Eddie's blond crew cut had darkened with perspiration, and he slid his own towel over his skull, but didn't look at Aiden.

Finally, Aiden leaned forward, elbows on knees, and admitted, "Something's wrong at the store."

Eddie raised an eyebrow, rotated his bare feet to the right, ankles popping, then circled them left.

Aiden swore. "Who am I kidding? Everything's wrong at the store."

"This one?"

"Yeah." Where should he start?

"We've got some new hires, through this woman running UpStart. Ever heard of it?"

"Nope."

Aiden grimaced. "I got sucked in on the first one. And then Butch hired two more people before I realized."

"What do you mean you got sucked in?" Eddie turned to him.

"This woman—Tori—is really something. Her company places homeless people who're trying to find steady jobs. So I interviewed this sweet woman and hired her." Aiden shrugged. There'd been no way to say no.

"Really something, huh?" Eddie's lips twitched.

Damn, Aiden thought, he'd said too little—a dead giveaway. He gave a wry smile and shook his head. "She's determined, feisty, and all Miss Do-Gooder."

Eddie squinted comically, quizzing him without words. Aiden ignored him. "She's also intelligent and incredibly hot— but in a clean, real way. Classy, without even trying, you know?"

"So? Go for it."

"Uh-uh. Trying hard to steer clear. She's got a kid and a dickhead ex—or almost-ex, it seems like."

"Everybody our age has kids and an ex," Eddie said as he

looked away. This conversation was making Aiden feel like crap. One of those things men like Eddie wished for, and other jackasses like him threw away or simply avoided.

"It's not that. I've gotten to know her son—good kid."

"Then what? You're too chickenshit to date someone you actually like?"

Aiden cringed at the look of disgust on Eddie's face. "You know my mom, man."

"This woman can't be that bad," Eddie said, and raised his drink again.

Spinning his bottle around, Aiden watched the last two inches of water climb the plastic like the start of a whirlpool before responding. "Jury's still out." Except he was beginning to realize she was the polar opposite of his mom—and that might be even more terrifying.

"She must really be great," Eddie said, "if you're this messed up."

Aiden slid his hand over his hair to rub his muscles, but was blocked by the towel he'd looped around his neck. "There's more." He told Eddie about the rat and the vandalism to Tori's car.

Eddie just stared at him. Finally he said, "Jesus, that's fucked."

"Exactly," Aiden said.

"So who is it?"

Aiden poured some water down his throat, let the rest douse his overheated face. He looked out at the trees, then directly at Eddie.

"Tori thinks it's Haley."

His friend's mouth dropped open. "That girl that's worked in your stores forever? In Philly, and then out here? That Haley?"

Aiden tightened his mouth, gave a curt nod.

Eddie was already shaking his head, processing. "She's a little stiff, but...whoa." He pinned Aiden with a look. "You're discounting it, I'm guessing."

"I have been." Aiden slid off the towel to grip his neck. "But I'm starting to wonder. I just don't know."

"That reminds me," Eddie said. "You ever call your PI about the Smelty woman?"

"Just heard from Nick yesterday. She's been dead over five years."

"No shit? But she stopped bothering you long before that," Eddie said.

"Apparently she'd been on disability for a few years and was pretty much housebound. Hit by a car." Aiden grimaced. He didn't wish something like that on anyone, and yet he was grateful the stalking had stopped.

"What about that woman with the camera outside The Granary?" Eddie asked.

Aiden shook his head. "Figment of your imagination. I haven't seen her or anyone lurking around."

All this talk about stalkers lately had made him sympathize with Tori. Even as a young male, strong and skilled in karate, it'd been unsettling. He remembered that awful, uneasy feeling—that someone was always lurking, always watching. The need to be constantly on guard, the sense that any minute something fucked up was gonna happen.

And Tori had a kid to worry about.

Aiden dipped his neck in a stretch, then realized he'd skipped something big. "One more kicker."

"Don't even tell me you saved the best for last."

Aiden nodded and debated how much to share. Fuck the detectives. He'd trust Eddie with his life. "Some detectives came to see me about Butch. He's running drugs—prescription—out of the store."

"That fucker! After all you've done for him." Disgust was evident in Eddie's voice.

Aiden shared a few more key details.

"No wonder you can't sleep, man."

"The worst part is having my hands tied."

Eddie gave a low whistle. "I bet."

"Word gets out about this drug ring, and this store's toast," Aiden said. "That's eating me too."

"Because of all the employees who'd lose jobs?"

Aiden nodded. "Especially the newest ones."

"The ones who need a steady paycheck the most," Eddie said.

"Yeah, and the hell of it is, somehow I feel like I'm letting Tori down."

Eddie just smiled—a knowing grin that spoke of things Aiden would rather not hear.

"I shouldn't care. I've done what I could for her." And why not? He had the resources and had enjoyed helping Tori. More and more, he was realizing it was the people he cared about. The people that had kept him at at the helm. Not the success, not the money. Aiden leaned forward, elbows on knees, but turned his face toward his friend. "I've made a decision to get out."

"Of Miller's? Entirely?" At Aiden's nod, Eddie said. "About time."

"Christ, Eddie, you couldn't have said that to me a few years ago?"

"Like you woulda listened."

Aiden rolled his eyes, then looked out at the forest. "Fresh-Rite made an offer years back to buy the chain. I'm gonna see if I can resurrect it." He shrugged. "If not Barry King, then someone else. Either way, I'm setting the wheels in motion."

"Good for you, man."

Aiden snapped Eddie's pant leg with his towel. "Don't say anything to Pops. I gotta figure out how to break it to him."

"Hey, whaddya take me for, anyway?"

But they both chuckled. They'd been snapping towels at each other for...man, like twenty-five years. Aiden hopped off the bleachers.

"Hey," Eddie said, "don't forget about the self-defense series. We start tonight."

Shit. He *had* forgotten. "What time?"

"Seven."

Aiden narrowed his eyes as an idea started to brew. "We got room for a couple more?"

Eddie nodded, knowing right where he was heading. "Always."

Suddenly Aiden felt lighter. Slim chance they'd be free on such short notice. But it'd be great to get Tori and Luke in here.

He headed for the showers, gait feeling far looser than when he'd arrived. Unbidden, he pictured toppling Tori to the mats, the look of surprise and then sexual awareness she'd wear. He wouldn't—not in a class, at least—but the idea sure was tempting.

Haley peered in the mirror, foggy after only a couple of hours of restless sleep, her new black eye makeup streaked from angry tears. Then she poked halfheartedly around the chaotic mess that was her lame one-bedroom apartment. Slashed pillows and cushions, her good-girl clothes strewn everywhere—that'd been fun. A broken lamp, leftover Chinese food smeared on the wall, the plate smashed below it. No wonder she was so hungry.

Yep, it had taken her all night to calm down after the fuck-up, and her apartment had definitely borne the brunt of her little...tantrum.

Haley shrugged. Childlike behavior, but whatever. She'd needed the release. And she hadn't smashed anything important. Her beautiful monitors were untouched. The tracers and alerts were functioning. She'd work around the mess until she felt like dealing. At present, her temper had cooled, but she still felt justified in wallowing.

Such total shit luck. That turd Luke had turned around at the last second, spotting her. As if he'd had a sixth sense. It was creepy. Haley had faltered, lost some momentum. Otherwise, Lukey boy would have gone down, ended up concussed or worse. There would have been a pallet's worth of family-sized

canned goods everywhere. Crushed boxes, splintered wood...
poor kid, wrong place, wrong time.

Instead, she'd been forced to go with the lame stuck mop
story.

Nothing had happened—yet. Repeated phone calls from
Miller, but he didn't sound suspicious or angry. As far as she
could tell, stupid Luke hadn't quit. Unreal. So apparently, the
kid was just smart enough to keep his trap shut. Her threats
earlier in the week must be to thank for that.

Haley wasn't so sure about Clarice. No way had she seen
anything, and yet she'd acted weird—well, weirder than usual.
Suspicious. Probably too chickenshit to say anything.

Still, Haley had a zero tolerance rule for prying eyes. Something had to be done. The question was, what? Another accident
so soon would draw too much attention.

She clicked a few times with the mouse and checked placement. Good. Miller and Radnor were both were they were
expected to be. Bonus: they weren't together.

Really, she only needed to get rid of the UpStart people—
including Radnor. Just needed them to turn in their time cards
and walk away. Haley gnawed on her fingernails. She *had* to
reinstate the status quo. With this melee going on, she couldn't
confess to Miller and expect a warm reception. She needed him
open to her...not all wrapped up in Radnor and her motley crew.

It would be ideal if the cops would hurry up and haul
Butch's loser ass off to jail. Even if she couldn't be manager, they
wouldn't be able to hire someone immediately. Besides allowing
her additional freedom and access at Miller's, it'd mean more
contact with Miller, more hours of his undivided attention,
more chances to bond.

So tired of waiting now, she'd have happily forced Butch's
exit—no one would think twice about some ex-con offing him in
the parking lot for past sins—but she couldn't take the chance.
She had to stay squeaky clean. It was why she'd gone the surreptitious route in the first place—setting Butch up with some

cohorts of an old friend—okay, fine, more like an old acquaintance, given that Haley didn't have—or need—any friends. That and there'd been plenty of time back when she'd first planned that scenario.

Not so much now.

Haley had seen the questions marks in Miller's eyes after the Luke screw-up. She hadn't lost his trust yet—she didn't think. But any more suspicion cast in her direction would be bad.

God, she could just kick herself. Why hadn't she come clean when things were calm? What had she been waiting for? Why hadn't she recognized good when she had it? Jesus, she'd only been waiting her whole life.

It'd take so much time to reestablish solid ground. She wasn't sure she could bear it. These last few weeks were just fucking everything up. So messy. Too many eyes, too many players, situations overlapping, problems creeping up faster than Haley could address them.

For instance, Aiden's other calls—the ones to Barry King over at FreshRite. Brief in length, it seemed he'd only left messages. Probably trying to get in Radnor's good graces—or at least in her pants—by putting in a word for UpStart with King. Still, it was odd. The two men weren't exactly buddies.

That wouldn't do. Miller working against her, helping Radnor, ensuring she'd stick by his side. Not when Haley had been working to kick her to the curb. Total bonus if she got run over.

Maybe that was it: Radnor's company. If Haley could deliver a solid blow toward putting Radnor's precarious little charity project out of business? She'd hit the hills, wouldn't she?

It could backfire, though. Radnor could grasp Miller and his job opportunities like a lifeline…

Haley's eyes widened as the perfect twist came to her. Hell yes—why hadn't she thought of it earlier?

She'd force Miller to cut them loose. If public sentiment—even public safety—was at risk, against Miller's, he'd fall in,

UNHINGED 189

wouldn't he? He might not pick Haley over Tori and Luke, but surely he'd pick his own company over them.

And if Miller's Markets was the demise of Radnor's brainchild—there'd be one dead relationship, too. The bitch would hate Aiden then. No matter how much she wanted his moneybags, Haley didn't think Radnor could forgive him that.

A ruined business, betrayed by her lover.

Perfect.

But how, exactly?

She cocked her head, listening...

Hmm. Mom was awful quiet on this one.

Haley tapped her pen against her thigh as she considered the possibilities. Usually you could control a situation without violence. A shame, really, when the alternative was so tempting. Getting physical with Radnor? That'd be an absolute pleasure, for she was the bitch that had changed everything. Logically, Haley knew it was best to avoid heightened suspicion, police, etc....and yet she almost hoped things would go that far, nearly craved that release—because, man, it'd been so friggin' satisfying belting Luke.

Well, a girl could dream while she laid out safer, more practical plans.

Haley righted her desk chair and settled in. Okay, yeah, things were complicated. But interesting. For once, she wasn't bored. She slid her hand up into her hair to think, twirling a big chunk around a finger.

Something would come to her. It always did.

CHAPTER 21

TORI SET THE PHONE down with a thud and blew out her breath. She crossed the last name off the list in her notebook, then pushed back the chair and started pacing.

This wide-open room at UpStart was good for that, as she could do mini laps around the perimeter. A few file cabinets and shelving units lined the walls, but all the workstations sat toward the center of the room. A combination of fun blue and funky green walls were meant to seem modern, motivating, and bright with promise. Today, Tori felt as if those same walls were closing in. She had some successful placements, nearly had FreshRite's commitment, but she needed an influx of cash, and soon.

And then there was Luke. Stitches above his eye, ibuprofen with his breakfast, and a grim set to his mouth, he'd chosen to go to school. Apparently Monday morning physics was preferable to another round of her badgering.

She'd forbidden him to return to Miller's, and he wasn't happy about it. She didn't care. She only wished she had as much control over Clarice and Alan.

A knock sounded on the door and in strode Stefan, always a balm to her spirits. His black hair was gelled and spiked, his clothes modern and slim-fitting—metrosexual, they called that look. Meaning this young single guy spent more time in front of the mirror than she did. Not that he needed to. With deep dimples and liquid brown eyes, a heart of gold, a solid work ethic, and a fun nature, he had it going on.

"Finally!" She'd begged him to intercept Luke at the bus stop this morning, and she'd been waiting anxiously for word.

"Sorry, *mi hermana.*" *My sister,* he often called her. "Crazy day." He shoved the remains of a bagel in his mouth. Lunch, apparently, and it was nearly two o'clock.

"I didn't mean to bug you, I'm just—"

"Shhh, I know," he said.

"So?"

He grimaced. "Nada."

Tori collapsed into her desk chair. "Damn."

"You just swore," Stefan chided, since Tori had admitted that she was trying to curb the habit.

"Shoot. Sugar. Crap. Dang." Tori complained, "It's hopeless—clean curses don't remotely satisfy."

Stefan slid into the kitchen and soon emerged with two mugs. Hers held tea, the string dangling from the side; his soda, but he used a mug, claiming solidarity.

"So what did Luke say, exactly?"

"It was early. He's a teenager. He was barely speaking at all. But he couldn't look at me. Definitely hiding something." Stefan shook his head, his funky hairstyle sticking out in all directions.

"Urggh," Tori grumbled—her attempt not to swear. "I'm convinced if Aiden Miller would just fire Haley, the problem would disappear like a puff of smoke."

Tori yanked out the tea bag and tossed it in her lined trash can.

"He still doesn't believe?" Stefan asked. He sat on the corner of the desk nearest to Tori's and crossed his legs at the ankles.

"I think he's coming around." Tori felt herself flush just from thinking about him—ridiculous, really, considering there wasn't actually anything between them. "But he's acting like his hands are tied. And I get that—to a certain degree." She sighed. "These days you can't just terminate without cause. You have to go through certain procedures, document absolutely everything, set up a plan for improvement, and on and on. Unless, of course, an employee has done something so grievous—"

"Slugging somebody doesn't count at Miller's? That's insane," Stefan said.

"Oh, it qualifies," she said, "but apparently no one saw it, and without proof..." Tori shook her head. "Aiden needs to confront her. Then maybe it would all stop."

Stefan winced. "Or backfire on Clarice and Alan, since Luke won't be there to pick on."

Tori dropped her head into her hands. "I'm rewriting my next placement contract for sure. I need veto power or something. It's torturing me that those two insist on staying."

"Unusual, extreme circumstances. It'll never be an issue twice."

She could only hope. "If I just had a solid yes from Fresh-Rite..."

"Nothing more you can do? Want me to go in there, slay him with my charm, and sing your praises?"

"Tempting, but no." She laughed. "I've pressed as much as I can, I think, without turning them off." She sighed and then blew on her tea.

Stefan said, "Let's hope something gives soon. If Haley did purposely hit Luke, who knows what she might do next." He gave Tori a pointed look, and she inclined her head. Yeah, she got it. She needed to be on guard herself.

"So, what's this Aiden guy like?"

"He's..." Tori peered down into her tea, looking for an answer to that question.

"Come on," Stefan said, eyes twinkling, "spill."

Tori laughed. "I'm that obvious, huh?"

"Clear as glass, *hermana*."

"Great," she mumbled, then leaned back and looked away to gather her thoughts. If there was anybody she could talk to, it was Stefan. Truth be told, he was a better friend to her than anybody ever had been. "Aiden's good-looking. Classy, dresses well—you'd approve—eyes that miss nothing. Like a businessman brokering high-powered deals. He moves like an athlete, though, with energy to spare, and he's got this crooked nose, like he's seen his share of brawls." She pushed at her own nose to illustrate.

"What?" she asked, when she realized Stefan was out and out grinning.

"Those are all *physical* pluses."

Tori rolled her eyes. "Can't help it. Seriously, he's hot."

"You movin' on that or what?"

"No way," Tori answered before Stefan had even finished the question.

"Why not?"

She frowned, thinking of the almost-kiss, the magnetic pull of him, the mixed signals he sometimes gave, her own messy feelings. She settled on the one thing she knew for sure: "He'd steamroll over me in no time."

"Then maybe *he'll* be moving in on *you*."

"If he were interested, he would have already." She waved, dismissing the idea, along with the unreasonable disappointment that edged under her breastbone every time she'd thought of it. He'd had his chance. More than one, actually. And she didn't want him, right? "He's a man of action, a risk taker. Just look at what he's done with Miller's Markets."

Tori threw up her hands in exasperation. "Which is why I can't figure out why he's not all over this Haley thing. He claims she's got years of perfect records—but come on. Really ticks me off." She crossed her arms. "But it's hard to stay angry, because he goes and does this really nice stuff, like fixing my car and loaning me his with no interest and no strings—to confuse me further. The fact that I'm wildly attracted to him—okay, yes, I admit it"—she made a face at her smirking friend—"makes me doubly mad."

Tori dropped her hands to the desk. "Listen, none of it matters. The minute I've got placements for my clients, I'm out of there. Done with Aiden Miller for good. I can't afford another man in my life."

"You say that, but—"

"No. I've got to make things work on my own before I even come close to considering another relationship. Besides, technically, I'm still married." She screwed up her face.

He snapped his fingers. "*Dios*, I forgot. What happened at the courthouse?"

"Holden responded to the notice I posted. Right at the last goddamned hour." Tori rolled her eyes. "He didn't contest, but he did request a hearing for the divorce."

"Why? To bargain?" Stefan asked.

"No idea. I hope he does his research, because it's a waste of time. He doesn't have a leg to stand on after what he's put us through." More worried than she cared to admit, Tori grasped her toasty mug between her cold hands and just held tight.

"Can you find him, see what he's up to, so you can prepare?"

Tori sighed as she looked at Stefan. "I imagine all I have to do is trail Luke. Holden's still following him."

———

Luckily Aiden had swapped the Harley for the sedan before he'd set out for UpStart. However, the Mercedes wasn't exactly an inconspicuous choice either. The industrial area had definitely seen better days. No wonder he hadn't recognized the address; he would have had no reason to come to this area before. As he scanned building numbers, he noted a man leaning against a doorway enjoying a smoke and a few other people sitting idly in rickety-looking folding chairs. Here and there a few businesses appeared open, but quiet. One man sat cross-legged on the sidewalk eating lunch. All of them followed his car like they were tracking prey. Eyeing up his hubcaps? Or simply curious about an unknown visitor in such a ghost town of a neighborhood?

No wonder Tori drove that dinged-up little Toyota, he thought, as he pulled in beside his own SUV in UpStart's rear lot. Why the hell hadn't she found a more desirable area for her business? Dammit, he thought, unclenching his jaw—his protective instincts were rearing up again.

The back door read "UpStart" and opened to a narrow staircase. Upstairs, in addition to the company name, the bright blue door boasted a slogan—*STAND UP. START FRESH*—and a small plastic sign that hung from a suction hook: *Come in, we're here.*

He cursed himself for an idiot. Why hadn't he just called?

Because he'd figured it'd be easier to convince her about the self-defense series in person. Plus, he'd wanted to see what kind of operation Tori ran. He'd known it was small, although his interest had been piqued all the same.

Aiden rolled his eyes. All true, and yet he was still a big, fat liar. He wanted to see Tori. Unreasonable. Ridiculous. Crazy. Stupid. Yet true.

He squeezed his shoulder muscles with his hands and rolled his head from side to side to ease the tightness. Chances were good she was out, anyway. He'd talk to a secretary or underling. Aiden reached for the metal knob, twisted, and entered—

And found himself in the middle of UpStart central, Tori seated only twenty feet away in the center of the room. She stared at him wide-eyed and open-mouthed. His own expression surely mirrored hers. A coworker had also turned at his entry.

"Aiden!" Tori said, popping up out of her chair. Her face was flushed, and she seemed nervous.

"Hi. Sorry to just show up."

"Is everything all right?"

"Everything's fine." Crap, he hadn't considered that showing up might suggest something was wrong—something other than his brain being scrambled.

She breathed a sigh of relief. "Well then, welcome to UpStart. This is my friend Stefan. He runs the shelter down the street."

Aiden strode forward and shook Stefan's hand. "Nice to meet you," he said.

Stefan wore a bemused expression. "You too." Then the younger man gave him a once-over. Aiden had the urge to stick his finger in his shirt collar and loosen his tie. Except he wore a modern-style golf shirt—as comfortable and as non-restrictive as business casual got.

"Did you talk to Haley?" Tori asked. "Have you found out something?"

Aiden grimaced. He explained that he'd found no witnesses, and that he'd been trying to speak with Haley but she'd only returned one text claiming a family emergency that would take a few days.

The little frown between her eyebrows deepened as he spoke. Her mouth pressed tight before she pasted on an upbeat expression and asked, "Well then, what can we do for you?"

"Uh, actually, there's no *we*," Stefan interrupted, grabbing mugs from both desks into one fist, and hugging Tori with one arm. "I have to run."

"Tomorrow?"

"Definitely," Stefan said, and widened his eyes at her. Then he darted into the kitchenette and back out again. Waved and left in under a minute.

Aiden said, "Nice place."

"Thanks. I'd show you around, except"—Tori waved an arm—"this is pretty much it."

"You must have done a lot of work." The inside was a serious improvement over the outside. Freshly painted with coordinated but simple office furniture, the place looked clean and smart.

"Yes, but it was worth it." Tori beamed, obviously proud.

"It's safe?" Aiden asked. "The area, I mean."

She bristled, pursing her lips and tightening her shoulders, causing her blue button-down blouse to shift. "Far safer than it looks. And we're near many of my clients."

He nodded.

Still, Tori narrowed her eyes. "Is this part of your background check on me and UpStart?"

Aiden held up his hands. "Easy. I had an idea. My friend runs Sunrise Martial Arts up on the mountain, and I thought Luke—"

She cut him off, big silver earrings glinting as she shook her head. "I can't afford something like that."

"Not lessons, just some self-defense clinics. They're free." They weren't, but he'd cover the registration cost himself. "There's one that starts tonight. Four weeks in all."

"That's… Thank you for thinking of him."

"I'm thinking of you, too," Aiden said.

———

Tori read the concern in his eyes. She frowned, not sure what to make of that comment or the traitorous thump of her heart.

"Last week, in the parking lot," he continued, "if you had been more prepared—"

"Holden wouldn't have hurt me," Tori said.

"That's not the point." Aiden sounded frustrated.

"I'm perfectly safe from him." Physically, of course. He'd caused her no small amount of emotional trauma, however. "I don't want to talk about Holden."

Aiden's eyebrows slanted down. "Then let's talk about this neighborhood."

"What about it?"

"It's seedy. You could be accosted coming to or from work."

She laughed. "That's ridiculous." She and Luke were familiar faces, neighbors who had proven themselves at the shelter. They weren't targets—if anything, they'd be protected.

"Assault is nothing to be laughed at."

"Everybody in this neighborhood knows us."

His face was set in a full-on scowl now.

"Listen," she said, "I'm far more worried about assault at your workplace. If Haley's dead set on trouble, she'll find a way."

Aiden held up a hand. "I'm not planning on Haley—or *whoever*—having the opportunity to pull any stunts."

So, he was considering Haley's involvement but leaving himself an out. Tori narrowed her eyes.

"However," Aiden continued, "self-defense is a good idea regardless. For you and Luke. Invite Clarice and Alan, too. There's room."

Tori sighed. Aiden was not going to be easily dissuaded—that she knew from experience.

"Come on, Tori," Aiden said, his voice turning smooth as he took a step toward her. "What could it hurt?"

Good question, she thought. Nothing—other than spending more time in close proximity to Aiden Miller. A bad, bad idea, if the tightness in her belly was any indication.

She watched his eyes. They held hers, steady and too warm for such a cool blue color. Were they talking about the same thing? Tori cleared her throat. "Is four sessions even enough time to get something out of the class?"

"Absolutely." Aiden crossed his arms over his chest. "Even one session can make a difference. We're not teaching martial arts, we're plugging personal safety, risk reduction, and free and flee tactics."

A sales pitch, except the least important word really caught her ear. "What do you mean, we?"

"I help out with some of the teaching sometimes. I'm part owner."

Another example of his wealth. The disparity between them. She laughed. Once upon a time, he would have been right up her alley—or her parents' alley, at least.

Tori moved away from him toward the kitchenette and mumbled, "Why am I not surprised?"

He followed. "I didn't catch that."

"You weren't meant to." She stopped and turned just inside the entry of the kitchenette, planting her hands on her hips.

Aiden braced his forearms high on the wall on either side of the opening, hands loose above, making him appear even broader and taller than he was. There was no door, and this space was tiny. He was too close for comfort, she thought, suddenly feeling overly warm.

"My involvement with the studio has nothing to do with this," Aiden said quietly, hard steel threading the quiet tone. "The classes are available. You should attend."

Tori shook her head, lips pursed.

"You're not acting smart, Tori," Aiden taunted. "Seems to me if you won't make reasonable decisions then you need someone to take care of you."

"That's the last thing I need!" Tori said. "And you—of all people—have no right to tell me what to do or where to be!" The gall of the man! She drew breath, then fought to speak with less volume. "Not me, not my son, not my clients."

His hands curled into fists above them as he leaned in, straining past the doorframe, his powerful chest crowding her space. His features set in hard lines, and his eyes blazed with intensity.

Tori's heart beat faster. Anger made him look predatory, but it was the heat in his look that terrified her. Like that day in the parking lot, he was a split-second decision away from taking what he wanted.

But she couldn't afford to give up an ounce of her hard-won independence for a man. No matter how sexy, no matter how misguided but well-intentioned, no matter his tendency to push like a bulldozer with the need to provide and protect. She *alone* would take care of herself and Luke.

Two steps, and he'd be backing her against the counter. She could see him, debating, weighing.

Her only fear, if Aiden decided to go for it? She was far too tempted to let him.

CHAPTER 22

AIDEN DIDN'T BOTHER to analyze the why. Fact was, the more she fought him on the idea of learning to protect herself, the more he wanted to kiss some sense into her. Screw the complications.

He unclenched his fists, dropped his forearms from the framed opening of the little kitchenette, and straightened. As he advanced, Tori shot out a hand.

Her words tumbled out in a rush. "How many stores do you own?"

Impatience reared up—he'd made up his mind, dammit—now what?

"Why?" he managed to ask without growling.

"Just answer me," she demanded.

"Close to twenty."

"How would you describe your house?"

"What do you mean?" He scowled. A second ago, he'd been so close to tasting her. What was with the interrogation?

"You know," she said, looking up as if she were thinking over options. "A double-wide in a trailer park? A three-room bungalow that hasn't been touched in fifty years? A cookie-cutter four-bedroom colonial in a housing development? A mansion with no neighbors?"

"You've seen my house."

She gave a tight nod. "I want to know how you think of it."

"Why do I feel I'm better off if I don't answer this?"

"Humor me."

"It's a cabin. A very big cabin."

She scoffed. "I'd call it a magazine-worthy Adirondack-style lodge."

He didn't want her to dissect his house. He wanted her

to think about him. Feel him. Feel his lips slanting over hers.

"Tori—"

"How much property do you own? An acre? Five? The whole lake?"

Aiden narrowed his eyes. "I have neighbors."

"Oh my God." She shut her eyes. "Renters. You own the whole lake."

"So what?"

She was shaking her head. "Move back."

She put a hand against his chest and shoved. She felt like a gnat, but he let her force him backward a few steps. That same hand, her left, stayed put, quite literally, he was sure, to keep him at arm's length, while her right shot out to point at two doorways.

He covered her hand with his own, pressing her palm to his sternum. His eyes followed her direction. Tiny rooms both of them, with dressers and beds. Bedrooms? His hand squeezed hers.

"This is where I live. Stop pursuing me. We have nothing in common."

Suddenly, he felt angry. Friggin' ticked. Scared, too. She lived here, at her place of business? In this crummy neighborhood, with her son? He already felt protective of her. He wanted to ring her not-soon-enough-ex's neck. He wanted to sleep over—in that goddamn single bed—and shield her from intruders with his own body.

He had been fighting this attraction to her since the moment he saw her steaming with frustration, cheeks flushed, in the checkout line of his store. Finally, he'd decided to ignore the warning bells and just...see.

And here she was saying no.

Didn't she know what a challenge did to him?

Aiden shrugged. "Homes. Cars."

He tucked a piece of hair that had escaped back behind her ear, then slid his hand to her nape and tugged her closer, forcing her outstretched arm to bend at the elbow. Tenderly, except now he held her fast.

"They're just trappings, Tori." He didn't give a shit about the financial disparity between them.

She might need him. But she didn't want him. Or, at least, she didn't want his help. He slid his thumb back and forth behind her ear, along her soft hair, tracing its way up into that clip.

Aiden felt a shiver under her skin, right through his palm to zing him in the region of his heart. Her expression was confused—probably because he wasn't reacting the way she expected. Yet her lips parted, her breathing came fast. His resolve centered and steadied.

She did want him. Deep inside, where they connected on some unexplored level, she did.

He definitely, positively wanted her, more than he'd wanted anything in a long time. He was hard at the mere thought of having her—like a schoolboy working himself into a frenzy, long before he'd sealed the deal.

Aiden placed his other hand on Tori's hip, squeezing hard over the crisp cotton of her white capris. She was perfect, all woman. Curvy and lush. Not too thin, just right. He wasn't letting her out of this. Not now that he was touching her, and she was allowing it. He stepped in, pressed his erection against the soft curve of her tummy, his chest flattening her perfect breasts.

See what you do to me? he thought. Feel me against you. Look into my eyes, he urged, and see how deep my desire runs.

Except she didn't raise her eyes to his. Under heavy lids, her gaze had fastened on his mouth. Her tongue slipped out, moistening her own lips. That was it—the green light he needed.

Aiden bent his head and claimed her, pulling her even tighter against him. He devoured her, sucking and licking at her mouth, lips, and tongue, dancing with her as if this wasn't the first time. He shucked that clip, loosening those straight strands of honey. Then he slid one hand well into her hair, to cup her head. The other squeezed her sweet ass.

When he bent his knees to align their groins, she mewled with yearning. Desire exploded.

He backed her up, through the doorway, to press her against the refrigerator, dislodging a flurry of magnets and papers to pin her with his hips. She gave back, grinding, her hands reaching up to into his hair, grabbing him tight.

Aiden touched her everywhere, sliding up under her blouse, cupping her breasts, thumbing her nipples. He trailed kisses down her neck. God, she smelled friggin' amazing. It wasn't enough.

"Wow, Tori." He caught her eye. An answering awareness flared in her own.

He dipped again to her mouth, freeing both hands to work the top buttons on her blouse, then spread the soft blue material to reveal creamy skin. A light tan faded to pale swells of breast cupped above her black lace bra. He traced the fabric curving over her, watching goose bumps erupt in his wake. He pressed with his hips, and she grasped his shoulders hard. He ground once, twice, three times, as he pushed her breasts up and out of their delicate cups.

He aimed to make a point.

Tori's unfocused eyes drifted shut just as Aiden bent, his mouth diving between the swells to nuzzle her gently, then, without warning, sucking hard on an already erect nipple.

She gasped, and her lids flew open. He released her breast, but held tight to her hips. He allowed a wicked glint to show in his eyes.

"Tori," he said. "We have plenty in common."

Tori registered his words, a frisson of fear cinching her lungs, even as she panted with desire. Because Aiden Miller, she suspected, could be focused to a fault—single-minded, deter-mined, and dead set on the end goal. Right now, however, she was flushed and fevered, every cell in her body straining for more, and she didn't care.

"Don't talk," she ordered, rocking her hips against his.

A flash of surprise widened his eyes, before he growled low in his throat and tucked his head to devour her mouth once more.

She grabbed fistfuls of his shirt and tugged it from his waist-band, the soft material slipping free easily. She ran her hands from his back to his front, ribs to belly button, and felt the hard muscles of his abdomen contract. The concave tensing created space behind his belt, so she slipped the backs of her fingers lower. Aiden sucked in a shaky breath and pressed his head alongside hers with a hand cupping her head on the other side. "Your touch is like fire."

Tori moved that hand in a slow caress, even as her other slid down his back to his tight ass. He sucked air in a hiss. God, but every muscle he had was as hard as steel. She was dying to see him naked. "Didn't I say no talking?" she murmured.

"Not even compliments?" He nipped at her ear, hit that sen-sitive spot on her neck. "Cinnamon, that's what I smell. Cinna-mon, vanilla, pine nuts. Delicious."

"We're in the kitchen."

She felt him shake his head, even as he tasted her collarbone, causing shivers to run straight to her nipples.

"Uh-uh," he said. "It's you. Although maybe we should find a more comfortable spot."

She froze—the idea both exciting and insane.

Aiden drew back at the change in her body. He held her eyes, looking very, very serious. "I won't push. You're ready here." He tweaked a nipple and elicited a gasp from her. "However, maybe not here," he murmured, and pressed a kiss to her forehead. His expression was tender, yet his blue eyes were intense when he sought her gaze again. "But just so you know. I want you, all of you."

"Aiden, I—"

"Your turn to shut it, Tori," Aiden said, that half-smile pulling up the left corner of his mouth. He didn't wait for her to respond, grasping her under the arms and hoisting her up. Her legs latched automatically around his waist despite her surprise, her arms around his neck. She started to protest; however, he didn't back up and head for the bed, only shifted to set her fanny on the counter.

Tori met his teasing eyes. She tugged at his neck, puckered her lips.

He complied, the kiss igniting heady desire all over again. His palms came around her ribs to cup her still-exposed breasts, and as his thumbs flicked her nipples, she groaned. Had her body ever responded this swiftly to the merest touch? Tori held tight to Aiden's head, hands luxuriating in the feel of his thick, soft hair, keeping his mouth focused on hers, giving as much as she took. Barely thinking, she yanked his shirt over his head to feel his hot skin against hers.

Their hips rocked together, the thin material of his dress slacks allowing her to feel how hard he was there, too. His hands lifted her and she pushed hard against him, craving and yearning deep inside, as she, too, swelled. Tori heard his fast breathing, basked in the heat radiating off him. She was this close herself, the rhythm and friction perfect—

Knock, knock, knock.

They both jumped, hips still connected, while their heads yanked apart and their eyes startled wide.

"Oh my God," Tori said, feeling her face turn bright red. Caught like a couple of naughty teenagers. In the middle of the workday.

"Ignore it," Aiden said, his voice low.

"I can't," she said, pushing at his shoulders. "The door isn't locked. Most people just walk right in."

Aiden frowned. "Your sign does say you're here." He stepped back and let her slide down him until her feet hit the floor.

Tori tucked herself back into her bra. Started buttoning furiously. She prayed she wasn't too rumpled.

"Coming," she yelled toward the front door, as she eyeballed Aiden. Drool-worthy. Absolutely. Defined pecs, taut skin, a dusting of dark hair that vee'd to draw the eye to a—yep—bona fide six-pack. Whoa.

"I need a minute," he said, looking pointedly at his erection. She laughed. He took her face in his hands and pressed a quick kiss to her lips. "Nothing to be done about your lips," he murmured, running a thumb over her lower one. Tori felt her face flame anew—damn, she must look every bit as devoured as she felt.

Aiden smoothed her hair away from her face. "Go," he said.

Tori took a deep breath and slipped around him. She scrambled for composure as she crossed the big room to the door.

"Alan, Clarice, hello!" she said, perhaps a little too brightly. Then, "You know you don't have to knock."

Clarice smiled shyly, then frowned, looking puzzled as she focused on Tori.

Alan, on the other hand, said, "I think we do."

Tori flushed yet again, although surely a little more heat couldn't possibly make a visible difference in her face.

Sounds came from the kitchen, paper rustling and snapping noises. Aiden must be putting her fridge back in order. Clarice's gaze shifted in that direction as her mouth made a little O.

"How are you both?" Tori asked, as she heard cupboards closing and the tap turn on.

"Fine, ma'am, and you?" Alan responded.

"Just fine, thanks." Tori cleared her throat. "Mr. Miller is here," she said, even as he rounded the corner with two glasses of water in hand.

Clarice actually took a step backward, before Alan placed a hand at her back, seemingly holding her in place.

"Hi, Clarice. Alan," Aiden said. "Care for water?"

"No thank you, sir," Alan said, though Clarice only shook her head like a terrified mouse.

"I'll just come back another time," Clarice stammered, wringing her hands and attempting to retreat.

"Now, now," Alan said quietly to her. "This is even better."

Tori frowned and exchanged a glance with Aiden. He looked as concerned as she felt. He turned to set the waters behind him on a desk, then remained a pace behind Tori.

"Clarice, what is it?" she asked, and stepped forward to rub the woman's upper arm.

Clarice turned her face to Alan, who nodded. She closed her eyes for a full moment and tucked her lips inward. Then she breathed deeply, obviously gathering herself.

Looking squarely at Tori, she said, "It's about last night. About…Luke's accident."

Tori nodded encouragingly.

"I'm sure there was no water on that floor. In fact"—her words gained steam and her twisting fingers stilled—"I'd already poured out the dirty water and wrung out the mop because my shift was almost over."

She glanced at Aiden, and Tori followed suit to find him frowning.

"I always do that," Clarice insisted, glancing away. Tori could see she felt the need to defend herself, and gave the woman's arm a little squeeze of support. Clarice explained, "I don't like to leave dirty water for the next person. And when I do fill a bucket, I use soap, like we're supposed to. That bucket of water was clear."

Clarice checked Aiden's expression, gauging. He nodded, and she continued. "I don't leave it by the doors, neither. Not ever—because someone could trip." Clarice looked down at her hands. The pause lasted long enough that Aiden and Tori both spoke at the same time. She'd been about to say thank you, but Alan broke in. "Tell them the last part."

Clarice nodded, though she avoided eye contact.

Tori dropped her hand, found herself holding her breath until Clarice spoke.

"I took a good look around after, at where the water was. There was no puddle, except right where the mop lay later." Clarice's arms wrapped around her chest, hugging herself. "There was water on the little windows in the swinging doors. A whole spray." Her hand demonstrated a rainbow-shaped curve.

Clarice raised her eyes, not to Tori, but to Aiden, and spoke, her voice firm and sure. "Weren't no accident. That mop was swung. Like a bat."

And they already knew, by Luke's admission and her own: Haley'd been the one wielding it.

UpStart's door flew open with a bang, and Luke stopped short, lacrosse stick in one hand, duffel in the other, his eyes widening as he took each of them in. Tori's worry meter surged. He wasn't supposed to be home.

"Hey," he said, and yanked out his earbuds and propped his stick against the wall. He set down the duffel, then slid out of the backpack, dropping it with a thud.

"No practice?" Tori asked.

The boy shrugged. "I skipped it."

"Your head?" she asked, refraining from leaping forward to take him in her arms, like she would have when he was little and hurting.

Luke nodded, but a look of relief gave him away. There'd been some other reason he'd chosen to come straight home. Enough was enough. They'd be getting to the bottom of all of this today.

"What's going on?" Luke asked.

Tori said, "Clarice believes Haley hit you on purpose."

Luke froze, then his eyes darted to Clarice. "What? No. Why?"

Clarice opened her mouth, shut it, opened it again.

Frustrated, Tori leaped in. "Why in the world won't you be honest about this?"

Luke's chin jutted out and his lips pressed together.

Aiden said, "We know it didn't happen like you said. Whatever Haley's up to, I really need to know. But no matter what, you're not in any trouble."

Alan spoke softly to Luke but inclined his head to indicate Aiden. "He's the one who can take care of things. Now's the time."

Luke huffed out a harsh laugh. "Great. A friggin' intervention."

"Luke..." Tori warned.

He pushed past her, threw himself into a chair, and spun it to give them his back. His big hands cupped the back of his head, but the posture was anything but relaxed. He bent, head and arms between his knees, then surged upward again onto his feet.

His eyes sought out Aiden's. "You have to promise that you won't let anything else happen. Especially to her."

Aiden frowned. "Haley?"

Luke shook his head, frustrated. "My mom."

Aiden said, "Of course. But—"

Her son plowed on. "Mom, promise you won't do anything stupid. That you'll stay out of it. Far away."

Tori was getting really worried now. "Okay."

"Okay. Okay then." Luke let out a breath and shoved his hands in his pockets. "Clarice is right. Haley wasn't mopping. She swung at me, hard. I saw her, but too late. Tried to duck, but she still got me." He jabbed a finger toward his forehead. "Obviously."

Tori's equilibrium shifted and she had to take a chair herself. Aiden looked like he was going to throw up. Alan squeezed Clarice's hand, and she appeared on the verge of tears.

"Jesus," Aiden said.

"Why?" Tori managed.

Luke shrugged. "Who the hell knows? She's been all over me pretty much since day one. Trying to get me to quit. Staring at me, whispering shit, leaving me messages and 'signs.' She wants us all out, but more me than them." He hooked a thumb toward Clarice and Alan. "She's, like, territorial or something. And she really hates you, Mom. She threatened—" Luke shook his head, as if he didn't even want to think about it. "She's seriously twisted."

"Why didn't you tell me?" Tori's voice rose and shook. "Why in God's name didn't you just walk out?"

"I couldn't. It would have ruined everything. You worked so hard to get UpStart into Miller's. Clarice and Alan waited so long for good jobs. And I also knew they wouldn't leave, so I had to stay to make sure they were safe."

"Oh, Luke," Clarice murmured.

"Your safety," Tori said, then pointed at her clients, "their safety, is far more important than a paycheck."

"What about your safety, Mom!" Luke burst out. "She said she'd hurt you if I told! That the damage to your face would match the scratches on your car, if I said even one word. So how was I supposed to quit without a reason? After I'd begged you to start working." He clenched his fists. "And I was going to tell, as soon as there were other jobs lined up. Then they'd be safe, we could all leave, you could stay away from there forever, and..." He broke off with a sound of frustration.

"I'm sorry. So sorry, for...all of this. I'm—" Aiden ran his hands through his hair, his expression pained. "I'll speak with the police, press charges immediately. As far as Miller's goes, Haley won't ever be allowed on the premises again. Ever. I'm sure she'll be required to see psychiatric help—I'll push for that." He shook her head. "You don't have to worry about her anymore."

"With all due respect, sir," Alan said, "I think we do."

All eyes swung to him.

Alan spoke quietly, but he didn't mince words. "We don't know why. But we know that the girl's got a vendetta and she's violent. She also knows where Mrs. Radnor lives."

CHAPTER 23

TORI AND LUKE showed up at Sunrise Martial Arts, largely because she couldn't stand being holed up and on edge, waiting for the fallout. She wasn't sure how worthwhile the class would be, but at least attending felt like taking action.

Finally convinced that Haley was both more and less than she appeared, Aiden had pressed assault charges. Officers had showed up to talk to Luke, and even Clarice. Haley would be issued a summons, but that only meant a fine and maybe probation. She'd still be roaming around, except now she'd be angry. Or angrier.

To that end, Alan had insisted on escorting them, wearing his tool belt—hammer at the ready. But he chose to remain in the car, like a guard dog, eyes on the front of the building.

Tori waved to him and sighed as she and Luke headed for the entrance. This was all so crazy.

Aiden greeted them at the door, looking sexier than ever in all black. A formfitting t-shirt showcased every hard muscle she'd run her hands over only hours ago and disappeared beneath the black belt wrapped around his waist and loose-fitting pants. His feet were bare—a fact that seemed oddly intimate, despite the fact that everyone else inside the studio had removed both shoes and socks—and heat stole over her. Thank God Luke was behind her and couldn't see the bloom on her face, nor the gleam in Aiden's eye.

"Hi." He leaned to kiss her cheek. An innocent peck to a bystander, yet to her it reinforced that they'd reached a new plane of their relationship—a physical one. A small thrill shot through Tori, as she stepped aside so that Aiden could greet her son.

More attendees entered behind them, allowing no opportunity to talk. As Aiden directed the newcomers, she and

Luke stowed their shoes in cubbies and moved onto the mat.

Tori felt silly in her old yoga pants and loose t-shirt. Once upon a time, she'd done Pilates, kickboxing, and yoga at the same gym that all the other wealthy moms in Philly frequented. These days she did nothing but work. Did it show?

She forced her eyes away from the mirror.

"Ready for this?" she asked Luke, who had lined up next to her in the front row.

Her boy nodded eagerly, ever-ready for anything new, especially anything physical.

A well-built male sporting a black belt approached and stuck out his hand. "Hi, you must be Tori."

She nodded.

"I'm Eddie."

"You're the other owner?"

"Yep. I also have the dubious honor of being Aiden's best friend."

"Dubious, huh?" She raised an eyebrow.

Eddie chuckled. "Good guy, but definitely a pain in the—" He caught himself. "Your son?"

After Eddie chatted up Luke, he turned to Tori. His smile remained, yet his eyes held a weight they hadn't a moment ago. "Aiden's told me a lot about you. I'm glad you're all here."

Tori refused to blush, choosing to assume Eddie didn't know this afternoon's development—the up close and personal one between her and Aiden. "Now I'm worried," she said, "that I'm doing all the talking, because he hasn't told me squat about you."

Eddie laughed. "Probably for the best."

He strode to the front of the room, faced the class with his legs spread and hands clasped behind him. Aiden joined him and the martial arts students, who stood out from the self-defense attendees in Sunrise uniforms and varying colors of belts, lined up along one wall. Like magic, the stragglers found spots and became quiet. The two men bowed—Aiden so tall with a full head of dark brown waves, Eddie a few inches shorter with his blond hair cropped close—both in supreme physical shape. The class returned the gesture, even the uninitiated like Tori and Luke.

After a series of warm-ups including basic stretches, jumping jacks, sit-ups, and push-ups—during which Tori discovered just how out of shape she really was—Eddie nodded at the Sunrise students. Some of them began to gear up, digging in oversized duffel bags to don padded masks, bulky vests, rectangular pads on their forearms, and booted ones on their shins.

"Welcome to Sunrise Martial Arts. Today we begin practical self-defense training. I say practical because we will be enacting real-world situations—scenario-based training—in which you will use full contact against your assailant. I see your eyes widening." Eddie said looking out over the group, and Tori realized she had definitely reacted.

"Unless you experience striking with all your might and utilizing your adrenaline, you will underestimate your power. Yes, a small female can take down a two-hundred-pound man. Yes, it's possible for a child to escape an adult assailant. It takes only strategy, knowledge that you have the ability, and a willingness to act."

He continued, "Your goal is *always* to escape as quickly and safely as possible. If that means handing over your wallet or your car, then that's what you do. Don't invite physical harm. If your attacker means to hurt you in any way, however"— Eddie nodded—"you will inflict as much damage as possible, as quickly as possible, in order to flee.

"We'll learn three techniques tonight: the palm strike, the groin strike, and the eye jab. Each week we'll review, then add, because repetition builds a comfort level, which in turn translates to instinct."

Eddie and Aiden squared off, demonstrating the palm strike in slow motion, targeting the soft tissue of the face.

"Will their nose break?" somebody asked.

"Doesn't matter," Aiden responded. "It's painful. The eyes water. The nose might bleed. Breathing could be impaired. Your goal is to gain time. Striking the nose will stun them. You only need that split second to follow up with another strike and take off."

"Okay," Eddie said, "small group time."

Aiden assigned their group a padded attacker named Cara— the only geared-up female. On purpose?

"Who's first?" Aiden asked.

"Ladies first," Luke said with a twirl of his hand.

Tori rolled her eyes and stepped forward.

"All right, first show me the move," Aiden said. Tori demonstrated, and he corrected her. "You want to swivel that hip, use the power of your whole body."

He nodded, indicating that she should try again; this time his big hands grasped her hips and twisted her as she moved.

"You've played tennis or softball? Same thing. Gotta rotate."

Earlier today when his hand had squeezed her in the same spot, they'd been lip-locked and needy. His expression was completely serious now. Tori redoubled her effort to concentrate, focusing on the proper form.

Aiden nodded, apparently satisfied. Cara stepped forward, pad held high.

"Go," Aiden said. Tori did, her palm hitting the pad with a smack and bouncing back.

Aiden said, "Follow through. Try and move her."

"Again."

"Picture the heel of your hand smashing right through that pad."

"Yes!"

"Again."

Tori was breathing hard by the time Aiden considered her successful. Luke went next, demonstrated, got the all-clear, and thrust.

"Harder," Aiden urged. Another thrust. "Harder."

"Stop," Aiden said. "Trust me when I tell you that Cara here could take you down in one second flat."

Cara, who was smaller and slighter than Tori at about five four, winked from behind the mask. She looked about sixteen, and wore a brown belt.

"Don't be afraid," Aiden said. "You won't hurt her."

At Luke's attempt, Aiden nodded, but said, "Okay, Luke. Let's pretend it's not you who's being attacked. Let's say this girl is trying to hurt your mom."

Tori sucked in a breath.

"You gonna pansy-ass it?" Aiden asked.

She couldn't see her son's face, but his next strike thrust Cara back a foot.

"Good. Again," Aiden said.

An hour and a half flew by. Surprisingly, Tori could honestly say she felt comfortable with all three of the techniques they had learned.

"Next week," Eddie said, "we'll discuss precautions to stay safe and avoid becoming a target in the first place. In the meanwhile, be well and stay safe." He bowed, and the class returned the gesture, thanking him. Then he mentioned that the Sunrise students would be sparring should the newcomers wish to watch.

"Can we, Mom, please?"

Tori pursed her lips. "Homework?"

"Most of it's done." At her look, he said, "Promise."

"All right, then."

They took off for the bleachers, Luke leading, until Tori veered off to snag her bag from the cubbyhole she'd tucked it into. Although Aiden was speaking with a male participant, he caught Tori's eye and pointed toward the back wall.

"Luke," she called, "I'm going to talk with Mr. Miller." He nodded, too excited about the sparring to care.

Two water bottles in hand, Aiden waited at the back door, holding her eyes as she neared. Sexual awareness rushed into her belly and excitement sang through her blood. Seeing him tonight—muscles not hidden by dress clothes, power and grace evident in each move, confidence of another sort lighting his blue eyes—had only made him that much more attractive.

Besides the physical prowess, however, she'd also been impressed by the way he'd worked with the attendees. There was depth and goodness to Aiden Miller. She sensed her heart slipping, and worked hard to remind herself that this afternoon's tangle had been a mistake. Getting further involved with him—sexually or emotionally—was *not* smart.

Aiden smiled as she neared, his expression mischievous, happy, and, Tori thought, hungry—for her, which was going to make keeping her good intentions intact harder.

He didn't speak, only pushed the glass door open and gestured her through. She stepped out onto stained decking in her bare feet and straight into a hidden oasis in the dusk, with wooden bleachers for viewing—

Aiden's arms came around her from behind, the two water bottles dangling from one hand, while his lips found her neck.

Tori gasped. "Aiden!"

He spun her in his arms and tucked her up against the wall of the building between the door and the risers. She was vaguely aware that he'd set the waters on the risers.

"No one can see us in this spot," he murmured.

He kissed her thoroughly, all those steely muscles pressed up against her, his hands cupping her face gently. By the time he pulled back, she'd wound her arms around his neck, her fingers into his hair, and had given herself over entirely.

So much for playing it cool and steering clear.

Aiden wore a rueful grin. "I can't leave you looking well kissed this time, but I was dying to taste you. All day, if I'm honest."

Tori's heart lurched as she looked away. A yellow wink flashed in the cleared grass, then another.

"Look, lightning bugs." She pointed. She wished he wouldn't be honest. God, the thought that he felt it too—this intense connection that hummed constantly. Only his presence was required for her to ignite all over again, glowing like a June bug herself.

"Should I go find a jar?" he asked.

"Aiden." She drew breath and found his eyes.

"Shhh," Aiden said, and pushed off the wall. "Come sit."

Just then her phone rang. Tori dug for the cell, searching awkwardly with the bag half open and hanging from her shoulder. She held it out, checking the caller ID, then let her shoulders drop as she pressed a button. It was only Stefan.

"Excuse me," she said to Aiden.

"Hiya," she answered.

"How'd self-defense go?"

"Great," she answered, "we're still here."

"Does that mean Midas is with you?" Stefan teased.

"As a matter of fact, he is," Tori said. "Want to speak with him?"

"No, ma'am." He laughed. "I only wanted to know if the FreshRite guy called."

Tori sighed. "No. Still waiting."

"Damn."

"My sentiments exactly."

They signed off, and Aiden gave her a hand to step up onto the bleachers. Settled at the top with her bag at her feet, they both cracked the tops of the water bottles and drank.

Tori scrolled through the call log on her phone. Sighed. Held on to it, just in case.

"Is the cell reception okay up here?" she asked.

"Yeah, pretty good."

"It's gorgeous." She waved a hand. "Almost as nice as the view of your lake," she teased with a wink.

Aiden chuckled. "I agree. There's something about the whole area."

She nodded. "I've always loved the Poconos, ever since I went to summer camp here as a kid."

Tori remembered that she hadn't checked voicemail, and hit a few more buttons in succession. She had the UpStart line set to forward to her cell so that she wouldn't miss the call. No texts, either. "Damn," she muttered.

"You're giving me a complex," Aiden said.

She doubted that, but she set the cell aside. "Sorry. I'm waiting on an important call."

"Hot date?" he teased. "I've got competition?"

"Actually"—Tori chuckled—"you do." Then, her tone more sober, she said, "I'm determined to find Clarice and Alan new jobs. They refuse to leave Miller's unless I have something comparable. Until we know Haley is…" She shook her head. "Well, there's nothing to be done about where I work or live, but I'll feel better if she doesn't know where my clients work."

———

Aiden grimaced. He felt the opposite—far more concerned about Tori's safety than her clients'. Still, he agreed. He could no longer argue with Tori's plan to place Clarice and Alan somewhere else. Not until they pinned down Haley's whereabouts and her intentions. Maybe not until she was behind bars or in a facility. Fuck Detective Lundgren and his rules.

Tori continued, "I'd already begun working on new jobs for them. I'm expecting a call from Barry King, the owner of Fresh-Rite. I assume you know him?"

"I'm actually expecting a call from him myself," Aiden admitted.

"Really? Why?"

How much should he tell her? Would she think less of him if he told her everything? He took a swig of water and looked into the darkening forest, past the soft blinks in the yard. "I'm hoping he'll buy out my chain." He looked at Tori and shrugged. "I want out."

Tori's mouth dropped open. Aiden reached over and touched the soft skin under her chin. "You'll let fireflies in."

"Why?" she asked.

Aiden shook his head. "It's time. The place is sucking me dry."

Tori nodded as if she understood, though he didn't know how. She seemed so passionate about her own business.

"Can FreshRite afford Miller's?"

"Don't know yet," Aiden said. "If not them, somebody else. It's not actually selling that's the trouble, it's..." He looked up at the evening sky. "Pops would take it hard."

"Your dad would understand."

"I don't know. The stores are all he's got. He's not actively working anymore—even so, it's all he thinks about." Aiden shook his head. "He practically crows when he walks around inside any of the branches. I don't want to take that away from him, disappoint him."

Tori looked at him like he was crazy. "Aiden, it's *you* your dad is proud of, not the stores."

"You met him once."

"That's all I needed. I'm telling you. *You* are his world." She shook her head. "What I wouldn't give to have parents that felt that way."

"Only Pops. My mother—" Aiden ran a hand through his hair. "She's a different story." Aiden had realized over time that Marjorie Miller was a good person. She just happened to be one of those who gave more of herself—her time, energy, and focus—to strangers than she did to her own child.

Tori tilted her head. "Still. To have that one somebody behind you, who believes in you, enjoys you, loves you unequivocally..." She looked away from him then, out at the yard.

"You didn't have anybody?" Aiden asked.

"So?" Tori dodged. "You'll retire? Spar and kayak and what? Read?"

Aiden allowed the change in subject, though this topic wasn't a comfortable one either. "That's the other problem. Figuring out what's next."

"Ah, the vast unknown." Tori nodded. "Nothing worse."

"Yeah. I'm way too driven to retire. I'd be out of my mind." Habit had him dipping his head in a stretch and reaching up to massage his muscles. In truth, though, he felt unusually calm sitting here next to Tori as night fell, with the light show in the yard drawing to a close.

"What are you considering?"

"I've got nothing."

"Come on," she said. "Money's obviously not an issue, so you can do anything that sounds interesting."

He shrugged.

She huffed. "Well, what do you like?"

"I like a challenge." Aiden leaned over and grasped her chin, kissing her pretty pink lips before she could protest. "Like you," he said, sitting back.

She grimaced. "I wouldn't occupy you for long."

"Meaning you're succumbing to my charm already?"

"Meaning," she said, swatting his arm, "that I'd bore you to tears soon enough."

Aiden erased the tease from his voice. "I don't see that happening."

Her mouth tightened, and she glanced away. "You like martial arts."

He waved a hand. "Yeah, but I see no need to take it further. The school is really Eddie's thing, anyway."

"You and your dad both love baseball, right? You could volunteer somehow. Coach little league or something?"

Aiden laughed. "You sound like my dad."

"Why is that?"

"I played ball in college. Was even recruited to the Frostburg Jacks, an Orioles Triple-A team, but by that time, we realized that Dad would need a heart transplant. He could no longer run the corner store, so I stepped out of baseball and into the store full time. I was ready and willing to make some money and see what I could do." Aiden shrugged. He knew part of that motivation was capitalistic—a desire to stick it to his charity-minded mother. It'd backfired, though. Marjorie had taken to money big time, funneling more and more into her causes and elevating her status along the way.

Aiden shook his head. "Pops still feels bad about it, so he's always after me to join a men's league. You know, the guys sponsored by the hardware store against the guys sponsored by the local pub? More about escaping the house to have a few beers than anything else."

"Torture for somebody who can really play, in other words."

Aiden nodded. "Pretty much." He lifted a palm. "I have to be moving my body. But there's no career in sports at my age."

"A line of outdoor clothing? Sporting goods stores instead of markets?"

Aiden scrunched up his face.

"Well, you're good at running stores." She bit her lip. "And making money. And you love baseball, but got rooked out of playing."

"That about sums it up, but there's no big neon arrow there, pointing out a direction."

"Ye of little faith," Tori said. "You forget, if the success of your chain is any indication, then you excel at thinking outside the box and taking chances. You'll figure something out." She smoothed her palms along her stretchy pants. "The good news is, you have time. It makes a big difference if there's no dragon breathing fire down your back."

He wondered at the shadow that passed over her face, but something else was niggling at Aiden, something she'd said.

"The lightning bugs are hitting the hay," she said. "It's getting dark."

He nodded. "The demonstration inside should be nearly over, too."

Tori reached for her purse. "Luke will be begging to join your studio after this."

Her phone rang, and she scrambled in her purse once more.

"It's him!" she exclaimed. "I thought it had gotten too late tonight."

Good for her. "Grocer's hours," he said. "Answer it."

"Tori Radnor," she said, looking up at Aiden with her face glowing. "Hello, Barry. Yes, I have a minute."

Aiden watched Tori's expression fall, before she angled away from him and walked out into the yard in her bare feet with those pretty painted toes. "Why? The news? No, I've been out this evening."

Tori curled in on herself a bit. "Just tell me, please."

She suddenly stiffened and her shoulders shot back. "What? That's not true!"

She spun and leveled a glare at Aiden, but spoke to King. "That's a complete fabrication. I can vouch—"

Tori listened, then pressed her fingertips to her forehead. "I understand. Thanks for your consideration."

Aiden strode toward her as she clicked off the phone. "What happened?"

Tori hopped back onto the deck and planted her hand on her hip, her eyes glinting. "Haley happened."

"What do you mean?" Aiden felt a twist of alarm. What now? Had Haley gone to see King to give the UpStart folks a bad report? How would she even have known Tori was talking with FreshRite?

"Apparently, it's all over the news," Tori said, "that your store is infected with both lice and TB. *Tuberculosis*, Aiden! Courtesy of a bunch of homeless workers from UpStart."

"What the—"

"And before you even ask, my clients do not have TB and they do not have lice!"

"Jesus, I know that."

"What happened after you left today? Did the cops serve her? Did you fire her? Is she lashing out?"

Aiden shook his head. "I wasn't able to reach her."

"What? How could you not—"

"I keep trying," he said, the words a frustrated growl. "She won't answer or call me back. And it's not a good idea to terminate employment via voicemail. She could say she never heard it." Aiden's neck and shoulder muscles bunched painfully. "That's one of the reasons I wanted to speak with you out here privately."

"Oh, so the kissing wasn't to distract me from asking about your out-of-control employee?"

Aiden clenched his jaw. "You and I are a separate issue entirely."

Tori scowled. "Goddammit, Aiden. Do you know what this rumor will mean for me? For my clients?" She stomped away, into the clearing, then spun back to face him. "If you'd just listened to me in the first place about Haley."

"You think I'd roll over at the merest suggestion that someone I've trusted for years is a little off?"

"Haley's more than a *little* off, Aiden. She's got serious issues."

"That's become clear." Aiden fisted his hands. "But you can't blame me for taking time to come around, for needing proof. If Luke did something wrong, or even one of your clients, you'd defend them to the ends of the earth."

Tori just glared.

He ground his teeth, deciding on the spot to share what he'd intended to keep to himself. "I've got a guy I use for employee relations in Philly. I've asked him to come up here. Look into things."

"Employee relations?" Tori narrowed her eyes.

"Nick helps with sensitive situations. Sometimes it's helpful to know what's really going on with an employee or what's behind a lawsuit or somebody's past history." Aiden shrugged.

Tori pinched the bridge of her nose. She didn't look up when she asked, "For what purpose with Haley?"

Good question. "I'm not sure." Aiden shook his head. "I'd like to have a better idea what we are dealing with. Just in case."

"She'll continue this crazy vendetta, no matter what."

"It's possible." Aiden thought of his experience with Audra Smelty. Crazy often meant dead-set determined. Where did Haley fall? "But the more information we have, the better. Maybe we can find out *why* she's targeted you. In the meanwhile," Aiden said, "I'll talk to King. I can vouch for—"

"No. Enough. It's best if we sever ties with Miller's entirely," Tori spat. *"Don't* help."

The door suddenly swung wide behind him, the sounds from inside spilling out. Aiden didn't budge, just stood braced and tense, staring down at Tori.

"Mom? It's over." Luke's words split the outdoor silence. "What's going on?" Both concern and suspicion were evident in the kid's voice.

Aiden forced his shoulders to relax, stepped aside, and pasted an even expression on his face. "Your mom and I were just talking."

Luke stepped out, his chest puffing up.

"Let's get out of here," Tori said. "I'll fill you in in the car."

She stalked past Aiden without a glance in his direction or a word of goodbye.

CHAPTER 24

AIDEN BOLTED UPRIGHT in bed, the idea that had been poking at his consciousness suddenly front and center, like a shadow that hardened into defined edges as soon as the fog cleared.

The TV was still on, the flashes of light from the box more pronounced than the low volume. He'd fallen asleep watching the local midnight newscast to find out what they were saying about a certain lice outbreak. Baseball scores, too, as he'd been too fried from today's bombshell about Haley to get up and check online.

The news that had jarred him awake, however, was old. Months ago, he'd heard a report that the Wilmington Warriors—the Triple-A farm team in the East Division of the International League that fed players to the Phillies—was in financial trouble. They needed a new owner, or at least some heavy-hitting investors, or the team would fold. He hadn't paid much attention then, wrapped up as he was in the stores and his own health issues.

Just last week, he and his dad had been to that Delaware ballpark—one of their least favorites. Attendance had been sparse and the stadium seemed as dangerous as a building constructed out of crackers. In fact, bits of cement actually crumbled from the steep steps in the aisles. The news bulletin had hinted that the current owner of the Warriors was in large part to blame for their precarious situation. Possible, as the place hadn't been nearly so bad when Aiden had played there with the Jacks. In spite of those things, the coach and players both seemed to have spirit in spades—any underdog knew passion could make the difference.

Aiden kicked off the sheet and swung his feet onto the floor. Grabbed the remote and killed the tube. Started pacing.

Baseball. Making money. Turning things around. A challenge. Thinking outside of the box.

Totally feasible. As soon as he said goodbye to the markets.

"Holy shit," Aiden said, a grin breaking free.

Excitement surged its way into his bloodstream, making each limb tingle with the need to move. He wrenched open the drapes, shoved open the sliders, and walked out to grip the railing hard as he looked up at the moon. The air of the wee hours packed a chill—crisp and alive.

A car engine flared then steadied, not as if it had been turned over, but with acceleration. Aiden craned his head to survey the sides of the house. Pointless. He couldn't see shit from this spot, facing the lake as he was. Tires churned slowly over the dirt-packed drive, unnatural against the sounds of the night—and so close that he was sure somebody had parked right up against the house.

Aiden frowned. The trees weren't illuminated—no headlights—meaning that the driver aimed for stealth. As the vehicle turned onto the road, the lights flipped on. The dark shape, he thought, was an SUV, but it was hard to see through the trees. Probably teenagers trying to access the lake via his property. Necking or skinny-dipping or smoking weed at water's edge. Likely his sudden appearance outside had startled the crap out of those kids. Probably what had woken him.

Perfect timing for his subconscious, though. God, but it had all came together in a flash. So simple, so perfect. It'd been there, waiting, but it had taken Tori laying out the puzzle pieces in a row for him to see clearly.

"Tori," he said aloud. "You're a fucking savior."

He laughed a loud bark of surprise that echoed over the moonlight water. Giddiness took hold—both elation and relief—and he hooted hard enough that his eyes watered. "Oh, man." Aiden lifted the edge of his t-shirt and wiped his eyes.

Talk about a new challenge. A farm team, a stadium... Baseball, he thought, his heart soaring. Hell yeah, that might ease the blow for Pops.

Selling the stores should be easy. Buying the team tougher, but not unthinkable. He'd need investors. Even if the sale of the chain covered it, that wasn't a burden he'd want to haul alone. Better to spread the risk.

If he got enough investors for the team and ballpark, he could keep Miller's. Maybe take it public but retain a controlling interest. Use Miller's as the official foods of the ballpark... *No, no, idiot, remember—you want out.* Aiden shook his head and smiled. What could he say? He got stoked easily when it came to making things happen.

He'd always loved a new venture, the challenge of growing a thing, making it work and succeed. Like he'd done with the store, and then stores, way back when, before the whole thing began to smother him.

He'd for damn sure always loved baseball.

If Tori could be true to a cause that fulfilled her, why couldn't Aiden do something he enjoyed? He didn't have to be saddled with the markets forever. Hallelujah, no. He was getting the fuck out.

Half an hour, maybe, until the sun started to lighten the sky. Aiden slipped back inside, slid the door shut with a thud, and strode to the kitchen, flipping on lights as he went. Coffee. Then he'd dress for kayaking. Caffeine, sunrise, and a steady glide over the lake, because yeah, he had a lot of thinking to do, in not a lot of time.

Trick would be finding a way to sell the stores before the world came crashing down with this whole drug bust. Yeah, he could shut down this one, Aiden grimaced, then sell the rest of the chain. Not ideal. He had an obligation to the Poconos employees—all of them.

He had to do damage control on the lice and TB issue with Barry King.

He still had to officially fire Haley—Christ, he still couldn't believe it. Assault on a coworker? And surely she was responsible for Tori's car, and now the rumors about Miller's and UpStart. He shook his head. It was all so nuts.

Plus, he already ached to get on the phone and find out more about the financials of the Warriors, which meant he'd better pay his dad a visit sooner rather than later. Because he absolutely needed his dad's blessing.

Last, but not least: despite her wish to "sever all ties," he intended to kiss the hell out of Tori Radnor.

———

The second she heard footsteps, Haley jumped up from her desk and put an eye to the peephole, waiting. The design of these seventies-style apartment units sucked—the open-air stairwells somehow echoed like they'd been made for rock band acoustics. Yet it worked for her—free security system.

Probably the police, trying to see in her windows again like last night. *Good luck, dickwads*, she thought. Exactly why she kept the heavy blinds closed at all times, the locks bolted, and the lights off. To anyone outside, it would absolutely look as if no one had been here in days.

There was no way in hell she was opening the door to sign a summons. Were they crazy?

On tiptoe at the peephole—what, were people taller in the seventies when this shithole was built?—she waited for a head to clear the landing.

Oh my God—it was him.

Here—at her apartment.

She'd called, and he'd actually come.

Her heart soared, even as she spun to snatch up her album. Frantically, she looked around debating where to hide it, and then realized—there was no way. She couldn't let him in. The place was trashed. That wouldn't do. Living in this kind of mess wouldn't seem...normal. Not to him, Mr. Always Perfect.

Should she go out?

Even with the distortion the peephole created, she could see that his lips formed a tight band and his eyebrows were lowered. Haley frowned. There was a movement and she tore her gaze from Aiden. Oh no, no, no.

Her initial, stupid excitement smashed as heavily as a cement block dropping to the floor. That bastard. He wasn't alone.

Knock, knock, knock. Then silence.

Knock, knock, knock. Another pause.

"Haley? It's me...Aiden." His voice was unsure.

Miller rapped harder, making her jump.

"Haley!" he called louder. "Open up. I just want to talk."

His pal moved toward the windows, out of her sight. Exactly like the cops who'd been here. Was this guy law enforcement, too? Undercover or something? Fuck.

She turned and leaned her back against the door, hugging the album so tight that it pressed painfully against her breasts. That was good—she needed to think anyway, and fast.

The door shifted ever so slightly, and she imagined him leaning in, palms flat.

"Haley, listen, if you're there, I don't claim to understand what's going on," he said, voice raised to travel through doors and windows. "You know I won't tolerate..."

She raised an eyebrow.

"...hurtful behavior."

Jesus, what a wanker. She snorted at the man's gall, even as the ramifications of that statement started to sink in.

"But I also know that you must be hurting, to have acted out this way."

She scowled, but he wasn't through.

"I'll make sure our healthcare covers you for counseling, mental health services. It's not too late."

Haley's mouth dropped open in outrage. She shoved the album away from her chest, her brain screaming.

Another voice, from inside: "He tried that angle with me, too. *You need help*, he said. But he *meant* the loony bin."

"Shut up! Shut up!" Haley said. "You're no help. I'm not the same as you."

"Haley? Haley, are you there?" Aiden called.

Shit, the thud of the album landing on the carpet must have been audible—or had she spoken aloud?

Haley wrapped her arms around herself and clamped her jaws shut.

"Open the door so we can talk, figure out how to help you."

Yeah, right, Haley thought, her ire rising in a swift wave. Here to help you as in, *here's the door to the psych ward*. Or *I'll clip on the handcuffs, soon as I get the chance.*

Haley dug her fingernails into her upper arms, the black nail polish disappearing, as her knuckles strained white. They waited, she waited, seething and still as a statue.

Finally, she heard footsteps descend with dull thuds. Two sets—no, wait. More than than two? Had there been someone else, hovering on the stairwell?

She counted out seconds, then ran to the window and peeked carefully between the blinds.

Cops! Two of them. Miller had coordinated with the fucking police. They all spoke for a minute, then the officers sauntered off to their patrol car and left.

Miller had a brief exchange with the guy who'd been at her door, then ducked into his Mercedes, reversed abruptly, and shot out of the parking lot. The street-clothes guy remained. Undercover cop? Friend of Miller's? Private investigator or some sort of hired thug? He leaned against a nondescript sedan, legs crossed at the ankles. Then he raised his cell phone to his ear and fixed his gaze on her windows.

Pulling back, she stood rooted there, clenching her fists, brain scrambling to find the sense in it all.

Apparently Miller had passed by doubt, waved at suspicion, and landed squarely on guilt. She'd assumed at first it was the

Radnors who'd pressed charges—goddamned kid must have blabbed—but here was Aiden Miller himself. Here to fire her. To commit her.

Fucker was awfully quick to throw her under the bus.

Haley let out a wail of frustration and ran to the album. It had flopped open to the page chronicling his last game with the Frostburg Jacks—though surely he hadn't known it at the time. One easy homer, two great saves. Giant smile.

Cocky fucking smug bastard.

Dropping to her knees, she pummeled the picture with her fists. This album—her most treasured gift—represented both her past and her future, and the tenuous link between them.

"I hate you, you traitorous dickhead! I hate you. You suck!" She raged until she bent and sobbed.

"Ripped your arm clean off, didn't he?"

A fresh wave of tears, the plastic over the newsprint getting slick.

"I told you. But you didn't listen. You got too close, started thinking he could be trusted."

"I know," she whispered. "But you also made me want him."

"He's not worth it."

"I've wasted too much time to give up now."

"That's how I felt, until I was stopped in my tracks."

Haley knew she was referring to the accident, when her mother had lost the use of her legs. She'd dashed out from between two cars to cross the street, and was hit. So intent on following *him*, she hadn't even looked.

Lots had changed then. Haley had been young, but she remembered.

"I'm not you," Haley said. "I'm. Not. You." She shut her eyes, head on the album, and hugged her knees to her chest. She whispered, "And you're not here."

CHAPTER 25

BY THE TIME Aiden entered the quaint bungalow he'd grown up in, it was past noon. He and his dad had always been tight, yet he was dreading this loaded visit.

He found Patrick Miller right where he expected—in the recliner, news blaring, and TV tray set up with lunch.

"Hey, Pop." Aiden leaned down and hugged his dad, surprised as always that he'd become frail and thin. In his mind, he'd forever be tall and sturdy like a tree. In fact, he'd climbed him when he was little, shimmying up his leg, grabbing fistfuls of his shirt...had to look up at him until he was nineteen and experienced a growing streak that well surpassed his dad's six feet. That was right about the time his dad started to shrink, Aiden remembered, from the heart problems taking their toll. Waiting for the transplant had nearly killed him. Since, he'd remained healthy and even gained a bit of weight back, but Aiden recalled the terror of nearly losing his dad—his anchor—only too well.

"What's with the rain barrel by the front door?"

Pat waved his hand. "Another of your mother's ideas. Reuse the natural resources. I'm not bathing in that chemical rainwater, though. I live here because I *like* running water."

Aiden's hand slid to the base of his neck. "So she's home?"

"For a few days only. You should see her."

"Yeah," Aiden said. "Maybe I will." *Not if I can help it,* he thought.

"Where is she?"

"Over at the Red Cross, figuring out where she's needed next."

Of course. "How're you feeling, Pops?"

"Real good. I spent some time at the store today," Pat said.

"I see that," Aiden said, glancing at his dad's plate, for he fixed a much simpler meal, like cold cuts and slices of cheese, if he hadn't visited the Westchester market.

"How'd it look?"

"Good, good. That guy Dusseldorf seems to be doing a decent job. Always clean, though I took a broom to some corners the kids had missed."

Aiden took a seat on the end of the couch to his dad's right. He could easily recall Pops doing just the same in his long canvas apron, when Aiden was young and racing up and down the three short aisles of their only corner store. Originally, it'd been a go-to for men on their way home from work. A *Honey, pick up some milk on your way* kind of place back when the phones were mostly still rotary and the men still pulled in at dinner hour. The kids came on their bikes for candy or ice cream, lots of folks for cigarettes and newspapers. A fifties-type place that had managed to hang on into the eighties. Eventually, though, strip malls with their behemoth groceries invaded and the corner store started to seem shabby and outdated. Who wanted a limited selection when they could go to a place with aisle after aisle of every boxed product made in the good ol' U.S. of A.?

By the time Aiden was in college, the store was barely hanging on. Had the stress of a failing store exacerbated the heart issues? Aiden had wondered...

"I'll check in there before I go," Aiden said, in case his dad was worried.

"How's things?" Pat tipped up his chin and inspected Aiden. "You join that men's baseball league yet?"

"No, Dad. Not yet," Aiden said, wincing. His dad still felt awful that his illness had ripped Aiden from his dream. Aiden had come to terms with it long ago. "Too busy." Which he was. But the truth of the matter was, like smart, insightful, wonderful Tori had guessed, that when you'd nearly played pro ball, a men's league was going to be downright painful.

"You look tense."

Baseball and stress—that brought things to a head nicely. "I need to talk to you about something, Pop. Something big."

Pat raised gray flyaway eyebrows. "That right?" He picked up the remote from its usual place on the arm of his padded chair, turned the tube off, and moved his tray to the side.

"Lay it on me then, lad."

Aiden cleared his throat and braced his hands on his thighs. "The stores. I'd like to sell them."

This time his dad's brows rose nearly to his silver hairline over his lean, wrinkled face. "Is that so?"

Aiden cleared his throat. "I'm tired. Overworked, but bored—and for what? This isn't my dream, it was your dream."

His dad opened his mouth, except, much like a shaken can of soda, Aiden couldn't be contained once that pop-top had been ripped off.

"I did it, Dad. I proved I could. I made the store a success. I made a whole friggin' chain a success. I made you proud—I hope. But I'm sick of it. I want to do something else, something new and different—for me, anyway." He took a deep breath. "I want to buy a farm team—the Warriors—and maybe relocate it to the Poconos."

His dad's eyes narrowed.

"I wanted to talk to you first. Because I believe that the bulk of the capital—for me to hold a controlling interest—is only possible if I sell the chain. You'd get a large chunk, of course, though I know that's not the part that'll get to you. I know how hard you worked, Pops. I know it's got the family name on it."

He searched his dad's light blue eyes, fading every year, for any sign of what he was thinking.

"I won't do it if you don't want me to." That was the hell of it right there. As badly as Aiden wanted this, as much as he knew he needed it, he wouldn't follow through if Pop couldn't get behind the idea. "I'm asking...for your blessing."

His dad's eyes welled up, and Aiden's chest tightened—he feared the worst.

"Ach, lad. We Miller men don't lay our hearts on the line with words too often. But that was a right fine speech."

Aiden held his breath, as his dad swiped a finger under his nose.

"Christ, I don't know where to start," Pat said, then shook his head yet again. "Am I proud of ye, son? Mother of God, I could not be more honored to call ye mine. As for the markets being my dream? No, never. I aimed to make a living, lad, to support my family, to provide a steady landscape for you when it became clear your mother—well, that she'd never settle down, that I'd have to be the one. The money? Gads, you send me too much. I barely touch it, just keep socking it away. For what, I don't even know. I suspect if I live to be a hundred, it'll never run out."

Patrick's gaze held his. Aiden's breathing and chest loosened, as hope gathered momentum.

"Sell the stores?" his dad continued. "Hell yes. Long overdue. I'm sorry, for I should have told you so. They're sucking you dry inside, and that's plain to see." He held out a large, gnarled hand to Aiden. "If I'd known that there was a way for you to be truly involved with baseball at your old age"—Patrick sniffed—"I would have told you to sell years ago."

Hands still gripped, Aiden pulled his dad out of the chair for an embrace emphasized by a few mutual, hearty back slaps. This was as affectionate as they ever got. But his dad's words were a great gift, indeed.

Both men were wiping a touch of moisture from their eyes when Aiden's mother spoke from behind them.

"What's all this?" Marjorie asked. "I'm gone a couple of months, and you've both turned into whimpering boys?"

Aiden and Patrick looked at each other and laughed.

His mother set down some sacks—reusable, of course—and put her hands on her hips. Her silver curls rioted out from under a wide and brightly printed headband and dangly wooden earrings. A similarly patterned caftan swirled around her. So, she'd been in Africa, where the need for aid never eased.

"Aren't you glad to see me? Come here and kiss your mother, Aiden."

He did, wrinkling his nose. She'd given up deodorant long ago as a show of solidarity with those she helped. At some point, she'd stopped using it on American soil as well, having decided that *those chemicals are sure to leach into your lymph nodes and cause cancer.*

"I've been home for three days and you haven't once checked on your father. Where have you been?"

"I don't need checking on, Marjorie," Pat said, at the same time Aiden retorted through gritted teeth, "I could ask the same of you."

She narrowed her eyes. She knew just how her son felt about her long absences. The way she gave and gave to every under-privileged, impoverished, natural-disaster-crushed community across the country—and the world—yet abandoned her family time and again.

Why his dad hadn't divorced her long ago, he never could figure. He'd never put up with a woman who didn't put family first.

"Aiden also doesn't live in this neighborhood anymore, Marjorie. He's been staying out in that place he built in the Poconos."

"I still wish you'd built more green—"

"He's going to be spending even more time there." Patrick rolled his eyes at Aiden, indicating that she'd go on forever if he didn't stop her. However, Aiden, for once, was content to let her rant. He wasn't ready to share. Certainly not with her. "Dad, I—"

"He's selling the stores."

Yep, that stopped her in her tracks—for a moment.

"Selling? But why? You've done so well with the stores, Aiden."

He shrugged. "I have my reasons."

Now his mother pushed, not to be left out of the loop when

her support strings might be severed. "What happened? Are the stores in trouble?"

"Nothing happened, except we've seen the light," Patrick said, and Aiden had to smile at that *we*.

"Aiden is going to be the owner of a baseball team, maybe even a stadium."

The look of shock on his mother's face was worth every second of worry. "It's not exactly a done deal, Pops. In fact, it's not even—"

"Ach, if I know my son, once an idea takes root…" Patrick turned up a palm.

Marjorie found her tongue, opinionated as ever. "You intend to *own* a bunch of men, who play games instead of working?" Her gaze swung to Patrick, disbelieving. "Is that a wise move?"

Patrick rolled his eyes heavenward, and Aiden shook his head.

"It's a business, Mom. And like everything I do, I'll aim to do it well. Your precious cash flow won't be stemmed." Besides first-class travel costs and designer dresses for fancy fundraisers, Aiden knew she donated the bulk of what he provided to whatever cause was most near and dear to her heart at the moment. In some ways she was utterly selfless. But she'd also come, Aiden believed, to crave the generous donor status his wealth afforded her, both here and abroad.

"This just seems so…so irresponsible," she said. "Sports can be so distasteful. You're a well-respected businessman, Aiden. Think of your reputation."

Aiden shook his head.

"Ach, Marjorie. Our son did everything you wanted. He's a black belt in karate, he studied languages and yoga, he even gave your ridiculous meditations a try. He gave up baseball—the one thing that speaks to his heart—for me. He's supported us both for years. We've asked more than we've given."

"Patrick! I cannot believe—"

"Enough." Pat's voice neared a bellow. "For once just keep your opinions to yourself and give the boy your blessing!"

She blinked and her mouth froze in an O.

"Sorry," Aiden said, biting his lip because he wanted to laugh wildly like he was thirteen again, "but I gotta run." He'd tell his dad the lice and tuberculosis thing was bogus with a phone call later.

Patrick frowned. Aiden knew he was shortchanging his dad a decent visit, but his mother made him crazy. He had enough to deal with: the health-scare situation to defuse at the store, an unstable employee he couldn't seem to fire, phone calls to make about his new venture—*bless you, Pops*—and a beautiful woman to make amends with—somehow.

Hell yeah, time to go.

CHAPTER 26

"AARRGH!" TORI SLAMMED the receiver down in frustration.

"Another one, huh?" Stefan asked, peering around a computer screen on another desk.

"Yes, all the local businesses seem to think we have lice, or worse, TB. Doesn't matter that it's not true; just the threat of creepy crawlies and a cough has sent everybody running."

"Can't you prove it somehow?" Luke asked, around a mouthful of burrito he'd warmed up as an after-school snack.

"The TB, yes. They've all had medical exams and been cleared to work." Tori dropped her head in her hands. "As for the other, I only wish it were that easy. I checked with LiceAway. Do you know what they charge to remove lice and nits? Two hundred and fifty—per head! Not that any of the UpStart clientele would actually need that. They do a check for a fraction of that." Tori looked up at both Luke and Stefan. "Even so, I just can't see us walking into LiceAway with a cell phone and uploading video to YouTube, can you?"

Stefan pursed his lips. "You're right. Not professional."

"You could have a real reporter come and film it."

Tori heaved a sigh. "I could, yet it still keeps the focus on lice. I know they say that bad publicity is better than none at all, that what you really want is for someone to simply recall your name..." She shook her head. "Awfully risky. If they only remembered UpStart, that'd be one thing, but I have a feeling in this case, it's the lice that'll hang on."

"No pun intended?" Stefan said.

"Nope." Tori laughed, though she almost cried. "Maybe I'll try again to ask my parents for money. A loan."

"Mom, no!"

"This time, they might see that I mean business, that we've got a good beginning here—something worth saving."

She looked at Luke. Saw the truth on his face. A fool's errand. An exercise only in sabotaging her self-worth. What was this, *Freaky Friday*? Where he was the adult, and she the teen reliving the nightmare over and over to learn her lesson?

Residing with her parents after the eviction had been hell—actually far worse than growing up there. Poor Luke got no pass as a grandchild. Rather, they aimed an extra-large portion of their judgment and disapproval arsenal at Luke because their daughter had already proved such a grave disappointment.

"I don't know what else to do," Tori said, resting her head in her hands. "I've got to start a positive press campaign, which takes money, to combat this thing. I've got to pay back Mr. Miller for the car repair next month. I still have this week and next to pay salaries for Alan and Clarice before Miller's takes over—assuming they won't leave, that is. I also can't get other clients placed without some serious spin-doctoring."

She slumped back in her chair and exhaled a long breath. She hated to burden Luke with all this, yet he'd been involved from the beginning. No point in hiding the gory details now. With a grimace, she admitted, "We are precariously close to drowning here."

"Hang on," Stefan said. "A campaign like that sounds like it'll take time to show results anyway, and you need an influx of money pretty quick."

Tori slumped. "True."

"You don't think your parents would give you the money? Even if it was a loan, instead of a gift or donation?"

She'd told Stefan some about her parents, but knew it was hard to grasp their coldness, their pinchpenny ways, and their singular disgust of the profession Tori had chosen.

"Uh-uh." Luke shook his head emphatically. "When we got booted, they didn't even want to house us. And UpStart is the last place they'd put money."

True. Tori—against her better judgment, but in an effort to speed the process of getting out from under the Winterspoons' roof—had gone out on a limb, presented her parents UpStart's business plan, and asked them for a loan. They'd been horrified. Offended, even. And without a single second of consideration, they'd refused—adamantly.

"What about your parents' friends?" Stefan asked. "Are they just as bad? Just as wealthy?"

"Their friends…" Tori shut her eyes. "There's that gala at Skytop Lodge that my mother called to harass me about, but I don't know that I can bear it."

"The Main Line Mickey?" Luke crushing the burrito wrapper into a ball.

"Yeah, that one."

"Sounds like crack," Stefan said.

"It's an annual fundraiser—" Tori began, but was interrupted by Luke.

"Where they 'slip mickeys' to all the rich people who live on the Main Line—the wealthy area of Philly"—Luke smirked—"so they'll empty their pockets."

"It wasn't originally called that, but it caught on, so eventually they called a spade a spade." Tori rolled her eyes. "People thought it was hysterical, but there's no drugs, just plenty of alcohol." She turned to Luke. "How do you even know that phrase 'slipping somebody a mickey'?"

He shrugged. "Maybe because you and Dad and every other person we knew *then* went every year."

"Why does your mother want you to go?" Stefan asked Tori, getting up and coming to stand with Luke in front of Tori's desk.

"Because"—Luke rolled his eyes—"she wants Mom to show up in some designer dress and fat diamonds and prove to all her friends that her daughter isn't wearing rags and begging on the street corner."

Huh, Tori thought, *Luke sure has a bead on things.*

"I'd still be begging," Tori declared, "if I go."

"Not with a tin cup and a cardboard sign, though," said Stefan, "and not from your parents." He rubbed a hand over his perpetual scruff. "Seems to me, more people give to a woman dripping with wealth than somebody truly in need. Backward, but accurate. Plus you already know lots of these people, right? So it's just working the relationships, nudging old acquaintances."

Tori sighed. "Yes. And although many of them have ties here, chances are decent they won't have heard yesterday's local news."

"It's a good idea, Mom," Luke said. "Just think, you can twist the knife in Grandma and Grandpa Winterspoon a little while you're there."

Tori shook her head. For years, she'd wished he'd had normal, loving grandparents. Sadly, no amount of wishing could make her parents people they were not, and Holden's folks were only marginally better. No surprise, since the blue-blooded Philadelphia Radnors had been practically handpicked by the Winterspoons.

"Some sticking points to this plan, guys," Tori said. "Even if I can still get on the list, I got rid of all the gowns and gemstones."

"Consignment store?"

"I guess. I'll just have to be careful not to pick anything Cynthia Sutton once wore." She made a face at Luke. "And it's still money I don't want to spend."

"I'll come with," Stefan offered.

"I don't know whether to be insulted or touched," she said.

Stefan laughed. "Heels?"

"I kept one black pair for weddings or funerals." Tori looked at her son. "There's still what to do about Luke."

"What do you mean what to do about Luke?" he asked, scowling.

"I can't leave you here alone."

He went bug-eyed. "The hell you can't. I'm sixteen. I'm alone all the time."

Tori wagged her finger, indicating that she'd noted the swearing, even as she inclined her head in agreement. "Normally, yes, but with wacko Haley out there somewhere, I'm not comfortable with that this time."

Luke frowned. "You said that Haley was MIA."

"That doesn't mean she's taken off for parts unknown," Stefan said. "She could be laying low right here, waiting to wreak more havoc."

"I'm inclined to suspect the latter," said Tori quietly. "And I'll be close to an hour away. If the meat proves anything, it's that she knows where we live."

Luke scowled, but didn't fight her. As Tori stood, she rolled her head, trying to dislodge some tension from her neck.

"I can stay here with him," Stefan offered.

"This event goes late," Tori said, reaching for her notebook and purse. She needed to get Clarice over to Miller's for her Tuesday evening shift. "Well into the wee hours."

He shrugged. "So I'll sleep over." At Tori's look, he said, "No big deal. Not like I've got somebody at home waiting on me."

She shut her eyes, as if she could block out this idea.

Damn. She was going to have to see her parents. And somehow sweet-talk their cronies into a good deed without Bernard and Grace being the wiser.

"You can do it, Mom."

Tori opened her eyes. Soaked up her amazing kid's grin. Thank God he was smiling again.

"You know what?" she responded. "I can. Damn well, too."

———

Tori waited anxiously for the six o'clock interview with the Midas of Markets. The preview clip had, of course, told her nothing—except perhaps that the merest glimpse of Aiden could leave her feeling warm and obvious, despite her frustration with him. She busied herself in the kitchenette, prepping sandwiches for herself, Luke, and Stefan.

"He's on!" Stefan called, causing Tori to dart back out to the common space, where they'd turned on the TV—one they normally used only for instructional or motivational videos for UpStart's clients, given the lack of comfy seating.

Aiden stood on the sidewalk in front of Miller's wall of windows, three reporters and their cameramen crowding him, microphones hovering below his chin.

Wasn't there anything newsworthy going on in the Poconos? *This* was really the big story?

After a brief introduction by one of the reporters, Aiden—to prove the community could trust Miller's—declared that he'd have every employee screened for lice. He offered a free day for the community to participate in the same. A healthcare provider would be on hand as well.

Stefan said, "That's going to be some bill."

Tori nodded. "Unlike us, moneybags there can afford it."

Aiden looked as handsome as always—dressed for work, but so physically, perfectly *male* that Tori's hormones did their little dance, despite television waves as a conduit.

Oddly, he looked...relaxed? Was that possible? At ease at Miller's, during a defensive media strike? Normally, his body language screamed stress, especially when he was at the store. What had changed?

"I'm confident not a single employee will be flagged," he was saying. "Today, like any other, you'll find that Miller's delivers exacting quality and the highest standard of service. We're as strong as ever."

That, Tori supposed, was a not-so-subtle message to Barry King, letting him—or any other big grocery conglomerate— know there was no point in lowballing an offer to buy Miller's.

By the time he closed with a thank you and began to turn away from the microphone, he hadn't mentioned UpStart at all.

Well, Tori admonished herself, she'd told him not to help, hadn't she? *Idiot.*

The reporters jumped to life, voices clamoring, one question rising above the others. "What incident caused the lice outbreak and tuberculosis scare to become news?"

Aiden turned back, spoke to the reporter directly. "There was no incident because there is no lice in our store. And it's June. I'd be willing to bet that not a single employee even has a cough due to a common cold."

"There must have been something," the woman said.

He paused a beat, then spoke, his face a blank mask. "We believe it was as simple as someone starting a rumor. That's all there is to it."

Another reporter. "Do you really have homeless people working at Miller's?"

"Bitch!" Luke whispered.

"Cool it," Tori admonished, even as she kept her eyes glued to the screen. "That fact was bound to come up."

Aiden's face hardened. He reached out and snagged a microphone. "All of our employees have roofs over their heads and are hardworking, responsible individuals. Furthermore, unlike some"—he gave the reporter a pointed look—"we don't discriminate."

Tears sprang to Tori's eyes at his defense and praise of her crew. He hadn't lied, either—the shelter might not be a roof they could call their own, but they were housed.

Aiden preempted the next obvious question. "I have contracted with a company called UpStart, who helps put struggling individuals back to work." He continued, his tone serious, his expression earnest. "I'm nothing but impressed with the operation and UpStart's clients, and recommend the program to any business owner in the community."

With an abrupt toss, Aiden returned the microphone. The audio feed caught his clipped words: "This interview is over."

Tori heaved a sigh of relief, and the news instantly flipped to another story. Luke squeezed her shoulder, and Stefan clapped. "See that? He *is* a good guy. He just gave you a positive press campaign."

Tori laughed and nodded. "He certainly got the ball rolling in the right direction. Now, we follow with action, because if there's anything we've learned, it's that people don't just offer up contracts and donations. They have to be chased down."

"That'll be easy," Luke said. "They'll all be in one spot at the gala."

"Right," she said, and slumped into a desk chair.

Easy would be the last word she'd use. Aiden's public support would help tremendously. However, UpStart still had a steep hill to climb—with only narrow shoulders and flimsy guardrails to keep them on track.

Haley's penchant for launching boulders made their path all that much more precarious. Why the girl had targeted her and Luke, and now UpStart itself, Tori couldn't imagine. But she knew, without a shred of doubt, that Haley wasn't finished.

What was next?

Worse—she frowned, watching Luke rip into a bag of chips—who?

CHAPTER 27

"THIS IS THE WORST idea you've ever had."

"I'm done taking your advice. Maybe if I'd stopped that a long time ago, if I was just honest and upfront, I wouldn't be in this situation."

Secretly, however, Haley was terrified her mother was right. Because Aiden had become so difficult to predict lately, and her own track record was tending more and more toward crash and burn.

I mean, holy hell. He was trying to fire her! After all she'd done for that place, for him. All these years.

She'd been dumbfounded last night after watching the six-o'clock news. Not only had Aiden *not* chosen Miller's over UpStart, he'd totally plugged Radnor's business. And he himself—as always—came out looking like his shit was gold-plated.

She hovered on the edge of the parking lot, in one of the dead areas for the security cameras, tapping the wheel of her SUV with her fingers, too jittery to sit still.

Hyper, but running on empty. No sleep, little food.

Telling Miller, using the thing she feared most, might be just the thing. Either it would swing his sympathies her way and she'd have her happy ending, or... Well, worst-case scenario, the giant question mark would become a giant slash mark of rejection. But at least she'd know...

All the years of waiting and planning would either be worth it or an absolute waste of her whole pathetic life. So yeah, this was either the worst or best idea. Which was why she was so goddamn anxiety-ridden.

She couldn't shut her eyes or calm down, kept flirting with

throwing up, and, worst of all, wasn't thinking straight enough to plan the right words.

She needed some courage, in pill form. Then, as soon as she hit an even keel, she'd be able to build some bravery. And go for it. All the way.

There he was, right on time.

She hopped out of her SUV and darted into the path of the oncoming truck.

"Jesus," Butch said, coming to a hard stop next to her and leaning out his window, "you're lucky I was paying attention." He squinted. "You don't look so good. Are you okay?"

"I will be."

"More piercings?" he asked, his massive brows sinking in a frown.

She'd forgotten. Thought the sharp pinch might help her think—and besides, she'd always wanted some piercings where they were visible. But the little diamond had been like a non-event, too sweet, too understated. And no one but her ever got to see the "M" charm at her navel. The lip and eyebrow piercings made more of a statement. Went with her new hair.

Mom hadn't approved of either. Said Aiden would never go for the dye job or the mauling of her face. Haley's response? *Fuck it, and fuck you.* Past time to start being herself.

"Haley?" Butch said.

She blinked. "I need you to hook me up."

He tried to cover his shock with a look of confusion.

She snorted. "Come on, I know you're selling." He didn't need to know what else she knew.

"Keep yourself clean. You don't need to be doing drugs right now; you got enough issues."

She scoffed. "Don't worry. I can handle it."

"That's what they all say." He shook his head. "This isn't going to help anything. Seriously, trust me. You shouldn't be here, but you do need to answer Aiden's calls."

"I will. I'm going to have a real heart-to-heart with him, but

I can't do it while I'm this worked up. Whatcha got for downers? Valium? Xanax?"

Butch rubbed his hand over his eyes. "I don't know. I'm low. Overdue for a shipment, but I have no idea what'll be in it."

She narrowed her eyes, started calculating, her mind sorting through the Miller's schedule. She thought this was Wednesday morning—when was he on alone at night?

"I need something now," she said, nearly growling.

"You gotta get out of here. You can't go assaulting people and then—"

Haley's nostrils flared and she erupted. "How could you believe that shit Luke over me?" She was still trying to wrap her mind around what had gone wrong, and when.

"Whoa—chill."

"That kid and his bitch mom are ruining everything!" She'd snapped. She heard it in her own voice, harsh and angry. No pretense of faking it anymore.

"Just calm down. What are you talking about? Radnor's people are good for Miller's, and she's good for Aiden."

Haley sneered. "No. Miller never keeps women around for long."

"This one's different."

Did Butch know something she didn't? "Why?"

He shrugged. "He's going to marry her."

"What?" Her heart curled in on itself. "He said that?"

"Nah. I can just tell."

"There is no way," Haley said, but inside, she shattered. If Butch was right…or even close…

She hugged her middle and bent over, trying to catch her breath. The remains of her hopes and plans had just been ripped out. Entirely. She wouldn't have asked for much from Miller. It would have been enough to just be—

No matter—he wasn't only going to yank her arm off, he was going to shred her heart to pieces, while Radnor snatched her dreams, took them for herself and her son.

She stood. Butch's eyes were narrowed as he said, "I defended you. I had a hard time believing it, but now... You don't need drugs. You need serious—"

Aiden had implied the same. In need of counseling. Mentally unstable. The fuckers, they had no idea. Haley let every ounce of hate she felt fly. "Don't even say it, you drug-dealing, weak piece of shit. You of all people have no right to judge."

Butch's face had gone hard. He shoved the car in drive. She put her hand on the window frame.

Haley's mind raced. "I need those downers *today.*"

Butch stared at her, disgust clear in his eyes.

"Give them to me," she demanded, "or you can kiss your job and your freedom goodbye."

He raised his eyes heavenward and muttered, "Screwed from all angles, huh? Christ, this is so fucking crazy."

"Shut up," she snapped.

He shook his head. "Meet me here on my lunch break." And he gunned the engine.

Haley stalked to her car. Thoughts pile-driving into her skull. *Miller can't marry, he can't. I won't allow it. He's mine. Belongs to me. I can prove it.*

She slipped into the driver's seat and laughed uncontrollably, sounding like a hopped-up hyena.

Unstable? Crazy? Nuts? Loco?

If she was a wack job, then it was all his fault. His and hers. For making her what she was.

Haley swiped the back of her hand against her tearing eyes, and sucked in air.

Going for the Big Reveal? Trying to tell Miller now?

That had been crazy. Mommy had been right.

So, back to taking pages out of Mom's book. Her manual for life. There was *Information is power, but only if you use it.* But the one she needed now was *The world is your playground, as long as you're the bully.*

Haley stared at the ugly brick lining the backside of Miller's.

Her hands gripped the steering wheel like she could strangle it, resolve settled and centered inside her with razored edges.

I'll show you unhinged, Aiden Miller. No way in hell do you get a happy ending without me.

———

Aiden rubbed his eyes and pushed up from the desk in the small security closet at the store, sending the wheeled chair flying into the wall. Giant swaths of video feed were fuzzed over. He'd hoped it was just a temporary glitch, but today's tapes showed more of the same. So, dammit...

Butch? Or Haley?

Mentally, he kicked himself. He'd believed that as long as the surveillance program was password protected and he had managers he trusted, this high-tech system didn't require an actual body to monitor it.

Stupid, fucking stupid. Aiden shook his head as he locked the door behind him.

Traversing the store, he found himself glaring at each and every mounted security camera on the way.

He'd finally given up and left a voicemail telling Haley that she was fired, but he felt it was necessary to deliver the message in person, as well. To that end, Aiden's private investigator Nick had been spending a lot of hours watching Haley's apartment, waiting for her to show. But he knew security systems. Maybe his time would be better spent here.

Surveillance cameras that actually worked, especially the perimeter ones, were essential. And not just for Detective Lundgren's purposes. According to Butch, Haley had been lurking around early this morning, just outside the back lot. He claimed she took off when he tried to talk to her, but Aiden found it disturbing that she'd been here at all.

Yeah, Aiden needed the video feeds working—pronto.

As he rounded a front endcap, he spotted Tori's son.

"Hey, Luke," Aiden said, "Here to pick up Clarice and Alan?"

"Hi, Mr. Miller. Uh-huh." He held a list in one hand, a basket with only a few items in the other.

Aiden gestured to it. "Mom sent you in to do the shopping?"

"Yeah."

The kid smiled, tossing his hair out of his eyes, presumably so that he could actually see. A shade lighter than his mom's, Luke wore it long, like many of the kids did these days. Aiden would bet that they'd regret those yearbook pictures eventually, though.

"She's waiting in the car?"

The boy nodded.

Aiden scanned the lot through the front window for his Land Rover. Yep, honey-gold crown bent, eyes down. Hopefully, car doors locked. Aiden shook his head. Playing with fire, she was.

"I wish she wouldn't do that," Aiden mumbled. He itched to scold her. Hell, he'd like to go talk to her period.

"Because of...Haley?" Luke's voice dropped to a whisper at the name.

"Yeah, and—" Yikes, he'd been about to mention Tori's ex, Luke's dad. Aiden craned his neck to the side, cracking it. "It's not smart for a person to sit all lit up like a beacon in a dark parking lot. You know, we touched on it in the self-defense clinic. Don't invite trouble, don't make yourself available as a target."

Luke nodded, very serious. "I'll talk to her."

Aiden laughed. "Better you than me. Have a feeling she'd take my head off." He also suspected she was avoiding him after the searing kisses and subsequent argument.

Luke said, "She's tough. But maybe not as tough as she acts."

"I know," Aiden said. Was that a warning to go easy, or a helpful hint from Tori's son?

They exited the aisle, and Luke glanced to where Clarice had been on checkout.

"She probably went to punch out. Alan, too. Did you get everything you needed?"

"Yeah, I'm good."

Butch came around the corner and greeted the boy, then told the cashier to stay open for one additional customer who was still shopping.

Butch asked Aiden, "Tori here?"

"Outside," Aiden said, inclining his head.

"Thought I'd check in," Butch said, and headed for the doors.

Good, Aiden thought. She wouldn't be alone out there—and yet he wished he'd beaten Butch to it.

The lot was nearly empty. Tori noticed Butch almost immediately, and hopped out of the car.

Why the hell not? Aiden thought, striding forward. He wanted to talk with Tori, too.

When Aiden exited the building, about ten feet separated Butch and Tori. He heard the roar before he saw it—an engine surged loud, accelerating, heading right for the pair.

White van.

Butch's head snapped up, even as Aiden bellowed and leaped forward into a full run.

A thud—Butch bounced back.

"Tori!" Aiden yelled.

Butch stumbled but kept his feet.

The van cleared them going—Christ, fifty miles an hour?

Aiden nearly hit the ground, knees giving way, when he spotted Tori.

Whole. Unharmed. Standing upright, eyes and mouth frozen open in shock.

Aiden yanked her to him, held her tight. "Okay? Tori?"

He felt her nod into his chest, latch her arms around him. He spun them to face Butch. "You all right, man?"

Perspiration glinted on the manager's forehead, which wrinkled like he was trying hard to solve a puzzle. "I slapped the side, pushed back." He held up his palm, ogling it, incredulous. "She didn't hit me."

Tori raised her face and turned toward Butch, her body instantly rigid against him. Aiden's gut twisted, his throat clogging against words. He already knew—this time without an ounce of doubt.

"She?" Tori asked.

"Haley. Had to be." Butch wiped a shaking hand over his bald head, his eyes meeting Aiden's. "Only a blur, but I saw the new hair. Freak-show purple-black hair."

CHAPTER 28

HALEY THREW HER LAPTOP, camera equipment, and stacks of pictures into a hastily packed duffel full of electronics, fighting the fury of frustration. She didn't think either Butch or Radnor could possibly identify her, but couldn't take any chances. She had to vacate this apartment.

Aiden's goon would probably be back any minute, and she couldn't risk getting stuck inside again. She'd be safer in the van, having already switched the license plate out.

Damn it all. She hated surprises, and Butch had really thrown her. She'd been gunning for Radnor, of course. But it'd seemed so expedient to just take him out with that bitch. Two pins at once.

She'd been too friggin' greedy, tried to split the distance because she'd wanted them both gone quickly. Getting neither. Fuck. Fuck. Fuck.

"You always mess up when you are impetuous," her mother sneered. "You *know* better."

"Shut up, *shut up!*" Haley shouted.

She grabbed her hair with both hands and spun in a circle, trying to think. What did she need? What could she leave?

Her eyes landed on the album, and she snatched it up, setting it beside the duffel. Too big to fit inside. She grabbed a backpack for clothes and toiletries, but halted midway to the dresser.

She had to get her life back on track. There had to be a way.

Think, think. She twisted both hands into her hair and squeezed her eyes shut.

Yes—the only thing more important than the album was her ticket to Miller: her birth certificate.

Dropping the backpack, she lurched toward the closet. Haley

turned over a full hamper and stepped on it, the plastic bowing, threatening to crack. She quickly yanked the old shoebox off the shelf and hopped down. Tossing off the lid, she held her breath as she ruffled through pictures of her and her mom. Very few, most of them from when she was quite young.

Yes. The certificate was here. She never kept it anywhere else, yet relief washed over her anyway.

Haley dumped the contents of the box into her shoulder bag. Nothing to do about cash. She'd used her savings from all her hidey-holes earlier today when she'd purchased the van. Only a couple of hundred left. Not smart to hit the bank now. Not until things died down.

She hefted the bag full of necessities. Heavy enough that she'd need to get that downstairs, and come back and grab some clothes and the album.

Haley took the stairs as fast as possible, her shoulder bag hanging from her elbow as she hugged the big duffel close. The lighting sucked, but she preferred the shadows anyway. She'd parked the van behind the other building—by the time she'd tossed the load on the passenger seat, she was panting. Soon as she turned to head back, she saw lights from beyond the passageway.

Red and blue, flashing in the darkness.

Haley scrambled into the van, slouched down low, and winced as the cranky engine complained before catching. She yanked the gearshift into drive and forced herself to drive at parking-lot speed, headlights off, to the farthest end of the apartment's lot. There was a side street here. An exit.

No sirens, but still—shit. Freedom was everything now. Because she had one last shot. One last chance to salvage this whole shit show. There was still hope, if Tori and Luke just… disappeared.

There were ways to get rid of bodies. As long as she could still get into Miller's with a few hours to herself, it was practically a no-brainer.

Haley grinned. Finally, *finally*, it had occurred to her that she could go ahead and get her hands dirty. Filthy and bloody. Because she had the perfect patsy.

Butch.

He deserved it anyway, the fucker. The slightest bit of evidence should convict him.

"See that, Mommy? My earlier plan was worthwhile," she said aloud, hitting the gas as she gained access to the highway.

Butch himself had handed her the magic bullet, mentioning the shipment. She'd been watching. She knew how it worked. All she had to do was tip off the police one last time, and Butch's sorry ass would land squarely in jail—where no one would believe a word he said.

In the meanwhile, she'd plant some incriminating evidence in Butch's truck, or maybe his office. Some pictures of Tori, Haley's crowbar, and maybe something new—something she could set up like a big, fat arrow.

Hmmm. She'd have to think on that.

About a mile away from the cops and her apartment now, Haley rolled down the windows and cranked up the radio.

Fingering Butch wouldn't explain absolutely everything. For instance, Luke's blabbering about that little mop incident was a problem. She'd just keep insisting it was an accident. Forever and ever. Until Miller believed her.

Because Luke would no longer be able to say otherwise. And neither would his precious mommy.

All together, it just might work. Yes, it *would* work. She'd make sure of it.

Her doubts, all of them, eased with a new plan in place. She drew breaths, big, calm ones now. She always felt better with a plan.

And it was a good one. Because there was an absolute bonus. With Miller's trusted manager in jail for killing his lover and her son? He'd be a perfect mess.

Ripe for someone new in his life…

It'd be oh-so-comforting then to find out that he had a daughter.

———

Tori's nerves felt as battered as the scarred courtroom table she and her lawyer occupied, as they waited for the afternoon session to commence. She hadn't been able to sleep, body and mind locked with fear and tension after nearly being run down. The police had taken their statements, but despite Butch's surety that it was Haley's hair he'd seen, they had no real proof. Haley's apartment still appeared empty. No sign of her SUV or a white paneled van. Hell, the summons for the assault on Luke still hadn't been served.

Today was loaded in a whole different way. Although she'd searched, she hadn't discovered Holden's current whereabouts, and, of course, he hadn't approached her again. Aiden had scared him off but good. No choice, then, but to attend the divorce proceeding at the Monroe County Courthouse in Stroudsburg unprepared. Concerned that things could get ugly, she'd refused to let Luke accompany her, insisting that he attend the last day of school. With luck, she'd bring home good news and no surprises.

To be safe, she'd asked one of the partners at the firm she'd temped at while they'd lived with her parents to accompany her. Wayne sat on her right, blocking her view of Holden, who had no lawyer, across the aisle. She'd already set out a folder with her notes and her copies of the law, mainly printed from the Internet. She knew she held all the cards here, given Holden's abandonment. But who knew what Holden might pull?

Nothing left to do now but squirm and fret.

Wayne, with his salt-and-pepper hair and beard, and bushy brows that had managed to remain jet black, looked like a kindly raccoon as he leaned over to pat her hand under the table. "Don't worry," he said in his gravelly voice.

She nodded, but the truth was, she did—worry. Her shoulders were tense, her palms clammy, and her breath too shallow.

The door on the opposite wall swung open, and the Honorable Judge Edmund Washorn was announced as he swept in. He had close-set eyes that peered up over a long nose, sweeping the room, as if he wore bifocals on his narrow face, though he didn't. The black robe poofed, then sank, as he sat and settled behind his desk for the case, Radnor vs. Radnor.

Tori had seen court TV. The ritual today was no different in this small, close room. She hadn't expected the smell, however. Stale and sharp, as if people's fears and loaded emotions had somehow seeped into all the wood and remained to add to the unease.

The judge greeted her lawyer and stated the facts of the case, before he asked, "Have you anything to add, Mrs. Radnor?"

Wayne looked at her, raising those dark eyebrows.

She cleared her throat. "No, your honor. The facts are straightforward, and I feel my petition has been adequately summarized."

Judge Washorn nodded.

"Mr. Radnor, you requested that we hold a hearing. What have you to say?" the judge asked, and Tori thought she detected a hint of disdain behind his words.

Holden pushed back his chair, grasping the edge of the table with both hands, then stood. "Judge, I simply wanted the chance to..." He drew a breath, then exhaled through his nose as his shoulders drooped.

Tori held her own breath, fingernails digging into her palms.

"To apologize, formally. On the record." He turned then, to Tori. "I...I'm sorry. For everything. Things got out of control, so fast. I was so...embarrassed and ashamed. I couldn't admit..." He shook his head hard, then tried again, palms out. "I realize I can't undo any of it. I just want you to know that I know now what I gave up by making the choices I did, handling things that way—or not handling them, I mean. I'm sorry for what I put you and Luke through."

Tears sprang to Tori's eyes. She hadn't known she needed this from him. It didn't even really matter, and yet, although her anger might linger for a long while, the apology from Holden did count for something.

He plowed on. "You're doing a great job, Tori, on your own. Luke, he's amazing—despite me, because of you." Holden's voice was choked. "I know I don't have the right and don't deserve the courtesy...but if ever Luke should change his mind...I'd love to see him...sometimes."

Holden bit off a sob, nodded twice, then drew a shaky breath. "That's all. Thank you, judge, for your time today."

The judge clasped his hands together, reminded Holden that both alimony and child support were due regularly, that he was getting off easy due to the forgiving nature of one Victoria Winterspoon Radnor, and that the legal system would indeed be nipping at his heels if he should further neglect his obligations to his *ex*-wife and family.

Tori had to put a hand to her mouth to stifle a swift urge to cheer. The judge declared them officially divorced, banged his gavel, gathered his papers, and left the courtroom without a backward glance.

"Congratulations," Wayne said as they stood. He hugged her, and Tori thanked him with a wide smile. Relief was her overwhelming emotion, not because of the additional income—justifiably; she had little faith in Holden in terms of financial help—but because the past was officially behind her now. She turned to gather her things, aware that Holden stood watching, waiting. For her response or for some hope? Or to say or plead something more?

Tori refused to really look at him; she simply couldn't—not right now. She allowed Wayne to usher her through the gate and toward the door, not at all sorry to close this chapter of her life.

They stepped out into the sun—so warm. Tori raised her

fists and looked skyward, feeling good—about everything, suddenly. Her luck was changing.

Although Tori would have preferred to rush home and share the news with Luke, Wayne insisted on treating her to lunch. She suggested they drive separately—then she could be home not even thirty minutes after they'd eaten. She jogged to her car—Aiden's car—digging in her purse for the keys. How wonderful to feel so light, so positive. Anything seemed possible, now that she was truly free of Holden and all that baggage. Surely the Haley thing would be over soon, too. Tori reached out, key fob in hand, then her fingers faltered.

Something was wrong—

"Oh, no!" she cried. Both tires were practically sitting on their rims.

She rushed to the other side of the SUV. Incredibly, all *four* tires were flat, as well as the ebullient sense of possibility she'd enjoyed only moments ago.

She bent and found a narrow black slit about four inches long, the rubber turning open just barely. Holy God, they'd been slashed.

Dread weighted her limbs as she slowly stood and scanned the parking lot. No white van, nothing unusual. People coming and going. A dark car pulled out, then paused as it passed the aisle. It braked, then slid backward, only to turn toward her.

Tori tensed to run before she realized: it was only Wayne, checking to see why she wasn't following. Tears sprang to her eyes at the absurdity—the ridiculous embarrassment that she'd have to admit this—this craziness—again, to someone else.

A shadow swept over her and she jerked her head up—

But it was only the clouds, thick, gray, and fast-moving, blocking out the sun.

One spare tire on the vehicle, not four. She'd have to call Aiden, see if he had AAA for towing. And the cops—she'd promised Mitch and Aiden both that she would call the police immediately if anything else happened. The last thing she wanted was to rehash each incident yet again. However, Stroudsburg fell under a different jurisdiction, so she'd have to provide her case number and the name of the property crimes detective—Jenner was his name—assigned to her originally. Then there was Luke's assault and the—what? Attempted murder?—of her and Butch.

God, it was all so crazy!

She bit her lip and fought the tears. She'd known better, and yet she kept hoping Haley would give up or move on. Such a fool she'd been. But what could she do? She felt horrifyingly helpless in this bizarre situation.

Tori rubbed her arms and tried not to panic, but she couldn't dislodge the terrifying questions from her mind...

Would Haley just continue to torment her? Or was there an end game?

CHAPTER 29

AIDEN HELD THE rear door of UpStart for Tori, his suit jacket spread like a sagging awning above them both. The gray clouds that had swept in had churned up the sky with a summer storm. Her stomach rolled in much the same way, rumbling with unease.

Too heartsick to smile, she murmured her thanks as she swiped the raindrops that had eluded Aiden's makeshift umbrella from her bare arms. He'd arrived at the courthouse parking lot, just moments before AAA, even though she'd told him that Wayne would drive her home. Turning, she climbed the stairs, leaving him to follow, or not.

Not would probably be best. She just wanted to wrap a towel around herself, curl up in a ball on her bed, and finally have a good cry in the face of all this instability. On the other hand, she could have that cry on his shoulder.

"Hey," Aiden said, catching her halfway up the stairs, grasping her hips, and spinning her around. He ascended one more step himself, putting them at eye level. "It's going to be all right," he said, smoothing her hair away from her face.

Tori shook her head and pressed her lips together. "I'm not so sure." Her voice broke, sounding weak. "It's all so out of control, so unreal. I don't know how to deal with a situation like this, because it's, it's…" She gulped.

"Not sane," Aiden said. "I know." He pressed a soft kiss to her lips. "I'm sorry, so sorry, it took me so long to understand just what we're dealing with."

"That's the thing. It's completely impossible to comprehend," she said, frustration edging every syllable. "Last night Haley's trying to run me down—to *kill* me—and today she's back to petty vandalism? To what end?" She shook her head.

"I'm going straight to the police, as soon as I leave you."

Tori wanted to shake him. "I already did that. I've filed a report now on every incident."

"Exactly. *You've* filed the reports. This time *I'm* pushing. Miller's is probably the biggest taxpayer in the county. Maybe I can at least get us some extra manpower."

"Midas of Markets on the case," she said mildly.

He grimaced. "It oughta count for something. I can't stand back and do nothing any longer. Not when it's clear that Haley won't stop, that's she's determined to..." None of them could imagine what Haley was determined to do. "We need a restraining order at the very least."

She snorted. "Like Haley would cooperate with something like that." Tori shook her head, feeling nothing so much as dread and despair. "It's pointless."

"No—it's not." He grasped her head in his hands, his eyes blazing. "I'll find a way to stop this. I promise you that. I won't let her keep taunting you. I won't let her hurt you."

He didn't kiss her on the mouth again, but her forehead, a long press of the lips, conveying—she thought—far more about how he felt in that simple gesture than she'd considered. She shut her eyes, soaking it in, blocking it out. The timing was damn poor.

Aiden tipped her face up to his. "Look at me, Tori."

Reluctantly, she met his weighty gaze.

He said, "I promise."

She nodded, knowing that *he* believed it, at least.

He pulled her in close, hugging her tight, rubbing her back. Tori gave in, accepting the physical comfort just for this moment, and laid her head on his shoulder—how odd to be at the same height level. She sighed. Aiden felt so good, so right. It'd be so very easy to hand herself over entirely.

The thought jarred her from the cocoon of comfort, and Tori pushed away.

The door below them swung open, hitting the wall with a

bang—*Goddamn it, Luke,* Tori almost said, expecting that she'd have to patch another hole in the plaster. But Aiden's arms tightened around her protectively, even as his head swiveled to see who'd arrived. She squirmed, pushing at him.

Luke appeared bearing his backpack and a large McDonald's cup. She felt the tension disappear in a whoosh from Aiden's body before he released her.

"Jeez, guys," her son said, rolling his eyes.

Tori said, "Say a proper hello, please."

"Hi, Mom," he singsonged, then, "Hello, Mr. Miller. Did everything go okay today, Mom?"

She sighed. "Yes and no. Let's all go upstairs," Tori said, turning. She'd been focused on the slashed tires, but Luke's question reminded her that today had been a stellar day before that. She was divorced—officially, truly, and finally—and if she wanted to wrap her arms around Aiden Miller, Midas of Markets, in the stairwell, she had every right to do just that.

Awkward, though, this stair-climbing thing, because Aiden could be checking out her rear right now. A tiny smile nudged at her lips. Knowing Luke wouldn't be able to see past his bulk, Tori threw a little wiggle into her hips. She might not want to get involved, but she couldn't deny enjoying the fact that Aiden wanted her. In truth, she ached for him to want her, at least as badly as she desired him.

At the top of the stairs, in the hall, she halted abruptly, causing everyone else to stop cold, too.

"Luke," she said, frustration surging instantly into her voice, like all moms whose repeated reminders were constantly ignored, "you left the door open. Not just unlocked this time, but open."

He laughed, indignant. "You left last, Mom."

She jerked her head to look at him, muscles from head to toe suddenly clenched. "You didn't come home after the half-day?"

He held up his drink, rattling the ice. "Some of us went and got lunch."

Tori's eyes shifted to connect with Aiden's, who already stalked forward, every movement stealthy, expectant, and sizzling with a silent current of focused energy. He slid past the open crack, then turned his back toward the door. Hands up and ready, knees bent, he nudged it wide with his shoulder, as he crept inside the office.

Tori held her breath, inched forward.

"Jesus," she heard Aiden say. Unsteady as her legs felt, she rushed in after him.

"Wait!" he said, the bark of it stopping her in her tracks so that Luke bumped into her.

Aiden leveled her a quick, fierce scowl, then moved fast to her right, presumably to check the bedrooms and kitchen. As soon as he no longer blocked her view, she spotted the scene on the far wall and gasped, stumbling backward.

Luke caught her against his chest, his hands anchoring her upper arms, even as she heard his cup hit the floor. Ice scattered with a racket, chilly bits hitting her bare ankles.

The wall directly across from them was…covered in chaos. Red paint and pictures. Her and Luke, Luke and Alan, Clarice, her and Aiden—God, kissing, out back of the martial arts school. Lots and lots of pictures, nailed to the wall—not just tacked up. The big industrial-sized flatheads speared eyes, cheeks, chests, foreheads. And the red paint: splatters everywhere, on the pictures, the walls, the nearest desks and computers, and the carpet below.

But the words. The smeary words, like child's finger painting gone berserk, slicing through blank wall and pictures alike, chilled Tori to her very marrow.

DEAD MEAT. DEAD MEAT. DEAD MEAT.

Over and over.

"It's empty. She's gone."

Aiden's voice registered somewhere in her subconscious, yet Tori could only stand and stare, fear icing her spine.

Luke squeezed her shoulders hard, then let go. He passed her, headed for the wall.

"No!" she snapped, instantaneously unstuck. "Don't look. Go, you have to get out of here." She grabbed at Luke's arm, but he easily twisted out of her grasp. "Please."

She felt frantic, unhinged, didn't want her baby to see this, face this.

"Aiden, make him—"

He reached for her, but she skittered away.

"Please."

Aiden blinked, the hard warrior eyes softening. "He's already seen it, sweetheart. It's too late."

The sympathy, coupled with that harsh bit of reality, did her in.

Tori made a sound she didn't know she owned—part sob, part growl—and hurtled into him.

———

He caught her, wrapping her tightly in the bands of his arms and between his thighs. He bent his head, curving his wide shoulders around her to envelope her as thoroughly as possible. She grabbed his shirt in her fists, buried her head, and clamped her jaws—to hold in the noise, he thought.

"Breathe," he demanded.

She forced open her teeth and gasped audibly, sucking in a great gulp of oxygen.

Aiden felt Tori's fists still twisting hard in his shirt, the thin cotton straining, but her shoulders stilled, and she drew in more air.

"Okay," he murmured, and released her just enough to get a look at her. Her face was still contorted as if she were in pain, her skin as white as athletic tape, her eyes a darker pool of green than he'd ever seen—like haunted waters. "Okay," he repeated, "everybody's okay. Time to call 911."

She nodded, and he saw determination take over as she straightened and moved toward the phone. Aiden went to stand beside Luke, who leaned toward Haley's sick display with his nostrils flaring and fists clenched, like he'd take it on, this second, if he could.

Aiden could relate. No matter how he'd tamped it down to settle Tori, Aiden pulsed with the physical urge to strike, to take action.

This scene had funneled out the last ounce of compassion he'd had for Haley and for whatever mental illness she might suffer, into an overwhelming need to stop her at all costs.

My God, she's been watching them, and even me, for weeks, Aiden realized, as he studied each picture in turn. They appeared to have been nailed to the wall at random. Tori and Luke leaning against her car in the store parking lot at night—surely awaiting Clarice and Alan. Tori alone, head bent, sitting in his car, completely unaware of the world—*Dammit, Tori, never do that.* Tori hanging out the window. Luke on the bus. From a distance, a shot of both Radnors plus Clarice and Alan in the vandalized Toyota with the windows rolled down, hair whipping around their heads.

Aiden could hear Tori relaying the details to the dispatcher. She still sounded shaky, although she adequately explained the particulars, and seemed to be gaining strength from simply doing something.

When she'd finished, Aiden gathered her up again.

Three minutes, tops, and sirens blared from the street. He went downstairs to find a fire truck, an ambulance, and two squad cars. He explained that no one was hurt, nor was there a fire.

"Procedure," he was told.

Tori seemed to know two of the officers, Wylan and Rogers.

"From the meat thing," Tori explained, shifting her eyes to the carpet.

"Huh," the female one—Rogers—said after they'd caught

them up, "so slashing your tires was a delay tactic. Suspect needed time for this little project."

Tori reached for Luke's hand. "Thank God you went for lunch. If you had come straight home…"

Luke's face got hard. "I wish I had. I'd have—"

"No, absolutely not," Tori snapped, and yanked on his arm before releasing his hand.

"Any of you see her, you call 911. Don't engage," Rogers instructed. "Things have most definitely gone from bad to worse."

"I'll say," Officer Wylan said, eyes sweeping the room. He poked his light brown mop into each bedroom and the kitchen.

He crossed back to the main door and squatted down to peer at the lock and the doorframe. "I don't want to touch this until we test for prints, but I'm guessing the lock isn't exactly secure at this point. Unless you can get a locksmith out tonight, I'd suggest you stay somewhere else."

"You can stay with me," Aiden offered.

"I can use the chain," Tori said.

"One kick would bust that chain," Aiden scoffed.

Officer Wylan confirmed with a nod.

"Look at that," Tori demanded. She thrust a pointed finger at a particular photograph—a close-up of Aiden's face that was especially marred, as if a nail had scratched and shredded it, smears of paint making the paper weak—then glared at him. "You're not exactly safe either."

"I have a security system. But if you feel better, I'll get us all hotel rooms. Be forewarned: I'm staying wherever you're staying. Physically, you're safer with me than without me."

Rogers said, "Now I remember, the Market Midas guy, also part owner at, at"—she snapped her fingers—"Sunshine Martial Arts."

"Sunrise," he corrected automatically, then ran a hand through his hair. Friday he had meetings with both FreshRite and the Warriors, but he'd cancel both if need be. No way was he leaving Tori and Luke alone. "I can't stand to think of you and Luke sleeping here tonight, with this"—he turned, shaking an open palm at the wall—"and you probably can't clean it up right away." He looked to the officers for confirmation.

"True," Wylan said. "Detective Jenner has to come out here. It'll be hours before we're done." And Aiden wanted Nick to come over. His PI needed to know what they were dealing with, in case he found Haley before the police did.

Aiden said, "I have room for Clarice and Alan, too."

Tori crossed her arms and studied the wall of pictures. "This isn't about them. And at the shelter, there's safety in numbers. I will give Stefan a heads-up, though."

Officer Wylan didn't wait for a resolution. "Man, we're really racking up the charges here: B&E—that's breaking and entering—criminal damage, harassment, and stalking. Then there's last night's attempted homicide." He puffed out his cheeks before exhaling over that list.

Rogers asked Tori, "You got security cameras on this property?"

She shook her head.

Wylan shrugged, then peered at a smear of paint. "If we're lucky enough to lift prints, and the suspect's match?" He whisked his hands together, miming an end to the trouble.

Tori crossed her arms and hugged herself. She glanced at Aiden.

No one would say it out loud, but they both knew. Warrants, fingerprints, arrests? None of it meant jack if Haley got to them before the police got to her.

CHAPTER 30

WHEN THEY'D DISCOVERED they were both attending the Mainline Mickey gala on Saturday evening, Aiden had insisted that Tori and Luke remain at his house one more night. That way his friend Eddie could stay with Luke. As a marine and a black belt, Eddie was far more qualified for protection duty than Tori's pal Stefan, or even Alan and his ever-present hammer.

When they were well en route to Skytop Lodge, misgivings reared like disturbing funhouse pop-ups. Logically, Tori knew she should attempt to enjoy the country drive with its lush, thick tree canopy hugging the two-lane road. Route 447 was a scenic route, after all.

Aiden was quite the view as well, perfectly at home in the driver's seat of his luxury Mercedes sedan, and so handsome in his tux. She should be reveling in the heat she'd seen in Aiden's eyes when she'd come out of the guest bedroom of his house in heels, smoky makeup, and a sexy sheath dress.

Except she hated to be away from her son at all, given the Haley situation.

Of course, she also dreaded contending with her disapproving parents.

And despite the fact that the Mickey was hands down the best opportunity for charity contributions all year, she didn't especially relish charming monetary donations from wallets fat with old money. Her heart just wasn't in it. No surprise, given all she'd been contending with lately.

Last but not least, as a woman, who was undeniably drawn to the man beside her? Well, a gala evening—drinks, music, dancing, and a festive atmosphere—sounded ripe with danger.

"Hey," Aiden said, slipping his large hand onto her leg, well above her knee—for this dress became much shorter once seated. His long fingers curved between her thighs, his thumb straddling the outside. Tingles became zings, shooting up to cause an involuntary clenching where it counted.

"Try to relax," he said.

She glanced hastily at his face—was it that obvious what his touch did to her?

He pulled his eyes from the road, his expression serious, blue eyes telegraphing concern. "Everything will be fine. We'll only be gone a few hours."

Tori breathed a sigh of relief, though this subject was loaded as well. "I know," she said. "Honestly, I know Luke will be fine with Eddie. I just…"

He squeezed her thigh, and her words tumbled out, as much with the need to say them as the desire to distract herself from focusing on his hand in such a possessive and intimate spot. "We've underestimated Haley all along," she said. "What we thought were just concerning but juvenile pranks were really escalating warnings. A series of attacks crafted to build confusion, paranoia, and fear. Well, she succeeded," Tori said, bitterly. "I'm off balance. I'm scared to death—even when I think everybody's tucked away safe."

"They are, especially tonight. You talked with Stefan about Clarice and Alan. The police are keeping an eye on both the shelter and your place tonight. Luke is in good hands with Eddie. The security system is on. And you've got me as a bodyguard."

"I just feel"—Tori pulled the tails of the light black wrap together, crossing it over the low neckline of this sleeveless get-up—"so out of my element. Most stuff, I can handle. Helping people. Running a business. Raising my son, the best way I know how. Even if we've struggled"—her voice wobbled a bit—"Luke understands right and wrong, compassion, and hard work. He knows his mother loves him."

Aiden's hand disappeared from her leg to grip her hand, but she couldn't stop now.

"Maybe in my own quest to follow my heart, I've failed him.

Somehow enabled a situation that I may not be able to protect him from." Tori expelled air as her eyes welled. "Those pictures terrify me." She swiveled her head toward her right shoulder, the trees now streaking by outside.

"Tori," Aiden said, "look at me."

She did, the tears she was holding back making him shimmer oddly in the stream of light from the lowering sun.

He took his eyes off the road again for a long moment. "You are the best mom I've ever seen. And Luke is a great kid. Don't be so hard on yourself. This situation with Haley is nothing any of us could have foreseen," he said, flinching. "And it's doubtful you could've prevented it either. But it's a temporary shit storm. She will be found, she will be charged, she will be locked up— God willing, somewhere they can help her."

Tori heard the weight of blame he heaped on himself in the brittleness of his normally sure voice. She squeezed his hand back, knowing Aiden needed comforting, too. "You're right," she said, "the situation has to come to a head. Hopefully soon, with no more incidents and no one hurt." Tori took a deep breath. She had to have faith.

He turned at the twin markers for Skytop Lodge. "Let's try not to think about it tonight. Just for a few hours," Aiden said quietly.

After they'd passed the lake on the right and curved around, the sprawling stone structure appeared. The warm glow of lights from the tall windows already lent a cozy intimacy, despite the lingering daylight. As always, the grassy area nestled inside the circular drive boasted perfectly manicured flowerbeds. Tori's memories painted in other bright, rioting colors.

Aiden looked over at her with warm eyes, tracing a finger along the already sensitized bare flesh of her inner thigh. Tori caught her breath.

Staying in Aiden's home—all that enforced togetherness— ample time for some stolen kisses—had only ratcheted up the sexual tension between them. Outwardly they'd acted low-key for Luke's sake, but underneath, desire had been gaining momentum, swirling into a maelstrom with every surreptitious look, innocent touch, and veiled innuendo.

"Let me make you forget," Aiden said.

Tori frowned. "Lest *you* forget," she said, shifting her shoulders to let the slippery wrap fall, "this is work for me. I have a mission."

Under the portico, the valet opened her door. She spun on the seat, sweeping her heeled feet, knees together, as she'd been taught, out onto the cracked asphalt.

Aiden's words escaped the confines of the sedan to taunt her, the sexual implications crystal clear. "So do I, Tori. So do I."

———

Aiden paused at the center of the curved south porch with his hand on Tori's lower back. One flight down was the garden where they held the Mickey in good weather, and already the area was full of people. He leaned in, his lips hovering at Tori's ear—closer than he needed to be, he knew. But with her hair swept up, all that sweet skin was exposed and tempting him. He whispered, "Ready?"

She looked past the billowing white swaths of fabric, hung and tied like curtains on the pillars to frame the outdoor event, and surveyed the crowd before she nodded.

"You forgot the most important thing," he said.

She turned toward him, eyebrows crinkling together with puzzlement. Taking advantage of her confusion, he snagged her chin in his fingers and pressed his lips—one long beat, two—to hers. She blinked, shocked, which made him laugh.

Yeah, he knew it was a caveman stunt to claim her like that in public. He'd realized—crazy as it was—that he wanted more than the usual cat and mouse game with Tori. It seemed big changes were afoot in every aspect of his life. The riskiest of all? Pursuing a woman he just might be able to have a future with—

hell of a thought for a workaholic loner like him. Tonight's venue was perfect for stepping up the romance, and Aiden wasn't one to waste an opportunity.

"Your smile, Tori. Turn it on," he instructed, and watched her lips curve up—forced, but lovely all the same.

Aiden pressed ever so slightly on her back over that silvery material, and they walked forward.

In no time, Tori was approached by old familiars, and Aiden watched as her unease dropped away just as naturally as she'd shed her flimsy wrap earlier. She spoke easily about UpStart and her clients, excitement and compassion shining through. Furthermore, she belonged here in this world, by birth, unlike him. Her parents' money was blue; his so green it might as well be undiluted food coloring—not that he gave a crap.

Despite that upbringing, she was a down-to-earth mom whose every decision centered on her son's well-being, safety, and sense of self-worth. He respected the hell out of her. Nothing like his own, single-minded, emotionally stunted mother. How he'd ever thought they were alike, he didn't know.

Tori introduced him to an acquaintance named Henry O'Connell, a parent she seemed fairly comfortable with from Demorrow, Luke's old prep school in Philly. Having asked what she'd like from the bar, Aiden excused himself. He'd barely turned his back when he heard Mr. Preppy ask, "So, Holden's back, I guess?"

Aiden paused, but heard Tori's light laughter. "That ex of mine is old news, Henry. Tell me how Camilla's doing, then I'm dying to tell you about my new venture."

That's my girl, Aiden thought, and worked his way around tuxes and gowns toward the bar, noting the positions of the men he intended to speak with just as soon as they'd all had time for a drink to broaden their minds.

Although he admitted to purposefully stoking Tori's imagination with the quip about having a mission, he'd been serious, too. He was here to gauge interest among the most wealthy and most likely—yes, he'd done his research—to invest in a soon-to-be-making-headlines Triple-A ball team.

Leaning on the temporary bar as he awaited drinks, Aiden surveyed the crowd. Hal Cain, with the loud guffaw, had played pro ball—one short season with the Pittsburgh Pirates. Martin Fink had donated the groundbreaking million to his son's college, for a hockey rink. Fink's Rink, they called it—no shitting. Manny Hallerman: not into sports as far as Aiden could figure, but a man who liked attention, especially the kind that bought him acceptance. Maritsa Wren, who loved flashing her ample cleavage for the camera from their private box at every Eagles game and who, by all accounts, had her husband wrapped around her jeweled finger. There were a few more he'd likely bump into tonight. Others, he'd simply call and suggest a meeting.

Tori had moved on to none other than Barry King. Good—there was hope yet for UpStart with FreshRite. Aiden would play dumb, though—Tori would have his head if he tried to help. He shook his head. If she'd just let him, he'd have UpStart well connected in no time.

As for Miller's, he and Barry had talked. Aiden was fairly sure they would come to a mutually satisfying agreement, despite the necessity of involving their lawyers.

Handing Tori the Pinot Grigio upon his return, he said, "Barry, I see you've met my date."

Aiden ignored Tori's subtle elbow to his side.

"Aiden," Barry said, and pumped his hand. "Good to see you. Actually, Tori and I are already acquainted. We're doing business together."

"That right?" Aiden glanced to Tori, and saw by her bright eyes and wide smile that UpStart indeed had a new client.

Barry nodded. "Hate to be always following in your footsteps—though I can't say it's a bad place to be."

"About to get even better, I hope?" Aiden chuckled.

"I suspect so." Barry gave a slight bow to Tori, then shook with Aiden once more. "We'll talk."

Alone once more Aiden raised his glass in a toast. "Congratulations."

Tori's eyes twinkled as they clinked. "Thank you."

As soon as she'd taken a sip, the pleasure in her eyes extinguished. Aiden raised an eyebrow as she took a second, rather large mouthful. She'd spotted something, or someone, she didn't care for over his shoulder. Her ex, maybe?

He twisted to look, but she stopped him with a hand to his shoulder. Leaning in, she whispered, "I apologize in advance."

Aiden frowned, turning as she pulled back, to see an elegantly dressed older couple bearing down on them. Aiden grasped Tori's hand, squeezing it once before letting go.

"Mother," she said. "Father."

"Victoria," her mother crooned, as they exchanged air kisses.

Her father said, "I didn't expect to see you tonight."

"I'm sure," Tori said placidly, although Aiden noted her white-knuckled grip on the fragile stemware. "Mother asked me to come, didn't she tell you?"

Gesturing with her glass—the other arm occupied in pinning her little purse between her elbow and ribs—she angled herself toward Aiden, expression tight. "Aiden, these are my parents, Bernard and Grace Winterspoon. Mother, Father, this is Aiden Miller."

Grace's eyes flicked up, then down, sizing him up; Bernard's, as the two men executed a firm shake, bored straight into his with the same purpose.

"Pleased to meet you both," Aiden said. "Is the Mickey a longstanding family tradition, then?"

Grace raised her chin to look down her nose at Tori. "It used to be. Victoria seems to find less savory ways to spend her time these days."

"Mother—" Tori began, then clamped her teeth shut when Aiden grasped her elbow, squeezing a warning. Tempting as it was even for him to tell the old crow to stuff it, Tori was better off avoiding a scene.

Tori smiled abruptly then, so sweetly Aiden expected sugar cubes instead of teeth, and said, "I'm finding this event far more fun than I used to. Perhaps because I have a purpose in being here now?" She sipped her wine.

Tori's mother's voice rose with ire. "Don't you think for one minute that we will allow you to harass our counterparts with your lowly—"

"Mother." Tori acted shocked, but Aiden saw the genuine curve playing about her lips. "No outbursts in public. Isn't that what you've always told me?"

Tori's mother glared—she looked like a thin gray hawk with her beady eyes and patrician nose over a plum-colored, flattened mouth that perfectly matched her dress. For that matter, Aiden decided, her father, a half-head taller, looked much the same—aviary, with a long neck, thin white hair, and a harsh, dry wrinkle for lips.

Dear old Dad said, "She's right, dear, now is not the time— but I will say, Victoria, that you never cease to disappoint me." Bernard's cold gaze sliced to Aiden. "Miller of Miller's Markets?"

"Yes, sir," he said, but Tori's father didn't speak or even blink. Neither did Aiden.

Grace sniffed and looked away as she spoke. "We are acquainted with your mother." Her tone left no doubt that she didn't approve of Marjorie Miller, either.

Finally, Bernard said, "Grace, come." Again the older woman raised her chin, leveling Tori and Aiden both this go round, before spinning to follow her husband.

"Phew," Aiden said. "Usually I make a better impression."

"I'm so sorry—" Tori halted the apology midstream when she realized he was teasing. She shook her head, her gaze fastened on his chest. "I told you they were awful."

He tipped up her chin. "I couldn't care less, except that they upset you." He rubbed his thumb gently back and forth.

She sighed. "They never ask about Luke when we speak," she said, tears gathering in those pretty green eyes. "That infuriates me far more than the rest of it."

"Their loss," he said, and tucked her against him. After a couple of minutes of people watching, he suggested, "How about we hit the appetizers?"

"I'm not sure I can eat after that." Tori crinkled her nose.

"Two drinks, no food, and the wickedest parents in the east?" he teased. "You need to eat. Come on."

On the south porch once again, Aiden gestured at the cheese and fruit display, the raw bar, the sushi table, and many others, all displayed like works of art. "What sounds good?"

"Cheese table first?" Tori suggested.

"Sure," Aiden said, though he'd probably follow this stunning woman to a landfill. He'd never seen her in heels, or a skirt for that matter—and this particular dress showcased just how perfect a figure she had. Long legs, curvy backside—

Cool it, man, not now, he berated himself as blood rushed south. *Focus on the food,* he thought, piling tiny plates with as much grub as possible. They nibbled as they perused, and she seemed to relax. Then, when silverware became necessary, they stood at a high table draped in white linen. Aiden ate with determination, aiming to dent his physical hunger, at least.

Sating his incredible craving for Tori, however, would take a lot more doing. If he thought she was remotely ready, he'd throw over the food, the party, the business, and haul her out of here right now.

Tori slid a grape between painted lips, and then smiled, ever so slowly. Aiden—supremely grateful for the barrier of the floor-length tablecloth—groaned.

CHAPTER 31

TORI NIBBLED ON APPETIZERS, toying a little with Aiden. She loved to see him react—it made her feel sexy and powerful, two sensations she hadn't experienced in ages. Eventually though, the heat in his eyes flared hot enough that she chided herself for playing with fire.

Aiden wasn't a man to trifle with, nor was she that kind of woman.

He ate at a rapid rate, obviously starving. Tori accepted every hot, passed hors d'oeuvre, taking one for each of them, then transferring both to his plate. Watching him virtually inhale the food, she chuckled.

"What?" Aiden asked.

"I was thinking of Luke. He'd consider this heaven and eat for two hours straight."

"Let me guess," Aiden said, wiping his mouth with a napkin, eyes crinkling above it. "I'm not far behind."

"I don't mind," she said. "Eat if you're hungry."

He shook his head. "I'm good now."

They stopped at the outdoor bar—she would *not* drink all of this one, she promised herself—before Aiden tugged her through the oversized open gates toward the rear gardens. Tori stepped carefully after they left the path, cognizant of sinking a heel too far into the grass. Soft strains of orchestra music filled the air, and the breeze felt gently euphoric. Fairy lights weaved into the landscape sparkled brighter than the June bugs they'd watched—what? Only days ago? Crazy, but she felt she'd known him far longer than the few weeks the calendar claimed.

Heat blossomed from the small of her back where his palm rested. Large, warm, and solid, it felt…perfect.

"Feeling better now?" he asked.

"Much," she said. "You were right about the food. And Barry King's change of heart was an unexpected boon."

"Sometimes, these things take time."

"Other times," she said, glancing toward the crowd, "you have to push."

Aiden laughed. "I see you're gearing up again."

"Sorry." She shrugged. "I have to make the most of my time here." Besides, given that she was falling under Aiden's spell—alcohol and atmosphere notwithstanding—a little distance might be a good idea.

"Don't apologize." He inclined his head slightly. "I see somebody over there I need to speak with anyway."

She raised an eyebrow. "Well then, by all means."

"You'll be all right?" he asked.

"Chances are good I'm safe from my parents for a while." She waved a hand. "Go."

At some point while Tori was bending more ears regarding UpStart, Aiden pressed a wine glass—filled with water and fresh lemon slices—into her hand and gave her a kiss on her cheek. Probably she should be swatting him away, insisting he back off. Instead, she tossed him a flirty look, because the truth was, his attention was delicious. Sweet, sexy, and promising. She'd felt his eyes on her all night, making her tingle with awareness, both of him and of the fact that she hadn't felt so beautiful and desired for a very long time.

Soon enough, all those beverages landed her in the bathroom, where she freshened her lipstick and pulled her cell phone out of her small black clutch. Maybe if she checked in at home, she could fully give herself over to enjoying the rare night out—and Aiden's company.

"Hi, it's Tori," she greeted Eddie when he answered.

"Hey, Tori. All's well. We're watching a movie."

"Good." Leaning against the sink, she pictured them in Aiden's comfy great room and let the last bit of tension ease away. "I won't even ask the rating."

"You shouldn't. Want to talk with Luke?"

"Please."

"Hey, Mom."

"Hi, hon. So all's well, huh?"

"Yep, drinking, smoking, porn. It's all good."

"Very funny, hotshot."

"Well, what did you expect?"

"Had to call," she said. "You know that."

"I know," Luke said, his voice sincere now. "Everything's fine, Mom. Chuck Norris kung fu marathon. Expert commentary. My own bag of chips."

Tori laughed.

"So, no rush, we're cool."

"Don't make yourself sick."

She suspected he rolled his eyes, but he said, "I won't. Bye, Mom."

"Love you, Luke."

"You too."

God she was lucky to have such a great kid, Tori thought, gripping the phone and shutting her eyes for a long moment.

Then she tucked the phone away, snapped the silver clasp on her purse, and gave herself one more check in the mirror. Dang, more of her hair had slipped out. It had always been too straight to hold well, and it didn't help that she despised hairspray. No lipstick on the teeth. Pink cheeks from the wine. Overall, she decided, she appeared as put together as when she arrived. Only she knew that her insides felt all melty with desire and charged with anticipation. Ever since that first kiss in her minuscule kitchenette, Aiden had been touching her, watching her, flirting with her…warming her up.

For what, she wasn't exactly sure, but if she listened to her body, and even her traitorous heart, she could admit that he was winning. Wearing down her resistance—like gravity pulling her into his orbit, the force of hot temptation becoming nearly impossible to resist.

Aiden was deep in conversation with another man when she returned. As soon as he spotted her, however, he extracted himself.

"So what *are* you doing here, exactly?" she asked.

"Besides enjoying your company?"

"Yes."

The half-cocked smile was back. "The same as you."

Tori realized that she hadn't seen him work on the muscles of his neck even once tonight. "What do you mean?"

"I'm here shaking hands, feeling out interest in a new venture."

Ah, no wonder he was so relaxed. "You thought of something, then?"

"I did, thanks to you," he said as he slid his palm down her bare arm.

"Me? I didn't do anything." She tried not to shiver. How his every simple touch made her come alive, she didn't know.

"You did, but I'll tell you about it later." His hand had lingered, and now he lifted her hand to kiss her palm.

"Tell me now."

"Can't." He suggested, "Let's dance."

She eyeballed the twirling couples on the dance floor that had been constructed in the main garden. "Just because you drove me here, doesn't mean you have to dance with me."

He raised an eyebrow. "My ego may never recover if you consider me a chauffeur only. At the very least, I consider you my date." He leaned in to whisper in her ear, his breath tickling her neck, and this time, the shiver erupted. "I want you…to be much more."

Tori wanted nothing more than to turn her head and press her lips to his, but she held steady, conscious of the many people around them, milling to and fro or chatting in small groups.

His eyes sparked with mischief, and his hand tugged her forward. He said, "Being seen on my arm will do more for your bottom line than anything else."

Ah, he'd switched tactics on her.

"I don't like it. *I* want to be the reason UpStart is successful."

"Tori, you have to learn to accept help, especially when it's freely offered. This is not violating your principles—it's making smart decisions. Decisions toward the greatest gain over the shortest amount of time. Besides, it costs me nothing."

"You don't feel like I'm using you?"

"Honey, you're welcome to use me a lot more intimately than this."

She swatted him lightly, but the telltale flush on her silly cheeks probably telegraphed the image that had leaped into her consciousness. The two of them entwined, skin to skin.

His eyes bored into hers—heated and knowing—as he swept her forward, his arm around her waist strong and sure, leaving her little alternative but to move with him.

Aiden slid into a perfect box step, though there was nothing boxy about the smooth steps and turns in his arms. His hand was firm, just under her shoulder blade, his legs moving in tandem with hers—perfectly in sync, nearly touching, yet always that hairsbreadth away, only the whisper of his pant legs teasing her bare shins.

"Truthfully," he said, "I'm using you, too."

Tori should ask *Why? How?* except she was mesmerized by the glint in his deep blue eyes, his palm pressed to hers in a strong frame that felt as much pull as push—an erotic tease, both sensual and romantic, that formal dancing could be if only fate delivered you the right partner.

She gasped at that thought—and stumbled.

"I know I didn't just step on your toes," Aiden said.

Tori shook her head slightly, words seeming to cave in on themselves as her heart swelled with possibility.

"I'm using you to keep me safe," Aiden said in a voice low enough that she was sure only she could hear him.

She frowned. From Haley?

"From all these other women." The upward twist of his lips

was both playful and self-deprecating. "Unlike you, they *like* my checkbook. They'd do *anything* I asked, if I shared just a little."

With Aiden practically pressed up against her, Tori's dirty mind took that *anything* and ran with it—as he'd surely intended. Heat burgeoned as she thought of Aiden's naked form, muscles straining during all kinds of sexual romps—but she pictured herself as his lover, no one else.

"You, on the other hand, hate my house," he said with a serious tone despite the fact that his eyes twinkled, "are terrified of my net worth, and refuse my help at every turn."

The music slowed and most couples shifted into the proper positions without missing a beat. Aiden, ever the one to forge his own path, bucked convention and pulled her to him, his hands gliding along the bare backs of her arms, lifting them to loop behind his neck. After she'd complied, his hands slid down her arms, over her shoulders, and smoothed down her back to rest at the small dip above her rear end.

His eyes shone, sexual intent clear as crystal. Tori could barely draw breath as they swayed. Only fabric separated them at chest and pelvis, his muscular thigh nestled between her legs, the other hugging hers from the outside. Tori could feel the heat of his skin, smell his spicy aftershave along with the hint of lime from his vodka and tonic, sense his arousal. Her nipples, sensitized by the rhythmic brush of fabric on fabric, ached. Warmth pooled deep where she desired him most, and the incredible urge to rock her hips shocked her.

But not here, never here. Appearances, she must remember, were everything. Still, he should know what he was doing to her.

"Aiden," she murmured, raising languid lids, and for once, un-shuttering her eyes.

"Yes." Aiden's voice was low and raw with promise. "Soon."

As her eyes dropped closed, Tori's knees buckled slightly.

"Whoa," Aiden said softly, his large hands holding her up. "Breathe, love."

Louder, he said, "Feeling faint? Let's take a breather."

Tori's cheeks burned as Aiden ushered her off the dance floor, up the stairs, and inside, his arm keeping her tucked tight to his side.

He deposited her before the door to the ladies' room. "Splash some water on your face. I'll be right back." He pressed his lips to hers, wet and intimate, full of promise. "*Don't* go anywhere."

At the sinks, Tori gulped some water from a courtesy cup, and used the complimentary mouthwash, too. She pressed a trembling hand to her chest as she noted her flushed face and bright eyes. *Dear God.*

A slight tapping on the door.

"Tori?" Aiden called.

She looked at herself in the mirror, nodded, and sauntered out, sure of what she wanted now. Let him see, come what may. He backed up as she came through the door, giving her space. They were the only two people in the hall, so she stretched out her legs and went right for him. Slid her hands up into his soft hair, raised onto her toes, and kissed him. Mouth open, sucking and teasing. For all she was worth.

Aiden—big, tough, confident, black belt Aiden—groaned, then kissed her back until they both fought to catch breath.

He pushed her away, hands grasped around her ribcage. His eyes had darkened. Stormy, sea blue now.

"I got us a room." Voice gruff, hands tightening on her. Desire emanated from him like heat rolled from the sun—yet she also saw a hint of doubt about her reaction.

"Thank God," she said.

CHAPTER 32

AIDEN MADE HER stand across from him in the elevator. He said, "If I touch you..." Tricky, as the space was about three by four feet, tops—a tiny antique lift with a manual sliding gate.

His gaze, though, roamed in a hungry caress, making her nipples and inner muscles tighten with longing.

Nerves hit when she walked into the hotel room—a suite, with a seating area, of course—and set her clutch on the credenza. That big bed dominating the room with its plaid coverlet, the click of the metal door behind her, his tux jacket suddenly tossed over a Queen Anne-style chair—all of it making her think, freezing her with a reality check.

Until Aiden kissed the curve of her neck... Tongue and lips in that sensitive spot, warm and wet, lighting her up from nape to freshly painted toes. His thick hair tickled her ear; his large hands squeezed her hips.

As her head fell back, he pulled her hard against him, nestling his erection in the cleft between her buttocks.

"Oh," she managed. Despite pinched toes, heels had their advantages.

Tori raised her arms to hold his head, as she angled up to kiss him. Aiden complied, devouring her mouth, sliding his hands up along her sides, under her breasts. Squeezing, kneading, teasing, until she was moaning. He cupped her neck in his hand, slipped the other under the shoulder of her dress and pushed it, along with her bra strap, off.

She wasn't wearing just any old bra. To make this dress look right, she'd had to splurge on a body-hugging slip with built-in push-up demi cups—the only truly solid material the piece boasted. The rest was stretchy peekaboo lace from breasts to her bare thighs. No way was she wasting it.

Tori took a deep breath and pushed away from Aiden. She walked forward three steps, turned. Slowly, he yanked at his formal cravat, unbuttoned his shirt, exposing the dark hair of his chest. Pectoral muscles tensed and tapered to a flat, ripped abdomen. His eyes, when she met them, teased. He let her look her fill, then returned the compliment, skimming his gaze over her every inch, traveling from her heeled feet to the skin of her legs, the swell of her hips and chest under silver shimmer. The heat in his eyes was all the courage she needed. She smiled and crossed her arms, bending forward to allow him a good view of her cleavage, as she grasped the hem of the dress at her thighs. Peeling upward, she shimmied the slippery stuff up and over her head.

By the time she tossed it to the bed, Aiden's jaw ticked and his fists were clenched at his sides. He said, "You're killing me."

She'd never felt so bold and in control as in that moment—tracing her fingers over the satin demi cups, from the hollow between to the curves outside, she cupped her breasts, lifting them once like an offering, then smoothed her hands down her lace-clad sides, and squeezed her thighs together. Rather Marilyn Monroe. Sultry, sexy.

"I'm going to need your help with this one," she said, angling a shoulder to show him the zipper in the back.

Aiden surged forward, although she noted his restraint, too. All that athletic power, held tightly in check.

"Let me touch you in it first," he said, taking her face in his hands and pressing a heated kiss on her mouth. He stepped back, just far enough to watch his own hands, trace the path hers had. Then he smoothed one hand hard down her front, bracing her from behind with his other.

"You are so sexy," he murmured, his fingers traveling upward, sweeping inside the lace at her breast. Although the demi cups allowed her to pop out easily, Aiden slid the other strap off her shoulder and peeled the bust down. Her arms were pinned, but her breasts free, the nipples aching as his lips descended.

He suckled and nipped, Tori nearly whimpering. "Mmm,

yes." Bristles had begun to darken his chin, and the friction on the sensitive skin further heightened her arousal. Tori arched, desperate and increasingly needy. She wanted more— everywhere.

Aiden straightened and spun her, nipping behind her ears and along her neck as he unzipped the constraining lingerie. He tucked his hands inside the slip over her hips and pushed. The material slid down her legs to pool at her feet. His hands rode forward, over her pelvic bones and down.

He stilled, hands halted, body tensed behind her. "You're not wearing underwear."

Tori bit her lip. "Even a thong felt visible under that damn dress."

Aiden's voice was leashed and low. "Damn good thing I didn't know that earlier."

Then, with his front pressed snugly against her back, his hands were everywhere, hot and demanding, leaving a wake of fire all over her body. Smoothing up and down in broad strokes, as if he needed to touch everywhere at once, until finally, he homed in on her most sensitive spots. One hand cupping a breast, twisting and pulling a nipple between his finger and thumb, the other hand busy working her nub. She quivered and writhed against him, dying for his cock to slip between her legs. However, he was contained in his pants, teasing and frustrating her. Still, she didn't want to budge from this delicious position. Both exposed and held tight—a total turn-on.

His lips continued the assault on her mouth. Sensations rocked her from all directions, stealing her ability to think coherently.

Aiden slipped a finger in and out, her wetness allowing him a silky glide back and forth up over her clitoris. Dipping again and again in determined, delicious strokes.

"Aiden," she cried.

"Come for me, baby." Aiden's fingers pulled hard at her nipple, increased their tempo down low. He sucked on her bottom lip and she whimpered, giving in, moaning. Lightheaded and swirling; her body imploded.

He spun her around then with her head feeling loose on her neck, legs wobbly in her heels, reeling from the most intense orgasm she'd ever had. A few kisses, intimate as they got, and she reached for him, pushing the crisp white shirt off his muscled shoulders. "You have too many clothes."

"Not for long," he said, and made quick work of his belt. He sat quickly on the bed, holding her eyes as he untied his high-shine shoes, kicked them and his socks off. Rising, he stepped out of pants and boxers all at once.

God, but he was glorious. All hard lines and perfect proportions. Seasoned, incredibly fit. A very impressive erection reminding her that only she had gotten relief.

Tori stepped toward Aiden, reached forward, and traced one finger along his length, watching it bob in response. She smiled, and put her other hand to his chest, moved in until his cock pressed into her belly. Aiden's eyes smoldered, and he cupped her head for a kiss, even as Tori gripped him tight.

He pulled away. "You're sure about this?" he asked, searching her eyes.

"Yes."

He shut his eyes, kissed her, and then moved past her to retrieve his pants from where he'd tossed them on top of his jacket. Digging in the rear pocket, he produced a handful of condoms, then crossed to toss them on the nightstand.

"I didn't presume," he said with that half-quirk to his lips that she'd found sexy from the first day they met. "I found them tucked into my folded receipt."

"Oh, no." Tori put her hand to her mouth.

Aiden raised an eyebrow, shoved pillows off the bed, and yanked the covers down. He crooked a finger at her. "Compliments of the head clerk," he said, wrapping her up in his arms. "Don't worry, I'm pretty sure he includes them anytime someone checks in after nine p.m."

A blush stole over her cheeks. "God, I hope so, otherwise we were too obvious."

"We?" Aiden asked, smoothing warm palms down her back. "You got to hide out in the bathroom."

Tori smiled, relieved. "True."

Aiden smoothed a hand over her rear, weaved the other into her hair. Bending her backward over the bed, he kissed her until she was limp, then laid her down.

"Still sure?" Aiden asked.

Was he kidding? If the foreplay was an indication, the sex would be mind-blowing. She was already throbbing, as if his kisses had jumped the normal circuitry to ignite a flame deep inside. Tori kicked off her heels, before scooting into the center of the bed.

"Get in bed, Aiden."

He crawled onto the bed and over her, paying homage to her body in kisses and licks, strokes of his callused palms. Tori touched him as well, his hair, his shoulders, back, and buttocks. He was so hard, chiseled like rock, though the skin of his cock felt silky in her hands. She rubbed him up and down, scraping lightly with her nails, then grasping hard with her whole palm, her other hand teasing his balls.

Aiden stretched his length along her, carefully propped on his elbows. Tori, though—she ached for him to crush her, to smother her, to lose control. She wanted him as wild and untamed as he looked now that he'd shed the stiff clothes— rough-hewn and naked, sporting a dark five-o'clock shadow and mussed hair. Tori spread her legs and angled him toward her—right where she wanted him first—stroking the tip along her. Oh wow, that felt good. She found a rhythm she liked, maybe too much. She watched his jaw clench, blue eyes darkening into stormy seas, full of still-leashed power as they narrowed on hers.

"Tori—I can't wait."

"Don't."

Like a flash he sat back on his heels, over her thighs, and grabbed for a condom. "I should give you more time to get ready for me," he mumbled around the foil packet as he tore at it with his teeth.

She propped on her elbows for a better view, watched avidly as he rolled it down over that impressive length and breadth.

He'd gained back too much control in the pause, Tori thought. She wasn't some fragile miss. She wanted him, all of him, no holding back.

"Aiden…" She slid a hand down his rock-hard thigh, then up her own, slipping it into her folds, then moving that finger to the tip of his wrapped cock. She watched his jaw tick, once, twice. "I've been wet for you since we danced."

He growled, actually growled, lunging forward with a "Jesus," to take her mouth hard in his, even as he slid home.

"Oh, thank God," she said, moaning.

"Tori, Tori." He grunted with each slam, as she thrust up to meet him, until the fierce yearning built and exploded, one into the other.

––––––––

For an in-charge kind of guy, she decided much later, her leg draped over his, his arm anchoring her to his side, he took orders well.

"We're missing the ballroom dinner." Tori sighed, head propped on a hand, as she traced a finger over his ab muscles. Still visible, even though he lay flat on his back beside her, sheet bunched around their hips.

"Don't care," he said, one hand in her hair, massaging the back of her head. "Nibbling on you is sustenance enough."

"But we'll be missed."

"Uh-uh," Aiden said, "I checked. This year there's no seating chart. It's buffet."

"My mother will be horrified."

"She won't even realize we're not there."

Tori flopped onto her back, laughing. "Oh, she will, but I meant that she'll be horrified that it's buffet."

Aiden levered himself onto an elbow and looked down at her, dark brows drawn together, eyes suddenly serious. "It took a lot of courage for you to forge your own path."

"It took me longer than I would have liked," she admitted. "I still struggle sometimes to shrug off all that fine breeding, the social pressure, those expectations."

"You've got an excellent start under the covers." Aiden gave her a devilish look that had her pulse in response where she was good and swollen. As if he could read her mind, he smoothed a hand down her belly, hovering just shy of cupping her pelvis bone with his deft fingers. "Maybe I should corrupt you some more to make sure it sticks."

Tori pressed her hips upward in invitation, her own wicked smile widening. "I'm not sure who corrupted whom," she said, secretly shocked that she'd been so free, so comfortable, so responsive with Aiden. Intimacy with him felt easy and...well, right, like not only their bodies were in sync, but their minds, too. Before, even as a safely married woman, she'd never felt this...honest.

Tori stilled as Aiden's finger began to move, her breath catching, muscles tensing. Aiden focused on her intently, gauging her body's reaction, watching her eyes to see how she felt where it mattered.

"If I'm lucky, maybe you'll become addicted," he murmured.

Tori's heart soared and sank simultaneously. Wishing this glorious night, this intense connecting, could last—knowing it was unlikely. As if to illustrate that fact, Aiden's phone bleeped suddenly.

"Dammit," he said, his gaze locking with hers.

Circumstances being what they were, ignoring the call wasn't an option.

CHAPTER 33

AIDEN'S PRIVATE INVESTIGATOR, Nick Shepard, didn't bother with a hello. "I'm in the girl's apartment. There's something you should see. How fast can you get here?"

"Not fast," Aiden said, calculating the distance from Skytop to home. "What do you have?"

"You're not going to like it."

Aiden sank to the bed, his head cradled in his hand, and switched to speakerphone. "Tell me something I don't know," he said, as Tori scooted up beside him, tucking a sheet around them both.

"The place is trashed. Stuff everywhere, food on the wall. Looks like she's taken off—there's some empty spots I assume held a laptop and other electronics. The desktop that's left was open to a surveillance system."

He and Tori looked at each other, both frowning.

"You're still up in Skytop, right?"

Aiden's stomach spun sickeningly. "Yeah."

"She's got a tracking device on your car."

"Jesus," Aiden said. Tori gasped.

"Uh-huh. And there's another stationary blink at your house. Safe bet it's Tori's vehicle."

Aiden swore again.

"There's more."

He held his breath.

Shepard said, "Photo album. Of you."

"All of us? Like the pictures she nailed to Tori's walls?"

"No. Just you. Newspaper clippings, articles, interviews. Your accomplishments with the markets and a lot about baseball."

Aiden scrunched up his face. "How the hell would she know

about my plans for the Warriors? I barely know myself what I'm doing."

"The Wilmington Warriors? That's not in here. Most of it's from when you played with the Jacks. Some college ball clippings, too."

Shock pummeled him like the reverberation in a bat from the wicked crack of a fastball. Aiden stood abruptly, running a hand through his hair. "What the fuck? Was Haley even born then? You're telling me—"

He spun, heart twisting, to look at Tori. "That this is all about me? That Tori is...targeted by association?" His mind raced. How did she get those things? What was that stuff you looked up at the library, microfiche?

"Don't know," came Shepard's reply. "But the album is the only thing I've found so far that seems to hold any clues. I should probably leave it here for now. I'll take pictures of some of it."

"Fuck."

"Yeah. Listen, probably best to come on home. I need to sweep your cars."

After he ended the call, Aiden sank to his knees in front of Tori and bowed his head into her thighs, his neck muscles already cramped with tension. She threaded her fingers into his hair, holding tight until he sat up.

Damn near tears, he managed, "I'm so goddamn sorry. I—"

"Shhh," she said, her face pale as she leaned down and pressed her lips to his.

He cupped her head in his hands. "I'm gonna make this okay. I swear it." He'd stop at nothing to somehow make her world right again.

The brief escape they'd experienced in each other's arms crumbled as reality hit home. They couldn't stay any longer. Not with Luke at home and Haley at large, and that tracking device clearly marking him out of town.

After they'd cleaned up, Aiden zipped up Tori's hot-mama undergarment. "Wear this again for me sometime," he murmured as he pushed aside her hair and kissed her neck, wishing the phone hadn't rung.

She shivered. "I thought you liked me naked best," she said, yet the levity of that remark didn't reach her eyes.

"I like you any which way," Aiden said, and meant it—naked, clothed, horizontal or upright, serious or laughing, fiery with anger or languid after she'd been sated. Even now, when she was upset and frightened, attempting a brave face.

He already thought highly of her, as a mother and a woman. Tonight, watching her work potential clients, he realized that she was a businessperson at her core, like him—didn't matter that the field was charity. And now, after finally getting his hands on her—every inch sweet, luscious, responsive woman?

Aiden gulped as he reached for his jacket. He'd never, he realized, have enough.

A few minutes later in the old-fashioned elevator, holding her tucked tight into his side, he said, "I'd planned to show you something on the way home. Won't take long."

She leaned against him. "I think you've shown me enough for one night, Aiden." She raised up on her toes to whisper in his ear, though they were alone. "I'll be lucky if I can walk tomorrow."

He groaned. "Damn."

She kissed him quiet. "I'm teasing. I wouldn't give up a minute."

As she leaned her head against his lapel once more, she said softly, "I'll cherish tonight always."

Aiden frowned. Why did that somehow sound like good-bye? Didn't she know what tonight meant? He wasn't letting her go. This wasn't the end, but the beginning—no matter what they were dealing with. Jesus, he worried now, had he managed to speak at all between the kissing and sex? What a fucking idiot.

No matter. He'd send flowers, wine her, dine her, kiss her every chance he could get, bare his soul as soon as the time was right—

The elevator lurched to a stop, and Tori tensed against him. The coast was clear, however, as many patrons either stayed the night or had already departed. Aiden had called ahead for his car, and Tori was tucked safely away in mere moments. By God, he'd keep her that way. Safe and close, come hell or Haley.

———

During the drive, Tori worked hard to push aside the disquiet Nick Shepard's phone call had brought. Time with Aiden was running out. Reaching for his hand, she traced each of his knuckles with her fingers. She loved his hands—long fingers, callused palms—from the kayaking, perhaps. Always warm, clever, and deft, she'd learned.

Tori breathed deeply, trying to focus on just this moment. She could smell his cologne in the cozy confines of the car, scented his more personal elements on her own skin. Spice, wood smoke, and lime would bring back his taste always, she suspected. Physically, she felt good all over—sated and sleepy, alive and jazzed, all at once. Thanks to Aiden. In one short night together, he'd made her feel more like a real woman than Holden ever had.

Tori sighed. She'd been so focused on her son, her clients, and UpStart that she'd never even considered the possibility of a full life for herself. Aiden made her think, want, wish…for more.

When he pulled off the road and coasted to a stop, Tori realized they'd made a detour. She looked over at him, eyebrow raised. At this point in her life, she was probably not flexible enough to enjoy sex over the console.

"Remember," he said, putting the car in park, "that I said I had my own mission tonight?"

"Pretty sure your mission was accomplished, Special Agent Miller."

"I had goals outside of you, my Bond girl." He leaned over

and planted one on her. "Climb out. I want to show you some-thing."

"You promise it's fast? I need to be home."

"Believe me, I know. A few minutes only."

Tori slipped her shoes back on and yanked up the wrap. Aiden met her at the door and walked her over to the shoulder, his headlights allowing her to pick along safely in her heels. She shivered in the cool June night, and he tucked her in front of him, flush against the furnace of his body. He smelled even bet-ter up close, but there was the fresh scent of the land and open air, too.

"See that?"

"See what?" she asked, eyeing acres worth of untended wild grasses.

"All that space. That, I hope," he said, his stubble catch-ing threads of her loose hair as he talked, "is the future site of the Wilmington Warriors' new stadium. I'll rename the team, though. Stroudsburg HardHats, probably."

Tori looked up at him, puzzled. He spun her around.

"You helped me figure it out, Tori. With what you said that night we talked—about thinking outside the box and playing to my interests and strengths. I'm selling—the whole chain. The Warriors have been failing, looking for a buyer. I mean to be their resurrection."

"Aiden, that's phenomenal." She beamed, so glad for him. Whoa, though—he could afford to buy a whole baseball fran-chise?

He nodded. "If things really go my way, I plan to move the team here, closer to home, and build a new state-of-the-art ball-park. You know, give this area a little boost."

She hadn't been sure about Aiden when she'd first suggested he hire her clients; however, she'd seen him with Clarice and Alan, and she heard him now. The man was a great, big softy inside, with far more philanthropic tendency than he probably realized.

"Is the land for sale?"

"Not yet." He shrugged with a cocky half-grin. "But almost anything is for the right price."

She shook her head. "So that's what you and Barry King were referring to. He's going to buy your chain."

Aiden shrugged. "We'll see what kind of offer he makes." He smoothed her hair away from her face. "You were amazing tonight, working that crowd. But I don't want you to worry so much. King has committed to you, so you've now got his stores and mine. If my chain goes to a third party, I'll insist that they honor your contract."

He squeezed her hands. "It'll take a while to sort out. But in the end, I'll be able to employ loads of your clients, whether I build a new stadium or not."

Tori drew her brows together, not quite sure if she should be elated or worried.

Aiden was on a roll. "Either location is a haul. I'm thinking some sort of subsidized housing near the stadium. It'd be great to get some of those folks out of shelters, give them a sense of security."

Concern leaped to the forefront. "Aiden, slow down—"

"Sorry." He kissed her forehead. "When the ideas start rolling…"

He lifted one shoulder, his smile wide and his eyes lively. His posture was loose, too, she noted, realizing that she'd never seen him as relaxed and engaged as he'd been tonight. Not just now, showing her what he hoped was his future, but earlier at the gala, and certainly when they'd been alone.

"Tori." He pulled her back to the present. "I'm not asking for any kind of commitment on UpStart's part. I realize it's too early in the game for that. I just wanted to ease your mind some. I'm going to fix the Haley situation, too." He lifted her face in his large hands to kiss her again. Soft and intimate, every press of his lips shot straight to her soul. "Thank you, for believing in me, for showing me the way."

Tori trembled. Her heart was a goner, she knew, even as she felt her armor rising up and fastening like clamps. Despite his proven track record and the Midas of Markets moniker, he was scaring her—big time.

Already? They'd known each other less than a month, they'd only just been intimate, and *already* he was making plans for *her* company? Mentally folding it in to his own new venture? As powerful and well connected as he was in this community, as used to being in charge and running things his way as he was—good Lord, he'd have the whole thing underway in a flash.

And here she was, susceptible to his charm and touch, and even his damn big ideas.

No. Just no.

Never again would she let someone else run her life, wield control over her bank account or her business decisions, leaving her and Luke vulnerable, unprotected in a sidecar hurtling out of control. Even if that meant growing UpStart in hard-won increments, instead of easy leaps and bounds. She wouldn't, couldn't do this.

With a flash of clarity, Tori realized the harsh truth. Aiden Miller might be a tuxedoed dream come true by fairy lights. However, in the harsh illumination of high beams, he embodied her very own tailor-made nightmare.

CHAPTER 34

BY SUNDAY MORNING, all that remained of Haley's disturbing handiwork at UpStart were nails and the messages in red—broken up by blank spots. The crime scene technicians, or maybe Detective Jenner, had removed all the mauled pictures from the wall.

Despite too little sleep post-gala and bags to unpack, Tori was anxious to get to work. From the high shelves in the supply closets that filled most of one wall in the main room, she dug paint cans, rollers, pans, and drop cloths.

Clarice and Alan arrived. "Oh," Clarice exclaimed, "Stefan tried to prepare me, but I just couldn't imagine."

Luke exchanged a glance with Tori. "It was worse when there were pictures."

"Don't you worry, Mrs. Radnor, we'll take care of this straightaway," Alan said, setting his own toolbox on a desk.

"Luke and I are pretty good with a roller, but thank you," she said. "We appreciate the help." In fact, they'd painted every inch of this place only nine months ago. She'd learned on the fly—hence two half cans of leftover rice blue.

As Alan started popping out nails with the back of his hammer, Clarice asked, "What can I do?"

"How about if you try the paint thinner on the desk splatters and monitors?" Tori bit her lip as she looked around. "I don't think there's much to be done about the carpet."

"Do you have any extra remnants?" Alan asked.

"A little. Unbound."

He nodded. "It won't be perfect, but I can cut the worst spots out and patch with pieces."

"Good enough," Tori said.

Just then, Mitch and Stefan each appeared.

"Hey guys," Stefan said.

Mitch frowned, eyeballing the remains of the evil art-work Haley had left. "I made some calls. No news. Still haven't located her."

Tori wrapped her arms around her middle. "I know, I talked to Detective Jenner again this morning." She needed to distract everybody, including herself. "Luke"—Tori turned—"why don't you spread the drop cloths over the desks nearest the wall that don't need work, and then stir the paint."

Mitch went to investigate more closely, though she suspected he'd seen the file. Stefan eyed Tori. "Soooo, how'd last night go?"

"Good," she replied, intending to leave it there for now; however, her face flushed, betraying her. Stefan's mouth dropped open.

"You didn't—"

Tori nodded wildly at the repair crew behind her. Stefan coughed to cover up the gaffe, though Tori saw Mitch turn with a raised eyebrow.

"Water," Stefan croaked, and they both slipped off to the kitchen.

He grabbed Tori's arm as soon as they were blocked by the wall. "You slept with him?"

Tori pressed her palms flat to her face. "I can't even believe it myself today," she whispered. Yet thoughts of Aiden had plagued her all morning, making her nerves tingle and her blood warm, even as her mind urged her to run as far and fast as she could.

Face it, you wimp, she thought. *Your heart is already securely on the line.*

"Good?" Stefan smirked.

Tori only arched an eyebrow in a what-are-you-crazy look.

Stefan chuckled. "Dang, girl! I'm shocked. I thought"—he wagged his head side to side—"you know, some dancing, some flirting, maybe a little pawing in a dark corner." His eyes bugged out. "You didn't do the deed in a dark corner, did you?"

Tori smacked him. "I can't believe I'm telling you all this. But no." Another furious wave of heat shot to her face. "Aiden got us a suite."

Stefan's jaw nearly fell off his face. "So you had *lots* of time together. Wow."

"It was wow, he's wow—but he kinda freaked me out, too."

"Too intense?"

"He's got all these ideas for UpStart."

"What do you mean?" Stefan asked, but Tori's attention was caught. A ping—the alert she'd set on her cell—then quickly another.

"Mom," Luke called, "want me to check your phone?"

"Hang on," Tori said to Stefan, slipping past him. Odd to be contacted on a Sunday.

She snatched her phone off her desk and unlocked the screen.

"What is it?" Stefan asked, having followed her out of the kitchenette.

"Hopefully good news. Let me check." She plopped into her desk chair and linked into the payment account that received donations direct from UpStart's rather rudimentary website.

"I think," she said, almost there, "we got a donation."

"Cool," Luke said, coming to stand behind her.

"Oh, and Stefan, I didn't get a chance to tell you yet," Tori said as she clicked through, "Barry King is back on board."

"Cool. How?"

"Saw him last night. He apologized—knew he jumped the gun. And"—she shrugged—"I'm sure Aiden's verbal support during that little press conference helped."

Tori leaned forward, then gasped. "Oh my God."

"Ten thousand dollars?" Luke asked, awe in his voice.

"Who donated?" Stefan asked.

Tori frowned again, zooming from one page to another, making sure she was logged in as the administrator. Except everywhere she checked, the reference only said *anonymous*, with today's date, and the amount. Ten thousand dollars.

"Has to be somebody from last night, no?" Stefan asked.

Tori bit down hard, logged out, and pushed out of her chair.

She'd gotten firm commitments from some of the people she'd chatted up at the Mickey; however, she'd expected nothing this large. Nor did she fool herself that they'd have made good on their promises without an additional nudge—especially not before their hangovers had even worn off.

Tori's stomach turned. There was only one person who'd be still thinking about her and her little company this early on a Sunday morning. With a post-sex buzz in his blood and a burning business plan rioting around his brain.

Aiden.

————

Having stewed all day Sunday about Aiden's "anonymous" contribution, Tori had built up a good head of steam awaiting Clarice's nine-thirty pickup. After dinner, she took Luke to hang out at the shelter with Stefan. He'd be safe there, and the apartment reeked of paint and turpentine anyway.

After she dropped Clarice off, she'd be meeting a young, pregnant woman who had no transportation to get to UpStart. Always willing to meet her clients' needs, Tori didn't bat an eye at the late evening appointment. Unable to locate her UpStart notebook anywhere, she'd finally grabbed an empty one, and left.

She stressed over that in the car. Had she left her notebook at Aiden's? Had it—God forbid—gotten tossed somehow in the chaos of today's cleanup of UpStart? It had all her ideas, the entire list of people she'd called in the last few months, details of conversations with prospective employers...

Now, she paced beside the Land Rover in Miller's parking lot, keys gripped tight in one hand, phone in the other, nearly sick to her stomach between the missing notebook and her anger at Aiden. The wind spun litter in tight circles here and there, tripping along the parking lot, sounding much like the skittering of leaves in the fall. Full dark already, the parking lot lights illuminated the lot in targeted spots only. The air felt heavy with moisture—definitely a storm brewing, which suited her mood just fine.

As soon as a large section of overhead fluorescents switched off inside the store, Tori headed for the front door. Aiden had taken to escorting out her clients. Perfect—because she had a word, or ten, for him.

He held the door for Clarice, who beamed at him like he was the be all and end all. The job had been good for Clarice. Even better? Aiden's praise. Her confidence level had soared under his attention over the last few weeks. Luke, too, couldn't stop talking about continuing at Sunrise Martial Arts, Aiden's cool house, the kayaking excursions Aiden had promised for summer break, and more.

Tori ground her teeth. She'd be denying her son again, on multiple counts, but it couldn't be helped.

Aiden smiled at Clarice, and then headed for Tori. Two strides and he met her on the sidewalk, a look of anticipation on his face, until she shot out her palm in the universal gesture for stop.

Aiden's brows snapped together, meeting over his crooked nose, as he halted. He scrutinized her expression.

"What's up?" he asked.

"Apparently you," she snapped, planting her hands on hips.

He angled his head to the side, considering. "You're gonna have to be more specific," he said, low and calm.

Tori threw out her hands. "The donation?"

His eyes narrowed further, and his lips flattened into a grim line.

"Don't even try to tell me that money isn't from you. How dare you! Right after we—"

"You want to do this right now?" Aiden shot out an arm toward Clarice, who'd retreated several steps and looked, once again, like a frightened mouse.

Tori wasn't backing down. "Things need to be said."

"Fine," Aiden snapped. He turned to Clarice, and in a softer, yet carefully controlled tone, asked, "Do you drive?"

She nodded, eyes wide.

Aiden stared down Tori as he tipped his head toward Clarice. "Give her your keys."

"Oh, no," Clarice said, her gaze shifting to and then quickly away from the Land Rover. "I couldn't."

"Drives like any other car," Aiden said. "I'll take Tori home, so we can talk—privately."

Tori stuck out her jaw, but held out the keys. "It's fine, Clarice. Park it at UpStart. I'll stop at the shelter and get my purse and keys."

Clarice nodded, finally accepting.

Aiden said, "We'll be right behind you."

"Thanks," Tori managed, watching Clarice bustle away, before pinning him once more with a withering look.

Tori felt the hard edges of his own anger in his glare. Another bank of lights flipped off inside, catching their attention.

"Before we get locked out," Aiden muttered, and pushed open the door for her. He stopped just inside, looking out the front window. Planted his legs wide and crossed his arms, waiting to make sure Clarice started the car.

Tori's heart gave a sad lurch. He cared and he showed it. He was a good guy where it counted. But that couldn't matter to her, because he was also the kind of man that needed to be in charge, running things.

She wouldn't let him take over. It simply wasn't an option.

As soon as Clarice pulled away, Aiden turned and strode past her. Tori followed, rubbing her arms. A darkened grocery at night felt like a ghost town—too quiet, shadowed, deserted.

Her flip-flop-style sandals slapped the tile floors as she struggled to keep up with Aiden's pounding stride.

By the time they reached his office, she was out of breath. He darted in to grab his keys and flip off the lights, then left her to follow once again. Although he held the swinging door to the back open, he avoided her eyes. Past the break room where Clarice had found the rat, into an industrially plain corridor. Floor-to-ceiling shelving, loaded with boxes of dry goods, lined one wall. A series of walk-in freezers marched along the other. Some other time, Tori would have enjoyed this behind-the-scenes peek.

He turned before they hit the double-wide doors of the loading docks, and shoved through the back door. They emerged into the lit alcove in the back of the building, part of a larger lengthwise lot, where his sedan was parked.

"All right," he said, facing her. "Let's have it."

"Ten *thousand* dollars? *Anonymously*?" Tori felt her nostrils flare. "Like I wouldn't figure out who had the biggest money-bags. And after last night? I feel like I've been paid for a good time."

CHAPTER 35

AIDEN'S MUSCLES WERE TENSE, and he knew he wore his frustration on his face. He didn't care. How could Tori think he was linking money to sex? Christ, he'd never.

"I was going to tell you about it." Aiden crossed his arms over his chest, feeling his dress shirt strain against his back. "Do you know how many groups come to me looking for sponsorships and donations every single week? The only way to manage the deluge is to say no across the board, and keep the details of what I do contribute private. *Anonymous.*"

Tori pursed her lips and narrowed her eyes. "Then why did you say yes to my placements in the first place? Were you angling to screw me even then?"

"Goddammit, Tori!" Aiden threw up his hands. "Don't do that. We didn't screw or fuck or get our damn rocks off. We made *love.*"

He stepped forward, grabbed her by the shoulders, and clamped his mouth over hers in a rough kiss, pouring as much of his heart into her as he could. The fight went out of her in seconds flat. She kissed him back.

Except she didn't—not really.

He was breathing hard. She'd held back and wore a resigned expression. She refused to connect, retreating.

Aiden released his grip. Still standing over her, he pinned her with a harsh look. "If you can't tell the difference, then something's seriously wrong with you," he said, bitterness too evident in his tone. Tori's eyes welled with tears.

"I told you," Aiden said. "I made an exception in your case. I make exceptions all over the goddamn place when it comes to you." He shook his head. "I can't believe that you'd think I sent money because I slept with you. That's the kind of man you think I am?"

She flinched.

He turned away and stalked toward the car. Damn, but he wished he didn't have to drive her home right now. He needed some friggin' breathing room—states' worth.

"Why did you do it, then?" she called out.

He stopped, planted his hands on his hips before turning. There was no point in discussion, little hope for them, if her opinion of his character was that low, yet he spoke anyway. "Because you needed it. You do good work, your employees need to be paid, and you were obviously stressing over money. That simple."

She searched his eyes. "Not so I'd agree to contract UpStart with the ballpark of your dreams? Cheap labor for a new venture?"

He could only stare, incredulous and disgusted. "Christ," he muttered, and headed for the driver's door of his car.

Aiden waited, hands gripped tight on the steering wheel, but she only stood in his rearview mirror, chest heaving under her short-sleeved blouse. He revved the engine. She snapped to attention and stalked away. Going where, exactly?

Shit. It was dark, deserted, and about to pour. Aiden threw the car into reverse and pulled up alongside her, lowering the passenger-side window.

"Get in the car."

He couldn't see her face. She kept walking, arms crossed.

He threw the car in park and jumped out. "I'm not leaving you here after hours without a way home, so get in the car." He nearly growled, "Or I'll make you."

She stopped, glared. "Only if you let me say my piece."

Oh great, there was more? "Have at it," he said.

She stomped to the passenger door, he to the driver's side. They both slammed the doors, and Aiden jerked the car into drive, his temper tightly clamped.

Tori took a deep breath, tucked her hands between the thighs of her khakis. He flashed back to his hand in that spot, on her bare skin, just last night. How the hell did they get from there to here?

"I'm sorry," she said.

Aiden shook his head. Little late for sorry.

"But you have to understand," Tori went on, "that you can't just jump into my life, my business, that way."

Aiden's mouth dropped open as he turned to stare at her.

He hadn't jumped—he'd resisted. She'd pushed and cajoled when it came to contracting UpStart, he remembered. Begged him to enter her body. And though she hadn't exactly sent an engraved invitation, she'd allowed him into her life, too. He said, "You invited me in, Tori."

"Not like this." She slammed a fist on her thigh.

"Like what?" he shot back. "You attended the Mickey to make a big push for donations. I support your cause. I donated. I can't see how that's wrong."

"Like doing things without asking me. You can't just take over and do what you think is right. It's not mine if you are forever butting in."

"For God's sake," Aiden said, "I'm not trying to one-up you. I see a need, I fill it. I want my employees paid." He scowled, taking a turn a too fast. "From what I can tell, given your stress level, you're not sure you can do that."

Tori crossed her arms over her chest.

Aiden asked, "You think I'd let you flounder and struggle when I can help you?"

"Yes!" she said. "That's exactly what you should do. *I* have to do this—*myself.*" She turned her whole body in the seat to face him. "Don't you see? Holden was able to decimate us because I *let* him. I wasn't standing on my own two feet, paying attention, and taking responsibility."

Aiden released a frustrated breath. "I'd never do that to you, Tori. I'm trying to give to you, not take away."

She shook her head. "It doesn't matter. I will not let you or anybody have a say in my business."

"I don't want a say. Use the money however the hell you want. You can't tell me you don't need it, that the contribution wouldn't make things better for your clients, easier for you, and even for Luke. He's a kid. He shouldn't be carrying your load."

"That's not for you to say. We make our own way. We don't get rescued. Not by you, not by anybody."

He clenched the wheel. There was no reasoning with her.

"It'd be best," Tori said, "if we just end this now."

Aiden gaped at her, completely incredulous, even as his heart dropped with a great thud. *What the fuck*. This wasn't just a fight. She was bailing. Abandoning him when they'd hardly begun. He could see putting her son first, but her business? Above love?

He pressed hard on the gas pedal to run a red light, and somehow managed to keep his voice level. "Agreed," he said.

Fat drops of rain began to splat on the windshield, and Aiden flipped on the wipers, scowling. His phone rang. Snatching it up, he answered—if only to break the charged and uncomfortable silence.

"Yeah," he said into the receiver, instead of the Bluetooth, like he should.

"It's Lundgren. We got a tip. They're unloading the semi tonight."

Aiden tensed, hands gripping both the phone and the steering wheel like iron bands. "At the store?"

"No."

Breath heaved out of Aiden with relief. At least that situation would soon be over. None of his people would be hurt in the process. "Where?"

"You don't need to know," Lundgren replied.

Aiden swore. But it was probably true—better that he didn't know.

"Any chance you know where Kovacs is supposed to be tonight?" the detective asked.

Butch had left work shortly before Aiden had. "No, but I can—"

"Stay out of it. I was just checking. He'll show at the unload, but I'll send someone to watch the home, in case."

Fuck that, Aiden thought, as he was disconnected. He tossed the phone in the cup holder, changed lanes, and ran another red light. He had to get Tori home fast. Aiden happened to be closer to Butch's house up the mountain right now than any patrolman would be. If Butch hadn't left yet, Aiden could keep him there, until the cops showed. After weeks of having his hands tied, pretending he knew squat—finally, he could *act*.

Aiden saw Clarice creeping along ahead, and pulled a quick maneuver to catch up. Perfect.

Tori clutched the armrest on the door. "What's going on?"

"I've gotta take care of something important," he said, focusing on getting Tori—who'd just skewered him anyway—the hell out of his car. Zooming alongside Clarice, he honked and gestured for her to pull off.

She looked like a startled deer behind the wheel, but she did as he'd indicated. Aiden slid over ahead of her and then reversed.

"Why the big hurry? What the hell is going on?"

"Nothing. Need to stop at Butch's house." He jammed the car into park.

"Uh, why?" she asked, sarcasm blazing.

"You don't need to know." He reached for his door, but she grabbed his other arm.

"The hell I don't. That didn't sound like a buddy on the phone."

Aiden bit down hard. She'd find out later anyway. Highly unlikely the press wouldn't get hold of the story and invoke his store. Better if the bad news came from him.

"It was a detective. Butch is into some bad stuff. They've

been waiting to bust him and his pals when it counts. We're not that far to Butch's now. I'm just going to make sure he doesn't take off."

Tori's stare seared him. "What do you mean, bad stuff?"

"Drugs."

"Drugs? Butch does drugs?"

"I haven't seen any evidence that he's doing them."

"Oh my God. He's dealing? To whom?" Tori was yelling now. "To whom, Aiden? The kids? People at the store?"

Aiden risked a glance—she was breathing hard and staring daggers at him.

"The cops involved *you*," she said. "He *is* selling at Miller's."

Aiden felt his jaw tick, and nodded.

"You bastard!" she said. "How could you? You let me put my clients at risk!" She slugged his arm hard. Aiden didn't flinch. In fact, he wished she'd keep it up.

"Why the hell didn't you tell me?" She gestured wildly. "I could have pulled them. I should have yanked them for the Haley thing alone. But this, this!"

"I'm sorry," Aiden said tightly. "At first I didn't even know, and then the cops insisted no one should leave. Status quo, so Butch would feel secure."

Aiden felt her eyes boring into him as she spoke, the words spiked with venom. "God help you, Aiden Miller, if any of my clients suffer repercussions from this."

He looked over at her. "They won't. I won't let that happen."

"You're gonna take care of that, control it, as you do everything else?"

Aiden wasn't sure she if was slamming him for failing to manage things, or if they were back to the earlier argument because she thought he was power hungry. Either way. She could yell all she wanted—on this, at least, she had every right to be livid. He shook his head and climbed out of the car.

He rounded to open her door, but she was already out,

stomping back to join Clarice, who stood twisting her hands between the two vehicles.

Aiden called out, afraid she wouldn't talk to him again. "Tori. Be careful. Haley—it's not safe yet."

"Oh, and going to confront a known drug dealer is?"

Clarice skittered to the passenger side.

"It's not me I'm worried about," he said.

Tori spun to face him, the wind whipping her hair, fury radiating from her face. "You should have thought of that long ago—*before* you exposed us all to drug dealers and psychos."

Aiden ached to shake sense into her. He'd never ever allow Butch or Haley—or anyone—to harm a hair on her head.

Why, then, did he already feel like he'd failed?

CHAPTER 36

THE PHONE RANG again as Aiden sped up the mountain toward Butch's house. Crap—a quick glance at the panel revealed only an unknown number—not Tori. He hit speaker.

"Mr. Miller?" A female voice, and a poor connection, probably due to his location.

"Yeah," he barked, annoyed. Probably a solicitation.

"This is Rayna from Cooper Hospital in Camden." Aiden's heart splintered, and the woman's pause was agony. "Your father's been admitted."

Alive, thank God. He wrenched the car to the narrow shoulder and skidded to a stop.

"What happened?"

"We're not sure yet, sir, we're trying to stabilize him, but…it doesn't look good."

Aiden could barely breathe for the pressure on his chest.

"He's asking for you. If at all possible, Mr. Miller, you should get here. Right away."

Dear sweet Jesus, Aiden thought as he hung up. And shit—from here it'd take him well over an hour to get to Camden. Not even a question in his mind that he'd go to his dad. The cops would deal with Butch.

There was no way to pull a U-turn, the road both too narrow and pinned by blind curves. Aiden sped forward.

Then he remembered—his mother. Was she still in town? If so, she should be able to give him more detail.

Slowing enough to pull up her cell number, he hit call and waited. It rang and rang. He prayed she was at the hospital holding Pop's hand tight, but with Marjorie, you never knew. So he called the house phone, just in case.

"Aiden, me boy."

His dad's voice, loud and clear, strong and healthy. *What the—*

He had to pull over again.

"Aiden? Aiden, can ye hear me, lad?"

"Pops—is everything all right?"

"Aye."

"No scares, no health issues? You haven't been to the hospital?"

"Hell no. I hope never to set foot in the place again. Why do ye ask?"

Holy Christ. "I got a call…from a nurse. She—" Shit. He shook his head, trying to wrap his head around the insanity. "Pop, listen, be careful. Remember that crazy stalker who broke into the house?"

"She's back?" His voice registered genuine horror.

"No. But I've got a similar situation, I think. It involves Tori, too. I don't know, but it's not good. Call me immediately if anything, *anything*, seems out of the ordinary, okay? Or better yet, call 911."

"Can't you fill me in?"

"I need to, but right now I've got a situation." Which was putting it mildly.

Aiden started to dial Tori, then remembered she might not be willing to speak with him until she had time to cool down. Or ever.

He texted, *Tell me you're safe. Got a scary phone call.*

The text came back. *Fine. Meeting a client soon. Luke at shelter, will pick him up when I get back.*

Aiden breathed easier, though he gripped the steering wheel as if he could squeeze answers from leather. *Nurse* Haley, undoubtedly. The crazy bitch. Besides screwing with him, though—to what purpose?

The phone dinged with another message from Tori. *Take care.*

He blew out a breath. Well, that wasn't exactly a love letter or even an apology, but it didn't spell out *fuck you*, either. At the moment, he didn't have time to read between any lines.

He dug his fingers into his neck. If Pops, Tori, and Luke were okay, then maybe Haley was trying to distract him from cornering Butch. That made no sense either. But Aiden leaned forward, head lowered, and hit the gas hard. Butch's house it was, then.

———

Haley kept the van, the lone vehicle on his quiet street, hovering at Luke Radnor's heels, the humid thickness of the evening pressing in her open windows. She chuckled watching him pretend to be unaware, even as his strides angled him away from the street and toward the building. He shifted his shoulders, both hiding his face and hunching from the first plops of rain— or from her eyes boring into his back.

"Lukey Radnor," she called in a spooky voice, grinning when he halted in place. Exhilarated, she laughed. It was time, finally. With all those days of interminable waiting while Radnor and Miller holed up for a giant fuck fest, she'd had plenty of time to plan. Cutting the power to the street had been easy. And she'd been prepared to deal with that fancy-pants shelter guy wherever Luke camped out. But here he was like a gift, entirely alone.

Luke turned his head, eyes leading, as if his body didn't entirely want to face her.

She pushed the brake pedal flat to the floor before the vehicle stopped. For a new purchase, this used piece of tin drove like shit. Haley held the kid's eyes. Didn't speak. Staring match.

Lukey lost. Facing her full-on, arms crossed over his chest, he blurted out, "What the hell do you want?"

"I have some news to share with you." She smiled, all sugary, delighting in the twinge of pain she felt at the movement. Brand-new piercings yesterday: lip and tongue. At least she thought it was yesterday; the days were blurring together some.

Haley watched Luke as he took in her new look. She thought

the black lipstick complemented the hair and piercings nicely. When his eyes sank to her chest and widened, she laughed. The white deli coat was covered in blood.

"I'm not playing your psycho games," Luke said, turning toward home. "Stay the fuck away from us."

She rolled the van forward a few feet. "Oh, this you need to hear."

Luke kept walking, angling halfway again. But there'd be no ignoring her this time.

Haley said, "I have her."

His eyes flicked again to the mess on her front. She stretched her face art once more, then said, "The blood's not hers, but it will make a nice addition if you don't cooperate."

In fact, it was animal blood—meat slop. Late last night, when she'd snuck into Miller's to plant a smear of red paint and a couple of nails—nothing too obvious—in Butch's office, she'd gotten creative in the deli in anticipation.

Her mother had only managed a few Halloween costumes— a baseball player with Miller's number, a cheerleader in his team colors, a karate girl... Haley had always wanted to go gory. This suited her present role perfectly.

Luke halted, eyes narrowed, like he was trying hard to see inside her.

Haley heaved a sigh and spelled it out, her tone bored and flat. "You're alone, dimwit. I have your mommy in my evil clutches." A small white lie, of course. She'd sent Tori on a fool's errand, so she could snatch the kid.

He sucked in air and reared back. She nearly chortled with glee. "If you want to see mommy again—in one piece, anyway— you'll come with me right now."

Luke stood rooted. She could see his mind chugging as if she watched it play out on a big screen. Trick or truth? Kids were warned against skeevy men claiming lost puppies and offers of candy—not mother-snatching young women.

Soon enough, Tori would figure out that she'd been duped

and return home to find that her precious boy had become bait. Just before approaching the kid, Haley had left instructions on UpStart's message system, voice disguised, message vague. But Radnor would understand; she'd know where to go. Aiden should be, if she knew him at all, headed toward Philly in a total panic. By the time he caught on—oops, wrong Mr. Miller, total misunderstanding, sorry—and returned to the Poconos, Tori and Luke would be...

Gone.

Haley grinned. She'd timed it all perfectly. Brains over brawn. If only Lukey here had some smarts of his own.

She rubbed her palm over the blood on her jacket. "I'm waiting," she trilled. "And so is she."

Luke glanced over each shoulder. Haley could have told him the street was deserted—businesses long past closed. She should know—she'd been waiting for Luke to emerge for what felt like ages.

"Three...two..."

She waved the notebook she'd snatched. Doodled from cover to cover and normally in his mother's possession, it should be as convincing as a ransom video. Totally worth the risk of getting it.

Just as Haley had known he would, Luke stepped forward, grasped the door handle, and yanked.

"Good boy," she said, patting the seat. He slid into place and pulled shut the door with a heavy metallic thud.

She could see him better now. "Only a few stitches, huh?" His lip curled, and she chuckled. "Yeah, as you know, I was hoping for so much more out of our little encounter."

"You're sick."

"So I've been told. Hand over your phone." When Luke attempted to play dumb, she said, "I'm not stupid, and I'm not taking you to your mother without some cooperation."

He shoved the cheapie into her outstretched palm. She dropped it out the window and was rewarded with a scowl. Boy, this was fun.

Haley hit the accelerator, lurching them forward fast. Nothing smooth about this ride, but then, what had she expected from a cash-only lot? Uncapping a water bottle as she drove, she plopped a pill into it. The white tablet dissolved instantly, and she held it out for Luke, swirling the liquid.

He shook his head.

"Come on," she said, "can't have you seeing where we're headed."

"Blindfold me, then."

"Mmm"—she tipped her head side to side—"no." Then she snapped, "Take it, or it'll go worse for you and Mommy dearest." That wasn't true either, of course.

He took the bottle, still hesitating. "What is it?" he asked.

"What are you, twelve?" She rolled her eyes. "Haven't you heard of date rape?"

Luke's eyes went wide, and she laughed uncontrollably, slapping her leg hard. "Oh shit, you're hilarious."

When she'd wiped her tears, she said, "I have better things to do than molest a twelve-year old, Lukey. I won't even peek, though I bet you've got a penis the size of an earthworm." She made a face at him, then played nice. "I just need you cooperative for a while."

He only stared at her.

"Bottoms up, worm."

At last, he took a few swigs. She knew it tasted slightly salty, but otherwise normal. She pumped her palm up and down in the air, indicating he should continue to drink. He did—as slowly as he could manage.

"You're a big kid. Drink it all," she said, telegraphing a warning.

He turned toward the window, drinking, and yet the neck of his shirt was getting wet.

"Stop fucking around. Every drop goes in your mouth."

He glared. "How long does it last?"

She motioned again, then slipped a six-inch serrated blade

out from under her thigh. It was dirty, brown, and bloody, because, hey, nobody was exactly going to be worried about infection setting in. He flinched.

"The rest," she snapped.

Luke drank, crushed the empty plastic in his fist, and hurled it to the floor.

With that done, calm settled over her. She was determined to save the bulk of her fun for Radnor, and the drug would help ensure that Luke couldn't go all teen hero on her. She did hope he woke in time for his turn, though, because if there wasn't fear and pain, it'd be just plain old work.

"Not that long," she said, answering his last question. "Might have to give you another. Wasn't sure of your weight."

Satisfied and pleased, she relaxed. "Woulda preferred to give you a roofie, but good-for-nothing Butch doesn't seem to have any of those in his stash. Only these weak-assed Gs."

Luke clenched his fists. "What's your plan?"

"That's my business," Haley said, "but I promise you, everyone will get what they deserve."

Drops of rain splattered on the windshield. Haley noticed that Luke stared hard at them, frowning and swaying with the car. His eyelids drooped—the drug was already working. Faster than she'd expected. She hummed with delight.

Soon, he looked just like a bobblehead. Haley laughed, picturing him bouncing on her dashboard in his lacrosse uniform—tiny body with a giant, swaying noggin.

His posture lost its tension, and he slumped some.

"Not bad, right? Sorta peaceful?" Haley asked.

He tried to focus on her; however, she was glad to see, he couldn't.

"It's kinda nice, if you're in a safe situation. Unfortunately, Lukey"—she shrugged—"you aren't."

A broad smile split her face. "Not even remotely."

CHAPTER 37

TORI PULLED INTO the isolated lot off the hill for the appointment with the new client and frowned at what she saw through the rain. A tired, boxy, little house, nestled into a random and uneven clearing. The front yard was expansive but more dirt and rock than grass, the gravel drive more weeds than stone. The mountain rose steep behind a brand new child's play set: a chunky plastic slide no more than four feet in height and a matching log cabin with an apple-red door. Plastic land—Toys R Us's solution to dollhouses for the toddler set, she knew. They'd had all of that when Luke was little, but for these folks the expensive items would be a luxury.

Even more odd, a luxury sedan and a decent truck both sat in the drive. Why wasn't this woman's family taking her in, if they had a roof and some financial means? There were no other houses on this stretch; this had to be it—

Wait. Tori peered through the rain and flopping windshield wipers, squinting as she rolled to a stop behind the Mercedes. The license plate—no way. She must have a digit wrong.

Pounding caught her attention from the direction of the house. Aiden—dammit, yes, Aiden—beat on the doorframe with his fist.

Butch stepped out and Tori reared back in her seat. What the hell?

The men had exchanged only a few sentences—Butch shaking his head furiously—when a young, very pregnant woman with dark hair pushed open the screen door, hand wrapped around the wrist of a towheaded little boy in SpongeBob pajamas. Tori flashed back to Luke's delight in the strange yellow character at maybe six or seven years old. He hadn't gotten half the jokes.

She shook her head. Was this her new client? Or Butch's wife? Or impossibly, somehow, both? Or maybe she'd been given an incorrect address?

Butch barked at her to go back into the house, as Tori flinched. He and Aiden both clambered down the wooden plank-style steps and moved into the yard. When Butch faced Aiden again, all the blustery denial seemed to have disappeared. He looked pained, distraught, and resigned.

Tori hadn't even known that Butch had kids. Now her heart lurched for them. Poor woman, sweet boy, and unborn baby—their lives were about to be irrevocably altered because of Butch's stupid choices.

Speak to the wife or take off? Her leg jackhammered against the brake pedal. Probably the wrong place; definitely horrid timing.

Her vehicle's windshield wipers were tucked low and silent now, so rainwater slicked the glass clear, plus the yard was illuminated some from the glow from the windows of the house—she could see them well enough. Most of their conversation was audible, too. Aiden was saying, "I'm keeping you here, until they come pick your sorry ass up."

Then Butch: "Aiden, I, I—listen—"

Aiden held up a hand; however, his voice dropped. She imagined that he, too, was overly aware of Butch's young family listening in. Neither man paid a bit of attention to the steady precipitation. Tori put the car in reverse, hoping to slip away unnoticed despite the gravel under her tires.

Her cell buzzed and rang all at once from her rear pocket, making her jump. She hit the brake and yanked the phone out. She didn't recognize the number, although it was a local area code. Maybe this was the client.

"Hello," she said, more abruptly than was polite, because she continued to glare at Aiden's broad back as he faced down Butch.

"It's Holden."

Tori tensed, then huffed in annoyance. "Your timing stinks. I can't—"

"Wait! It's important—it's Luke!"

He sounded upset, nearly frantic, and Tori shot into full alert, bracing herself.

"What do you mean?"

"Someone took him."

"He's with our friend Stefan, down the street," Tori said, cursing him, but relieved. "Stop following him, Holden."

"He's not. He—I *was* following him." Holden's words tumbled fast. "So, I saw it. You dropped him off at the shelter. He was inside a long time, because I went to eat. When I came back, the lights were out. There was a van, and when he came out, it pulled up."

The breath was sucked from her lungs, paralyzing her. Every parent's worst nightmare. No—it couldn't be. He was supposed to stay there until she returned.

"He talked to the driver," Holden said. "Then he got in. He doesn't seem to have regular friends here, so I knew it wasn't right. I tried to follow, catch up to them, but—"

The death clamp on Tori's voice suddenly exploded and she demanded, "The driver. A girl?"

"Yes, young woman. Wild black hair. Piercings."

The ground seemed to hollow out beneath her, even as a cry wrenched up and out. "No!"

She looked around wildly, tried to get out of the car. "Call 911," she shouted at Holden.

Fumbling, she finally located the lock button and jumped out, screaming at Aiden and Butch, "Call 911!"

Aiden spun at her raised voice. "Tori? What—"

"She has him," she yelled through the rain, anguish tearing the words like razors from her throat.

———

Aiden crossed the yard in seconds flat and lunged to grasp Tori's arms, holding her still, even as one part of his brain kept tabs on Butch behind him. "What happened?"

She struggled to get free, frantic eyes searching and darting, obviously terrified. "She has Luke! Haley has him!"

"Are you sure?" Aiden shook her slightly—he needed her to focus. "How do you know? Who's on the phone?"

She nodded, seemed to remember the phone gripped tight in her fist between them. "Holden saw it. Luke got into a van with a dark-haired, pierced girl. Yes, I'm sure," Tori managed.

Her fear surged into Aiden like a crack of lighting, becoming his own.

"Let me go!" she cried. "I have to disconnect. Holden, call 911," she called toward the phone. Aiden released his grip, shock making him slow, and watched Tori hit the end button with shaking fingers.

Tense with dread, Aiden asked, "Stefan?"

Tori shook her head. "At the shelter, I think."

"Thank God, that's something…" However, that small measure of relief did nothing to offset his fear for Luke. Weeks ago, he'd have scoffed. Now, well, God only knew what she was capable of.

"Okay, think, goddammit," Aiden said, feeling shell-shocked. Running both hands through his damp hair, he willed himself to make heads or tails of Haley's next move. It wasn't about Luke; that he felt sure of. The boy was a pawn, like a dangling carrot—

"There's no drug bust, man," Butch said, interrupting Aiden's thought.

He spun, blocking Tori from Butch—instinct, rather than logic—yet Butch stood stock-still, looking as dumbfounded as Aiden felt.

Shock gave instantly way to fury—at Haley, at Butch, at all of it. "What?" Aiden said, his voice like a taut wire, as he clamped every muscle against exploding.

Face tight, eyes hard, Butch said, "Seriously, man, they already rerouted the shipment. They knew the store'd been made. I swear. This"—he waved his arm between himself and Aiden—"has to be a decoy, a distraction so that your focus is on me." His eyes flicked over Aiden's shoulder, to Tori. "I'm sorry," he said with a deep grimace. "I never dreamed…"

"Fuck," Aiden said, clenching his head in his hands. "Where? Where would she take Luke?"

"Her apartment?" Butch said.

"No, the police and my PI have been watching it. And I bet she's got something bigger in mind," Aiden said, thinking aloud, his mind spinning fast, hands fisting in frustration. "She must have planned on us being caught up for hours with the police. It's only because Tori's ex—"

Aiden halted mid-sentence as it clicked. His eyes bored into Butch's. "After hours—the store. It's private, and practically a fortress."

A car door slammed. Aiden spun as the Land Rover jerked backward onto the spotty grass.

"Tori!" Aiden leaped and caught the rear of the car as it braked, switching from reverse to drive.

He pounded on the slick back window. "Stop!"

She peeled away, clumps of grass and mud and sprays of gravel shooting over his feet.

"Dammit!" Aiden slammed his fist into his thigh. Haley expected him to be headed to the hospital. She likely expected Butch to be headed for jail. This was exactly what Haley wanted—Tori. Alone.

As the roar of the car lessened, Aiden heard gravel churning yet again behind him. He launched into a run as he spun, sure Butch was trying to get away. The stocky man raced toward the front door, thick legs pumping fast. Aiden surged forward, tackling him just shy of the house.

"Ooof," came out of Butch as they went down. Aiden flipped him easily and straddled him. Then smashed his fist into Butch's cheekbone, before the shit managed to get his forearms up in a block.

"You bastard," Aiden spat as he grabbed Butch's shirt—knuckles scraping the Miller's nametag he still wore. Store manager—a fucking joke. He hauled him up, then slammed him down into the soft earth, wishing for concrete behind the jailbait's skull.

"You are not getting out of this," Aiden said. "As soon as I deal with Haley, you're going to jail, fucker."

"Lay off." Butch grunted, struggling to get free. "I'm getting the keys to my truck. We gotta get to the store."

"Not you. Me," Aiden said, scowling. He climbed to his feet, glaring, but he held out a hand and heaved Butch up when he took it.

"I'm coming. I have to." Butch held his eyes with a plea. "So much, my fault. Shoulda been doing my job, paying attention." He shook his head hard. "I might be able to help."

Aiden snarled. "I doubt it. I'm driving."

Butch spun, pounded up the wooden steps. Aiden didn't wait, only bolted for his wheels.

He heard the screen door slam and Amy's voice, questioning. Butch's response: "I'll explain later, if I can. Baby, just know I love you, and Tommy, and I'm so sorry. Remember that. Please."

The man's voice held anguish, but Aiden couldn't think about that. And he damn sure wasn't waiting around for Butch. He yanked open his car door, thoughts on both Luke and Tori, wondering what the hell Haley could be thinking, doing.

Aiden started the car even before he'd slammed the door. He hit the accelerator as Butch dove into the passenger seat, the door swinging wide as Aiden flew out of the drive. He took the turn too hard, fishtailing, then worked to put a vise on his fear and temper. Couldn't help Tori and Luke if he didn't get there in one piece.

Butch, now that his secret was out, spewed like an uncapped fire hydrant. "I never meant for this to happen. Any of it." Butch went on, swiping the rain from his face. "I thought I was good to go, with my own crew still in the slammer. These guys came out of nowhere and tapped me. Said a *friend* told them I was available. I've never been able to figure out who, man."

Aiden drove fast, taking the curves hard.

"Told them to fuck off. I was done. Out. I did my time, wasn't going back." Butch shifted in his seat to face Aiden.

"Until they threatened my wife and kid." He slammed the heel of his hand into the dash. "I caved. What was I gonna do, huh?"

He glanced over at Aiden, eyes pleading for understanding. "I had to keep them safe. No matter the cost."

One hand on the wheel, Aiden rolled up his wet sleeves. "You could have gone to the police, man."

Butch waggled his head furiously. "You don't know these kind of people. The code they live by—"

Aiden knew he should be paying attention to Butch's blathering, details he could glean for Lundgren and Smaltz. He just wanted him to stop, though. He had to think.

"So later," Butch said, "tell Amy my plans got all fucked up. I was trying to save her, and I love her."

"Jesus, Butch, you're heading to jail, not your grave. Tell her yourself."

"I'm not going to live through jail this time."

"Cooperate with the police, tell them what you know. Maybe you'll get off easy."

"I rat, I'm not going to even make it to jail, man. Seriously, you have no idea. Tonight's it. Before I go down, I've got to do something right, for once. Something to leave Amy with."

"I'm not going to let Haley hurt anybody."

Butch shook his head. "I have a bad feeling. Just tell my wife what I told you."

"Fine. Now shut the hell up, so I can focus."

What he didn't say was that Butch wasn't the only one. Aiden's instincts, too, were screaming, as if an overloaded bar of bench-pressed weight hovered inches above his windpipe, seconds away from dropping.

CHAPTER 38

"I'VE BEEN WAITING for you," Haley said, a smirk on her face and an odd light in her eyes, as she held open the front door for Tori, the store gaping like a dark cave behind her.

"Where's my son?" Tori demanded as she slid past her, chill bumps erupting on her damp skin under her sticky clothing.

"Give me your keys," Haley said.

Tori hesitated. Haley looked disturbingly disheveled—as if she'd gone mad at the butcher block, jacket smeared, hair both sticking out on end and falling down from a top ponytail. She'd need those keys to get the hell away from this girl, just as soon as she found Luke.

"Now."

Reluctantly, Tori complied, noting that Haley kept hold of them, even as she thrust a store key in the door, then punched in some numbers on a keypad. Haley kept one eye on Tori the whole time.

"Where is he?"

"He's waiting for you. We knew Mommy would come," she said in a baby's voice.

Tori looked hard at her. Her eyes were too bright and yet sort of blank. The girl was either losing it or high. Or maybe she was just toying with her.

Tori said, "If you've hurt him—"

Crack! Tori's face snapped to the left with the force of Haley's open-handed slap. She gasped as her own palms flew up protectively and her eyes watered.

"You'll what?" Haley said, spit spraying Tori's face. "I'm calling the shots now. You don't get to make threats."

Tori just stared. Haley's eyes were lit up like bonfires, a raging madness suddenly visible. She'd have to be careful, avoid fanning those flames, yet take her down—somehow—as soon as possible. With or without Haley, she'd find her son.

For a split second, she wished for Aiden. Then not. She couldn't bear the thought of anyone else she cared about being at risk. She'd find Luke and get him out fast—faster, please God, than Aiden could follow.

She'd had trouble getting service on the mountain. And then the 911 dispatcher had wanted her to wait, but that was insane. Haley had her son!

So she'd left the line open, the dispatcher squawking, phone face up on the seat of the car. If the police found the phone, they'd eventually find her, right?

Haley grabbed Tori's shirt, pulling her off balance then shoving her ahead. Tori stumbled, found herself yanked back by the hair. Tears welled once more at the pain, then she felt cool metal pressed against her neck, where the underside of her chin met throat—dear God, a knife.

Tori tried to glide, not bounce, as she was propelled awkwardly toward the rear of the store; however, Haley was unrelenting, shoving too fast from behind. Tiny rivulets of warmth—blood—trickled down to Tori's collarbone.

She shuddered, prayed that no more blood than this would be shed. And yet, come what may, her resolve hardened as they marched forward. As Aiden and Eddie had instructed in that self-defense class: she would not underestimate her power. And by God, she surged with the willingness to act. She would fight, claw, kick, risk injury, anything—even death—to get Luke free of this monster.

Haley pushed her through a freezer filled with hunks of meat on tiered rolling carts, through a set of swinging doors— the black rubber between them making a sucking noise—and into the butcher's cold domain. Tori's breath stalled as her eyes locked on to a large magnetic strip on the wall that suspended a series of knives, each bigger than the last, glinting with menace.

———

As he zoomed into the store parking lot, Aiden peered through the pouring rain at his other car, parked haphazardly in front of the store. Empty. No Tori. Only the outer lights illuminated the storefront—those lights always remained on at night. Inside, the store looked dark. Haley must be using the back.

Aiden swung around the building, causing Butch to grip the door handle. There were more places to hide if they went in the rear—they might be able to gain the element of surprise. Haley wasn't expecting him so soon, Butch, not at all. They both leaped out the second he threw the car into park. Aiden punched a series of numbers into the rear entrance's security keypad.

It only blinked, and he swore. "She's changed the code or disabled it," Aiden said, smacking the brick alongside the door with his palm. He pulled at the handle, but it was locked tight.

"She couldn't have," Butch insisted. "I changed her security access, blocked her, just like you told me."

"She's got your password or mine, then. Probably reset them."

"Do you think she's watching on the cameras?" Butch asked, turning his face into the rain to glance at the mounted box.

"I'm guessing she's occupied." Aiden clenched his jaw so hard he should've cracked some teeth. "She may have shut them down anyway—wouldn't want her actions recorded."

"What now?" Butch asked.

"The side door by the docks," Aiden said. "It's key only. Can't be locked down."

Butch's hand went to his belt, where he usually wore the store keys on a chain. "Shit."

Aiden raced the few steps back to his car, cursing every wasted second. Leaning in, he rummaged in the console for his heavy set of store keys, fumbling in his haste. The second he grasped the ring, he and Butch took off running, heedless of the puddles.

Where the fuck where the cops? Surely Holden had called 911? Hadn't Tori reported the location to either Holden or emergency services? What if she'd been too distraught?

He mentally berated himself and Butch for the blabbering. They should have called, too. He couldn't wait for help, and yet—terrifying thought—they might need the EMS.

"Find the right key." Aiden tossed him the ring as they took off for the loading docks. "I never use that door."

He swiped the screen of his phone, intending to call 911. Seconds later, however, they were in. He disconnected—couldn't risk being overheard. Their soles squeaked a bit on the tile, drenched as they both were.

Aiden stopped to listen for a moment. He heard only Butch's breathing behind him and the buzz of electricity needed to run even a closed store. They were in the rear corridor, storage and freezers the whole way. Tense expectancy kept him on full alert as they snuck forward.

Spotting something unusual, he halted suddenly, caught Butch's eye, and pointed—padlock on the third freezer.

Every walk-in compartment had a safety release button on the inside of the door. But the freezers had holes built in to the handle on the outside, in case you needed to secure goods. His store had no theft, therefore, little need for locks.

A padlock from the outside meant anybody inside was fucked.

"Shit," Butch whispered. "Not ours. Brand new."

Only someone who worked around freezers would know to put the long-shackled padlock on upside down. Keyhole visible from the top, so you didn't have to squat and search underneath. Anger surged anew. Haley would have the key—on her.

The freezer had no window in the galvanized steel door. No question, though. Luke or Tori—or both—would be inside, their body temperatures dropping. They needed that key, fast.

Suddenly a noise—a heavy whir from beyond the row of freezers. Aiden and Butch locked eyes.

Holy God almighty. The meat prep room—specifically, the band saw.

A piece of machinery so beastly, it was audible even through a closed metal door. Dread slid over Aiden, the cold steel in his stomach doubling its weight.

Later, an officer could shoot off that freezer lock, eliminating the need for a key. EMS could deal with hypothermia.

The precision blade of a band saw, however—its speed and strength designed to make cutting through meat and bone as easy as slicing cotton candy—that, Aiden refused to contemplate.

"Call 911," Aiden said in a fierce whisper, thrusting his phone at Butch, who hesitated.

"We can't be sure Tori took time to report the location," Aiden said. "Plus, they need to know her life's at risk now, too."

Butch nodded and scuttled back down the passageway. Instantly, Aiden regretted the directive. Would Butch take off or only pretend to call, in order to avoid the police himself?

Aiden turned and set his jaw, putting that part of the equation out of his head. He'd trusted Butch once—he had no choice but to trust him one last time.

CHAPTER 39

HALEY PROPELLED THEM both forward until Tori was face to face with a scary-looking piece of equipment. The worst part: a wicked length of serrated metal stretched taut between a metal table and an enclosed box above.

"We're going to have a little fun," Haley whispered in her ear. "We have plenty of time."

"What do you mean?"

"Your fuck-buddy," she sneered. "I made sure he's occupied. By the time he misses you, you'll be gone. As in gone-gone. Not a trace left of you or your son."

God, no, Tori thought, her heart sinking even further. She should have attacked Haley as soon as she'd opened the door. Instead, Luke, and even Aiden—because Haley was wrong, he knew and he'd come—everyone she loved would be caught in this terrifying nightmare.

Haley pulled a big, round, black button out—

The machine whirred to life like a monster, the blade blurring before Tori's eyes. Instantly, terror beyond anything she'd ever known flooded her body.

She pushed back against Haley, hands braced on the cold metal edge of the table. Frantically, she tried to see how the contraption's parts worked. The cord did her no good, running as it did straight up from the top of the machine to plug into the ceiling. She could see nothing loose within range to use as a weapon. Sweat erupted under her arms and on her face, even as her blood went as icy as the freezer room they'd passed through. A metal tang filled her mouth—had she bitten her tongue, or was this the true flavor of fear?

She snaked out an arm to the side, reaching for the black

button to kill the power on the monstrosity. Haley grabbed her wrist easily.

"Uh, uh, uh," she scolded, wrenching both of Tori's arms behind her back.

"I thought we'd start with fingers, but maybe not." She dragged Tori backward.

Tori looked around wildly, the knives on the far wall now beckoning as instruments of freedom. As soon as the knife at her throat disappeared, Tori thrust her hips backward and threw her shoulders side to side, but Haley kneed her hard in the lower back and yanked her shoulders nearly out of their sockets.

As Tori cried out, Haley quickly wrapped something tight around her wrists. Twine? Plastic? She couldn't tell; the lacing so tight sensation was lost in the pain. In order to accomplish that, Haley must have set down the knife or secured it on her person somehow. That gave Tori hope.

Haley was slightly smaller than Tori, but strong, younger and spurred on by madness—or evil.

She breathed through the pain, nostrils flaring. Tori was wiser, smarter, and beyond motivated. Fighting for her son's life, her own life. A warrior. No way in hell would she let Haley win.

"Don't worry." Haley chuckled. "I'm sure you'll pass out before the worst of it."

"Haley," Tori tried, "I never meant to cause you any trouble."

She judged the distance to the black button—could she slam it off with her foot? She didn't think so. Haley kept an upward thrust on her wrists, making Tori's upper body bend forward. Plus, the distance was only a couple of feet—too tight in this position.

Haley snorted. "Right. Just like I haven't been fucking with you since you had me demoted to meats in the first place."

Take any and every opportunity. "I'm sorry about that. Really."

Haley clucked. "Like you're sorry about nearly ruining my future?"

"I wasn't trying to ruin anything for you," Tori said. What else? What else? Keep her talking, buy time.

"Ha," Haley said bitterly. "Bad-mouthing me to Miller."

"He's been on your side the whole time. Defending you constantly."

"Moving in on him? Twisting him around your little finger? Fucking up everything!" Haley was practically spitting in Tori's ear, pushing her forward. Tori resisted every step, using her legs, even as her worthless sandals slid on the terra cotta tile floor and bit deep between her toes.

Haley shoved hard between Tori's shoulder blades, wrenching up her wrists at the same time. Tori fought back, yet still found her face flat on the frigid stainless steel of the table. Too goddamn close to that hyper blade.

"I've fantasized about this, Mrs. Radnor." Haley laughed wildly. "But now, such decisions before we make you disappear. A nose job? Wrinkle removal?"

Tori wiggled her hips, trying to smush that button—the power source—but her pelvis and thighs were too far from the edge and Haley's weight pinned her down.

Out of nowhere, a blade slashed down an inch in front of her eyes, thudding into the table. Tori felt the echoing thump in her cheek. Shocked, she stopped struggling.

"I could drug you into oblivion like I did your son, but I'd really prefer you alert."

Tori nearly sobbed—that was the first tangible information she had of Luke. He was alive. Drugged, yes, but alive.

"Cooperate now, whore," Haley said, as her hand slid into Tori's hair from behind. She pushed her head toward the blade as Tori pushed back.

"Don't!" came a shout, made small from the noise of the machine, but Tori knew—it was Aiden. He'd come. Relief swamped her, even as her fear ratcheted up.

Given her position, she couldn't see him. However, he must have moved closer, because his next demand was loud and clear. "Let her go."

"What are you doing here?" Haley sounded horrified. "No, no, no, no. You're supposed to be driving. Away."

"Haley," Aiden said, raising his voice over the mechanical buzz, "this is a no-win situation for you. Drop the knife. Give Tori the key to the freezer, and send her over here to me."

"Shut up! This isn't happening." She shook her head. "Go away. Just leave."

"I can't do that."

"You have to. This isn't the way I planned it. You aren't supposed to see this—me. Not yet."

Tori thought Haley sounded panicked, and the girl's grip on her head had slackened some. Now or never.

———

Aiden leaped forward even as he sorted it out. Tori must have swept out a leg—just like they'd shown in self-defense—using his arrival to her advantage. Haley faltered to the right, suddenly off balance. Tori arched upward. The two women almost went down.

"Stop!" Haley shouted, her hand twisted in Tori's hair.

But it was the knife Haley pulled out of nowhere and pressed to Tori's neck that halted him in his tracks. Dammit—there'd been too much ground to cover. Still, Tori was upright now, and thank God, a foot from the band saw's blade instead of mere inches.

Aiden raised his hands, stepping back—into a comfortable ready position, Haley none the wiser. He noted Tori's watering eyes, her pained expression. Anger flared, but he zeroed in on

Haley—taking in each tic of her face, shift of her eyes, twitch of her limbs. Gauging, waiting.

"This is all wrong." Haley's eyes darted around wildly. "This is not my ending."

She yanked Tori's head. "*She* showed up out of nowhere and ruined everything. All my plans. It was supposed to be just you and me. You and me together like it should have been from the beginning."

Where the fuck were the cops? Had Butch bailed? Or could Aiden just not hear anything in here—deep inside the building with the band saw whirring so loud?

Aiden forced his voice to sound gentle and still be heard. "I never meant to lead you on. But you're young. You'll find some-one of your own someday."

Haley laughed hysterically. "You idiot. This isn't a stupid crush."

Adrenaline pumped through every cell in Aiden's body, primed and ready. "What is it, then?"

"Can't you see it?" she asked, the words full of frustration.

"See what?"

Haley's eyes shone with tears, and her voice shook. "I'm your daughter."

Shock flooded him, and, if possible, he thought Tori's face had drained of its last ounce of color.

"Still blind? You bastard," Haley said. "Why don't you ever see it? How don't you recognize me?"

"I don't have any children."

"You do! Me!" she insisted. "My mother told me you wouldn't accept me." Bitterness in her face, her voice.

There was no way. No way. Aiden had always, always been careful. Never had there even been a scare.

In his peripheral vision, he saw a shape pop up on the far side of the swinging doors. Butch. No chance Haley would spot him from her angle.

Aiden asked, "Who is your mother?"

"Audra," she said, as if he should have known.

But he couldn't have possibly known, he thought, wanting to hurl. Because it was nuts. That wacko? The psycho. The stalker. "Audra Smelty," he managed.

Out of the corner of his eye, he saw Butch raise three fingers. Aiden lowered his head infinitesimally—as much of a nod as he dared. "You're Audra Smelty's daughter?"

"And yours." Her eyes speared him.

"No, not mine."

"Yes. I am! She said all her trouble was because of you, and still you abandoned her."

"She lied," he said, as gently as possible. "She was already pregnant when I met her."

"*You're* lying." Her voice became shrill. "You're listed on my birth certificate."

"She must have put down what she wanted, what she wished."

"No!" Haley screeched. "No, that's not possible."

Two fingers from Butch.

"The only paperwork I signed," he said, "was the restraining order against her."

"No! Why are you lying? You're my *father*. She worshipped you, even after you rejected us. She said I was just like you. Brown hair, blue eyes, the same half-smile. Smart, stubborn, too high and mighty."

He shook his head. Tried to lace some sympathy into his voice. "Your mother was delusional. She stalked me. And she deceived you."

"Stop it," she screamed, and shook Tori. The blade seemed to sink dangerously into Tori's neck, her green eyes widening even more.

"Don't talk about her like that," Haley screeched. "She said you weren't to be trusted."

"Okay, okay, maybe we can—"

One.

The door burst open, Butch's bull-like torso leading. Haley's face swung toward him, even as Aiden sprang forward.

A second before Butch barreled into Haley, the girl shoved Tori to the side—toward the band saw.

Aiden twisted mid-leap, he and Tori coming at the blade from opposite forty-five-degree angles.

He saw it all as if it played out in slow motion—single frames jerking forward one by one.

Tori fell, arms still tethered, momentum pulling her face toward the blade.

His arm shooting out, hand splayed over her face, shoving her out of harm's way. His forearm pressing into the blade, even as his feet found purchase and he attempted to pull back. Blood spraying—like a rooster tail of rain water shooting from a car's tires, only bright red. Tori's knee snapping up—landing squarely on the kill button.

The machine's buzz changing in frequency, the higher pitch lowering to a quick hum before it shuddered to a stop. The nasty hook of each tooth of the blade becoming visible in its stillness, marching down to disappear into his arm. Blood welling, bubbling, over his skin, onto the metal surface. So warm.

In the abrupt silence, he heard sirens. Also, grunting and scuffling—Butch and Haley.

Tori straightened—white face, wide eyes, open mouth.

"No!" she finally cried, eyes locked on his arm.

He tried to move, but flesh and maybe bone held him captive on either side of metal. "Don't worry, sweetheart. Doesn't hurt." The truth.

Aiden yanked hard—straight out this time—releasing the arm and a whole new gush of blood.

Tori sprang into action, eyes searching around wildly. "Towels? First-aid kit?" She turned her back to the band saw and worked the plastic binding her wrists against the blade, until her arms were free.

Aiden tucked his arm against his torso, pressing his other palm hard against the wound. The movement and pressure sent a wave of searing pain to his brain, nearly buckling his legs. He groaned, waiting for it to pass. Shook his head slowly and forced his legs to move.

Butch was on top of Haley, but she'd gone berserk, kicking and squirming, trying to stab him. He had her right wrist held between his hands and was bending it hard. Any second, Aiden thought, it would snap like a twig. She dropped the knife, sensing the breaking point, and it clanked onto the floor.

Yet Butch screamed and lurched back, releasing Haley's wrist. A different knife, one she must have had hidden, protruded from his chest—from his heart.

Haley snarled, reached for the blade that she'd dropped in the struggle, and lifted it high. Her bright eyes collided with Aiden's—taunting him, even as she aimed to pierce Butch again, this time aiming for the abdomen. In a split second, he processed the madness and hatred she normally concealed behind a placid mask. She couldn't be reasoned with. She'd gone beyond— mentally passed the point of no return.

Aiden lunged and front-kicked, slamming her arm across her body. He snapped his foot back and immediately launched a second thrust, his heel connecting hard with her face. The knife fell free. She groaned, blood bubbling from her nose, and seemed to lose consciousness.

Aiden turned away. He searched for Tori, feeling unsteady. She stood stunned, pale face splattered with red dots. The large blue first-aid box hung from her hand.

"That's not enough," Aiden said, his voice sounding like it was in a tunnel. "Go let the medics in. Butch needs—"

Aiden registered movement behind him. He ducked and spun instinctively, crouching low and rolling to his back, the engulfing pain of swift movement making his vision flicker.

Tori flew past him, on attack, already swinging the heavy metal box in a wide arc. It smashed into the side of Haley's head with a thud, sending her flying. Another sickening thwack sounded as her skull struck tile.

Now only Tori's ragged panting.

Aiden shut his eyes and let go.

CHAPTER 40

AIDEN GROANED, bringing Tori instantly alert. She lifted her head from the hospital bed, where she'd nestled on the mattress by his good arm, which was all wired up.

She stood, grasping his hand in hers, smoothing his hair off his forehead with the other. Dear God, but she loved this face, she thought as his gaze cleared and connected. Tears sprang to her eyes.

He furrowed his brow over heavy lids, and croaked out, "Luke?"

She squeezed his hand. "He's okay." Reaching for a cup of ice, she pressed a melting chunk to his lips. He pursed his lips, slurping it in, then let his head fall back. His dark scruff was heavy now. She'd lost track, but given the cheery sunlight streaming in between the slats of the blinds, it was midmorning. Surgery to microscopically repair the nerves and vessels in his arm had taken hours. She'd been alternating between Luke's bedside and searching out news of Aiden, using the time to sort out her heart and mind.

"Tell me."

"Haley drugged him. Apparently she wanted him cooperative. They think she gave him Rohypnol or a similar drug called GHB." She fought a shudder, still plagued by thoughts of what *could* have happened to her powerless son if Haley hadn't wanted Tori first. "He wasn't hurt, but he feels terribly guilty for stepping into Haley's trap and putting everyone in danger."

Aiden shook his head, just barely. "She would have found a way, regardless."

Tori nodded. "He's also pissed he didn't see any action. And he feels like total crap—the aftereffects of the drugs will last for days."

Aiden shut his eyes, then blinked, fighting grogginess. "Butch?"

"Critical condition. They won't let me see him. The cops posted outside his door won't even confirm that it's him, but I caught a glimpse when they wheeled him into the room after surgery."

"Witness protection, maybe."

"Makes sense. If he makes it."

"Need to call his wife."

"I'm sure the detectives have taken care of that. You don't need to do anything but rest."

He shook his head. "Haley?"

Tori flinched. "Dead," she said, her voice cracking.

Aiden's hand—too cold for him—found her arm. "You did what you had to," he said. Then, so quietly she could barely hear him, "So did I."

"I know." With a do-over, she knew she couldn't, wouldn't, change what she'd done to stop Haley. Still, to reconcile ending a life—even one as disturbed and dangerous as Haley's—well, she'd need some time to come to terms with that.

"Never could I have imagined. Audra Smelty... Haley—she never had a chance." He shut his eyes.

"The damage must have been done early. The police told me Audra's been dead for years." They'd also told her about the photographs they'd found in Haley's bags when they'd searched her van. Pictures spanning over two decades, from early Polaroids to current borderless glossies, cataloguing Aiden's adult life. Begun by Audra, continued by Haley. Baseball games, beach and skiing trips, excursions with his dad, walking in a business suit in Philly, and even sitting at a local bar—dated only a few weeks ago. The most disturbing, according to the officer she'd spoken with, were the close-ups of a very young and obviously excited Haley framed against an unaware Aiden in the background. Tori felt strongly that that information could wait, at least until he was out of the hospital.

"Do they think Haley"—Aiden's face creased, like he was pained—"could have…"

Tori said, "No. Audra's death certificate lists natural causes. I asked."

Aiden nodded and squeezed her hand. "She was a fan, at all the games. I sensed she was someone to keep at a distance, but eventually she guilted me into meeting her for a drink. The minute she took off her coat, it was obvious. Pregnant, and in complete denial. I got out of there as fast as I could. She wouldn't take no for an answer. Knew absolutely everything about me. Showed up everywhere. She was fucking terrifying."

"Shhh. We can talk about her later." She fed him another ice chip. "You haven't asked about your arm."

He winced. "Don't need to. It hurts like hell, so I know it's still there."

And thank God for it, she thought. He'd not only lost a lot of blood, flirting with death, but the surgeon had explained that if the blade had done more than just graze the bone, he likely would have lost the arm. He'd be damn lucky if all he suffered long term was numbness or tingling in his hand.

"You're not supposed to be in any pain," Tori said, scrambling for the corded remote and pushing a button. "I'll call the nurse."

"I don't even care, Tori. They can have my goddamn arm," he said, the fingers of his good arm lacing with hers on top of the sheet. "I'm just so friggin' grateful you're okay. If—"

"Don't even say it. I know, I know exactly how you feel, because I feel that way, too."

And she did. Here was a man willing to risk life and limb, literally, for her. He wasn't a Holden: he wouldn't turn tail and run at the first sign of trouble or insecurity, he'd never bury his head in the sand, or even live in the clouds. He was a realist, and a sticker. Somebody who tackled things head on, and stayed, through thick and thin.

If he'd still have her, she was his.

"In that case"—he smiled in that half-cocked way of his—"I'll just say thanks—for kneeing the kill switch on the band saw."

"Is that what it's called?" She shuddered.

He nodded. "Thanks for the other save, too."

Tori shook her head. "I should be thanking you. For coming after us, even after I was so awful, ungrateful, and hardheaded. For saving my ugly mug, warts and all."

"Gorgeous woman. Not a single wart." His eyes twinkled, although Tori could see exhaustion in his face. "I should know."

"You might need to check again when you're feeling better." Tori felt a modicum of lightness touch her soul at the sexual banter.

Aiden raised an eyebrow as the nurse hustled in. "Mr. Miller, glad to see you awake." She headed straight for the monitors behind Tori's chair, glancing over them before looking down at Aiden. "How are you feeling?"

"Damn good," he said.

Tori rolled her eyes and relayed his comment about the pain.

"Ah. Can't have that, can we?" The nurse pushed a couple of buttons, then patted Aiden's good arm. "You'll be feeling better in no time. I'll be in regularly, but you can reach the nurse's station with the touch of a button, too." She showed him the correct one on the remote, then exited.

"Your dad will be here soon. I talked to him, told him not to worry."

"Thanks. Have a lot to explain." Aiden winced. "My mom?"

"She's...not coming."

"Good. He and I will be able to talk."

Tori made a face, and Aiden said, "You'll see. She makes things difficult."

"Just rest."

"Tori." Aiden squeezed her hand until she met his eyes. "I need to say *my* piece."

His voice was gravelly, so she fed him another chunk of ice. As soon as it had dissolved, he held her eyes and spoke.

"I know you don't want help. You want to save yourself. I get that. You've certainly proven you can—and I don't just mean tonight." He smiled, then his expression turned serious. "I promise—I'll do my best to ask you, consult you, honor your wishes when we disagree. But I can't *not* help you. I want to make your life easy. I want to do right by you and Luke. Love you. Take care of you and protect you. Save you if it's in my power. It's what I do, who I am."

"That sounds serious," Tori whispered.

"It is," Aiden said. "Even though I'm goddamn horizontal—it's a proposal. Tori, I want to marry you, if you'll have me—and when you're ready. But you can't ask me to be someone I'm not. You have to take the whole package."

Tori's eyes filled and her heart swelled to bursting. "How about a prenup?" she asked.

He nearly growled. "I'm telling you, what's mine is yours."

She knuckled a tear. "But I don't want *yours*."

Aiden shook his head without much oomph. "Let me get this straight. If we divorce, you want to be as poor as when we started?"

"Pretty much."

He sighed, eyelids lowering for a long moment, before he levered them up again. "Need to think about that. Maybe an addendum. Like anything that might have gone to you can roll over to UpStart. Or to Luke's college education or his kids…" He trailed off, slurring. The drugs were taking hold.

"Don't you see?" he asked, rallying. "The details you make me agree to aren't going to matter. I'm not letting you go—ever."

She could live with that last part. "Good."

"Say yes, then?" Aiden's blue eyes twinkled, and the quirking smile she loved most twisted up his scruffy face. "So I can go to sleep?"

Tori laughed. "Yes, Aiden. Yes."

UNCOVERED
(Unlikely Series, Book 2)

To find a murderer, marine Eddie Mackey must enlist the help of Miranda Hill, the reluctant photojournalist who filmed his wife's last words. The investigation soon lands them both in a world of danger, and he must take on the role of protector. If only he knew how to protect his heart.

UNDONE
(Unlikely Series, Book 3)

Modeling agency owner Maxine Ricci and her bodyguard Shane O'Rourke must put the past—and their tangled sheets—aside in order to stop a serial killer who has targeted her models...and ultimately her.

RUNAWAY
(Retrieval, Inc. Series, Book 1)

Detective Mitch Saunders uncovers a disturbing link between his missing sister and one of his cold cases. The runaway—or victim?—now known as Charlie Hart— holds the key to his sister's safety. Except she refuses to help him. Too much is at stake to look back. Nor can she consider a future with Mitch—a man who will expose her to evil, if that's what it takes to bring his sister home. He leaves Charlie no choice but to run—again. Or is it already too late?

For more information about JB Schroeder
and her books, visit:
www.jbschroederauthor.com

Newsletter subscribers are the first to receive news and
updates, however, if you'd prefer only new release alerts,
simply follow JB on Amazon or BookBub:
amazon.com/author/jbschroeder
bookbub.com/authors/jb-schroeder

Please also consider leaving an honest review at your
retailer and on Goodreads. Besides word of mouth, reviews
are the best way for others to find new reads, and
authors greatly appreciate every single one!

DISCLAIMER

Being somewhat sports challenged myself (there's always a book to read or a story to write), I knew I couldn't fake my way through baseball adequately enough to satisfy any true enthusiasts. A five-minute conversation with my sports-loving husband cemented my initial thought: the safe bet was to invent a Triple-A team for Aiden. Of course, in order to avoid an odd number of teams within an existing division, I had to create an entirely new division within the International League. Only a fraction of my creative license within the East Division shows up in this story, but what fun I had naming the Frostburg Jacks and their competitors, plotting out their locations with my atlas, and letting them roll from Patrick Miller's mouth as he bragged a bit about his son...

Anyway, please forgive the liberty—this is fiction, after all.

A NOTE FROM JB

Despite that fact that my Unlikely series tagline reads "Evil lurks in the most unlikely places," these books are inexorably linked in my head with my "Do-Gooder" protagonists. Just try putting "Do-Gooder" in a series title, though! Hardly an exciting way to brand a book, but it *is* worth noting that although Tori's placement agency was built from my imagination, I discovered while writing just how similar my local Dress for Success is. Their mission statement reads: *To empower women to achieve economic independence by providing a network of support, professional attire and the development tools to help women thrive in work and in life.* —*www.dressforsuccess.org*

Pretty cool, huh? To all of you who give to those in need—thank you for your generosity!

ACKNOWLEDGMENTS

Ever grateful to the following:

Sue Weidman for the head start on Philly's Main Line. Jessica Orbock and Amber Leechalk, my go-to legal eagles. Eli Jackson for sharing her martial arts knowledge. Jenna Sullivan for human resources stories, info, and a good, tipsy visit. Jill Rathyen MD for handling my surprise attack questions with grace, and of course for the information on arm wounds and ER procedure. Erich Hradecky, for key information about walk-in freezer padlocks and restaurant machinery power cords. Ralph Bartlow for humoring me with a grocery store tour during which the band saw idea was planted (no, he didn't break any rules—I had to look from a distance!). Crime Scene Questions for Writers and Wally Lind for answering my bizarre meat-rotting questions, as well as police procedure and charges. Lee Lofland and the crew involved in the Writer's Police Academy, thank you from all of us writers attempting to get it right.

My dear critique pals, The Violet Femmes, who suffered through the most boring draft of this story, and later, my fab beta readers, Maureen Hansch, Beth Harness, and Julie Cahillane, who hopefully had a bit more fun.

My friends at New Jersey Romance Writers, as well as Marie Force and all the indie authors who share their knowledge and guidance so freely on the Self Publishing Info Swap loop.

Anne Hawkins and Bev Katz Rosenbaum for pushing me even further editorially, Arran McNicol for fixing my mistakes with some fine copy editing, and my dear friend Barbara

Greenberg of BJG Publishing Services, whose proofreading is top notch.

Last but never least, my family, whose support is invaluable.

As always, any mistakes in grammar or research are mine and mine alone!

JB SCHROEDER, a graduate of Penn State University's creative writing program and a book designer by trade, now crafts thrilling romantic suspense novels. Blessed with a loving family and a home in NJ, JB has no idea why her stories lean toward gritty, and her characters keep finding evil—but she wouldn't have it any other way.

JB loves to connect with readers and can be reached through her website:

www.jbschroederauthor.com

CPSIA information can be obtained
at www.ICGtesting.com
Printed in the USA
JSHW02091314121
2950JS00001B/6

9 781943 561032